CRAZY IN LOVE

LUANNE RICE

Crazy in Love

VIKING

VIKING
Published by the Penguin Group
Viking Penguin Inc., 40 West 23rd Street,
New York, New York 10010, U.S.A.
Penguin Books Ltd, 27 Wrights Lane,
London W8 5TZ, England
Penguin Books Australia Ltd, Ringwood,
Victoria, Australia
Penguin Books Canada Ltd, 2801 John Street,
Markham, Ontario, Canada L3R 1B4
Penguin Books (N.Z.) Ltd, 182–190 Wairau Road,
Auckland 10, New Zealand

Penguin Books Ltd, Registered Offices:
Harmondsworth, Middlesex, England

First published in 1988 by Viking Penguin Inc.
Published simultaneously in Canada

LIBRARY OF CONGRESS CATALOGING IN PUBLICATION DATA
Rice, Luanne.
Crazy in love.
I. Title.
PS3568.I289C7 1988   813'.54   87-40612
ISBN 0-670-82131-4

Printed in the United States of America by
Arcata Graphics, Fairfield, Pennsylvania
Set in Granjon
Designed by Amy Hill

For my mother,
Lucille Arrigan Rice

CRAZY IN LOVE

My husband, Nick Symonds, commuted to work in a seaplane. This was unusual, of great interest to people who lived in our small town on Connecticut's shore and to the people we met at parties in New York. They loved to hear about how he and three other Wall Street lawyers, all of whom had pilots' licenses and lived in Black Hall, beyond reasonable commuting distance to New York, had bought and refurbished a third-hand seaplane for less money than it would cost to buy a new station wagon. Only during bad weather and when the bay iced over did they drive into the city. Still, I considered the seaplane an ominous portent. It symbolized the extremes to which Nick would go for Wall Street. The trouble was, we loved each other madly, but the Street was stealing him from me.

It was early May; the leaves were out. I stood on the wide porch watching Nick go through his briefcase. Every morning he inventoried its contents. I stared at his wavy hair, wild in the wind. I saw the scene as a tableau, as an outsider would see it. My black hair and white nightgown were whipping behind me as if I were a heroine about to be left. I wanted to pull him inside, take off his dark topcoat, have him with me all day. We could go back to bed for an hour, eat a big breakfast, fish for snapper blues, ride bikes along the Shore Road.

"Baby, don't go," I said. I always called him "baby" when I wanted to make light of something I felt murderously strong about.

He stood and hugged me close, and then I pulled back so I could see his eyes. They were black, nearly purple like India ink. They held my gaze for a while, but then I heard the plane taxiing across the choppy bay.

"Why don't you drive today?" I asked. "It's too windy to fly." The Tobins' flag was snapping like gunfire.

"There's not time now, Georgie," he said. He sounded a little sad; lately I had become more anxious about his flying. I could hear the voice of a Coast Guard commander: "We're sorry, madame, the plane and all passengers were lost."

"I have to go," he said. He kissed me and ran for the plane. Nick was tall; his strides were long. His black coat flapped in the wind. For a few steps he ran backwards, waving at me. I watched him climb into the rear seat behind my brother-in-law, Donald Macken. How incongruous it looked, that shabby yellow plane full of pristine lawyers! I could see them only from the chest up, wearing identical dark coats, white shirts, dark ties. Nick was identical to no one; he only dressed that way. The plane taxied into the Sound, gaining speed as it bounced across the waves, then took off. It circled once over the pine trees, casting a black shadow on the bay. Then I did what I always did when Nick flew in windy weather: I walked next door to visit my mother.

·   ·   ·

Pem, my grandmother, stood at the kitchen door. "You ought to cover yourself up," she said, holding the cuff of my nightgown between her thumb and forefinger. I kissed the top of her head. She had once been five feet six, my height, but she had shrunk to five one and developed a humpback. She was eighty-six. Her white hair was sparse and wild, her nose prominent. She resembled Einstein.

"No one saw me," I said.

"Those birds in the plane did."

"True, but one of them is Nick and one of them is Donald."

"Who are they?"

"Your grandsons-in-law."

"My granddaughters are married?"

For eight years, I was about to answer, but then my mother called from the living room. She sat in a wicker chair, wrapped in a red plaid blanket, a tiny portable radio on the table beside her. She had a famous smile, wide and radiant and nearly square, but her expression was pained that morning. For effect, she swept back her thick shoulder-length chestnut hair with one hand and held it there. "A winter sea in May," she said.

"It's not that bad," I said, feeling vaguely angry that she should bring up the subject so abruptly, as if I wouldn't be worrying myself.

"I don't think those guys should be flying at all," she said. "No jobs are worth risking their lives in that plane. I have to say, Georgie, that you and Clare should tell them what's what. The plane is a rattletrap, winds on the Sound are fluky . . ."

"You're not helping, Mom."

"Another thing—remember the hurricane season begins in June."

I thought, not for the first time, of how incredulous her audience would have been to know that Honora Swift, the woman they had watched nightly as Channel 6's weather forecaster and Saturday mornings as Weather Woman, placed weather at the head of her ever-changing list of One Hundred Things to Fear Most. This list included the dangers of walking barefoot on the beach at night, the dangers of pigeons, the dangers of cans left too long in the refrigerator.

Clare walked in, followed by her two sons and Pem. "You know what Mom did?" Clare asked, kissing my mother, then me. "She called before dawn to tell us the wind speed and wave heights."

"I wish they hadn't flown," I said, hating to admit it in front of Honora. Clare smirked, slipping off her down parka. Casey came to sit on my lap and Eugene pressed my nose hard. "Ouch," I said and did it back to him.

"Hey, hey," Pem said, laughing.

"I'm not saying the wind is actually dangerous today, but it's important to be aware. You girls of all people should know how dangerous weather can be." She was referring to our father, who had died on a North Sea oil rig in Force 10 weather.

"I think that's a really mean thing to bring up," Clare said.

"Your father was a scientist—he knew the dangers. My God, they had been predicting that storm all week. But those precious bottom samples were so important, so almighty important to him. Just like Wall Street for Nicky and Don."

"Shut up, Mama, and eat your peanuts," Pem said, a bland expression on her face.

Honora looked at her with hurt eyes while Clare and I tried not to laugh. "That is a very vulgar saying," Honora said.

Ignoring her, Pem spoke to Eugene. "It's an old Irish saying. My mother used to say it to her mother."

"Your mother was English and she was lovely," Honora said. "My grandma would never say anything like that. Mrs. Dawkins told us that story, it was about a bridal shower where the mother kept mentioning the girl's old flame, over and over again, until the girl finally said, 'Shut up, Mama, and eat your peanuts.' "

Put out, Pem watched Honora across the heads of her great-grandsons. She stuck out her tongue. Still wounded by the story, my mother looked away. "Do you believe my mother is making faces at me? Who would believe the dignified matriarch makes faces at her daughter? Two days ago the librarian called her 'the grande dame of Bennison Point.' "

Our great-aunts had told us that Pem had been a hellion as a child, but none of us had really believed it until she had started to get senile nine years ago. The white-haired matriarch became a naughty girl. She would start boxing matches. She would say "Oh, I'll smash you," and mean it, if she didn't get her way. Having always admired the color pink, she one day dyed the living room's predominently ecru chintz curtains and slipcovers damask rose. Then she dipped the sponge mop in a bucket of leftover dye and pinkened the white patches on the hooked rugs. She had always loved our family, but now she loved us exclusively, if pugilistically. In public she became overly polite, as if she knew that once her guard dropped the antics would start. She stopped wanting to go out. She was happiest when we were all together at her house. "Is the family coming home tonight?" she asked Honora every night, never mind that Clare and I had families of our own, that we lived in houses my grandfather had built on his property during the years Clare and I were born. Our proximity gave her no comfort; we had to be under her roof, and that included Nick, Donald, Eugene and Casey, even though she could never remember their names. Although Pem was frantic for our presence, no one but my mother would have been surprised if Pem decided to smash all the sherry glasses or started putting lit matches between our toes. My mother continued to treat her like a normal person, like her mother, as if she hoped the condition would go away and they could get back to their regular shopping-and-lunch days.

"I'd better go home and change," I said.

"Waiting for Nick to call?" Clare asked in a funny tone, as if she were teasing me about having a crush on him.

"Doesn't Donald call when he gets to his office?" our mother asked, leaving no doubt that she thought he should.

"That's the worst trap a woman can get into," Clare said. "You spend your time waiting for the phone to ring and if it doesn't you're sure he's dead. Or kissing someone. Same thing anyway—Donald kisses someone else, he's dead."

Clare and I laughed; Honora tightened her lips and shook her head. Then I left. To go home and wait for Nick to call.

. . .

Nick and I had a fine telephone romance. This was fortunate, considering the twelve or so hours he spent at the office every day. For six and a half years he had worked for a securities law firm where he specialized in Tender Offers, top secret transactions in which one company would take control of another, often in an arrogant, hostile manner. Every deal had a code name: Project Hamlet, Project Broadsword, Project Blue Lightning. Telling anyone about the deals was forbidden. Before joining the Tender Offer Squad, Nick had had to swear on the Bible never to talk about the deals, even by their code names, to anyone outside the firm. He had to specifically swear not to tell me. The senior partner who had administered the oath told him that wives were the worst: they were always giving inside information to cab-drivers, hairdressers, Park Avenue doormen. The senior partner had held the Bible before Nick and said solemnly, "You must swear, son, never to tell Mrs. Symonds about your work, no matter how curious she becomes." Nick had sworn, but the oath was invalid, since Nick had sworn not to tell Mrs. Symonds, and I had kept my own name, Swift, after our marriage. Besides, we always told each other everything.

The phone rang. I knew it was Nick before I answered. "Hi," I said.

"Safe and sound," he said quickly.

"It's incredibly windy here, Nick," I said ominously.

"But if I hadn't flown, I would have had to get up two hours earlier. Think of what we did in that time."

We had made love and fallen back to sleep. But the memory didn't make me smile. "Will you be busy today?"

"Very, and it's already starting. The clients are here from Project Broadsword. They're going into the conference room now, but I have a few minutes."

We sat there, silent, connected by the phone line. Nick never put me on the speaker phone. He said he liked talking to me through the receiver, something he could hold onto.

"Is this a big deal?"

"Very big. Four billion dollars will be exchanged." He laughed. "That's what we say—'exchanged.' Doesn't that sound totally unrelated to money? Like wampum, or chickens exchanged for medical care in rural Spain?"

"It does, exactly." I smiled, but he had missed my point. I didn't care about the money involved in his deals, but the figure he quoted gave me an idea of how late I could expect him to be each night. Four billion dollars was a very, very late deal.

I heard someone in the background at Nick's office. A male voice telling him they were ready to leave for the meeting.

"Are you interviewing anyone today?" Nick asked.

"I have a few possibilities, don't worry."

"I'm not worried about keeping you busy, Georgie." He paused. "I love you," he said, even though someone was standing right there.

I hung up feeling angry; I had started to notice I often felt angry after talking to Nick. That was one secret I kept from him. He knew I was bothered, but he didn't know how much. I barely knew myself. At the beginning his job had been an adventure, not to mention being the type of work about which every law student dreams. Everything about it felt larger than life: the clients he represented, the amounts of money involved, the way we lived in a house directly on Long Island Sound while many of his law school classmates had small rent-stabilized apartments in the city, the way he flew in and out of Black Hall by seaplane, the exotic places we went on business trips. But gradually the stakes had grown higher. He had been at the firm for nearly seven years, and he was thinking about partnership. That meant longer hours and major pressure. A tiny mistake could cost a client millions and Nick his chance.

Occasionally we considered returning to New York, where the commute would be twenty minutes by subway instead of an hour by seaplane, but I loved living in the country. Our shingled house perched on a rocky point jutting into the Sound. My grandparents, Penitence (Pem) and Damon Bennison, had built houses for Honora, me, and Clare, and prayed we would always love the place. We had flower and vegetable gardens and an entire hillside covered with heather. Migrating birds passed through every March and September. Every winter, seals came down from Maine to swim in the bay. For years I had been working on a profile of the bay, from the rocky bottom to the water column itself, but now I had another job. I operated the Swift Observatory, an institution that observed neither galaxies nor constellations but human nature.

It began with a lie. I lied to Nick. Or, rather, I failed to tell him the whole truth. Six months earlier I had answered a classified ad and started working as a maid. I did not tell Nick. Later I saw this as an act of pure defiance, a private protest against his endless working nights, but at the time I felt nearly out of control, in need of a secret. When Nick would call late in the afternoon, asking where I had been, I would say, "The fish store." It astonished me, the fact he never suspected. I hid my wages in an envelope in my desk drawer. I imagined whipping it out some day, handing it to Nick and saying, "Pack your bags, baby, we're going to the Bahamas." Sometimes I considered buying him an extravagant birthday present. Mainly I saved the money for our future.

Working as a maid, I experienced the thrill of observation. My first client was Abel Darty, a banker who was never home. The house empty, I could sustain the illusion that it was a museum of his life. Ashtrays, dirty socks, the gallery of family photos standing on the grand piano, the history and science books in the library: all were artifacts.

I took on other clients. Mrs. Burns, whose father was dying; the Corellis, a couple with twin teenaged daughters; Liza Jordan, whose marriage was breaking up against her will. Housekeeping was the precursor of the Swift Observatory. The simple facts of my clients' lives seemed extraordinary. Their different ways of arranging their kitchens compelled me. I began to make notes about them instead of doing my profile of the bay. How Mrs. Burns spent mornings making delicious, clear, concentrated broths to take to her father in the hospital. The secret things I found hidden in Gabrielle and Cecilia Corelli's room: a do-it-yourself voodoo kit, three failed biology quizzes under Cecilia's bureau scarf, a vial of water-soluble green hair dye in Gabrielle's gym bag. One day Liza had started to talk about the separation, and two hours passed before we even noticed that I hadn't done the upstairs. Although the daily transformation of my hands from smooth to abraded satisfied me in a way I couldn't define, the work bored me. I had already decided to quit. But by then my interest in other people's lives had become so consuming, I had to tell Nick.

At first he was devastated by my secret career as a maid. He could not begin to understand why I hadn't told him about it. Two nights in a row he came home from work and tried to get to the heart of some terrible truth. His first fear was that I was in love with Abel Darty. When I remember those conversations they seem warped, spoken by people entirely unlike me and Nick. Wickedly, I enjoyed his jealousy. I took to greeting him at the door wearing lipstick—certain proof of a serious transformation.

Finally we talked until dawn one Thursday. I had expected to tell him about the great interest I had developed in my clients' lives, but instead we talked about his absence from our house. How he always seemed to be gone. How we both were too tired to have any fun by the time he landed in Black Hall. We accused, denied, disavowed, then finally, agreed, for the truth was quite obvious: we missed each other like crazy, and all because of his work. For the moment we would change nothing, but at least we had raised the problem. Like a still-activated undersea mine brought to the surface by scuba divers, danger remained, but at least it was in plain sight.

Stepping close to me, Nick chased away the melodrama. I caught a glimpse of us in the bathroom mirror: Nick, so tall, with softly curling black hair, me with hair as black as Nick's but eyes pale instead of dark.

"You really like cleaning bathrooms?" he whispered into my hair.

"No, I like looking through medicine cabinets."

"It's your cataloguing instinct," Nick said. "It sounds to me like a human version of your profile of the bay."

"I want to do profiles of people, Nick. Study the most ordinary people I can find. I learn the most amazing things about high-school girls—"

"Your parents named you right, Agassiz."

My mother, who had had me during her graduate years at the Woods Hole Oceanographic Institute, had let my father call me Georgiana after his mother under the condition my middle name be "Agassiz" after Louis Agassiz, the great naturalist. His motto had been "Study nature, not books." Much to Honora's dismay I had adopted it and not gone to college.

"Honora will love this idea," Nick said. "Maybe she and I can be your patrons for awhile. You can do a newsletter for the family until you think of something broader."

"I already have. I've written up a grant proposal, and I'm submitting it to the Avery Foundation. I want them to fund the Swift Observatory."

"You have? Maybe this will take your mind off my work," Nick said.

"Maybe," I said, but I doubted it and so did Nick.

Kissing goodnight in pajamas and glasses we reminded me of those couples in black-and-white home movies: stocky, jerky, the wife in a shirtwaist, the husband in a white shirt and tie, bumping glasses and noses during the kiss, smiling at the camera. Safe. Old-fashioned. A real married couple.

· · ·

In March I got the money.

I could hardly believe it.

Two thousand dollars paid by the Avery Foundation to the Swift Observatory for the study of human nature, and all they expected in return were quarterly reports on my progress.

· · ·

The study of human nature deserved more than a few quarterly reports, so I decided to narrow my focus. By that windy May morning I had started to specialize in families. My first reports covered three sisters who had traveled around the world together, a couple whose Christmas tree farm had just been repossessed, a man whose new bride had drowned in a white-water kayaking accident, and a woman accused of helping her terminally ill husband kill himself.

I let myself in my front door, changed into jeans and a sweater, and walked into my work room. Battered wicker furniture covered with faded summer fabric filled the small space. The surface of every table was covered by shells, sharks' teeth, vases of dried heather, tendrils of dried seaweed, framed snapshots of us and our families. On my desk, an eighteenth-century French work table, piles of notes about families covered old notes and sketches of marine life in the bay. Through two windows I saw the bay, the rocky headlands that protected it from the open Sound, Clare's house farther out the western headland. My mother's house, hidden from my sight, nestled in a pine grove. Pem's house, big and dark and empty now, lorded it over the entire scene, its widow's walk barely showing over the treeline.

Yesterday's newspapers covered the seat of my chair. I went through them in search of stories about families. Since giving up my maid's work, I had to take my ideas from the media. The relationship between Senator Hearne and his troubled son interested me, but of course it interested everyone in the state. The dynamics of life in the Children's Home, where brothers and sisters were allowed to stay together, seemed brave and poignant, but too public. Social workers studied that place every day. Newsprint had turned my hands black by the time I came to the story about Mona Tuchman.

Mona Tuchman had tried to kill her husband's mistress. She stabbed the woman with a butter knife. Despite the weapon's bluntness, Mona Tuchman had cracked one of the woman's ribs and left her bleeding. This had happened in the woman's own kitchen. The woman remained in the hospital; Mona Tuchman had been in jail but now was free on bail. She had three children. She was my age. The other woman, whose name was Celeste Stone, was a close friend. A source said Mrs. Tuchman had been so shocked to hear about her husband's affair that she had gone straight to the friend's apartment, just four blocks away on Central Park West, and confronted her. One thing led to another, and Mona Tuchman grabbed the nearest weapon. "We're grateful it wasn't chicken shears," the source said. Apparently the other woman was an excellent cook, in the process of boning partridge breasts when Mona Tuchman burst in.

The newspaper reporter found this situation hilarious. Why quote "We're grateful it wasn't chicken shears" in a story about real tragedy? I sat there holding the newspaper, listening to waves slap the rocks, thinking about desperate Mona Tuchman. One day she thought she was happily married, that night she was an attempted murderer. Her husband had custody of their children. They had been married six years; he was an eye surgeon, she ran a mail-order patchwork quilt business. I imagined her choosing that line of work because it would allow her to stay home with her children. I imagined her at that moment: alone in the West Side apartment she had, until two days ago, shared with her family. Now they were gone. I conjured up this picture of her: huddled in a chair by the window, knees drawn up to her chin, dark hair greasy because she didn't have the strength to wash it. A woman named Mona Tuchman would have dark hair, or maybe I was just thinking of the Mona Lisa.

I have always believed that anyone, sufficiently provoked, could be capable of murder. Clare and I once laid the groundwork to murder someone. When we were thirteen and fifteen, our mother came close to marrying a man named Carson Bleyle. We hated him. He made himself too comfortable in our house too soon. At the same time, he owned a house in New Haven and wanted us to move there. He couldn't keep his hands off Honora, and thinking back on it, Clare and I have agreed he was overly touchy with us as well. "Bring me some tissues, lovey," he was fond of calling through the bathroom door. Whenever he visited he would take a solitary stroll to the end of Pem's dock. He would smoke a cigar and stroll back. Clare and I decided he would meet his fate on one of those moonlight strolls. We bought marbles at Malloys, poured them into a mesh bag that had once held onions, and tied them underwater to a piling. Within days the bright glass turned murky with algae. Tiny sea plants attached themselves to the smooth surfaces. After a week the marbles looked as though they had been in salt water for a year. Our plan was this: we would retrieve them, spread them over the dock and lie in wait for Carson. He would slip on the marbles. When he fell into the water, we would bash him with a rock. Upon investigation, the police would discover the marbles, but Clare would swear she had lost them when she was nine. Although Honora broke up with him before we came close to acting, planning Carson's demise gave us much pleasure.

Mona Tuchman had acted, not planned. Hers was a crime of passion, brought off in mere seconds. Sources said they doubted premeditation. In the heat of the moment she had grabbed a butter knife and driven it into her friend's ribs. How much better it would have been for Mona in the long run if she had simply fantasized killing the other woman. Perhaps nothing could stop the romance, but at least she wouldn't have to go through life known as the woman who tried to kill her husband's lover. And a laughingstock as well for having used a butter knife. Why did I care nothing for Celeste Stone, the other woman? Alone in my room I could have cried for Mona Tuchman, but for the woman who lay injured in her hospital bed I thought only, "Homewrecker."

I reached for the Manhattan white pages. There were listings for Richard Tuchman MD and Tuchman Country Quilts at the West Seventy-fourth Street address. From past experience I knew that today was the time to call her. In a week she would figure out how to ditch the interviewers: change her phone number, move out of town, refuse to comment. But for now she would answer obediently, as if cooperation would improve her luck. I dialed the business number.

"Tuchman Country Quilts," the voice said.

"May I speak with Mona Tuchman, please?" I asked in my
most respectful tone.

"This is she."

"Mrs. Tuchman, this is Georgiana Swift calling from the Swift
Observatory—"

Long pause. "This is my business line. Are you calling to order
a quilt?"

"No, I'd like to interview you."

"I know, I can tell from the tone of your voice. Reverential,
you know? The way you talk to someone at their mother's funeral.
I'll bet you write for a woman's magazine, you're after the sis-
terhood angle. You've got the sensitive approach."

"I don't write for a magazine. I'm doing a study."

"Well, get off my fucking business line. I'm taking orders
today." Her voice cracked into a sob, and the line went dead.

I sat very still, holding the receiver and shaking all over. What
kind of a creep was I? I felt like the paparazzi who followed the
Royals down the slopes at Klosters, who hounded the families of
murder victims. Who was I to envision Mona Tuchman curled
into a pitiful ball, hiding from the world? She was trying to keep
her life together. She was conducting business. She was an ordinary woman. She had just tried to kill someone.

DRIVEN TO VIOLENCE FOR LOVE OF HUSBAND

LOVES SO INTENSELY SHE'D KILL FOR IT?

WHAT ABOUT HER KIDS IF SHE GOES TO JAIL?

HOW DOES HER HUSBAND FEEL ABOUT HER NOW? HER KIDS?

FAMILY AT ALL COSTS

BREAKUP UNTHINKABLE

BRAVE LADY, BUT CRAZY

I sat there writing notes about Mona Tuchman, listening to
the storm gathering force. I couldn't stop thinking about her,

writing about her. I put myself in her place: if Nick had an affair, wouldn't I want to attack his mistress? That stopped me for a moment because of course the answer was no, I would want to attack him.

Then I remembered that Celeste Stone had been a close friend of Mona's. They had met at their daughters' playschool. How sordid that made it seem, the image of adultery combined with images of pitch pipes, colored construction paper, poster paints, rocking horses. After our father had died, Honora had told me and Clare that he had been unfaithful with the mother of one of our friends. Then she had refused to tell us which friend. Also she had refused to tell us how she had felt about it, except to give us the message that men, even good men, should be watched carefully and not quite trusted. The fact that she had stayed married to him, had not tried to stab anyone with a butter knife, said something. Why did I think that interviewing Mona Tuchman could tell me what?

.   .   .

I could hardly remember my father, but I know I loved him. When he was alive we lived in Woods Hole. Timothy Swift was a top geologist-geophysicist at the Marine Biological Laboratory, and Honora was a weather girl with a red-and-blue uniform and a stage name—Wendy Swift. She also did a series called "Weather Woman," now a camp classic, in which she played a good character able to affect events by controlling the weather. Her beauty and eccentricities made her a natural for the talk-show circuit. Every time she appeared on television, my father, Clare, and I would watch. We witnessed her forecast hurricanes and clearing trends, we saw her banish the Princess of Heat Waves to Lapland, we watched her on "Live at Five," "Midday Talk," and, at the height of her fame, on the Dick Cavett show. "That's my wife," my father would say out loud in a puzzled voice, but we knew he was proud. He took care of us on all her publicity trips. When she was gone he let us stay up late; sometimes he let me stay in his office instead of going to school.

My father's office was just across Eel Pond from my school, and I remember waving to each other every morning at eleven. The few times he forgot I felt terrible. My teacher would tell me he forgot because he was a "dedicated scientist." In Woods Hole the greatest compliment anyone could bestow was "dedicated scientist." They all accepted that my father, with his books and yellow pencils, deserved the appellation, but most felt that Honora, with her glamorous job and stage name, did not. Clare and I assumed they were jealous that a dedicated scientist like our mother could make so much more money than they could, get picked up in a black sedan, and be recognized at the Cape Cod Mall in Hyannis. Even now, as adults, we couldn't believe that our father could have found any woman in Woods Hole more attractive than she. But of course that's not what adultery is about. Need is what adultery is about. It has taken me all this time to find out.

My father was tall and solid. He rowed around Eel Pond every morning at dawn to keep from getting fat. Sometimes he would take me and Clare in the boat. I remember his oars splashing the still surface, making too much noise. We felt thrilled with embarrassment that he might be waking the town. He had a wonderful black moustache that turned up at the ends, so he always looked like he was smiling. Honora called him "Timmy." Pem called him "Tim" or "Tim dear," but we all knew she resented him for keeping us in Woods Hole instead of at Bennison Point in Black Hall.

I must have sensed some trouble between our parents because I was always praying they wouldn't get divorced. I prayed and found comfort in Catholic rituals and symbols, the secrets and mysteries, the story of Mary, the concept of an all-loving God who kept families together, the beautiful tales of Lourdes and Fatima. The church in Woods Hole had a Mary Garden, a peaceful place planted with flowers whose names were associated with Mary. The Madonna Lily; St. Mary's tree (rosemary); Lady Never Fade (wild strawberry); the Dear Mother's Love (wild thyme); and Lady's Cushion (thrift pink). I felt dizzy in that garden. I'd walk carefully around the grass walk wishing for Mary to appear to me the way she had to the children at Fatima, praying for everything to be "all right." I never defined "all right," but I knew it had something to do with my parents staying happy together. Or at least together.

Then my father took the job with Ordaco. Leaving research for a high-paying job with an oil company was perceived in Woods Hole as selling out. Honora told us one day, "Your friends might tell you that Daddy has 'sold out,' but that is because their parents are envious of him. The way they are of me. So hold your heads high." He spent a lot of time in Texas and Scotland. For some reason his absence was a relief to me. It seemed entirely job-related, nothing like the emotional separation I had feared. Development had begun in the North Sea; his involvement caused great excitement for Honora, Clare, and me. We couldn't wait for his letters, his phone calls. Oil gushed at a tremendous rate. He studied new sites, new sediment samples, and determined whether the company should dig. Honora told us he was "in charge."

Off the coast of Scotland he lived on an oil rig equipped with movie theaters, restaurants, and a health spa. He wrote that the men could order anything they wanted, including North American lobster, and the chef would prepare it. He wrote that he was getting a little fat without Eel Pond to row around. Even though Clare and I were young, we could see that Honora loved him more after he started his glamorous job. He would return from Texas with cowboy hats and Indian jewelry, from Scotland with tweed and shortbread. Honora paid more attention to him than she had when he was doing research, but I still sensed trouble. It came from him. He never seemed peaceful in our house. His letters were wonderful, full of love, but at home his eyes betrayed that he wished he were elsewhere.

Then a North Sea gale, Force Ten, had swept away the oil rig and all the men on board. For years I had nightmares of tidal waves, great whirlpools sucking the men underwater, murky black seas that reflected no light from the sun or stars. I kept picturing my father treading water, waiting to be rescued, wind screaming in his ears. Sometimes I thought that if he had wanted more than anything to come home to us, he would have been saved. He drowned. Lying awake on certain nights I would think of his eyes, darting to the window, the door, the chimney. On those visits home, only his moustache smiled. I would think of him leaving a hole in our family, and I would drown him all over again. Perhaps that was why I couldn't forget Mona Tuchman. She couldn't bear her husband leaving her, leaving a hole in her family. She would rather kill someone than let that happen.

The following Friday was my turn to have the family dinner. That night I was happy. I remember it so well. Everyone was gathered together under my roof. Nick walked around passing nuts. Honora and Pem sat at opposite ends of the sofa with Eugene and Casey between them. The boys grew restless with embarrassment watching their parents lipsynch "Strangers in the Night." Nick came to sit beside me on the floor. One big pillow of faded cotton paisley leaned against the french doors, and we rested our heads on it. Sitting outside the circle of direct light felt intimate, and I pressed closer to him.

"We all ought to be home where we belong," Pem said crossly. Naturally she meant we should all be at her house.

"The family's together, Mother," Honora said. "Georgie's cooked a lovely dinner. Can't you smell the lamb?"

"I'm glad I got off easy today," Donald said. "I almost had to fly to Zurich."

"You boys are ridiculously devoted," Honora said. "I know

that's what it takes to make it on Wall Street, but still. Am I being a boring mother-in-law?"

"Yes," Donald, Clare, Nick and I said at once.

"It's cold in here," Pem said.

Nick walked over to her, shook out the black shawl I kept folded on the bannister, and laid it across her shoulders. She nodded but started to rise. Anticipating her mission, Nick pushed her down. "Sit down, Pem," he said. "I'll get you another martini."

"Another? It's my first," she said, indignant.

"It's your second," Eugene said. It didn't matter, since Pem's martinis were now one tablespoon of gin floating in a glass of tonic water.

"I'll get it," Nick said. Pem started a little boxing match, but Nick turned it into a waltz. She rested her head on his shoulder, her eyes rolling as though she wanted us to see she thought it was a big joke, but everyone knew she was enjoying the dance.

"Make it a good one," she said as Nick headed to the kitchen for her drink.

"Have you read about Mona Tuchman?" I asked.

"The woman who tried to kill her husband?" Honora asked.

"No, she tried to kill his mistress," Clare said, "though I question how seriously she wanted to. She used a butter knife."

"Butter wouldn't melt in her mouth," Donald said. "Is she the subject of your latest study?"

"I'm interested in her, yes. I called her. How do you think she'd sound on the phone?"

"Weepy," Honora said.

"No, quite strong. I was a little surprised."

"Women whose husbands cheat on them can find amazing reserves of strength," Clare said. "You shouldn't make it out to be the end of the world, Georgie."

I watched Honora for her reaction, but there was none. Her hands rested on her lap, palms up. She seemed to be avidly watching Eugene jiggle two ice cubes in his glass of lemonade.

"Do you think she'll go to jail?" Clare asked.

"Doubtful," Donald said. "Her lawyers will use the classic 'heat of passion' line of reasoning. She'll get off." Donald had a stiff way of speaking; he always sounded like a lawyer, even within our midst, but after Nick he was the best man I knew.

"How can you remember that?" Nick asked, coming into the room with Pem's drink. "I haven't read a criminal case since law school."

"I don't know anything—I'm just bluffing. Trying to sound like a wise lawyer."

"They'll use the 'extreme emotional distress' defense, don't you think?" I asked. Nick and I had married between his first and second years of law school, and Criminal Law and Evidence had been my favorites of his classes.

"Why don't you hang out your shingle?" Honora asked, her eyes sparkling.

"The mere matter of no law degree," I answered. "No law degree, no college degree—thank heavens I didn't decide to snub education until after I'd finished high school."

"Why do you say that?" Honora asked, frowning. "What did you need high school for? You've always had your eyes open, sweetie." She turned to Eugene and Casey. "When your auntie was your age she knew more about fish than any kid in Woods Hole. Not to mention birds, seaweed, rocks and electricity. She could make you a battery right now—out of materials in plain sight in this room."

"This morning we saw a scarlet tanager," Casey said.

"Now your mother, on the other hand," Honora continued, smiling at Clare, "was quite different. She got straight A's in math, English, history, everything. Also, she was a very good sculptor. But she wasn't so interested in nature."

"That's why she had the time to get two PhDs," I said. Everyone laughed, and Clare gave me a secret smile. Even with her advanced degrees, I knew she valued knowledge and the task of learning more than diplomas. She had never used her art and biochemistry degrees professionally. In another family that might have been considered a strange waste of time and talent, but Honora had come to understand Clare's decision to be a stay-at-home wife and mother. We had been taught that learning mattered; it was essential, but whether we wanted to use our accrued knowledge in careers or in the most private way was up to us.

Still, no matter what Honora now said, she had railed and gnashed her teeth when I had refused to go to college. My decision terrified her. Perhaps she had doubted one could learn without the structure of a university. I glanced at Clare's small smile and figured she was thinking of Honora's evolution.

On Bennison Point Pem and I represented the unschooled. I tried to get her attention, but she was engaged with her weak martini.

"You know, Mother," Clare said. "I was interested in nature, but that was always Georgie's province. Georgie was the nature lover, I was the bookworm. Georgie was the tomboy, I loved pretty dresses. It's strange how we attribute different characteristics to each child. Even here," she said, casting a significant glance at her two sons, playing with drink coasters. "One is the scamp, the other the gentleman." I thought I saw Eugene, the scamp, sharpen when he heard that, but he continued to play.

"I think Georgie would be a good lawyer," Nick said. "She knows a lot of law. She sat through the bar review with me, and I know she could have passed the bar exam. In some states you don't need a law degree—you serve an apprenticeship, then pass the bar."

Honora leaned forward, grinning. "I'm just waiting to see what happens with the Observatory. I think it will put the Swift name on the map."

"Thanks, Mom," I said. For no matter how plain I saw Honora, she was still my mother, and I wanted her to be proud of me.

· · ·

In a week the weather was clear and fine. I lay on the floor of my work room, reading old newspapers. The sun had come around the Point and was streaming through the tall windows. It glittered on the bay. Shore birds appeared in bold relief against the brightness. By their silhouettes I recognized mallards, mergansers, buffleheads, brants, loons, and cormorants. The kingfisher perched on the pier. I found no updates on Mona Tuchman. The phone rang.

"It's me," said Nick.

"What's cooking?"

"Tonight will be very late. I won't make it home."

"I'll make a reservation," I said. Whenever Nick had to stay so late that he would miss his flight, I would book a room at the Gregory and take a train into the city.

"Georgie, are you sure you want to? It's going to be late, and I mean late."

"Don't ask such a ridiculous question," I said.

"Ah, well." He paused, then said, "Project Broadsword is taking off. A corporate raider is getting into the act."

Corporate raider. I thought of the language of tender offers: white knight, golden parachutes, shark repellents, scorched earth, sale of crown jewels. It had a poetry that belied the brash doggedness of the participants. "Don't tell me the details. Discretion is paramount. Someone might have your phone bugged."

"Which train will you take?" Nick asked, ignoring my sarcasm. I couldn't stand the way he used those phrases, like a boy playing King Arthur or Arabian Nights, playful little phrases that trivialized his work and made too light of the disruption it caused in our lives.

"The next one. The one that gets in at two-thirty."

"I'm sorry about this. It's just that meetings are scheduled all day, and then I'll have to turn the agreement around. They need a final version tomorrow morning."

"That's okay," I said. "We can have a late dinner tonight. Clare gave me a book about New York restaurants open after midnight. There are more than you'd think." Nick laughed. I pictured him leaning back in his brown leather chair, his back to the window facing Trinity Church's dark spire. I knew exactly which glen plaid suit he had worn that morning, which navy foulard tie, which socks. His white shirts were interchangeable; even I could not tell them apart. The instant a fray appeared, he would give me the shirt to wear on the beach. I found his dislike of frays endearing.

"Should I call you when I get in?" I asked.

"Of course. Leave a message with Denise if I can't come to the phone."

"I will. I love you."

"I love you."

I love you: We said it so often I sometimes expected the words to lose their meaning, but they never did.

We had a regular room at the Gregory, a small hotel on West Twentieth Street named for Yeat's Lady Gregory. Before the west side marshes had been filled in, the hotel had stood at the edge of the Hudson River. Now you couldn't even see the water from our room on the top floor. A ten-minute walk from the river, and I felt landlocked. The hotel had a genteel shabbiness: faded brocade draperies, mahogany walls and lobby furniture, polished brass lamps, leather chairs at the writing tables, sad-eyed portraits of Lady Gregory. Nick sometimes suggested we stay at a fancy hotel on Central Park, but I liked it here. I felt totally anonymous. The bellman barely greeted me; I carried my own bag upstairs. In the dark shadows of Manhattan, I tried to not

feel anger about leaving bright, sparkling Black Hall. Wasn't it
my choice to join Nick? He had never insisted that I come to
town; in fact I could not remember him actually suggesting it.
He was happy that I wanted to, but the idea was mine.

I paced the room for a few minutes. The desk was antique,
in need of new brass drawer pulls. I used a plastic pen cap to
pry open one drawer, to check whether the previous tenant had
left anything behind. Once I had lost four sketches of marine life
in that very drawer, but today it was empty. I spread my papers
across the desk. My first quarterly report was due in a month.

I called Nick's office and left a message with Denise. Then I
picked up the Manhattan phone book. I called Mona Tuchman's
number. She answered.

"Hello, this is Georgiana Swift calling from the Swift Observatory," I said, expecting her to hang up.

"Mmmm."

"I wondered whether I could interview you."

"I don't know. Maybe. What does the Swift Observatory want
with me?"

"To ask you a few questions. Talk to you a while."

"I notice you don't have the rapid-fire approach. You could
have already asked me some questions."

"I thought we could meet. You could come to my hotel, or I
could go to you. Whichever you prefer." I could hardly believe
I was arranging a meeting with Mona Tuchman. After our last
conversation I had been steeled for an attack.

"You might as well come here," she said. "Okay?"

"Okay," I said, already planning my subway route.

She lived in a big building on the Upper West Side where
stone gargoyles, angels, and rams leered from rooftops and lintels.
A brilliant green patch of Central Park was visible around the
corner. A terra-cotta planter of begonias stood outside the entrance. The doorman directed me to the eighth floor.

She was waiting in the foyer. I had been right about the dark hair; short and curly, it framed her round face. She wore tortoiseshell glasses. Gentle lines indicated that her face was accustomed to smiling, but it was at that moment expressionless. She wore a full green corduroy jumper over a nylon turtleneck. I wondered whether she was pregnant.

"Entrée," she said, preceding me into the apartment. We introduced ourselves.

"What is the Swift Observatory?" she asked, gesturing at a brick-red wing chair. I sat, watching her settle herself onto a straight-backed desk chair. The decor was vaguely colonial. Patchwork quilts hung on two walls.

"It's an organization that studies human nature."

"Yikes. What kind of human nature are you after here? Human nature. I don't know, I thought this was going to be an ordinary interview."

"It is. I don't want to intimidate you," I stammered. I felt intimidated myself, and pompous at the same time. "Actually, I am the Swift Observatory—I'm all there is. I needed a name for my work because it's funded, you see." As Clare had said, the foundation would be more likely to give grant money to the Swift Observatory than "Georgie Swift, Nosy Bitch."

"I never planned to kill Celeste Stone. My hand was stabbing her, then all of a sudden I realized what I was doing and stopped. In one instant I ruined my life. Well, not an instant exactly. I was hitting her for about thirty seconds, we think."

"We?"

"Celeste and I. We haven't spoken to each other, but we communicate through our lawyers. I've already been told that I probably won't go to jail, but I'll go on probation and lose custody of my children. Celeste says she doesn't want me to go to jail. She's being very big about this. She's lying in a hospital bed at this very moment. They're letting her out tomorrow." Mona looked out the window as she spoke. Her voice lilted slightly, betraying no emotional connection to the words.

"Did you know her well?"

"Very well. We met at the nursery school. The mothers take turns volunteering, and she and I usually had the same day. Her husband is a doctor too. A dermatologist. Dick's an eye surgeon."

"And the couples became friendly."

"That's right. We took ski trips together." She looked at me for the first time. "I don't want to talk about the romance."

"All right."

"I'll just say that I knew but I didn't know. In other words, I now realize that subconsciously I knew something was going on, but I refused to recognize it. Then someone told me about it—my mother, in fact—and I went crazy."

"Your mother told you your husband was having an affair?"

"Yes. Isn't that unbelievable? I feel ashamed that she knows anything about it. She saw them . . . kissing . . . outside a restaurant. She told me, then everything became clear. Everything I had known but not known. Dick had just left town for a conference, so I couldn't confront him. I went crazy and headed to Celeste's. I'm a great believer in the subconscious. I think I chose a butter knife because I didn't really want to kill her. This is the most ridiculous thing to be talking about. I hardly believe I did it—I know I did, but I still can't believe it. I'm not the type to stab someone."

"Are you pregnant?"

She looked away again. "I don't want to talk about that," she said.

I had the feeling she wasn't being totally sincere, that she was using me a little. I could hardly blame her. She would benefit from sympathetic news stories.

"Excuse me, Mrs. Tuchman," I said. "I should tell you that my account of your story will probably not be published."

"Really? I didn't know that." She sounded upset.

"Did your lawyer tell you to give interviews?"

"Yes, but hardly anyone seems interested. Last week they were, but I wasn't ready. Too much time has passed or something, and they're on to a new story." Her voice shook and tears glazed her eyes. "He thought I'd stand a better chance if the public liked me. He said if they identified with me instead of Celeste, I'd get off easy and maybe get to keep my kids. Oh, God, that's the worst part," she said, really sobbing now. "What are they going to think of me?"

"They'll understand," I said calmly. "They'll understand that you wanted to keep the family together."

"That's it," she said, sounding bewildered.

"Tell me about that," I said.

"It's so simple. I love Dick. We have a wonderful family— two girls and a boy. I'm his wife, he's their father, they're our kids, we're parents, they're sisters and a brother. We're a family. That's exactly it," she said, as if the thought had occurred to her for the first time. "We belong together."

"That's what I figured the moment I read that article about you."

"What makes you so interested in my story?" Mona asked me, frowning, cleaning her glasses with the hem of her dress.

"Because I think I understand exactly how you felt," I said.

"No one has said that to me. I realize that most people wouldn't actually have done it, but I thought they might understand how I felt. My neighbor shuddered when she saw me. Even the people who really know us, know how close Dick and I are, can't understand how it happened. I haven't seen my kids yet, but I've seen Dick. He looks like he's in shock. He says there's been a problem between us for a long time, but he doesn't love Celeste."

"Why did you decide to confront her?"

"Good question. I have no idea. I was standing in my kitchen, talking to my mother. She told me about seeing them. After she left I was sitting there thinking. I didn't feel sad or hurt exactly. Just rage—I felt as though a cyclone was inside me, whirling me over to Celeste's apartment. I have this picture of myself running down the Park, flailing like a rag doll."

"Then what happened?" I asked. I could see her exactly, floppy with fury.

"She was in the kitchen. She was wearing a checkered apron, standing at her butcher block island, peeling the skin off partridge breasts. She's a fabulous cook." Mona sighed.

"What are you thinking?"

"Oh, just remembering some of the dinners we had at her house. Anyway, I said, 'I just heard the news' or something like that. She said 'What news?' with a terribly bright expression and a happy voice, as if I were going to tell her the Bolshoi was coming to town. I mean, what other news could it possibly be? That made me even angrier. I guess I screamed something about her and Dick, and then I just grabbed the butter knife off the butter dish and began hitting her with it. That's how I think of it—hitting her. I hate the thought of stabbing. I hate it."

"But the papers said you drew blood."

"I gave her a bloody nose." She paused. "I did hurt her with the butter knife, though. I heard her rib crack. She doubled over, and she looked like Lee Harvey Oswald in that picture where Ruby shoots him. It was horrible. See, when I think about it I remember quite a lot. I'll always remember that look on her face."

"When I called the other day you said you were trying to get on with business."

"I am. I think that's important. I've sort of given myself an assignment: get up, make coffee, do my work. It's the only way to get through this."

I wanted to ask what she imagined her future would be, but

the question was too cruel. Here she was, talking about making a good start each day.

"I expected this interview to be different," she said. "I thought I could portray myself in a certain way, and you would print it. Instead we've just talked. I've enjoyed it."

"So have I. I wish I could help your cause. I should go now, but I'll leave my number just in case—" I wrote down my numbers at the Gregory and in Black Hall. Then I stood to leave and we shook hands. She followed me to the elevator. She gestured at a closed door.

"That's Dick's office. He's in there right now, seeing patients. Unless he's at the hospital," she said, frowning, as if she were unused to not knowing his whereabouts. "One of us will obviously have to move. God, before this happened I could call one of my friends to talk. You've got me in the mood to talk, but I don't know who to call. Everyone is afraid I'll bring up the event. They don't know how to react—they're afraid they'll sound too sympathetic or approving." Suddenly I couldn't wait for the elevator doors to close. How terrible it seemed, for a woman who was used to the company of friends and, especially, her husband and children, suddenly to be left alone. She didn't even feel free to make a phone call. It seemed like the worst punishment on earth.

The air outside was fresh, and I crossed to the sunny side of the street. I heard sparrows cheeping; I looked up to see a pair nesting in a hollow section of the traffic light. This seemed normal, a standard rite of springtime. I decided to walk through the park, anything to get my mind off Mona Tuchman. In a shady bog not three yards from Central Park West I saw a jack-in-the-pulpit. Then pigeons in a mating dance. Then a young girl standing on her toes to kiss her boyfriend. The girl was wearing a pink dress. I heard birds singing, horns honking, children playing, when all of a sudden I knew I had to talk to Nick.

I'd done this before, when the specter of infidelity reared its unwelcome head. I needed to know that Nick wasn't doing it, would never do it, to me. Cheating on me. Kissing someone else. Honora was in there, pitching her message: keep track of your man. I began to look for a cab.

At the Gregory I waited for the elevator with painful nonchalance, then hurried to the phone in my room. A strange pattern had just been set in motion: I was going to call Nick, seek reassurance that he loved me and would always be faithful, then hang up feeling like a fool. I could view it objectively, the way a lab technician views a specimen, but I was going to do it anyway.

Denise told me he was in a meeting.

"Did he say he wasn't to be disturbed?" I asked. "Because this is pretty important, Denise." I rarely disturbed Nick when he was in a meeting, but suddenly I felt that unless I spoke to him, I wouldn't be able to breathe.

"The thing is, Georgie, he isn't here. The meeting is uptown, at the client's place."

"That's okay," I said, hanging up.

Every once in a while, when Denise was vague about where Nick had gone, I started thinking about the women on Wall Street. They were sleek, beautiful, accomplished. They dressed well. Some of them spent more late nights with Nick than I did. I hated imagining them huddled over documents, their heads nearly touching. I called Clare.

"Where are you?" she asked. "Eugene and Case just swam over for a visit, but they said you weren't home."

"In New York. I'm at the Gregory."

"Georgie, you're nuts. So Nick has to work late one night. What's the big deal about sleeping alone?"

"You read my mind. I've got affair-paranoia again."

"You want me to run through the usual things?" Clare asked.

"If you wouldn't mind."

"All right. You and Nick love each other. It's obvious to anyone who looks at you. You've been honest with each other. You have to trust him more. He would be so hurt if he knew you had these doubts."

I laughed at her tone of voice, which was deadpan. "Thanks. I feel better. This started because I just met Mona Tuchman. I feel so sorry for her, Clare."

"I know. Her situation sounds dreadful. Has she seen her kids?"

"No."

"God, I'd die if I ever lost the boys. Have you ever noticed you call me more from New York than you do from home?"

"I have. It's weird."

"It's because when you're at Black Hall you know I'm there. If you look out your window you see my house. When you go away you think maybe I've disappeared. You're a really insecure traveler. Honora is the same way—whenever she leaves the Point she calls constantly. You two must have some phone bills."

"That's putting it mildly."

"Quit mooning over Nick, will you? It's really undignified. Not to mention unnecessary. When you have something worth worrying about, you'll know it."

"What you say makes perfect sense."

"But it doesn't sink in, eh?"

"Not completely. But I'll get to work on my report and try not to think about it."

"I marvel at the fact that my sister's husband can't spend one night without her, she rushes to his side at the drop of a hat, and then she spends her time looking for lipstick on his collar."

"That's a little parable about me?"

"You're the only sister I've got, honey."

We said goodbye, and the second we hung up the phone, Clare disappeared. She was absolutely right: if I didn't have the person with me, anything might be happening to him. The minute Nick flew out of sight every morning, he could crash-land, be pounced upon by brazen hussies, forget me. Honora had trained my imagination well. I reached for my notebooks and arranged them on the desktop. I held my pen very tight. I concentrated on every word. I reported all my recent cases, winding up with Mona Tuchman. Hours passed. I barely noticed. By eleven that night, when it was time to meet Nick for dinner, everyone who had disappeared was coming back. They were all there, in place but invisible, at the edge of my consciousness. Nick, Clare, Honora, Pem. Reunions brought them back.

"Do you think we should have a baby?" I asked Nick across the table at Vinnie's in the Village. Candles burned in wrought-iron sconces, casting romantic light on his face. The restaurant was lively, considering the hour. I had to speak in a louder voice than I would have liked. Nick stopped twirling his tagliatelle. He grinned.

"That's a nice question," he said.

"Well?"

"You know I'd like to, but I'm afraid of how my hours would affect raising a child. You'd have to do a lot more than your fair share."

"What's a fair share when it comes to a child?" I asked, scoffing. I sipped some Barolo. "We'd each do everything we possibly could."

"Consider whether you would have come into the city today if we had a baby. I'm not sure it would be possible. In fact," he said, with deliberation, "I've been thinking about it—the way you come in whenever I work late."

"Are you saying you don't want me to?" I asked, more sharply than I had intended.

"Georgie, we're just having a conversation. I want a nice dinner—" His lips tightened, then relaxed into a smile. He took my hand. "We're not setting anything in stone. I just think you shouldn't come to New York every time I work late. Other lawyers manage it. Jean and her husband spend two days a week apart, and they seem happy," Nick said. Jean was one of those Wall Street females I most hated to imagine huddled with Nick at the conference table.

"I guess tonight is not the time to talk about having a baby," I said, because he would know how furious I was if I kept talking.

"Georgie." Deep sigh. "Shit. Forget it. Do you want me to quit my job?"

Guilt found fertile ground. "I don't want to be responsible for you quitting Hubbard, Starr."

"Give me some credit, okay? Don't you think I question the way we live? It's crazy, me flying in and out of Black Hall, bringing home work every weekend, spending so much time away from you. You coming to New York just so we can have a quick dinner together. It would be much easier if we lived in the city, but we both love the Point so much."

"I know," I said. It was typical of Nick to not take unfair advantage in an argument. He could have said "but you love the Point so much." He knew how much I loved my family. Another man might have resented that, blamed our difficulties on my unwillingness to leave them, but he loved them too.

"It will be easier on us both if you stop checking into the Gregory every time—if we don't always count on having dinner together," Nick said. "I'm so tired right now I can't taste what I'm eating. And I have to be at the office by seven tomorrow morning."

"Have you been dying to bring this up?" I asked. "Just waiting?"

"It's been on my mind," he said.

Can you pinpoint the moment when a marriage begins to change? It can be an instant or longer, a period that marks the end of the relationship as you've known it and the start of something new, something that could turn out to be sweet or dangerous. To observers, even to people who knew us well, that night at Vinnie's in the Village might have seemed ordinary. But it was not. Sitting across that cozy bistro table from Nick I felt anger but also a sort of grief. I was losing something I loved.

Dining together, no matter how difficult the logistics, had always been important to us. It disciplined us. Where other busy couples would lapse into one dinner a week apart, then two, then three, we had an unspoken commitment to share the evening meal.

Nick paid the check and we left Vinnie's in silence. I felt unhinged with sadness and worry. I wanted to ask him what he had meant, suggesting we not plan dinner together every night: Exactly what had he meant? I knew the answer he would give me: he was just being sensible. The time had come for us, for Nicholas Symonds and Georgiana Swift, to give in to what other couples, probably no less loving than we, had accepted much earlier. Sometimes the demands of life kept people apart. It was that simple.

But not to me. In the taxi I imagined motives: dark, heavy as sex, and furtive. I thought of Young Goodman Brown, who had imagined his wife Faith to be pure, then discovered she had joined the witches' sabbat along with the rest of the neighborhood sinners. Had we been special, Nick and I? We didn't speak, but we sat close to each other and rode uptown with our shoulders touching.

"I know I've hurt you," Nick said when we were alone in our hotel room.

Then, because he was sounding like the Nick I wanted, I started to cry. "Explain it to me," I said, which was really stupid because I knew just what he would say, and I knew that it would make good sense.

He said nothing. He turned off the bedside light and walked

to me. He held me for a long while. When he began to stroke my arms in a slow, gentle way, I began to feel mad with desire or maybe violence. Energy pulsed along my veins; I could have chaneled it into wild sex or a fistfight.

"Nick," I said, pulling back because I felt afraid. I kept my head down.

He was unbuttoning my dress. I felt his big fingers undoing the delicate buttons easily. His other hand cupped my shoulder, then pulled the dress away. I saw it fall to the floor, a puddle of blue and white cotton around my feet, and I stepped out of it. I wasn't wearing a bra. I brought my arms across my breasts, but Nick held my hands and pulled them away.

"Have I made you want to hide?" he whispered.

"No. I don't know," I said, standing stiff and hearing my sullen tone. What would happen if I hit him, I wondered. After that thought I felt more like making love. I kissed him. I was standing naked against him, and he was fully dressed. I felt his erection through his trousers. He lowered his head and kissed my nipples. Sometimes with Nick I thought of nothing and felt joined, truly joined with him in spirit, but not that night. That night he undressed me and then himself, and every place he touched me seared, and I paid attention as if I were committing every sensation to memory.

"I have always loved you," he said later, just before he fell asleep.

Watching him as he slept, I thought about dinners past and dinners yet to come. Smoked turkey and appenzellar sandwiches at the Library of Congress. During Nick's third year of law school we lived on Capitol Hill. Studying late, or preparing a journal article, he would say he was too busy to take a dinner break. I would take him sandwiches. Walking past the Senate office buildings, the Supreme Court, and the Capitol, all floodlit, white and stark, my mission seemed greater than the mere delivery of din-

ner. The Library of Congress guard would admit me with barely
a glance through my bookbag. I would cross the rotunda to the
law library where I would find Nick, at his favorite carrell beside
the mezzanine's wrought-iron balustrade. Then we would go
into the stacks to feast and talk.

Cold lemon chicken during the New York Bar Examination
review course. By this time Nick was working until midnight at
the firm, with four hours off for a nightly Bar Review course.
Circles deepened under his eyes, he lay awake every night, utterly
exhausted, worrying over the Rules of Evidence while at the same
time worrying what it meant that the head of the Tender Offer
Squad had invited Jean Snizort to lunch at the Broad Street Club
but not Nick. We were living in New York then, downtown
from the theater where the Bar Review was held. I loved that
time. Nick would take the subway up from Wall Street, I would
walk to Times Square. I would bring dinner with me, things
that could be eaten tepid or cold, and sit through the class. With
Nick taking fast notes while gobbling his dinner, I would turn
off the lecture and think about our life. Even with Nick's busy
pace we were managing to have dinner together every night. All
it took was a certain amount of creativity and flexibility. How
smug I had been! I had sat there, wondering how many wives
would plan such portable meals, so delicious that their husbands
wouldn't even notice the entire dinner had fit into two small
plastic containers.

I conjure the business trips I've gone on with Nick by remembering sirloin steak at Morton's in Chicago (a leverage buyout of
Frankenthaler, Weiss); the tandoor chicken at London's Bombay
Brasserie (negotiations with a prospective White Knight for the
ailing Rosco Corporation); turbot *grillé* at Hôtel des Indes in The
Hague (meetings on the purchase-and-sale agreement of a four-
billion-dollar transaction involving sixteen countries); Lobster Sa-
vannah at Locke-Ober's (a hostile tender offer for shares of Boston

Chemical); ravioli *de ris de veau* at Jamin in Paris (meetings to quell the general panic that hit the Firm's clients after the Socialists came into power).

I can remember vacations, periods when we had unlimited time together, without thinking of a single meal. When I think of our free time, I think of the clarity of that day's light, the species of birds we counted, the Rembrandts we gazed at, the hills we scrambled. But for a running account of our marriage, I think of the dinners.

I lay in bed beside Nick, listening to a movie playing in the next room. I could hear the voices perfectly. The story was about a farming family in Nebraska in the thirties. The father had just been shot by bandits. I lay awake, crying for the mother and children. Then I realized: I feel as though Nick's abandoned me. He's left me to keep our little vigil on my own. Our good marriage vigil.

In the following weeks, no story absorbed me the way Mona Tuchman's had. I thought of her often. I related to her: as a woman in love who had sabotaged her own marriage. It was a matter of degree. Mona had alienated Dick and her children by an act of attempted murder. Surely they must feel they no longer knew her. But Nick: he knew me. When had I wanted anything but sheer closeness? If I was willing to make the trip into New York to have dinner with him, why should he mind? I felt as though I were pushing too hard, and that that delicious, almost unbearable closeness I had had with Nick, that I had lived by since our marriage, seemed in deep jeopardy.

One morning I stood in my yard, waving goodbye to him as he flew away. Although the weather was clear and fair, I walked next door to visit my mother. I felt sad; I wanted distraction. Honora stood in her driveway, cutting yellow daylilies with garden shears. She wore lightweight white trousers, a navy blue blouse, and, although the sun hadn't risen enough to evaporate dew from the flowers' leaves and petals, a straw sunhat.

"Good morning, sweetie," she said, kissing me. "The boys have a nice day to fly. Winds will be light, out of the northwest, and the visibility should be about fifteen miles."

"Oh, good," I said.

"Your grandmother is still asleep."

"You're kidding!" I said, feeling alarmed. I had never known Pem to sleep past dawn. "Are you sure she's still. . . ." I couldn't bring myself to say "alive."

"I checked, and she was fine half an hour ago. She's been sleeping late recently." She preceded me into the house and began arranging the lilies in a tall glass vase. "I have to admit it's good to have some time without her."

"It must be," I said. The year before, Clare and I had tentatively suggested that maybe Pem should go to a rest home, and we had been relieved when Honora had said absolutely not. Knowing it was not a possibility, I felt fearless raising the subject. "Do you think it would be better if she were in a home?"

"No, of course not. But she's a day's work, Georgie. I'm not that old. If I weren't taking care of Pem, maybe I could travel or teach or something."

"Mom, you know Clare and I would help out."

"No, she's my mother. It's my responsibility."

"She's my grandmother."

Honora regarded me with blank eyes. "She wets her bed."

This came as an enormous shock. "You're kidding."

"No. She's done it twice this week. She can't take baths by herself, so I have to bathe her. We've got mice because she makes herself a little sandwich, then hides it when she hears me coming—it seems that old people feel guilty about eating. Then she forgets where she hid it. I find these dried crusts all over the house."

"I know about the sandwiches—I find them in my house every time she visits."

We heard Pem's bedsprings creaking. Then her feet shuffling into slippers, then the window being opened.

"How's your report coming?" Honora asked. "It must be due soon."

"I still have a week. I'm typing it over now."

"I can't wait to read it. Did you read that Dr. Tuchman was granted custody of the children?"

"Yes," I said, thinking of how Mona must feel. If he wanted custody, that meant he was leaving her. I remembered that day in her foyer, the small hope she had felt because her husband didn't love his mistress. But that didn't mean he loved Mona, either. I watched my mother getting Pem's breakfast ready. "What do you think of her story? Can you understand how she could have stabbed Celeste Stone?"

"Mmmm, I suppose," she said, pouring orange juice.

"I mean, how did you feel when you found out Dad was having an affair?" My heart went faster as I asked the question I'd been waiting to ask.

"Well, I didn't want to kill her, if that's what you mean," Honora said, laughing a little. "She was very unimportant to me. She could have been anyone. It was your father. He shouldn't have done that to us. It was humiliating."

"You mean people knew?"

"I have no idea. But they might have. That idea made me furious. The main thing was that Timmy betrayed me. He cut himself away from us by seeing that woman."

"Who was she?"

Honora was carefully scraping thin curls of butter from the cold block. "Alice Billings."

I gasped. "You're kidding! Mrs. Billings? I didn't like her at all." Suddenly I remembered the time Mrs. Billings had driven Rachel and me to the skating pond and my father was waiting for us. I hadn't expected to see him. After helping me lace my skates, he had said he was going to sit in Mrs. Billings's car and watch me. It had been cold, with snow on the hills and tree branches. I remember skating as daringly fast as I could, wishing I was in Mrs. Billings's nice warm car with her and my father.

"She was a scrawny little mouse," Honora said. "She worked as a research assistant at the Fisheries. I used to wonder how your father could go for such a boring person, not pretty, without even an interesting job. But then it occurred to me that he wanted someone who would adore him. Who would think he was a real catch."

"He was one," I said, feeling strangely defensive of my father.

"That may be true, but it's irrelevant. He behaved like a bastard. I never trusted him again after I found out."

"But you stayed with him."

"That's true. I stayed with him for three years afterwards. I'd probably be with him still if he were still alive."

"Why? How could you stay with a man you didn't trust?"

Honora smiled her beautiful square smile. "I was raised a Catholic, dearie. Those rules stick, even when they stop making sense. Plus I'm half Irish. And you know they say Ireland is a vale of tears."

"That's why? That's the reason?" I asked.

Honora's smile collapsed. "And I loved your father. I loved him very much."

"G'morning," Pem said sweetly, shuffling over to kiss us. "It's bitter cold."

"Pem, it's nearly the Fourth of July," I said. As she turned to Honora I saw the wet patch on the back of her nightgown and looked away.

"Come on, let's have breakfast," she said.

"I have to change her," Honora said.

"I'll run upstairs and get her a clean robe," I said. By the time I returned to the kitchen, they were already in the bathroom. Honora opened the door a crack, and I handed in the robe.

"Goddamn it, I don't want to change," came Pem's voice.

"You have to. You'll be warmer if you do."

"But I don't want to!" Pem shrieked.

"Oh, Lord," I heard my mother say wearily.

I sat at the kitchen table, stirring my coffee, thinking about my father and Mrs. Billings. I hated to think of Honora feeling so betrayed. As a child I had always thought her as being incredibly strong. People say that children feel responsible when their parents' marriages go sour, break up. Sitting there at Honora's kitchen table that summer morning, I was thinking, what did Clare and I do wrong? By the time Honora and Pem emerged, I had become a waif, the product of a broken home.

"Don't look so gloomy, Georgie," my mother said. "Try to cheer her up."

Pem's face was sullen. She refused to meet my gaze.

"She's embarrassed," Honora mouthed silently.

"Good morning, Pem," I said. "Isn't it a beautiful day?"

"Beautiful," she mumbled. Honora placed a tray with toast, juice and coffee before Pem. Pem prodded the toast with her index finger, as though she were inspecting something vile and inedible, then stuck out her tongue. "Stinks," she said.

Honora pointed significantly towards her own eyebrows.

I glanced at Pem, her white hair splendidly wild that morning. Then I cocked my head and wrinkled my nose. She looked over, interested now. "What?" she asked.

"I was just wondering, what do you do to your brows?" I asked.

"So many people ask me that, it's funny," she said, her voice rising with mirth. "I do nothing to them."

"But they're so dark!"

"Well, my hair turned gray when I was only thirty years old, but my brows stayed dark," she said, beginning to be absorbed in the story. "People always say, 'What do you do to your brows?', but I do nothing!"

"They're just naturally dark?" I asked, trying to sound skeptical.

"Yes! Go on!" she said, indicating that I should test for myself by rubbing them to see in any charcoal or bootblack came off on my fingers. I touched them, then held up clean hands for Honora to see.

Pem chuckled. "So many people ask me that, and they call you a liar if you say you do nothing." She took a bite of toast. The query had done its work. Honora and I breathed deeply. Casey, a poor eater, had had to be cajoled into each mouthful by images of planes flying into the hangar, pirates delving into the cave, here comes the pony express. Persuading Pem to eat her toast was getting to be the same sort of adventure.

"Look out there," Honora said. I joined her at the window. Across the lawn, at the edge of the bay, Clare was sitting at her easel. Eugene sat at her feet, drawing on the rocks with chalk.

"A future graffiti artist," I said.

"He is a rascal," Honora said. "How did Casey turn out so sweet and calm? Eugene keeps Clare on her toes. He takes after his great-grandmother." Pem had finished her toast; we heard her rearranging the living room.

"Did you see the portrait Clare did of the boys?" I asked. "She's planning to give it to Donald for their anniversary."

"It's a beautiful painting," Honora said. "She caught their personalities, didn't she? Also Eugene's likeness to Donald. Does Eugene have a cowlick?" Honora asked, reaching for the telescope she kept on the shelf beside the toaster.

"That's a funny question," I asked. "Of course he doesn't."

"Because I could swear Clare painted him with one. Of course it was probably artistic license, giving him that Tom Sawyer look. Freckles, cowlick and all. What a kid," Honora said, turning from the window. Sunlight burnished her chestnut hair. "Is it wrong of me to wish Clare would do more with her painting?

I love her sea paintings. And I'm sure Dina Clarke at the gallery
would give her a show."

"Clare's never seemed to want that," I said. Clare, who always
seemed in perfect control as a sister, daughter, wife, and mother,
had shied away from succeeding as an artist. As her sister I was
probably unqualified to rate her painting, but I had never seen
a seascape I liked more than hers. One night after she married
Donald she confessed to me that during graduate school she had
been offered a one-woman show at Boston's Drake Gallery. I
had known enough never to tell Honora: Honora would have
lost her mind with the idea her daughter could decline such an
opportunity. Clare knew how to wisecrack, and she loved to tease
me about "affair-paranoia," but my own theory was that she bore
her own scars of my parents' troubles, and they kept her very
close to home.

"Well, she's a wonderful artist," Honora said. "It's ungenerous,
in a way, to keep her work hidden. When so many people could
enjoy it. But you're right out there, honey. My little chicken, the
Swift Observer."

"Mom, do you really think it makes sense? I mean, I've set
myself up to observe families. I love doing it, of course, but I
don't want to give myself the voice of authority."

Honora gazed at me for ten long seconds, her mouth set to
speak. "Of course it makes sense," she said, "but you do seem to
be devoting an inordinate amount of time to Mona Tuchman. I
mean, I'm wondering how Nicky feels about that."

"How Nick feels about what?" I asked, my back stiffening.

"Well, about the fact you're so fascinated in a story about
adultery. Isn't that begging for trouble?"

I sputtered. I guffawed. I was laughing so hard that Honora,
now frowning, had to give me a glass of water.

That was Honora—she said what was on her mind. She made
it her business to tell Clare she should show her work in a gallery,

to tell me my choice of subjects might be coming between me and Nick. God, how she annoyed me! But did I want the perfect mother, one who would say just the right thing without taking risks, without the cliff-edge passion that for me came along with love? Even family love, the kind that was supposed to be safest?

"Do you find it so funny?" Honora asked glumly.

"No. I find it disgusting, but I have to laugh," I said. "Daddy hurt you. That doesn't mean Nick's going to do the same thing to me."

"I hope he doesn't. I'm sure he won't, but it doesn't hurt to be on guard, sweetie."

"Okay. Thanks. Come on—let's go take a look at Clare's painting."

"You go. I've got to get your grandmother dressed."

I paused. I almost offered to help her, but instead I kissed her cheek and walked outside into the fresh air.

"Hey, there," Clare said, not looking up from her watercolor. I stood beside her, saw it was of the rocky archipelago that led from the bay into the Sound.

"Doesn't Mommy's painting look like turtle shells?" Casey asked.

"Well, yes," I said. "If you look at it a certain way, the rocks do look a little like turtle backs. Gleaming in the sun."

"I told you, I told you, Mommy," Casey said.

"Mmm," Clare said. "Box turtles? Sea turtles? Any particular kind?"

"There are sea turtles in the Galapagos Islands," Eugene said. He reached for my hand, pulled me close to the water's edge where he had drawn chalk pictures. One of them showed a dog with a remarkable penis. Eugene grinned when he saw me notice it.

"Isn't that cute?" I said. "Want to have lunch at my place today, Clare?"

"Sure. I'll bring the brownies." Clare loved to bake; brownies were her specialty. I started to walk away; Clare was concentrating hard on the view she was painting.

"See you," she said after I had turned the corner. Her voice drifted to me; she had barely noticed me leave.

In my own kitchen I puttered around and wished I had someone to talk to. I started to call Nick, then remembered he was in an all-day meeting. We had not yet had to test his suggestion that I not check into the Gregory; work had not kept him away since our dinner at Vinnie's.

I began to imagine him in the meeting. Over the years he had described his work so vividly to me, I felt able to conjure any given situation.

The Meeting: He would be nervous, just a little, before it started. He would go through the file, arranging documents in the order in which they would be discussed. He would check with Denise to make sure she had supplied enough legal pads and papers for the participants and to make sure she had arranged for coffee and doughnuts. He would fix his tie. He would feel sorry he had worn the red tie with the tiny stain. Then he would gather the documents, walk down the hall to the big conference room, and arrange the proper papers on the enormous oval walnut table. He would squint at the window, adjust the blinds to let in enough sun but not too much.

The clients would enter with John Avery, the partner in charge. Since this was a friendly meeting, everyone would shake hands and people who had met before would ask about spouses and vacations. Nick would still be feeling nervous, but no one would know it because he could hide his nervousness extremely well. Nick would be asked to fill everyone in on what had happened since the previous meeting. He would start to talk. He would discuss the deal's structure, the tax aspects, the percentage participation of each company. Within a few seconds, he would cease feeling nervous. The meeting would continue until lunchtime. Then Nick would ask everyone what kind of sandwiches they wanted. He would leave the room to call a messenger with the order, but first he would call me.

I cut myself off there. I began to mash tuna fish for the sandwich I would serve Clare. With equal clarity I could imagine negotiations, smaller meetings between Nick and one partner or one client, Eastern shuttle flights to Washington, lunches at the Downtown or Broad Street Clubs, places I had never set foot in but could envision perfectly, based on Nick's descriptions. Following him through the day in my mind had once given me pleasure, but now I felt ashamed of it. It seemed like a secret vice, akin to following him into the city on the nights he had to work late. To Nick, the love of my life and husband of eight years, I now felt I was displaying my heart on my sleeve.

I wanted to talk to Clare. I couldn't wait for lunchtime. But the phone rang; it was Clare saying that the babysitter had a bad bee sting and couldn't come to work, that Clare would have to take the boys to their swimming lesson. That she couldn't come for lunch.

I made myself a tuna sandwich, and I turned to the newspaper. I quit thinking about Nick, and I became the Swift Observer. I found the window on other peoples' worlds quite consoling.

Four

One evening that week I completed my report. My last case involved seventy-year-old identical twins, separated at birth, who had lived in the same Bronx apartment complex for thirty years but hadn't discovered each other until they wound up playing bingo at the same table one night. The news account said they were dressed identically, including their jewelry. I tried to imagine a seventy-three-year-old woman dressing up for another night of bingo. Perhaps it was her only night to socialize. At the bingo table she had glanced up, and there was her mirror image. Information gave me a number for Doris McNaughton.

She answered the phone, and I identified myself. "Excuse me for bothering you," I said, "but your story is fascinating. How do you feel, meeting your sister after so many years?" The idea of it delighted me.

"It was interesting, to say the least. I couldn't believe it then, and I hardly believe it now. The phone has been ringing off the hook. You can't imagine."

"Sure I can! I'm sure every reporter in New York wants to hear your story."

"But only one of us wants to tell it." Pregnant pause.

"That's you, I take it?"

"Yes. You see, I'm the one my parents kept, and Herself is sulking over the fact. She's refusing to talk to any reporters at all. And believe me, the offers are much more lucrative if we talk together."

"Your parents gave up one of their twins? Do you mind if I ask why?"

"We were on Ellis Island. Need I say more? The point is, you have to get on with life. I'm living on a fixed income, so naturally I want to sell my story. But Vivian is being a regular wet blanket. She's crying day in and day out, refusing even to get out of bed."

"Well, think of how happy your parents would be," I said.

"It's turning out to be a mixed blessing, to say the least. We're not getting off on the right foot one bit."

After we hung up I lay on the floor, watching the sun's declining light turn the bay's surface silver, then purple. I felt empty and sad, thinking of rootless Vivian. I imagined Vivian lying across her bed, tears streaming from her eyes. I wondered whether Vivian had at least known she was a twin; that knowledge might have mitigated the shock. I wished I had asked Doris.

Clare's voice came from the back door, and then she entered the room. "The little boys are sleeping out at Billy Mendillo's house, and the big boys are flying in late tonight. What say you and I keep each other company?"

"Good idea," I said, rising from the floor. We walked onto the porch and sat on rattan chairs. "I just spoke to a woman who was separated from her twin on Ellis Island."

"How horrible." Clare shook her head. "God, you have a lifetime with a sister—like you and me. Can you imagine if we'd never known each other?"

"I can't imagine that."

"What made you call her?"

"Her story is about sisters. Also, it's sensational."

"Ah, escaping the old 'Journal of Lipid Research Syndrome,' " Clare said, and we both laughed. As the daughters of scientists, we had been surrounded by people who appreciated the minute, the insignificant, the esoteric. We had spent hours in the cavernous library beside Eel Pond, wandering through the stacks of scientific publications while our father did research. There were years' worth of the *Journal of Liquid Chromotography, Geomarine Letters,* the *Journal of Great Lakes Research,* the *Journal of Insect Physiology,* the *Journal of Lipid Research.* How, I had wondered, could so many volumes be devoted to Lipid Research? What was Lipid Research? There it was, in the Marine Biological Laboratory Library, that I learned my love for the large, the grandiose, the extravagant. I had sat at one particular scarred linoleum table in the northwest corner, listening to the wind scream through the windows, watching my father work on his latest article for *Paleontology Today.* Clare would do her homework while I had fantasies of Hollywood, New York, and St. Moritz. My fantasies were panoramic, like movies by Louis B. Mayer. One daydream could include Jean Claude Killy, Bob Dylan, Prince Charles, John Lindsey, Virginia Woolf, and Roger Tory Peterson.

Clare and I sat on my porch, looking west across the bay. It felt comfortable to be silent with her. She hummed a tune I couldn't recognize, something she often did when she felt relaxed.

"Get ready for a bombshell," I said. "Honora told me the name of Dad's mystery woman."

Clare's mouth dropped open. "She did? Oh, I'm not sure I want you to tell me who it was. We knew her, didn't we?"

"Yes, but her identity won't devastate you. I promise. Want to know?"

"I guess so."

"Mrs. Billings."

After a considerable pause, Clare wrinkled her nose. "That drab little thing? God, I can barely remember her. That was his great romantic downfall? No wonder Honora could never bear to tell us—it's shameful, to lose your husband to someone like her. I remember going over to Rachel's and seeing her in the rattiest bathrobe I've ever seen."

"I remember how frail she looked. I was afraid she'd blow away in a storm."

"Maybe it would have been better if she had. How did Honora seem when she told you?"

"Fine. It didn't seem to upset her at all."

"So much time has passed." She slapped my forearm. "I'm jealous she told you instead of me. She must be taking your role as the Swift Observer very seriously. She's not confiding in her daughter, she's confiding in an entity."

"Maybe that's true. Heaven knows we've been trying to get it out of her for years."

"Why didn't you call me the minute you heard?"

"I was going to—the day I invited you for lunch and you threw me over for swimming lessons."

"I almost wish I didn't know. Now I'll always have to picture Dad kissing little Mrs. Billings. It's a letdown in a way—I used to imagine him with an Elizabeth Taylor type."

"So did I. Knowing her true identity makes it seem more real, I think. I feel worse for Honora."

"I don't. It's too bad Dad cheated on her, but it's not the worst thing that could happen. Honora has always drummed it into our heads that men are scheming sex fiends, ready to leave you at the first opportunity. No wonder you're paranoid about Nick."

"I'm not exactly paranoid," I said, beginning to hear the faint hum of the plane's engine.

"Listen, the fact that you even doubt him is ridiculous. Donald says Nick begins dreaming of coming home the second he gets into the plane in the morning. Give him a break and don't have affair attacks anymore."

"I'll try." The plane banked into sight, the port and starboard lights now clearly visible. "I'm not really worried anyway."

"Bullshit," Clare said, smiling at me. Then we held hands and said "Safe landing" at the same time, a ritual we followed whenever we were together as the plane came in. The plane chattered across the glassy bay.

"When does Nick's firm has its summer outing?" she asked.

I had nearly forgotten about the annual summer party for lawyers and spouses. "Sometime before the end of June. Next week, I guess. How about Donald's?"

"Next week also," she said, making a face that reminded me of one of Pem's.

Nick and Donald stepped onto the jetty. The ferry to Orient Point chugged along the horizon. Dark clouds had gathered over Plum Island, covering the early stars. Nick came towards me. He held me close. "You feel wonderful," he said.

"Say it like you mean it," I said, and he bent me over backwards, supporting my shoulders with one arm, and kissed me hard. Then we stood up.

"Let's have dinner. I'm starving," I said. We said goodnight to Clare and Donald. With our arms around each other we walked up the stone walk, across the porch, into our house.

·   ·   ·

The days of early summer passed quickly. My first report to the Avery Foundation submitted, I now worked on the second. It gave me pleasure to work each day before the heat came, filling the air with white mist. One day I called every woman whose engagement announcement appeared in the *New London Day*, to ask questions about love, family, what she wanted from life. The answers ranged from thoughtful to absurd. "We just want to be together," said Judy Delancray, with shy pride in her voice. "I got to get away from my parents," said Marlene Arturo. "We want to fuck with the church's permission," said Noreen Jackowski in a voice so deep that I suspected I had reached her brother or a male cousin, someone grabbing the opportunity for fun on the telephone. I laughed with him, remembering how Clare and I had adored prank calls as children. None of the betrothed, however, could distract me from the well-publicized news that Mona Tuchman had suffered a miscarriage. One night I was standing at the sink, chopping vegetables, imagining the conversation she and I would have, when I heard the seaplane. I checked my watch: nine-thirty.

For a moment I tried to ignore the droning engine. I had a terrible superstition, from which I was trying to escape, that the plane would crash if I weren't actually watching it. When I was young I had believed the Red Sox would lose if I didn't watch them on TV, that my father's ship would sink on a trip to the other hemisphere if I weren't standing on Water Street waving goodbye when he left. On his last, doomed trip, he had flown to Scotland from Boston. I had kissed him goodbye in Woods Hole, but in order to attend a birthday party had stayed behind while Honora drove him to Logan Airport. Remembering that lapse in vigilance, I dropped the knife and hurried to the porch door. Through the trees I saw the plane's lights angling down. They seemed to skim the top of the privet hedge. Then I heard the small splash as the plane landed.

Nick came inside and shook off his jacket. His lean face was tired but smiling. By this time of June it was usually more tan.

"It's good to have you home," I said.

"Oh, what a day it was," he said, following me into the kitchen, watching me start dinner.

While dinner cooked we changed, Nick into striped blue pajamas, I into my white nightgown. I always washed it with strong bleach to keep it looking nearly blue, a prediliction I had picked up from Liza Jordan during my days as her maid. We sat on the sofa. My back against the sofa arm, I stretched my legs across Nick's lap. He touched my toes. I stared at the white fabric draped across my knee, its folds deep lavender in the shadowy lamplight. Just one lamp burned beside us, and I loved the way it isolated me and Nick together, leaving the rest of the room dark.

"No one looks as comfortable as you do," Nick said. "The way you snuggle into a sofa."

"I'm a sloth."

"No, that's not it. Remember that Whistler exhibit at the Freer?"

During law school one of Nick's favorite ways to relax was to visit the Freer Gallery on Sunday afternoons. We had loved the Chinese screens, the lacquered writing boxes, and the Peacock Room, but Nick had especially enjoyed an exhibition of Whistler's watercolors. I knew what he was going to say.

"I think of those paintings a lot," he said. "The women looked just like you, even if they didn't resemble each other. The way they reclined on those chaise longues, or curled up in chairs to read. They were beautiful, such small paintings, but vivid. The expressions on the faces . . . you looked at one woman, all comfortable in a chair, and she'd smile at you with the most intelligent eyes. Or maybe she'd just been crying. That's how I think of you. Your face can't hide anything. Right now you look so happy. Your face is so pretty and happy."

"You're home. We're together."

"I know. That's what makes you happy."

"You know that and yet you begrudge me the chance to rendezvous with you on late nights in New York. Some husbands would actually find that romantic." We were together and times were easy; I could joke about it when Nick was touching me.

"I find it romantic. But sometimes I find it exhausting. You know there are times when all I want to do is call room service for a BLT."

"What did you do today?" I asked. "Are you exhausted?"

"Not really. Broadsword is on hold, so I negotiated the basics of an agreement between two companies who want to form a joint venture in Great Britain. It was pretty exciting—we drafted and signed a letter of intent before lunch."

"You mean their two companies will be joined as one?"

"Only in a matter of speaking. The two companies are joining forces in one area they have in common—fiber optics—in the EEC countries. The company that hired us—our client—will actually own more shares in the new company that will be formed. That means that they'll hold the controlling vote."

"The controlling vote? Like Honora?"

Nick laughed. "She'd make a dandy chairman of the board. And she does exert a certain amount of control around here. But I don't hear anyone complaining."

"We humor her. But go on with your day," I said, smiling at the idea of anyone thinking they could humor Honora.

"Let's see. After the signing we all went out to lunch at the Windmill. I made sure to order spa food so I could eat a good dinner tonight."

"That's commendable. We're having chicken."

"And after that we returned to the client's office on Park Avenue and he told me a few war stories about his days as an arbitrator in London."

"Oh? He's a lawyer?" I asked.

"Yes—he's general counsel for the corporation."

"Company lawyers work less than lawyers at law firms," I said, dismayed to hear an accusatory tone in my voice.

"True, but their deals are not so big. Not so exciting."

"I know," I said. "I wouldn't want you to give up what you

do. You love it so much. Even if the price is BLT's from room service."

He leaned across my outstretched legs and gave me a long kiss. His hands held my knees as if they were breasts, then moved to my breasts. His tongue parted my lips, and with our lips touching he said, "Right now I don't want a BLT."

We sat on that sofa kissing for fifteen minutes. Having enough free time to kiss is one of the great luxuries of a busy marriage. We knew we'd wind up making love, but we didn't want to rush into it. I lay back, not touching Nick with my hands, and felt him kiss my mouth, my eyelids, my collarbone. We sat side by side, our arms around each other, kissing with our eyes closed, then open. He kissed one corner of my mouth, then the other. Running his finger down the length of my spine, he made me arch against the pressure.

The timer sounded to tell us the chicken was ready.

"I don't want a BLT and I don't want roast chicken," Nick said. And we walked into our bedroom.

·   ·   ·

The day of the summer outing dawned clear and fine. The air held no trace of humidity. I lay awake, enjoying the novelty of Nick still asleep beside me. Today he wouldn't go to the office; it wasn't allowed. The invitation, printed on Hubbard, Starr cream vellum stationery had read:

> *Our annual summer outing will be held Thursday, June 25, at Stoneleigh Bath and Tennis Club. We hope all of you, together with your dates or spouses, will be able to attend. As always, attendance at this affair is mandatory—so please make your plans accordingly. Those who do not attend will be subjected to heinous sanctions currently being developed by the Corporate Coordinating Committee in plenary session.*

There will be golf and tennis available to all, as well as appropriate intra-team athletic contests to be organized by the Super Athletic Coordinating Committee.

All of this will be followed by cocktails on the Club Terrace commencing at 6:30 p.m. and dinner at 7:30 p.m. The club requests that jackets and ties be worn on the Club Terrace.

Sincerely,
Corporate Coordinating Committee

Lying still beside Nick, who was snoring, I reflected that tonight would be the first weeknight in months that any Hubbard, Starr associate had eaten dinner at 7:30.

.   .   .

Our bags packed with tennis and evening clothes, we began our journey. We took one train into New York and transferred to the Long Island Railroad.

"See that blond girl towards the back of the car?" Nick asked.

Pretending to look for the conductor, I saw who he meant. The young woman was slight, with blond hair and a pink sundress.

"She's a summer associate," Nick said. "Her name is Michele and she's starting her third year at Harvard."

Summer associates were law students who worked at firms during their summer vacations, hoping to be offered permanent positions. Qualified law students were valuable; Wall Street firms wooed them with outings, summer memberships at exclusive clubs, and theater tickets. Summer outings, such as this one, were crucial for summer associates who vied for the highly coveted permanent jobs on Wall Street. Here they could hope to impress the right people.

"We should probably invite her to share a cab to the club," Nick said.

"Good idea," I said, not meaning it. My time with Nick ceased feeling special once we joined the throng. I felt too obliged to act sweet to summer associates and charming to partners to really enjoy myself. But at least the Stoneleigh Bath and Tennis Club had good food and lovely grounds.

When the train reached Stoneleigh, we stepped onto the platform and waited for Michele to emerge. She didn't. The train began slowly to pull away.

"Shit, she must have missed the stop," Nick said, looking worried.

"So what? This train stops every five minutes. Let her take a cab back from the next station." I took his arm, leading him towards the taxi stand. The train inched past.

Suddenly Michele hurled herself out the moving train's open door. The train's brakes screeched. A conductor leapt to the pavement. Nick ran to help Michele, who had crumpled on the pavement. Before he reached her, she stood up. Blood trickled down her face; it had stained her blond hair rust and dribbled onto her sundress. Covering the wound with one hand, she held her other hand out to me.

"You must be Mrs. Symonds," she said, smiling graciously. "I've seen your picture on Nick's desk."

"Sit down," I said. "Right here." I pushed the girl onto the train platform. My heart pounded in my throat.

"Are you a lawyer too?" the girl asked, still smiling brightly. "It's just incredible how many lawyers marry other lawyers."

"You must be in shock," I said, amazed that the girl would try to act normal.

"All of a sudden she just jumped off," the conductor was saying to Nick. "I turned around and she's running down the aisle and she takes a flying leap."

"The train wasn't moving very fast at all," Michele said, as if confiding a secret, her voice perfectly controlled. "I missed the stop because I was reading some securities regulations. You know, for the Southport Electric case, Nick. Anyway, I'm just fine. If I can just find a ladies' room, I can freshen up."

I pressed my white tennis shorts to the gash in her head. It looked deep and purple, about an inch long.

"Listen," Nick said. "We have to take you to the emergency room."

Michele stood, holding my shorts to the side of her head. She laughed. "Don't be silly. Give me a minute, and maybe we can share a cab. Unless you two want to go on ahead."

"That's ridiculous," Nick said. I heard impatience, anger, in his voice. "We're going to the hospital. Head injuries can be really dangerous, Michele."

"I have to take down her name," the conductor said. "It's a regulation." The train stood still; passengers watched avidly through the grimy windows.

"I'm sorry," Michele said, smiling. "Give me a minute while I find the ladies' room." She weaved speedily around a corner.

"There is an Observer piece in this," I said, hurrying after her, leaving Nick to fill out the train man's forms.

He caught up with us at a gas station two blocks away. Michele had locked herself in the ladies' room. "This is unreal," I said. "She's obsessed with the summer outing. She refuses to go to the hospital. Did you see the blood?" I pressed my head against Nick's chest. The experience had left us both shaking.

"Michele, we're going to the hospital," he called.

She emerged, having changed into a red-and-white seersucker suit. She had washed her hair in the bathroom sink. She smiled sternly.

"I appreciate your concern, but I will not go to the hospital. It is that simple. Now, where can we get a taxi?"

I had to marvel at the tyranny of this frail, wounded blond. She would make a fine lawyer. During the ride to the club, she sat in the front seat chattering about the wonderful experience Hubbard, Starr had provided so far. It was as though the accident had been a mere hiccup in her plan to bowl over the partners and senior associates. Nick and I sat in the back seat, astonished. To me it seemed the perfect metaphor of the cutthroat Wall Street spirit: that a woman would risk concussion and maybe brain damage to ensure a job offer at Hubbard, Starr. Nick whispered that he planned to find the hiring coordinator and suggest that she force Michele to have her head examined, yuk, yuk.

The cab sped up a long drive bordered with mountain laurel and rhododendrons. Through the bushes we glimpsed emerald fairways and grass tennis courts. All tennis players wore white; even the balls were white. This was, after all, Long Island's north shore, home of Jay Gatsby. I had been here on many summer outings. I knew just when the clubhouse, a rambling white clapboard building with green shutters and trellises of roses, would come into sight. The cab stopped at the main entrance.

Couples dressed in white strolled past. Barn swallows swooped down from the eaves. Michele bid us farewell and went off in search of more influential members of the firm.

"That woman is a first-class maniac," Nick said, watching her extend her hand to Greg Gerston.

"You'd better tell someone about her head," I said. "I can just imagine her keeling over in the middle of cocktails and you getting blamed for not getting medical help."

"I suppose so. I'll be right back."

I sat on a white bench beneath a tall elm. A cab discharged a group of associates. Two of them approached me.

"Hello, Jean, Pete," I said. Stocky Pete Margolis was dressed to play golf, his bag swung over one shoulder. Jean Snizort, the most beautiful of Nick's colleagues, wore a stunning off-the-shoulder red blouse and full print skirt. It looked sensuous and bold.

"Well hi, Jessie," Jean said, smiling sweetly.

"It's Georgie," I said, correcting her, the way I always did.

Jean touched her forehead. "I am so sorry. Why can't I get that straight?"

"You have a rather unusual name," Pete said, kissing my cheek. I smiled at him, recognizing the private joke. Pete had once occupied the office across from Nick's, and we had gotten friendly on the Saturdays I spent at the firm. He was irreverent and had once confessed to me that he purposely forgot people's names to throw them off guard. He had said it was common practice among lawyers.

"Where's your fellow?" Jean asked.

"Oh, he went to find someone," I said, telling them the story of Michele.

"Sounds demented," Pete said.

"Yes, but I must say she did the right thing, coming here," Jean said. "Any summer associate who fails to show up here, I don't care if her father just died, is dead meat. Kiss the job offer goodbye. Anyone planning to play tennis?"

Pete and I said no, and Jean walked away. "Do you agree with her about Michele?" I asked, watching Jean enter the clubhouse. Suddenly, in my white sundress, tinged red along the hem by Michele's blood, I felt drab. My simple outfit broadcast the fact that I was a wife, not a lawyer, that I lived on Connecticut's shore, not in New York. I imagined Jean finding Nick, convincing him to play tennis with her.

"That's a tough question," Pete said. "I think she's right about Michele not getting an offer if she didn't come here. But what does that say about priorities? I mean, Michele should care more about her health than one legal job."

"And the firm should be more understanding."

A slight breeze rustled through the leaves overhead. Sunlight filtered through, making patterns of shade on my knee. Far off, someone yelled "Fore!"

"No offense, Georgie, but the firm doesn't have to be understanding. To the firm, associates are apple seeds. Chew them up, spit them out. Lose one, another is waiting in line. You know how hard it is to get a job at a place like Hubbard, Starr?"

"I remember," I said, grinning. I thought of the summer Nick had worked at the firm, between his second and third years of law school. How we had sweated through the last weeks, ignoring Pem and Honora's pleas that we spend at least one weekend at Black Hall, hoping that he would get a permanent offer.

"And now I leave you in the able hands of your husband," Pete said, greeting Nick who approached from the clubhouse.

"Fortunately the club has a club doctor, and he's going to check her out."

Sitting on the bench I gazed up at him. Next to Pete, who had the compact body of a wrestler, Nick looked ravishingly tall and lean. And relaxed. Happy. We were together in the middle of a weekday.

.   .   .

The day passed in a bucolic blur. Since my tennis shorts were stiff with Michele's blood, I forewent tennis and walked the grounds with Nick. Then we played nine holes of golf with two partners from Nick's squad. Then I sat on the ground watching Nick and the Tender Offer Squad play volleyball against the General Corporate Squad. Naturally, being the most aggressive, the Tender Offers won. Then they played and beat the Litigation Squad, the Leverage Leasing Squad, the Taxation Squad. Victorious, the Tender Offer Squad formed a circle by grasping one another's biceps. They did a gleeful little dance that made me laugh because it reminded me of young English children frol-

icking around a maypole. Nick, sweaty and happy, joined me
and some other wives.

"You play a mean game of volleyball," said one, Virginia Grant,
a nice stockbroker who was married to a litigation partner. "Where'd
you grow up—California?"

"No, Massachusetts," Nick said.

"Excuse me, folks," called John Avery, head of the Tender
Offer Squad. He stood ten yards away, beside the volleyball net.
Addressing the group, which covered a wide area, he spoke in
a low voice that carried magnificently. His body was trim, dressed
in a khaki safari suit. "Our match, superbly executed though it
was, seems to have gone on a bit longer than anticipated. Cus-
tomarily, one of the—I don't like to say *losing* squad leaders—"
here everyone laughed, "presents the trophy here, at courtside.
However, time constraints and the fast-approaching cocktail hour
force us to postpone that ritual. So, with haste, I bid you to take
to the locker rooms. We shall convene on the terrace in seventeen
minutes."

"Bravo!" called Jean Snizort, a vision in a tight, sleeveless navy
blue jumpsuit made of some irridescent synthetic.

A ribbon of lawyers and their mates began winding up the
hill towards the clubhouse. Nick and I held hands, walking faster
than the others. We passed Jean.

"Hi, Nick, hi, Georgie," she said, emphasizing my name,
twinkling at Nick.

"What was that about?" I asked when we were alone.

"Oh, Jean asked me yesterday if my wife, Jessie, was coming.
Then she made me promise not to tell you that she always gets
your name wrong."

"Honora would say she has her eye on you," I said. I did not
say that Jean was the embodiment of every fear I had ever had
about Nick working late.

"Honora would be wrong," Nick said.

Parting in the corridor, we kissed, then entered separate locker rooms. I found mine filled with women in various stages of dishabille: naked in the shower, pulling on pantyhose, slipping into summer dresses. I took a quick shower. I hoped my lilac linen shift would look pretty.

"Well, hi," Jean said as I walked out of the shower. She was applying gold eye makeup in a long mirror. Her creamy white skin looked flawless as a Spanish princess's. Her lips were garnet red.

"Hi, Joan," I said, walking directly towards the bank of gray-green lockers.

. . .

A vivid purple and orange sunset blazed in the western sky. I leaned against a stone balustrade at the terrace's far end, talking to John Avery. He had changed out of his safari suit into a coral silk blazer and white slacks. He drank a frozen daiquiri. I drank dry vermouth with a twist. My lavender dress looked darker in the purple light.

"Now, last thing I heard about you," Avery was saying, "you were doing science. Marine biology, is that it?"

"It was. I was profiling a bay in front of our house."

"How do you profile a bay? If you'll forgive my ignorance? . . ." John Avery chuckled, sipping daiquiri through a slim straw.

I smiled. I knew that John Avery was being amusing, that he considered himself ignorant about nothing worth knowing. "A profile is basically an inventory," I said. "You know—marine life, rock formations, seaweed, that sort of thing. But I've put the bay profile aside for something else. I've started the Swift Observatory."

His jaw literally dropped. "Oh my dear sweet Jesus, of course. Your name is Georgiana Swift, not Symonds," said John Avery, and at that instant I made the connection: the Avery Foundation.

"You don't—do you?" I asked.

"My family endows the Avery Foundation," he said. "I sit on its board of directors. I read your report last week. I'll be damned."

Nick joined us; he listened in silence.

"The material on Mrs. Tuchman was most interesting," John Avery said. "I must admit I didn't read many news reports about her case, but other board members said your piece was the most personal, the most revealing piece they had read."

"Thank you," I said, struck by situation's oddness. John Avery was Nick's boss, my patron. He was the master of both of our professional destinies. I cast a sidelong glance at my husband, to see how he was taking it. I could not read his face.

"We're looking forward to your next report," John Avery said. "How about this, Nick? Fascinating turn of events, eh?"

"It's amazing," Nick said. "I've never connected you with the Avery Foundation."

"Many people have never even heard of it. We're a very small operation. What made you try us for a grant, Georgie?"

Suddenly it occurred to me that maybe he thought Nick and I had known of his connection all along, that we had exploited Nick's closeness with him to get me the money. I felt myself blush deeply. I would have to tell the truth, which was embarrassing and might offend him. "I read a description of the Foundation in a book about grants, and it said you favor unorthodox projects that probably wouldn't get money elsewhere."

John laughed. "Worse things have been said about us. Some people think we're a venture capital organization, funding fly-by-night inventions or research projects—no offense, Georgie—then profiting from them down the line. It's the lot of a grant-giving foundation. We're nonprofit, of course. There's no way we could earn a cent. But there are lots of sour grapes among people who apply and don't get the money."

"Why did I get the money?" I asked, feeling daring.

John looked me straight in the eye. "Because your project was unorthodox and probably wouldn't have gotten money elsewhere." He smiled.

"Oh," I said.

"But we think it's important. We take your work very seriously."

"So do her family and I," Nick said.

"Between you and me, Nick," John said, "we are lucky men. A lot of lawyers have nothing in their lives but law. No outside interests to speak of. But I have the Foundation, where I'm in touch with creative minds and the outside world. You have a wife who does interesting work. I don't understand lawyers who marry lawyers or, worse, accountants. What do they have to talk about?"

"Georgie shows me her work hot off the presses," Nick said, and I detected pride in his voice.

John tapped the side of his head. "The workings of the creative mind." He glanced around. "I'd better talk to some summer associates. Can't forget what this party is all about. We'll talk again, Georgie. See you tomorrow at the clients' office, Nick." He walked away.

Seeing John Avery disengaged, hordes of summer associates made straight for him. Michele whizzed by, not noticing us in her zeal.

"This is weirder than words," I said. "I had no idea, absolutely no idea that John Avery was that Avery. Are you mad at me?"

"Why would I be mad? It poses a slightly awkward situation, with both of us essentially working for John, but I'm not mad."

"I don't work for him. He funds my work, but that's it," I said, feeling huffy, though secretly sensing truth in Nick's assessment.

"If I had checked the firm directory, I probably would have discovered John's affiliation with the Avery Foundation. It always lists memberships, directorships, things like that. I probably should have known," Nick said, looking worried. He was thinking that he had committed a disastrous gaffe, not realizing John's connection.

"Don't worry—there's no reason why you should have known," I said.

"Partners notice things like that. After all, if my wife applies to some foundation, I should be reasonably expected to know that my boss sits on its board. Shit."

"Nick—"

He glanced at me sharply. "I'm mad at myself, not you, all right?"

"All right," I said. But I wondered why he would be mad at himself if nothing were wrong?

Five

For four nights, sleep was dangerous, my dreams haunted by images of Nick and I on opposite sides of a desk, not speaking or even acknowledging each other; of leaving the room by separate doors; of Jean Snizort waiting, unseen but quite tangible, behind Nick's door; of a butter knife in my pocket. I would waken and press close to Nick. He would open his arms and sleepily pull me against his chest, where I would lay until his dark and sparse chest hair tickled me away.

How anxious I'd felt to see Nick rattled at the outing! Every word spoken to a partner contained a million nuances. How would John Avery perceive the fact that Nick hadn't known his position with the Avery Foundation? Associates were supposed to be impressed by such things. The biographical information published by the firm was a gold mine for eager associates. Nick denied that he was seriously upset, but he was. I knew.

Then one afternoon came the moment of truth. He called to tell me he would have to work late that night and wouldn't be home.

"Are you sure you don't want me to come into town?" I asked, pleasantly enough.

"Maybe tonight is a good night for you to stay in Black Hall. Project Broadsword is heating up again, and I know I won't leave the office till midnight. It would be much easier for me if I just eat Chinese or something at my desk."

"I can't believe this is happening, Nick," I said. "That you don't want to be with me tonight. I don't care how late it is."

"Georgie," Nick said, sounding weary.

Rage, hurt, and fear battled for the lead. "You seem so upset these days," I said, trying to sound reasonable. "I can't help thinking you're staying away on purpose, that you don't want to come home."

"Georgie, that's not true," Nick said, his voice making me trust him. "I do want to come home. It's rotten, having to work so late, then going to some hotel alone. You sound self-centered, accusing me of that. Why can't you see it from my point of view? The clients from Broadsword are so fucking nervous they can't see straight." His voice rose and rose.

"Don't sound so mad at me," I said.

"Well, I *am* mad at you. You could show me a little sympathy. You always need plenty of reassurance, and don't I always give it to you? I think you should give me what I need right now— understanding. You could say, 'Oh, I feel so bad you have to work all night with lousy demanding clients and I wish we could be together.' Instead you turn it into an accusation."

"I'm sorry."

"Forget it," he said, still sounding angry.

"We can't hang up feeling this way. I don't want to stay angry at each other when we're going to be apart all night."

"That's too bad, because I'm still angry and I have to get off the phone. The clients and John are waiting."

I felt a sob rising. "Is this because of John Avery? Are you upset because of that?"

"Jesus, Georgie! Why can't you take someone's word for it? It's not deep, it's not complicated. I'm upset because I have to work late and I can't come home. Goodbye."

He hung up. I sat there, holding the receiver, feeling cold as ice. I was shivering. Waves broke on the rocks outside; I listened, wanting them to soothe me. I hated myself. I felt as though I was driving away the person I loved most in the world. I called his office, but Denise said he had just gone into the conference room. "Just tell him I called," I said.

For a moment I regretted calling, like a high school girl who likes a boy but fears appearing overeager. But of course Nick and I had been married for eight years. We called each other ten times a day. In the natural course of events, whenever we fought, we would stew separately, each feeling wronged, perfectly justified in the feeling, certain the other was skewed. Then the moment Nick came home he would tell me he understood my point of view, I would tell him I understood his, we would talk and reach a compromise. Then we would kiss. We would snuggle into bed, touch each other's body, show each other the real meaning of vulnerability. That night it wouldn't happen because Nick would be staying in New York. It scared me to think I wouldn't see him until late the next night. I calculated the hours: at least thirty hours until I saw him. How bad could things get in thirty hours? I envisioned his anger hardening, growing bigger than a house, so that when he did come home he wouldn't even fit through our door.

The thought of having dinner alone seemed terrible, so I called Honora to invite myself over. Nick would call me there if he didn't get an answer at our house. If he called. On my way across the yard I met Clare.

"You alone too?" I asked.

"Yes. Mother just called to tell me you were eating there, so I decided to make it a foursome. Nick has to work late?"

"Yes. Donald?"

"He's in San Francisco. The boys are having a cookout at the Fortnums.' "

Pem and Honora were sitting on the terrace. The sunset splashed gold and rose across the sky. The water tower on Plum Island, eight miles across the Sound, glinted like the edge of a knife. Everyone wore sweaters. Pem was wrapped in her wool coat and a blanket.

"Ah, my two Nereids," Honora said, rising to kiss us. The Nereids, to the ancient Greeks, were personifications of breezes. Clare held up her peach silk scarf to let it flutter in the light wind. "It's been so long since the four of us had dinner alone. Seems like since you girls were in high school."

We tried to remember a more recent time, but always Nick or Donald or Eugene or Casey or a friend of Pem's or Honora's had been there. "Three generations of Bennison women are on this porch," Clare said. "One of us should have a daughter, Georgie, and make it four."

"I'd love a granddaughter," Honora said. "Not that I don't adore the boys. But I loved having little girls. Other people would say, 'Don't you wish you had a son?' But I didn't, not a bit. Your father didn't either."

I sat on the glider beside Pem. "Hi," I said.

"Hi," she said, smiling. "Where's the boy?"

"Nick? He had to work late."

"Dare we ask why you're not at the Gregory?" Clare asked.

For a second I felt too close to tears to answer, but then I managed to lie. "He called too late for me to get the train."

"Oh, sweetie," my mother said.

Clare leapt to her feet. "Quick! We'll take my car! Honora can ride shotgun, watch for speed traps, you and Pem in the back seat, we'll be in New York in two hours—tops."

"Shut up," I said.

"If the boy were here, he could make us a drink," Pem said.

"Not a bad idea," Honora said. "Care for a cocktail? It's a little early, but so what?"

"If you're serving bourbon, it's never too early," Clare said.

"Martinis all around," Honora said, knowing Clare never drank bourbon. Clare went to mix them. Honora came to sit on the glider beside me. She tucked one bare foot beneath her and started the glider moving with the other. Afraid she would try to begin an intimate conversation about the troubles she imagined between me and Nick, I felt my back stiffen. I'd been on guard ever since she'd said "Oh, sweetie."

"I had the loveliest swim today," she said. I waited to see how she would segue from the swim to marital tensions. "I didn't see one jellyfish—odd for this time of year, don't you think?"

"They usually come around July fifteenth," I said.

"Well then. Anyway, I swam out to the big rock, then across the bay to Tobin's jetty, then back to my house. The water was perfectly clear. I kept my eyes open the entire time, and I think I saw an octopus. A very small one."

"Wouldn't that be rare, in these waters at this time of year?"

"Perhaps. Are you terribly upset?" she asked, lowering her voice.

"About an octopus in the bay?"

"About Nick."

"No, I'm not. Not at all. Nick has to work really late—what am I going to do, sit in a hotel room waiting for him? It's much better to stay on the Point," I said crisply.

"I've always thought it clever of you to follow him into the city. Something I think Clare should do more of, but of course with the boys. . . ."

"The way you put it—'follow him into the city,' " I said, feeling disgusted.

"Why deny it? I'm not criticizing you. I think it's a very good idea. If there were a later train, I'd say take it."

"There's no later train. You make it sound as though I shouldn't trust Nick."

"I'm not saying that. Not at all. I love and adore Nicky, he's ten times better than most men, but there you are."

"Aaargh," I said, to let her know I wanted to drop the subject. Pem jiggled the glider as she stood up. I reached for her arm, to pull her down.

"Let her go," Honora said. That meant she wanted to talk about Pem; although Pem was hard of hearing, Honora disliked talking about her in her presence. I watched Pem shuffle into the house, stopping to break a long tendril off the honeysuckle vine. She liked flowers tame and spiky. The screen door banged behind her.

"I nearly killed her today," Honora said. "I had all my papers spread across the dining room table, bills and canceled checks, all my financial stuff organized month by month. I went out for my swim, and when I came back I discovered she had bundled everything up and set the table for eight. She does that every night; it's my fault for leaving the papers out. I just forgot."

"Martinis!" Clare called, Pem trailing close behind.

"Many happy returns of the day," Pem said as we toasted.

Honora repeated the story of the octopus for Clare, who said Eugene had claimed to have seen one while snorkeling.

"I miss your bay profile, Georgie," Honora said. "Time was, an unusual sea creature couldn't pass by without you telling us about it. Remember the sunfish? And the summer of the blue lobsters?"

"Eugene and Casey were so upset when we cooked them and they turned red," I said, laughing. The sun had nearly set now. I glanced west, down the horizon towards New York. The ferry to Orient Point was passing Plum Island.

"There's the ferry, Pem," I said loudly.

"The ferry!" Pem said. "There used to be three steamers leaving the dock at Providence for Newport and Block Island, and if you weren't there by nine, they'd be jam-packed."

"What were they called?" Clare asked.

"Let's see . . . The *Mount Hope*, the *New Shoreham*, and . . . the *Penguin*," she said without a trace of uncertainty. I smiled; she had never mentioned the *Penguin* before.

"Did I ever tell you Nick and I once stopped by that dock on our way to Fall River?" I asked. "It's right off the Wickenden and India Streets exit, and the steamer still runs. There's only one now."

"Donald and I once stopped," Clare said. That dock had great significance to our family beyond Pem's happy memories of the ferries. Pem's mother had stepped off a boat there after crossing the Atlantic from Plymouth, England. The boat had docked on Christmas Eve. My great-grandmother had celebrated her ninth birthday on board. Her people were Catholic, and they had left England to escape religious persecution. Promised jobs at a hosiery mill in Providence, Rhode Island, they had looked forward to arriving in the New World. I imagined their joy at landfall on Christmas Eve: they would be able to worship in a church. The mill owner greeted the ship. My great-great-grandfather asked where they could find a church. "You're Catholic?" the mill owner had asked with dismay. Of course he had expected workers from England to be Protestant. If persecution met them on the shores of New England, it also made them tougher, I thought, looking at the last survivor of her generation in the family. Pem of the wild hair and noble nose and dark brows.

Oh, the pleasure of sitting with my family on that terrace! Lights blinking on Long Island, the sound of the waves, the gentle breeze making me glad of my sweater, the predictability of Pem's stories and Honora's worries. Nick's absence was the only blight. I imagined him sitting in a smoky conference room, arguing for hours over the same paragraph, eating food soggy with steam. Missing me and the Point. Missing an evening like this.

"I lied before," I said suddenly. "I didn't miss the train. Nick didn't want me in New York tonight."

Clare and Honora leaned toward me, their chins jutting forward, worried expressions on their faces. "What's wrong?" Clare asked.

"He's just decided it's best that when he works late I stay here instead of at the Gregory." I felt tears running down my cheeks.

"Honey, I said such awful things!" Honora said. "All that jawboning about not trusting men—I was just carrying on. I'm sorry."

"When Donald and I were first married we went through something like this," Clare said. "He had to spend a month in Tokyo—do you remember?"

"I remember," Honora said.

"I was dying to go," Clare said. "I mean, there I was, staying home, being what I thought was the perfect wife, with all the time in the world to travel with my husband. Especially to Tokyo—I planned to illustrate a travel diary with brush and ink, and to learn Japanese lacquer. But Donald told me I couldn't go. The reason, I later learned, was that he was embarrassed. No one was taking a wife along, and he didn't want to be the only one."

"That's a very uplifting tale. Thank you *so* much, Clare," I said, grinning sarcastically.

"My point is, they're under a lot of peer pressure," Clare said. "Sometimes Donald tells me his biggest regret is that he didn't buck the trend and take me to Japan."

"Is your biggest regret that you didn't go?" I asked.

"No—it's just one regret of many," Clare said. Clare was

motherly and voluptuous, but when she smiled at me that way
I remembered her when we were girls: skinny, taller than I, with
an expression that told me she loved me more than anyone in
the world. "Nick's all right," Clare said. "He probably feels better
knowing you're on Mom's porch than in a stuffy hotel room."

"Clare's right," Honora said. "Nick's thinking of you." Then,
because the time had come to change the subject, she clapped
her hands. "The coincidence!" she said, pronouncing each syllable
with force. "I can't get over it, the partner at Nick's firm over-
seeing your grant. Isn't it bizarre, Clare? Have you ever heard
anything like it?"

"I nearly fainted when I found out," I said. "There I was,
standing on the club terrace, making what I thought was small
talk with John Avery. I mean, he is always very polite, very
interested in what the associates' spouses are doing."

"That is a real talent," Honora said, "making the other person
feel important. That time I was on Dick Cavett, he made me
feel that I was the most interesting guest he had ever had. Me,
Weather Woman. Hah! Go on."

"Then I mentioned the Swift Observatory, and at that instant
I connected him with Avery and he connected me with Swift
and we both about fainted."

"It's unreal," Clare said. "And he said he liked your work?"

"Yes."

"Great, great," Honora and Clare said together.

Honora stood. She collected our empty glasses on the tray. We
started into the kitchen. I gave Pem a hand, and she slipped her
arm through mine. "Take my arm and call me Charlie," she said.

After dinner both Honora and Clare invited me to spend the
night at their houses, but I said no. We all kissed, and Clare and
I left at the same time.

"That's a terrible story about Tokyo," I said. "I wonder why
I never realized it at the time." Honora's grass needed mowing;
the long grass, wet with the night air, tickled my bare ankles.

"You were single then. You didn't want to hear about married problems. Remember how upset you were when I first married Donald?"

"I was jealous of him."

"I know, but you never said that. What you did was tell me how foolish I was to get married instead of working. Of course I saw no reason why I couldn't paint and sculpt at home. Not to mention keep up with biochem. An architect came to design a studio in the garage, but we never had it built."

"That portrait of the boys is great," I said.

"Oh, thanks."

We had come to the spot where Clare turned right and I turned left, but we stood still, listening to the waves. "You start off thinking you can plan the way your life will be," Clare said. "But I don't think you can. Sometimes things just happen. But we're lucky, Georgie. More good things happen to us than bad."

"Think of the sisters who don't live near each other. That's sad, isn't it?" I asked, kissing Clare.

"Sleep tight, Georgie," she said.

The emptiness of my house struck me because I would be alone in it all night. The hook where Nick wouldn't hang his coat that night, the table where he wouldn't place the plane's chart case, the sofa on which he wouldn't sit beside me. I walked through the rooms aimlessly, accompanied by my own amber reflection in each window. Settling in my work room, the room where I was always alone and would be least likely to feel Nick's absence, I glanced through old newspapers. In a way it felt good, to be relieved of worrying about plane crashes for one night. Then I came to a news story about a retired firefighter who was killed by a falling brick on Fifth Avenue. It could happen any time, anywhere. As I sat in my cozy house a meteor could crash through the roof. I thought of what Clare had said: you think you can plan, but you can't.

The phone rang.

"Nick!" I said into the receiver.

After a long pause, a woman spoke. "Is this Georgie Swift?" she asked.

"Mona?" I asked, recognizing her voice.

"Is this a bother, me calling you?"

"No, I'm glad to hear from you. I'm sorry about your miscarriage."

"Thank you. This is awkward, but it's late, I just had a bottle of wine with dinner, and I feel like talking. So I thought of you. We had a nice conversation that day."

"Yes, I've thought of it often. How is everything?"

"Pretty shitty, but not as bad as it could be. My lawyer has managed to arrange for the charges to be dropped if I agree to counseling. So I'm not going to jail."

"Oh, that's wonderful!" I said, feeling genuinely thrilled for her but uneasy about being on the phone when Nick might try to call. I knew what his meetings were like, how difficult it was for him to step away from the conference table. Sometimes he had only one chance an hour.

"They've let me see the kids, and Dick is going to be reasonable about it. He keeps saying 'you're their mother,' and I get the feeling he'd let me have them if it weren't for the severity of the charges. If I'd only hit Celeste instead of stabbing her. He has such unpredictable hours. Everyone thinks an eye surgeon can plan his time, but you wouldn't believe the calls that would come in at night. Eyes injured in brawls, in car wrecks. Of course he could schedule routine things, like cataract operations, but not the others. So it's tough for him to take care of the children and keep up his work. He would be better off if we were back together."

"I know that, Mona. I've always felt that way, ever since I met you. I hate to do this, but I have to get off the phone. Could we talk some other time?"

"Oh, sure. I don't want to bother you." The change in her tone told me I'd offended her.

"I wish I didn't have to go. Can I call you tomorrow?"

"Sure, bye."

The click as she hung up sounded final and mocking, but I didn't care because the phone rang one minute later and it was Nick.

"I love you," he said.

"I love you," I said.

We said more, but those were the words that mattered.

· · ·

That summer the telephone was the sorcerer's apprentice, and I was the sorcerer. The alchemy started with newspapers, full of stories about faceless people, victims of tragedy, winners of lotteries, yesterday's ordinary people made extraordinary by events in their lives. I used a pair of Pem's old white kid gloves, to keep my hands clean while I paged through the papers. That was part of the ritual. So was the coffee I sipped while I read, the chair in which I sat, the pile of newspapers that grew until Thursday, when the garbage men came. I would list stories that captivated me, and eventually I would call the people involved. My bookshelves became clogged with phone books from many municipalities. I would dial, transported by the hollow ringing into another person's life. I envisioned each person I called. They had definite features, families, political views. The minute I heard their voices, they became entire.

The telephone company installed a second line. I wanted to leave one line free, in case Nick or someone from the family tried to call. For the first time in my life I was putting people on hold. I instructed my loved ones to call me on Line One, while Line Two was the meeting ground for people I had read about but would never see or meet. "Hold, please," I said to Clare when she called in the midst of a conversation with Alfred Hoberg, winner of the New Jersey Jackpot. "Can I call you back? I'm on Line Two," I said over and over to Nick, once I had established that nothing was wrong and he was just calling to talk.

Nick seemed amused by my obsession with the telephone, and perhaps relieved. He thought it was curing me of my obsession with him. "Obsession is not love," he had said to me the night after our night apart. "It's driving me crazy, the way you imagine my motives. It scares me."

It scared me as well. I had thought that people grew comfortable after many years of marriage. In worst cases they became bored with each other when nothing new was left to discover, but mainly they could rest easy, having learned a common language, developed a pattern of days and nights, put down the terrible fears of early love. The vigor with which I telephoned my people, the diligence with which I transcribed those conversations into reports, the effort I made to forget Mona Tuchman because she reminded me of the violence of love: all of these kept my fear in check.

·   ·   ·

When I think of it now, that summer, I try to understand the frenzy. What stirred us up? Had I been a distant observer, I might have seen a normal young couple, living happily among the wife's family, suffering the usual trials of the man's demanding career. Even to me, in the midst of everything, that is how it appeared on the surface. But it was beneath the surface, where tensions seethed and poisoned, that counted. How could powerful love be a poison? I thought of it as strong and bracing, life-giving, a sweet, delicious and sinful nectar. Sometimes I thought of the people I loved and the feelings were so strong I would cry. Sometimes I thought I would die of love for them.

Nick's parents invited us to a Fourth of July barbeque at their home in the Berkshires.

"The Fourth is Pem's favorite holiday," I said. "But we haven't seen your parents in a long time. Since Christmas."

"That's true, but it's a long way to go. I can't take the whole weekend off."

"But they're your parents."

"True," Nick said.

That exchange typified the debates we would have every holiday. From my cajoling, would you guess that the last thing I wanted to do was leave the Point? In a perfect world I would choose to spend every holiday with my family, but in the real world Nick had parents and brothers and sisters. He seemed oddly indifferent about seeing them. Perhaps that was because he felt so close to my family; we talked about it often, but Nick never seemed to care about the answer. It was always I who told him we should visit his parents, spend Christmas with the Symonds instead of the Swifts-Bennisons-Mackens. I did this partly because I felt it was penance for the great majority of time we spent with my family. I made bargains with myself: if we visit the Symonds for this one holiday, we won't have to go back until December or March or June. I liked his family very much, but they weren't mine.

We borrowed the seaplane. The day was perfect: bright sun and a deep blue sky. Nick wore a golden suede jacket and aviator sunglasses. Checking the instruments, he frowned with concentration. I sat beside him, holding the chart of the Connecticut River Valley across my lap. I wore blue jeans and a black teeshirt covered by a woven shawl.

"Ready?" Nick said, leaning across me to make sure my door was locked.

"Kiss and fly," I said, just before he turned the key.

The engine whirred and the propeller began slowly to turn. Our pontoons slapped the bay's flat surface as we gathered speed. Motorboats and small sloops, thick in the water, gave us right of way. Then came the lift, and we were soaring straight into the sky, leaving Bennison Point beneath us. Nick banked left, then right, giving me a chance to wave goodbye to everyone: Donald and the boys in their Dyer Dinghy, Clare standing on the rocks, Honora in the rose garden. Pem stood by the stone wishing well, shielding her eyes to watch us. As we wheeled north I lost sight of everyone, but the land's contours gained sharper focus. I saw the rooftops, the groves of pine and oak, the craggy rocks dipping into the sea. I saw the Point in relation to the rest of Black Hall. Then the sea was behind us.

We followed the Connecticut River north. The plane's engines were loud, making conversation difficult. I loved flying with Nick. I experienced no fear, and I wondered, as I always did when I flew with Nick, about the bald terror I felt every time I watched him take off. Hartford, with its tall buildings and gold domes, came into view. We flew straight past, past the Connecticut-

Massachusetts border, and took a left turn over the Massachusetts Turnpike. Nick seemed so confident as a pilot, as he did in all his walks of life: lawyer, pilot, family man. I viewed each occupation as separate. At his office I looked at him and thought "lawyer," just as in law school I had looked at him and thought "law student." In a plane he was the pilot. In bed he was a wonderful lover. At the dinner table he was my dear husband. I couldn't seem to integrate his selves into one person with many aspects. I did that for the people I studied, but not for my husband.

We landed on a black lake ringed by parasol pines in the heart of the Berkshires. Gently rounded mountains, made velvety green by the thickness of trees, surrounded us. We coasted to a buoy, set in place by Nick's father the year Nick invested in the seaplane. Already Bart, Nick's father, was rowing towards us. He held out his hand to help me into the boat. It felt pleasantly rough, a measure of how he was enjoying a rural retirement after years as a hospital administrator in Springfield.

"Hey, Nick, Georgie, how about this weather? Terry bought some fireworks on his way back from Florida, you should be able to see them for miles."

"Great," I said, even though we planned to leave before dark.

"How are you, Dad? How's Mom?" Nick asked, sitting beside me on the boat's aft seat. Bart rowed fervently, as if lives depended on it. His round face gleamed with sweat and sunburn.

"We're good. We're just fine. Your sister Eleanor made it home for the party, and so did you and Terry. But Beth couldn't come. She has a party to go to on the Cape. Did she tell you she's renting a house with some girls? They're having a ball."

"No, I didn't know that. I should stay in better touch with the others," Nick said.

"She sent us a postcard," I said, leaning against him. "It showed fishing shacks in Provincetown, remember?"

Nick shook his head, laughing quietly. His father rowed and

rowed, hardly noticing our joke. Nick had a funny habit of
reading his family's letters and immediately forgetting what they
said. He said it was because he knew everything that was going
to happen: every summer until Eleanor got married, she had
rented a house on Cape Cod, and so would Beth until she got
married.

Nick's parents now lived year-round in what had been their
summer retreat. It stood two hundred yards away from Lake
Temperance, a modern house with a lot of windows, in an enclave
of similar houses. Nick's mother, Sally, was playing badminton
with Eleanor and her husband, Paul.

"Oh, hi, get yourselves a drink or find a racquet," Sally called,
a greeting I thought understated considering we hadn't seen her
since Christmas. Further proof of the worthiness of my family:
Honora showered us with hugs and kisses even when she saw
us every day.

Bart poured us beers, foamy from the keg. It seemed touching
to have a keg capable of serving fifty people, with only six of us
there. Light came through the trees, dappling the dry grass. Bart,
Nick, and I sat on the picnic table's hard benches.

"How's retirement, Dad?" Nick asked. "You chasing that white
ball around the course?"

"No, I don't play much golf. I'm taking care of this place
morning, noon, and night. Chopping wood for next winter, weed-
ing the garden, you know. Your mother is the golfer. Cut her
handicap by two since last year."

"But you're enjoying yourself, right?" Nick said. I knew he
was remembering his mother's fear that Bart would wither without an office to go to, that he would be dead of boredom within
six months.

"Nick, I love it," Bart said earnestly, leaning across the table.
"It's the best thing that ever happened to your mother and me.
We feel like lunch in Vermont, we just drive up to Grafton. We
feel like a show in the city, we just drive to Boston. Last week

we took in a double-header at Fenway, spent the night with your sister Eleanor."

"Who'd they play?"

"Yankees. Yankees killed them. You see the Yankees play much in New York?"

"No, we've switched to the National League," I said. "We follow the Mets now. Isn't that terrible? Two lifelong Red Sox fans rooting for the Mets."

Bart shook his head. "You'll come to your senses one of these days."

Sally came to stand behind Bart. She bounced her racquet lightly on his head. "He's not telling you all about the hospital, is he? Because if he is, I'll brain him. I tell him, the hospital is no longer his problem. Hello, you two."

"Hello," we said. I climbed off my bench and walked around the table to kiss her. Nick stayed where he was. She went to him, gave him a crushing hug from behind.

"It's a crime, the way you don't visit more. I want to hear everything. Get me a drink, Dad. I want to sit right here and listen to everything that's happened, from start to finish."

"I'm working too hard and Georgie has a new job," Nick said.

"You do, dear?" Sally said, and I thought I saw her eyes narrowing. I know she approved heartily of wives who stayed home, taking care of their husbands. For that reason she had always encouraged me to do my profile of the bay. After Nick had explained the Swift Observatory, she frowned. "I'm not sure I like you telephoning strangers out of the blue," she said. "With so many nut cases out there."

"Thank god, or there'd be nothing interesting for her to study," Nick said.

"That's not true," I said. "The more ordinary the better. Ordinary people faced with extraordinary strife. That's becoming my motto." I punched Nick playfully on the upper arm.

"He always bruised so easily," Sally said, staring into space.

Leaning against Nick, I felt him stifle a giggle. He reached around me, hooking his thumb through my belt loop.

"The woman is a terror," he said. "Just look at her."

Sally looked at me and smiled. "I know she's a good girl."

Everyone decided to swim. They changed into bathing suits, but I stayed dressed. I couldn't swim in lakes. Fresh water lacked the buoyancy of salt. It felt sinister to me, although it tasted pure as drinking water. Perhaps if the lake contained a spring, or was fed by a waterfall, anything to make it move, I would have swum in it. But I hated thinking of its muddy bottom, nurturing plants that bloomed on the surface. A nickel dropped in that lake would rest in the mud until eternity. A nickel dropped in our bay might turn up in the Outer Hebrides. I felt frightened of freshwater fish, which I found tasteless to eat: trout, pike, bass, none of which I could identify. Snapping turtles. Water bugs. Swamp adders and pit vipers. Frogs. Lily pads. Branches rotting beneath the surface. In the sea, branches would be tossed onto a beach and saved or pulverized by the tides, waves and currents.

I sat in a mesh lawn chair watching the Symonds tread water. They formed a circle of heads; their voices carried to me, but not their words. Then Nick struck out from the group and came towards me. He walked onto shore, his bare chest dusted with silvery particles of mud.

"This is nice," he said. "I'm glad we came. Thanks for suggesting it."

"I'm glad we came too," I said, thinking of the Point and Pem's traditional Fourth of July cake, but absurdly happy to be given credit for our visit with his family.

"We'd see my family much less if it weren't for you," he said.

"They're your family. It's very important to stay close to them." It was a philosophy I believed with all my heart, even when staying close to Nick's family interfered with a day of seeing mine.

We cooked hot dogs and hamburgers on a gas grill, but after that first beer Nick, the pilot, refused to drink another. His mother tried to convince us that we should spend the night, partly so that Nick could help drink the keg, but we stood fast to our plan. We said goodbye at six o'clock. Everyone acted disappointed that we wouldn't stay to watch Terry's fireworks, but Nick had to go to the office early the next day. Flying home I watched the clock and wished for the plane to fly faster. Reading my mind, Nick glanced at me, smiling. "The throttle's opened up. We're going as fast as we can." Mountains turned to hills, farmland to suburbs, we followed the highway to the river and the river to the sea and we landed in our bay at Bennison Point in time to watch Pem cut the Fourth of July cake.

. . .

The Fourth of July cake was white and gooey with red, blue, yellow, and green squiggles and twirls of icing. Paper flags of all the states flew from toothpick standards, circling Old Glory in the center. Pem had made the cake, or supervised the making of it, every year since I could remember. That night everyone sat on her porch: Clare and Donald, the little boys in their summer pajamas, Honora and Pem, me and Nick.

"We can't cut the cake until the fireworks start," Eugene said, sounding injured.

"That's the rule," Honora said. "That's always been the way it is." The sun had set, but light reflected in the sky, clinging to the water's surface, to the trees, to the yards and houses, to everything on earth.

"Come on, let's cut the cake," Pem said, a telltale smear of white frosting in the corner of her mouth.

"What do you do to your brows?" Nick asked, peering into her eyes. She laughed merrily, distracted from her sweet tooth, and spun into the story.

"So many people ask me that!" I heard her say, but I was remembering other Fourth of July cakes.

Everyone in Pem's family would drive from Providence to Black Hall for the Fourth and the days surrounding it. Our cottages were full of her sisters Gert, Nettie, Lil and Kat and the husbands and children of everyone except Lil, who had never married; her brothers Edward and Henry and their wives and children; her father, Achilles (pronounced "Ash-heel" in the French manner), a big man of noble proportions whose profile fittingly resembled the Indian on the Buffalo nickel. He was half American Indian. Present also were Pem and Damon, whom Clare and I called "Granddamon," Honora and Timothy, me and Clare. The generations were staggered in such a way that there were no children our age. Honora was the oldest of her cousins. Many of those cousins were still unmarried; two were married with little babies. Clare and I received a lot of attention. Everyone brought us presents: little chamois sacks of marbles; sweatshirts that said "Narragansett Pier" across the front; tin rings with plastic rubies; our great-aunts' castoff sunglasses, pointy and trimmed with rhinestones. They brought boxes full of doughnuts, rolls, and cheeseless pizza. The moment they arrived a card game would start—canasta, pinochle, or thirty-one—and not finish until they left.

Clare and I were aware of small intrigues and rivalries. Everyone vied for Lil, the unmarried great-aunt. Everyone sought to please her by letting her sleep late, bringing her lemonade and beer on a cute little silver tray I never saw except when she visited, offering to buy her nail polish. No one could stand Edna, Henry's wife. Edward, Gert's husband Buddy, and my father steered clear of Granddamon. Pem and Honora seemed always to be on opposite sides of the room, making sure everyone had what they wanted. Aunt Kat and Uncle Homer were the most fun, constantly swearing, smoking, and gossiping about Lil and her secret beau, Nettie's son's dyslexia, and the connections of various well-known politicians to the Providence mafia. Achilles, whom all his great-grandchildren called "Grampa," would play cards with everyone, sitting in the same place as long as possible to avoid moving his wondrous bulk. He was totally bald. Clare and I would stare admiringly at his shiny scalp for hours.

Pem would wait until the fireworks were in full swing before carrying the Fourth of July cake onto the porch. Everyone would cease watching the show and remark how beautiful her cake was that year. It seemed the most reverent tribute, that anyone could take their eyes away from those explosive fountains and sizzles long enough to look at a cake, but that is the sort of attention Pem commanded. No matter who was speaking, Pem had merely to clear her throat for silence to fall over her family.

"She was a holy terror when she was little," Aunt Gert told us.

"In fourth grade she got caught passing a note that called the teacher a namby-pamby blackassed grumble midget," Lil said.

"Oh, she used to take my dolls and switch their heads," Nettie said.

"We took her on canoe rides and she always capsized," Henry and Edward said.

"Ain't she sweet?" Grampa asked.

Clare and I would hear those stories, and although we didn't quite believe them, we respected them, for Pem certainly had power over everyone. Part of it came from their affection for her, but part of it came from something else.

Only my father would continue watching the fireworks when Pem brought out her cake. He would sit in his corner, beside Uncle Edward and me or Clare, smoking a cigarette, watching the sky. "Look at the cake," I said to him one year, when his arm held me tight and kept me from jumping at every crashing boom. "Mmmm," he had said, gazing skyward.

Pem always noticed that he refused to look. She never said a word, but I could see her lips tighten. Then she would forget to cut him a piece of cake. I'm not sure whether my father ever tasted the Fourth of July cake.

After the fireworks, Clare and I would each have the lap of our father or Granddamon. Cards would shuffle softly. The pitch of Providence accents formidable, stories would commence. The great-aunts and -uncles told about block dances in Thornton, skating on Silver Lake, bonfires on Neuticonkinet Hill, taking the steamers from Providence to Newport. With much screeching they told about Harriet Grady's quest to do her brother out of the family inheritance. Aunt Gert told us about the origins of belly buttons, of how babies came out of an oven and God tested their soft tummies with his finger, saying, "You're done, you're done. . . ." Even then Clare and I had thought it brave of her to tell that story in the presence of two dedicated scientists, although both our parents had laughed at it. Honora was the beloved niece, Clare and I her children, Timothy her brilliant and therefore distant husband. Clare and I adored those gatherings. Every year we saved a piece of Fourth of July cake, precious as wedding cake, and froze it, to keep until the next year.

· · ·

All the great-aunts and great-uncles, Grampa, Granddamon and my father were dead now. Many of them had died in their nineties, but Grampa had lived to be one hundred and Gert, his oldest daughter, one hundred and two. She had died last year. Granddamon had died in his sleep at seventy-one, and my father had died at forty. He was the youngest and the first to die.

The year his oil rig toppled, Clare and I looked forward more than ever to the Fourth of July. Honora quit the New Bedford television station, and we moved from Woods Hole to Black Hall. What had been our summer place was now our home. Pem and Granddamon lived right next door. After school every day I

would sit on Pem's lap in the Boston rocker, my head against
her big soft bosom, and tell her how much I hated school. She
had hated school too, so she understood. Pem showed me the
best trees to climb, and Granddamon shagged fly balls for me
when he came home from the bank. Clare and Honora were
nearly inseparable, speaking French to each other or making
botanical drawings, until a New Haven station picked up "Weather
Woman" for its Saturday morning lineup and Honora went back
to work.

Then school was over and it was the Fourth of July. Clare
and I had been counting the days. We had even cut new state
flags out of a *National Geographic* and attached them to virgin
toothpicks. Wearing red, white and blue bathing suits, we waited
in the yard for the first cars. Edward's blue Cadillac bearing his
family and Grampa arrived first, followed immediately by the
others. The great-aunts and -uncles filed up the hill, and we
instantly knew something was wrong. How solemn the proces-
sion, how silent! Everyone kissed us, cooing about our father,
and Clare and I started to cry. Other people could kiss and coo,
but not the great-aunts. From them we wanted whoops and
shouts, card games and gossip and presents. After everyone hugged
Honora things improved, but not much. All the stories seemed
to be reverential ones about Timmy. Clare and I had loved our
father, but even we could recognize that he was not the proper
subject for stories told by Pem's people. He was too reserved, too
quiet, too kind to inspire the sort of malicious joy that infused
their customary tales. All that day I sulked on the rocks, feeling
angry at everyone for spoiling the tradition. I had expected them
to be the same as ever, to save their phony polite restraint for
the funerals of people they knew and loved less than us. But it
wasn't phony. Everyone was truly sad.

That night, waiting for the fireworks to start, I sat between
Granddamon and Uncle Homer. The sun set fast that year, and

the show started right away. I jumped at the first explosion, and
my grandfather held my hand. The rockets flew with clashing,
terrible sounds that reminded me of trees crashing, of the worst
thunderstorms, of Moby Dick sounding for the last time, dragging
Captain Ahab behind him. Oh, I heard the sea crack and part
and swallow them both, and I shuddered and began to cry. My
grandfather squeezed my hand tighter. "Shh, little one," he said.
"They're just fireworks."

"You love fireworks," Honora said from across the porch, from
her safe spot between Aunt Lil and Aunt Nettie. "Remember we
told you how they're just a chemical reaction?"

I remembered, and I stopped crying, but the terror I felt grew
and grew. The great-aunts were quiet that year, the big man
beside me couldn't stop my fear with the gentle weight of his
arm across my shoulders, and when Pem brought forth the cake,
everyone would be watching her.

· · ·

"Oh, they're wonderful!" Casey called, watching the twinkling
blue ash darken and fall into the bay. A red starburst turned
green, then gold, then disappeared. Four bright rockets exploded,
followed by a gentle silver fountain.

"Pretty," Pem said. "Did you see that red one?"

"How about a little cake?" Clare asked.

"No, watch the fireworks!" Eugene said.

"The rule is, cake as soon as the show starts," Honora said
sternly. She lifted the silver knife, the same one Pem had always
used, and handed it to Pem.

"The show's nearly over," I said. "Why don't we wait?"

"No," Honora said, nudging Pem's forearm, but Pem was
spellbound. She sat there, her mouth barely open, watching ashes
shower the bay. "Mother!" Honora said.

"Here comes the finale," Donald said. Everyone watched lights fill the sky, flashing every color, the noise ferocious, and then the lights stopped, the noise grew muffled, then stopped.

"Well . . ." everyone said.

"Now can we have cake?" Eugene asked.

"Cake!" Pem said, waving the knife over her head.

Clare and Honora were glaring at me. "What?" I asked.

"You know, it's been three years since you spent an entire Fourth here on the Point," Clare said. "And I think you're forgetting the traditions."

"We never wait until the show is over before we cut the cake," Honora said. "Never. This is the first time in my life that I ever have eaten Fourth of July cake without watching fireworks."

"You could have cut it before if you wanted to," I said, amazed at the direction of this conversation. "I just suggested we wait because the boys were so wrapped up in the fireworks."

"How are the boys supposed to learn traditions if we don't teach them?" Clare asked.

"Well, I'm sorry," I said, feeling as though I might burst out laughing. I had the feeling they were miffed that I had visited Nick's family instead of spending the day with them.

"Clare has a point," Nick said. "The Fourth of July is a nice tradition. Georgie and I flew like the wind to get back in time."

"How is your family, Nick?" Honora asked, leaving her cake untouched, in protest.

"Fine, fine."

"I hope you gave them our love," Clare said.

"Of course we did."

Pem cleared her throat, then started to sing: " 'No matter where I wander, no matter where I roam . . . I was born in the land of Uncle Sam, the good old U.S.A.!' "

Then Eugene asked if we could sing "It's a Grand Old Flag," then Clare started "Yankee Doodle Dandy." We all sang along, Pem at the top of her lungs.

"Oh, think of the ghosts that are smiling at those old songs," Honora said sadly when we had finished.

"Shut up, Mama, and eat your peanuts," Pem said.

Then Nick held my hand, squeezing it to let me know it was time to go home. We made our way around the porch, kissing everyone, telling everyone what a wonderful evening it had been. I wrapped a piece of cake in my napkin and handed it to Casey. "Put this in the freezer and save it till next year," I said.

"You're a good girl," Honora said when I got to her.

Nick and I walked home through the dark, his arm tight around me. Waves splashed the jetty, sending spume into our faces. Our path seemed darker, the night stiller, after watching fire in the sky. I thought of the family ghosts who had visited that night, of Nick's and my journey across two states and two families, and I loved him more than ever.

Seven

In the heat of deep summer, I was summoned to meet the Avery Foundation's board of directors. Since their offices were in New York, I booked a room at the Gregory. Nick, consumed by the insatiable Project Broadsword, had brought work home every night; he was relieved when I provided him with the chance to stay in the city—my reasons were legitimate and impeccable. My business required it. I asked everyone what I should wear. Clare thought my white cotton skirt with a blue lisle pullover would be best—not at all sophisticated, giving me the look of an unworldly scholar. Honora advised me to wear something unusual, like a sari or clamdiggers. Nick said to wear my black linen suit, and since he was the most experienced in matters of business and making a good impression, I followed his suggestion. The humidity was so oppressive, it was like sitting in a bath. Although I took an air-conditioned cab from the Gregory to the Foundation, my backbone and the backs of my thighs were drenched by the time I arrived.

I buzzed and was admitted into the narrow stone building on

East Sixty-fourth Street. One glance told me this was the perfect place to house a foundation. A pale oriental rug over hardwood floor, furniture covered in gray-striped satin, a receptionist with the correct head-tilt: efficient, not curious. After I gave her my name she offered me a glass of Bristol Cream sherry. My skin began to dry. I leaned back, sipping. I wondered why they wanted to meet me. The letter had been quite pleasant, like an invitation to tea. "Could you possibly come by our offices 24 July, so that we may have the chance to meet and talk with you?" It had been signed "Cordially yours, Julia Avery Buchbinder, Secretary." Nick and I had speculated whether John Avery would be present. John had said nothing to Nick at work, and Nick thought Project Broadsword was too hectic to allow John to attend a family board meeting. Perhaps they would demand I account for the money they had granted me: Spent it on phone bills and my new telephone line, I would tell them. Actually I felt unconcerned. The Swift Observatory had existed before the Avery Foundation had heard of it, and it would exist without their money. Mainly I enjoyed the credibility the grant had given me, and, now, the chance to wear a nice suit, be served sherry, hobnob with my patrons.

One minute after I set my empty glass on the leather-topped side table, the receptionist led me down a corridor. Vivaldi played in the distance. We entered a large bright room where six people including John Avery stood around an oval table.

"Hello, Georgie," he said, shaking my hand.

"Hello, John," I said, and then I was introduced to the board of directors: Julia Buchbinder, Jasper and Helen Avery, all brothers and sisters; Ralph Gower and Tucker Chase, cousins. There were empty sherry glasses in front of each of their places at the table, and I wondered why I had had to drink my sherry alone, in the reception area. Ralph, Tucker, and Jasper had the same sort of solid, confident good looks as John Avery. They all wore dark suits and red ties, as if they had just run out of their law or investment banking offices for this meeting. I looked more closely and realized that each of them wore exactly the same red tie: dark red background with horizontal gold and navy blue stripes. Julia and Helen stood together but appeared very different. Although older than Helen by at least ten years, Julia had chestnut-brown hair and Helen had gray. Julia wore pearls around her neck and a shirtdress that clung to her broad figure. Badly applied blue eye makeup emphasized her puffy eyes, but she had a glorious smile. Helen looked about forty, too young to be totally gray, and she had a pale complexion. She wore a brilliant yellow, green and orange caftan.

"Now, to business," John said, placing both palms on the table. I recognized that he was the family ringleader. Everyone sat, with me between Helen and Jasper.

"We think the Swift Observatory is a fascinating enterprise," Julia said, with patrician emphasis. She fumbled for gold-rimmed half-spectacles, which she put on. Smiling, she glanced at me and began to speak, referring to a sheaf of papers before her. "As you may know, the Avery Foundation funds a variety of projects. Some of these are very important. We underwrote the exhibition of Etruscan Art at Bartlett Hall in 1982. We supported Leo Guziewicz's research during his lean years."

I gasped because she had paused expectantly, and I tried to recall: hadn't Leo Guziewicz won a Nobel Prize for something? She went on. The list of whom they had supported included accomplished artists, writers, and musicians, research projects, fledgling newspapers and magazines, small specialized museums, and inventors.

"You see you're in good company, Georgie," John Avery said.

"I truly am. Thank you," I said, fighting the urge to bow my head.

"It is practically unheard of for us to meet grant recipients face to face," John continued. "I can think of four, maybe five instances."

"Four or five," Tucker Chase said. He seemed about John Avery's age; I wondered whether they had been the sort of cousins who had grown up together, sharing everything, closer than brothers because they didn't have to battle for their parents' attentions. They seemed to check with each other now and then, glancing across the table and analyzing the other's expression. Jasper Avery, on the other hand, looked everywhere in the room except at John. John played the part of oldest brother, but Jasper appeared older by several years. I heard him crunching, not jingling, the coins in his pocket.

"Perhaps my connection with Nick makes it easier for us to invite you here. We have some cards that we want to lay on the table, and it seemed provident to do that with you present."

"Maybe I should have brought my lawyer," I said, and although everyone smiled, no one laughed.

"We both know that your lawyer is up to his ears on Wall Street," John said. "I promise you, one day the deal will be done, and he'll be all yours again."

"I hope so," I said, wishing Nick were with me to hear the proposition.

"We want to increase your grant," John said.

Everyone was watching me: Julia, with a small smile; Tucker, John, and Helen with generous grins; Ralph and Jasper, both expressionless.

"You do?" I said finally.

"Your first grant was very small," John said. "Two thousand dollars—a pittance, really. Some would call it 'seed money.' We plant a seed, we watch it grow. That is how we commonly operate. Sometimes we fund a project just once, then never again if it doesn't meet our expectations. You see, we never want to exert influence, but we do expect a certain standard of quality. We think the Swift Observatory has untapped potential. Tucker?"

Tucker Chase cleared his throat, and his left hand jostled his tie knot. "All through the world are venerable institutions called 'think tanks.' They take a problem, analyze it, examine it from all angles, and come up with a solution. We think of the Swift Observatory as a 'look-see tank.' " He smiled. "I'm not trivializing it, Miss Swift. To the contrary—we think it could take its place among important centers of thought."

"On a smaller scale, perhaps," Julia said.

"Tell us some of your ideas," Helen said. "Are there more stories like Mona Tuchman's?"

I mentioned my series on Mom and Pop groceries, the piece on what goes on in a family when one of the children joins a religious order, the interviews with brides-to-be. "I've been trying to arrange an interview with Caroline Orne—you may have read about her?"

"Yes, the woman who shot the man who killed her mother," Helen said excitedly.

"She's in prison in Chicago," I said. "I haven't been able to speak with her on the telephone, and she hasn't answered my letter."

"See what I mean?" John said, more to Jasper than anyone else, I thought. "With a larger grant, more could be accomplished. The scope could be larger. The Observatory would not be so regional, so East Coast."

"Wasn't Caroline Orne a teacher?" Helen asked, frowning.

"Yes, eighth grade. She lived at home, she was just out of college at the time of the murder. Her mother was robbed and killed coming home from the theater one night. They caught the man who did it, and Caroline bought a gun, went to the prison, and shot him," I said.

"Gad, what sort of security do they have at that prison?" Jasper asked.

"You're missing the point as usual," Julia said dryly.

"We shouldn't take up more of Miss Swift's valuable time than necessary," Tucker said. "Let's get to the point. We would like to increase your grant to twenty thousand dollars."

"That would enable you to travel if necessary," John said. "Let's see what happens when you spread your wings, study humanity on a nationwide scale. Is human nature different in Chicago than, say, Tallahassee?"

I was considering how to answer. I was flattered, certainly, but I felt as though something were being taken away from me. They all seemed too interested, almost proprietary. Looking around the table, I imagined that each person present, with the exception of Jasper, had his or her own ideas about what I should observe and where I should observe it. And how could I agree to travel when the point of the Swift Observatory was that I could work at home? If only I hadn't mentioned the Caroline Orne idea. Added to these worries was the fact that John Avery was Nick's boss, and I felt leery of saying anything that might offend him.

"We'd like you to expand," Julia said, almost apologetically. "Take on some additional observers, perhaps. There are people who would do it without pay."

"I'm afraid of these conditions," I said. "Travel, expansion. I'm not sure I want the Observatory to change."

"Change is crucial to all of us," Ralph said.

"Let her think about it, let her think about it," Julia said.

"No, this is a no-strings-attached offer," John Avery said, firmly settling the case. He leaned forward, resting his chin in his hands. "You might say we're acting as the *Avery* Observatory now," he smiled at me. "We're going to give you the money and watch what you do with it."

"Fascinating enterprise," Tucker said, tossing his head.

"This is unexpected," I stammered. "And wonderful. Thank you."

"You're welcome," John said, rising, giving me my cue to leave. I shook everyone's hand.

"I'll walk Georgiana out," Helen said. She took my elbow and we walked down the cool, dark corridor where Vivaldi still played. "We always have pet projects going," she told me when we reached the reception area. "And yours is our pet just now. Ralph and Jasper don't quite approve; you probably picked up on that. They like projects more easily defined, like a failing ballet company, or a promising young artist. Things they can point to years later, saying, 'Oh yes, remember when we saved the Portland Ballet?' " Deepening her voice, she did a remarkable imitation of Jasper. "Your project is too unconventional, and I think it embarrasses them to tell people they fund an observatory that has nothing to do with the heavens. But that's exactly why the rest of us love it."

"I'm surprised, to tell you the truth," I said. "I never expected the Foundation to take such an interest."

"We take an interest in every project. Even John, Tucker, and Julia, and you know how busy they are. Tucker's a lawyer at a firm as big as Hubbard, Starr, and Julia's the president of Jazzline Graphics. The Foundation comes first, always."

"That's really wonderful," I said, wondering how the Foundation could come first to a man who had to work as hard as John Avery. What if Nick had a foundation that came first, in addition to his law practice? Where would love and family fit in?

"Is John married?" I asked, feeling awkward but needing to know.

"Divorced. Poor John. All alone, but then so am I. Maybe that's why we all love the Foundation so much. It really is our family. Our ongoing, never-ending, family without end." Her face turned several shades redder; her eyes flickered around the room—from the window to the portraits on the wall to the brass doorknob. "Our mother died when we were very young—was murdered in fact. Maybe that's why we all are so drawn to your tales of vengeance. There's not one of us that wouldn't have liked to stab that devil's black heart." She stuck her index finger into her open left palm. "Well, I should let you go."

"Yes," I said, feeling dazed. I shook her hand, then walked out the door into a barricade of heat.

The humidity was brutal. I dragged down Fifth Avenue, trying to make sense of my meeting with the Avery Foundation. Two black limousines drove by, tinted windows shielding their air-conditioned occupants. I imagined John and Tucker and Julia riding downtown to their offices. If they weren't paying me, I would have liked to do a study of the Averys. I wondered when their mother had died and how old each of them had been. Why had Jasper, the oldest brother, been stripped of his stature? No one paid him any attention at all. Why was Helen's hair gray? The one question I didn't have to ask was why John was divorced; considering his work load at Hubbard, Starr, if the Foundation came first, what lunatic would stay married to him?

Back at the Gregory I called Nick to tell him the news, but Denise said he was in a meeting. I turned the air conditioner to high and lay across the bed. The machine rattled, but I discerned no movement of air. Closing my eyes, I pretended to have a fever. I was lying in the jungle, dying of malaria. Because I was delirious, I allowed myself to have these thoughts: I would use my grant money to travel around the country, interviewing the most extraordinary people I could find. The ordinary man made exceptional by events in San Francisco, Tulsa, Green Bay. I would fly to Chicago, visit Caroline Orne in prison. In my fever state, I began to envision her: long blond hair, prison garb of blue and white ticking, like a mattress cover, bruised eyes. Imagining her made her real, and I imagined visiting a travel agent, booking a flight to Chicago, choosing my hotel, buying a Chicago restaurant guide. Then the fever broke.

I sat straight up. What was I doing, planning trips around the country? I thought of Nick. I would eat alone in my hotel room, he would eat alone in his. I had no illusions that he would bother to fly home to Black Hall if I weren't there. He had enough work with Project Broadsword to keep him in New York twenty-four hours a day and in the office twenty. Our little cottage on Bennison Point would be vacant, filling with dust and cobwebs.

The telephone rang, and it was Nick.

"They increased my grant!" I said.

"I know. John told me," he said, sounding dismal.

"What's wrong?"

"I have to fly to London. We have some business to do there."

"Great!" I said. Of all the places Nick went on business, I think I loved London most. My fantasy of flying to Chicago was replaced by the reality of London. The Basil Street Hotel, with its Edwardian facade and cozy country-house interior filled my mind.

"Georgie, you can't come," he said. "I can't even talk about it right now, but I'll tell you when I see you in an hour. I have to leave tonight."

"I can't believe it," I said. Something was sucking the air from my lungs, and I couldn't get my breath. I choked.

"Georgie? Are you okay?"

I didn't answer.

"I'll be there soon," he said, and hung up.

Until Nick arrived, I treated myself like a very sick person, someone with jungle fever. I lifted things with extreme care, as though I might drop them. Not wanting to injure myself, I moved slowly around the room, leaving wide spaces between me and sharp corners. Every few minutes I would lie across the bed, thinking of nothing at all, trying to regain a little strength. I heard his key in the door. He lay beside me on the bed and hugged me hard.

"We always go to London together," I said, thinking of Clare, of how Donald had not taken her to Tokyo, of how that was his greatest regret.

"I have to tell you some things," Nick said, and he led me to the table, as if what he had to tell me was so important that we had to be upright to discuss it.

"Project Broadsword is a very large tender offer," he said.

Not for the first time, I wondered why they were called Tender Offers. What was tender about them? Nothing.

"John and two other partners have told me, unofficially, that if I do well on this deal, I have a very good chance of making partner." His eyes glowed with excitement.

"That's wonderful. I'm really happy about that, Nick," I said. "But why can't I go to London?"

"Because what we're doing over there is so top secret, it would look bad if I brought you along. Everyone would assume that you knew what was going on. No spouses on this trip, we've all been told."

"That sucks."

"I think so too."

"What's so top secret?"

"The target company is Bombay Petroleum," he said, naming one of the largest oil companies in the world. He watched for my reaction.

The fact that he watched me, wanting me to be impressed, assuming that the deal's magnitude would make me understand why he had to go to London alone, filled me with rage.

If it weren't London, I wouldn't be so angry. We loved London. We always found time for a walk in Hyde Park, a night at the theater, and dinner at Scott's. But suddenly I remembered that Nick had gone alone on his last trip to London: I had volunteered to stay with Pem while Honora attended a meteorology conference in Montreal, a commitment that couldn't be broken. I remembered feeling disappointed that I couldn't go with him. But nothing close to the killing rage I was in now.

"If it makes you feel any better, I won't have time for the theater on this jaunt. Back-to-back meetings have been scheduled, as John puts it, 'far in the night.' " Nick had an air of distance to him, as if his involvement with the deal was total; he barely registered my fury. He had been so busy recently, he hadn't had a haircut, I thought, noticing the way his black hair curled just above his collar. I wanted to touch it in spite of myself. "Besides," he said, "Honora and Clare will be happy to have you all to themselves. I can see it now, the three of you taking Pem for a ride to Newport one day. . . ."

And all at once I realized why I felt so panicked at the idea of Nick going alone to London. It meant I had to go to Chicago. The anger left me. I uncoiled like a snake, and started to cry from the relief of understanding. "I have a few things to tell you," I said. I began with a description of the Avery family and their office, and then I told him about their offer.

"I'm so proud of you," he said. "John told me today that they consider you a bright light."

"That's nice," I said, wondering how he had missed the point that I was afraid of going to Chicago alone. It came to me: because I hadn't said it.

"I've never taken a business trip on my own," I said. "It changes everything—my entire concept of the Swift Observatory. Why do you think I started the thing? Because it gave me the chance to work at home."

"That's not entirely true," Nick said. "Your profile of the bay gave you the chance to work at home. You want to branch out a little, Georgie. The only subject you've met face to face was Mona Tuchman, and everyone says that was your best study. I think you need more contact than a voice over the telephone."

I smiled and hugged him tight, my lips against his damp neck.

"Off you go to London," I said, my voice muffled by his skin and collar.

"What? I didn't hear you," he said.

I knew he hadn't, and I didn't repeat it. That was all the blessing I was able to give.

Eight

I allowed myself barely enough time to pack and inform Honora and Clare of my plans to go to Chicago. Forward motion, that was the key to maintaining sanity. If I allowed myself to sink into a chair, like one of Nick's Whistler women, I would see my center of focus shifting from Bennison Point to the world at large. I would think of Nick staying at the Savoy, two doors down from Jean Snizort. Of course Jean had gone—how could I have thought she wouldn't? I had known she was a colleague working on Project Broadsword. "Who else is going to London?" I had asked Nick that night at the Gregory. His expression told me even before he opened his mouth.

Clare couldn't come when Honora drove me to the airport.

"She wanted to," Honora said, "but Casey has that dentist's appointment."

We headed north to Bradley Field. We allowed plenty of time because Honora had several stops to make along the way: the bank, the dry cleaner's, the pharmacy. At first I felt annoyed that she insisted on doing her errands before taking me to the plane, but then I realized she wanted to prolong the ride, wanted us to have more time together. She told the bank teller I had an important interview to conduct in Chicago; she gave the druggist an oral history of the Swift Observatory.

"Mom," I said. "You're embarrassing me."

"Honey, I bragged when you won the Eel Pond Science Fair, and I feel like bragging now. Mothers have the inalienable right to brag about their daughters."

I smiled, looking across the front seat at my mother. She drove like a college kid: a little too fast, window down, elbow resting on the window ledge. Her chestnut hair blew in the wind. I remembered when I was small and felt lucky for having such a fun, beautiful mother. She had seemed to be, but was not, younger than my friends' mothers. I also remembered dimly one night when Clare cried, accusing Honora of flirting with her boyfriend.

"Do you like Chicago?" I asked.

"I adore Chicago. Any town that puts a Chagall mosaic in the middle of the business district is okay by me."

We finally reached the airport. She insisted on parking the car, accompanying me to the check-in desk.

"Be careful," she said, giving me a big hug.

Of what? Of strange men? Of high winds? I didn't flinch or bother to ask what she meant because "Be careful" was as normal a farewell for Honora as "So long" or "Goodbye."

· · ·

The flight passed quickly enough, but stepping off the plane in Chicago I felt impossibly far from anything familiar. In my hotel room I reached for the telephone book, as if holding it connected me to all the names it contained. Maybe I knew someone listed: an old teacher or someone I had gone to school with. The impulse to grab the telephone and dial randomly came over me. Instead, I ordered a drink from room service and forced myself to breathe

deeply. "You are not alone," I said out loud, foolishly, since of
course I was alone. But was I? Closing my eyes, I conjured Nick.
I saw his lean face and broad grin, his mop of black hair, his
dark eyes. He leaned close to kiss me. Then I heard Pem asking,
"Who's the boy?" "My husband," I answered out loud. "Nicholas
Symonds, my husband. Go away, Pem." She shuffled off, sullenly,
in the direction of the kitchen, no doubt to make a secret sandwich. But Nick must have gone with her, since he was no longer
kissing me and I truly was alone, waiting for room service to
deliver my drink.

All that night I couldn't stop observing myself. I couldn't get
over the feeling that I was at once going through certain motions
and watching myself go through them. While I was brushing my
teeth, I was also two paces away, sitting on the edge of the bathtub,
my knees crossed, my chin resting in the palm of my right hand,
thinking, "Let's see how she brushes her teeth." I was alone in
a very nice hotel in a strange city, on a different continent than
Nick, because of my work. The different format of Chicago's
telephone books gave me a strange thrill. The unfamiliar newspapers seemed heavy with promise. I had traveled west without
knowing which prison held Caroline Orne; I was not sure that
I would be allowed to visit her even after I found out. Never-
theless, lying in bed that night, I thought of myself as an adven-
turer, climbing a mountain in order to plant a flag at the summit.

Before I left the hotel the next morning, Nick had called me
and I had called Honora and Clare. I felt better, knowing that
I had everyone pinned down. Then I went out. I took my satchel
of notebooks and the morning papers down to a bench at the
edge of the lake. Lake Michigan is enormous; I could see no land
on the other side, the way one sees Plum Island across Long
Island Sound, but I wanted to deny that a lake could be greater
than any body of salt water. I sat in the shade of a walnut tree
and opened the first paper. On page five I found a story about

her. The photo showed a pretty girl, pert with small, regular features and straight hair held back with barrettes. She was smiling at a spot somewhere beyond the photographer, and I decided it must have been a yearbook picture. The article said her lawyers claimed that she was not guilty by reason of insanity; she was being held for observation at St. Ursula's hospital.

I considered calling her lawyer, to ask permission to see her. I thought of visiting the University of Chicago law library, to check any statutes that might prevent me from meeting her. Sitting on that shady bench I complicated matters terribly until I saw a cab cruising past, hailed it, and told the driver, "St. Ursula's, please."

The hospital's shiny, sterile environment seemed hardly the place for an intimate talk, the sort I had had with Mona. I was prepared for some sort of screening: what if I were the daughter of the man whom Caroline had killed because he had killed her mother? I could be the latest link in the chain of vengeance. But the nurse on duty simply asked me to sign a guest book and take a seat in the lounge. Waiting for Caroline Orne, I wondered if I would have flown to Chicago to interview brides. Probably not. Sitting in that gleaming room, I thought of Carson Bleyle, of my sister's and my very real plan to murder him with marbles. Loss had not moved us, because if he had married Honora we would, in fact, have gained a stepfather. Still, loss was what we had feared: the loss of our family as we knew and loved it. Carson Bleyle would have removed us from Bennison Point, from our home with Honora, Pem, and Granddamon. Those strange memories came back to me; I was feeling the weight of slimy marbles in my hand when Caroline Orne walked towards me.

She looked twenty-five, was my height, and she wore blue corduroy pants and a beige sweater, clothes too warm for the season. Her hair was feathered in the manner seen on young women in shopping malls, and she wore tinted turquoise contact lenses. She smiled, waiting for me to introduce myself.

"That's an interesting profession," she said after I had explained my mission. "Did you major in sociology?"

"No, I didn't go to college," I said.

"I was a sociology major before I switched to Spanish. I must say, I left sociology because I didn't think the career possibilities were very interesting. But I'd never heard of anything like the Swift Observatory."

I didn't tell her that I had invented the Swift Observatory, that I in fact was the Swift Observatory. I had never connected my work with any discipline as defined as sociology, and the definition made me uneasy.

"Are you willing to talk to me?" I asked.

She stood still for a minute, not speaking. I thought she was going to walk away without answering, but she shrugged and said, "Okay. Let's go in here."

I followed her into a smaller room, equally clean and smelling of disinfectant. A television played to the otherwise empty room. A nurse stuck her head in, saw that we were sitting quietly, and left. For some reason, that nurse's vigilance comforted me.

"You taught eighth grade?" I asked.

"Yes, but only temporarily. I was taking masters' courses at the university." She leaned forward, grabbing her ankles with both hands. "I have to tell you, I'm interested in your study. I can understand how a sociologist might be pretty interested in someone like me."

"But I'm not really a sociologist," I said, not wanting to deceive her.

"Maybe that's not your label, but that's what you do—you study society, people, behavior. Or you could call yourself an anthropologist before the fact, the fact being death or maybe extinction. Anyway, go on."

"You lived at home?"

"Lived. Hmmm, you're putting it in the past tense. I think of myself as still living there. It made a lot of sense, when I decided to do it. All my friends from college have their own apartments, or else they live on campus if they're in graduate school. But I get along very well with my family, and it seemed like a good way to save money." She laughed. "That's what my parents kept telling me, 'Live at home and start a bank account,' as if they weren't dying to have me back home. It was hard for all of us when I went away to college."

"Why?"

"Well, it was the first time I'd ever gone away from home. I never went to camp, never went on a long trip without my family. Still, going to college was easier than I had thought. God, I really dreaded it! All the summer before I left I would lie awake thinking about what would happen at home when I was gone."

"Good things or bad things?"

She shrugged, impatient because I had missed her point. "It didn't matter. Just that things would change. Like the first time I came home for vacation, my father had been on a diet and lost about ten pounds. Also, my brother had fallen and cut his chin, and he had a terrible red scar. And no one had bothered to tell me! I know none of that's important, but I cried when I saw how different everything was."

"I think that's important. You want to keep track of things in your family," I said, thinking of Nick, Honora, Pem, Clare and Donald and the kids, glad that I had them in place, the way a radar operator tracks aircraft on a screen. "Who's in your family?" I asked.

"My parents, me, my brothers Guy, Brian, and Peter, and my sister Bonnie."

"Do you see them often?"

"Of course. They all come, every day. Even Guy, who's in college. He goes to the University of Chicago, and he lives there, even though it's so close to home. My parents thought it would be a good idea. But I'm sure they'll encourage him to move in after he graduates, to start his bank account." She grinned, and I noticed her unconscious use of "my parents" and "they," as though they were both alive.

"What do your parents do?" I asked, going along with her use of the present tense, but I watched her register my mistake as the grin slid away.

"Well, my father is a musician. He plays French horn in the Chicago Symphony. My mother was a pediatrician. She had her office in our house." She paused for a moment, smiling. "The sound of crying babies used to drive us crazy. It used to upset Bonnie horribly, thinking of Mom giving injections to all those babies. I loved hearing about her cases. She'd tell us about cradle cap, and failure to thrive, chicken pox and whooping cough, and once a case of meningitis that worried her so much she evacuated the family to a hotel near the airport. Failure to thrive was the worst. It meant that a baby wouldn't take nourishment. God, we hated when babies failed to thrive." She frowned, remembering those sad babies. "All those little lives that came through our house. It seemed wonderful, having a mother who specialized in taking care of children. When Bonnie was little she was afraid that other kids would hate us, because our mother gave them shots. She had a real thing about injections. But I didn't see it that way at all. I thought if the worst happened, and one of us contracted a deadly disease, she would be able to cure it. I thought having a pediatrician for a mother was about the safest thing in the world."

"What happened?" I asked.

"Which part?" she asked, snorting, a sound that seemed half laugh and half sob. "Well, she had gone to see a play one night. My father had a performance, so she went with her friend, Linda Donatello. After the play ended, they were heading for their car, and the man robbed them. He had a gun, and he told them to hand over their jewelry and money. They did—very calmly, Linda said. Linda said my mother was very careful to not make any fast moves. The guy had everything in his pocket, and he started to walk away. Then suddenly he turned and shot her. Shot my mother."

"I'm so sorry," I said, wanting to hold her hand.

"I know. It only happened two weeks ago. They caught the man right away, even before he was out of the parking garage. A guard heard the gunshot and then heard him running. His name was Warren Castile, but you've probably read that already. My lawyer says he has a long record of robbery and assault, and if anything will help my case, that will. I really want to get out of here."

Although I didn't feel capable of judging Caroline Orne, I thought the chances were good that she was just where she should be, for that moment: in a psychiatric ward. "Do you know why you did it?" I asked.

She smiled. "Everyone asks it that way: 'Do you know why you did it'? Instead of 'Why did you do it?' I wonder why."

"Maybe in order to give you the chance to stand back from it. To give you an escape hatch."

"Escape from what? My mother was murdered, and I hate her murderer so much, I shot him. Now he's dead, and I guess I'm glad." Her voice shook a little, and she clasped her hands tightly; otherwise she seemed calm. "Here's what I did: I took my father's gun out of the gun case. I didn't know anything about loading it or shooting it, so I had to read the brochure. The night before, two police detectives came to our house to tell us the news. My father hadn't gotten home from work yet, and I was doing lesson plans. They told me, and I had to tell my brothers and sister and later my father. It was the worst thing in the world. I thought about that guy all night, sitting in a nice warm jail, then I thought of my mother in the morgue. I thought, that's where he should be. So the next day I took my father's gun to the jail, and I shot him."

"You wouldn't have felt any satisfaction to see the court convict him of murder and sentence him to prison?"

"No. The best thing I ever did was pull the trigger. You know, I never expected to get past the guards. But the metal detector was broken. Can you believe that? They had a little hand-held thing that they waved over all the visitors, but I snuck through in a crowd of patrolmen. I told them my name was Cathy Lake, and they let me see him."

"An eye for an eye?"

She shook her head, and for the first time since I'd met her, Caroline Orne started to cry. "I don't see it that way at all. An eye for an eye? I found out that he had killed another woman twelve years ago. I'll bet her kids are happy about what I did."

"I'm sorry," I said again, and then I walked away. On my way out I told the nurse that she should look in on Caroline, because when I left her she was sitting in her chair, gripping her ankles, head dropped down, rocking back and forth.

· · ·

I had a hypothesis I wanted to test: did everyone who lost someone in a terrible way, through treachery or violence—someone they loved, a member of their family—want revenge? I returned to my hotel and searched my meager two-day supply of newspapers for any reference to Warren Castile's family. Two papers ran the same picture of him, his mug shot; it showed a gaunt, hollow-eyed man, staring blankly at the camera. It might have been a photo of his ghost. The accompanying article mentioned his wife, Dora, and their two children. The Chicago telephone directory listed one Warren Castile, and I dialed the number. A woman answered.

"Mrs. Castile?" I asked.

"Yes?" she answered suspiciously.

"Are you the widow of Warren Castile?"

"I'm his mother. She doesn't live here. You've got the wrong number."

"Could you please tell me her number? I don't see any other listings for Warren Castile."

"That's because they don't have a phone. Are you a reporter?"

"No," I said, feeling vaguely like a liar because I wanted the same information a reporter would.

"Then give me your name and number, and I'll have her call you. I'll be seeing her around suppertime."

"Thank you," I said, gave her the information, and hung up.

I could have asked his mother about the desire for vengeance, but that question belonged to his wife. Why did every situation, no matter how far off the path of normal life, make me think of me and Nick? I thought of the revenge I would seek if someone hurt him. If someone tracked him down with her father's gun, the way Caroline Orne had done, I could imagine wanting to kill that person. But of course Nick was no murderer; the two men were not comparable. But perhaps the feelings of their wives could be.

Many hours passed; I spent that sunny afternoon in the air-conditioned hotel room, afraid that if I went out I would miss a telephone call. I told myself the call I feared missing was from Mrs. Castile, but in fact I hoped to hear from Nick. Sitting at the blond wood desk, I wrote pages about Caroline Orne on my portable typewriter. My trip to Chicago, and the discoveries I made about Caroline Orne and Dora Castile, would comprise my second quarterly report. I actually looked forward to submitting it to the Avery Foundation. I especially wanted Helen to see it. Although it wasn't due until September, I would send it as soon as possible.

At five o'clock, eleven o'clock Greenwich Mean Time, my telephone rang, and it was Nick. I sighed at the sound of his voice. Why? With the relief of knowing that he was alive? Knowing that at that instant he belonged to me? I lay on the bed, my head against two soft pillows, and closed my eyes.

"I miss you so much," he said. "Last night was terrible. The meeting broke up earlier than we expected, and everyone went to Simpson's for dinner."

"Did you have roast beef?"

"Of course. I kept looking over at the table we had last time, but there was another couple sitting there. It made me jealous to look at them."

"Did everyone go?"

"Just John, Jean and I. Tonight, if we ever get out of the office, we're having Italian food at some place John knows in Chelsea. I feel like ordering a sandwich from room service, to tell you the truth."

"I miss you like crazy," I said.

"But everything is fine? You're enjoying yourself in Chicago?"

"I'm not sure 'enjoying' is the right word," I said, and told him about my sad session with Caroline Orne. "She really seemed around the bend, Nick. I felt so sorry for her."

"Maybe you should treat yourself to a really nice dinner and a movie tonight," he said.

"Maybe," I said, thinking of how characteristic it was of Nick to say that, of how cheered he always was by small pleasures.

"Do you know when you'll be in Black Hall?" he asked.

I had planned to stay in Chicago another night, to spend tonight listening to music under the stars at Ravinia, to see tomorrow's game between the White Sox and Boston, then make a quick visit to the Art Institute and the Chagall mosaic, but talking to Nick across half the continent and an ocean made me want to go home.

"I wish I were there now, Nick," I said. "With you." I hesitated, then said what was on my mind. "I hate thinking of you in London with Jean."

"Why did you have to say that, Georgie? God." He sounded disgusted or discouraged. "Do you trust me or don't you?"

"I do," I said, but then there was a commotion in the background, someone calling his name, and he had to get back to work. We hung up. I was frowning at my reflection in the mirror when the phone rang again.

"Hello, this is Dora Castile," came the tired voice, and I nearly told her I had to go, had to catch a plane. But instead I sat on the edge of the bed, facing my reflection in the mirror.

"This is Georgie Symonds," I said, needing to link myself with Nick, if only by name. I explained my work for the Swift Observatory, and she listened without interrupting. "Will you talk to me?" I asked.

"What do you want to know?"

"Anything you want to tell me," I said, thinking that her choice of topic would be interesting.

"Warren was bad news. Everyone knows that, everyone tells me that. My mother-in-law feeds my kids every night because Warren put no food on their plates. Ever. From day one. But there's no saying what makes you love a man."

"You loved Warren?"

"Yes."

"And you're sad he's dead?" I asked, knowing the question was abrupt and rude, but I was thinking about getting to the airport.

"Yes, very sad."

"Even though he killed the mother of the woman who shot him?"

"Oh, you've been appointed Judge of the Land? I didn't hear one word about a trial. I didn't hear one word about that."

"How do you feel about his assailant, Caroline Orne?"

"I'll tell you how I feel. I feel like she's a murderer. That's because she is one. She confessed, but she didn't even have to do that because the jail has every second of her crime on videotape. Warren never got a chance to confess, and there's no one except the dead lady's friend to say he did it."

"What about the gun he fired? I've read he had it in his pocket. I've read he shot Dr. Orne with no provocation whatsoever."

"Maybe he found that gun in the garage. I don't know about that."

"Mrs. Castile," I said, feeling nothing good for the woman on the other end of the line. "Do you want revenge against Caroline Orne? Do you want harm to come to her?"

"Yes, I do. I want that spoiled brat to rot in the nuthouse, and I want to sue the living shit out of her for the pain and suffering she has caused me and my children." She delivered her speech with grace and emphasis.

"Thank you, Mrs. Castile," I said. I hung up the phone, thinking of how she was proving a point I had never set out to make. Probably no one, even the wife of a murderer, could help hating the person who hurt their beloved. Did it matter to Dora Castile that Warren Castile was a criminal and Dr. Orne a loving mother, wife, and healer?

I lay down for a second, and I fell into a deep sleep. When I wakened it was dark, and I lay there for a moment, reliving my dream. Caroline Orne and her entire family were in a prison and some of us—me, Nick, Honora, Pem, maybe Eugene and Casey, were in the next cell. Our jailors, Jean Snizort and Warren Castile, laughed maliciously. My father was nearby, in solitary confinement. Clare and Donald were nowhere close, and that made me uneasy, because I was unsure of whether I should be happy because they had escaped or scared because they were facing worse punishment.

Slowly I sat up. I faced my reflection in the mirror. My posture straight, I looked very young, like a child quite frightened of being alone. I wore one of Nick's cast-off oxford shirts over khaki shorts. My legs looked bony, and I identified scratches I had gotten while playing wiffle ball with Eugene and Casey, the bruise from bumping into the stove one night while rushing around the kitchen, and my scar. It was the only scar I had. When I was small I had jumped into a pile of leaves my father had been raking, and gashed my leg on the rake he had left buried there. I remembered that day exactly: the blue October sky, the smell of burning branches, the happiness I felt when my father lifted me out of the leaves and hugged me close to him. "Oh, honey, oh, honey," he kept saying. My blood stained his wool jacket as he ran with me to the car, Clare following as fast as she could, calling, "Will she be all right?" At the hospital the doctor numbed my leg with novocaine, and my father held my hand, telling me a story about the time he and my mother hiked to the top of Mount Hawk one Thanksgiving day when the weather was warm as August and the air so clear they could see five states. Staring at my scar in the mirror brought back happy memories and made me sad for the Ornes. Everything, even a scar, brought me back to the family. It would be the same for Caroline Orne. All through her life she would see a baby and think of the babies her mother had healed, see a horn and hear the symphonies her father had played. I felt tired enough for more sleep, but first I dialed Nick at the Savoy.

"Hello?" came his sleepy voice after the fifth ring.

"Hi, Nick. I'm sorry about what I said before."

"What's wrong, Georgie? Why do you have to sound so suspicious?"

"It was thinking about you in London with Jean."

He was silent for so long, I thought he had fallen asleep. "It's late here," he said finally. "We've been working all day and most of the night, and I'm jet-lagged. It's hard to talk about this over the phone."

"That's it," I said, desperately wanting to end the conversation on a normal note, as if nothing were or ever had been wrong. "You'd better sleep now. Sweet dreams, I love you."

"And I love you, if you'd only believe me."

Nick hung up before I could say I do I do I do I do believe you. I do.

.   .   .

The nights grew cooler than usual for early August, and the first scarlet leaves had begun to appear in the trees of Black Hall. When I was a child those leaves had been heralds of the end of summer, the beginning of school, and I had always felt sad to see them. Now, sitting on my porch, typing the last pages of my report, I felt excited by the change in seasons. Like birds changing their plumage and migrating to southern marshes, I felt as if something fine were about to happen to me. Perhaps it was the pleasure of work progressing well. Clare and Honora left me alone most of the time; when we did meet, we would talk about my interviews, and they would tell me their impressions and try to place themselves in the situations of my subjects. Nick had returned from London and, although his work load remained heavy, he flew home to Black Hall every night. But his eyes were sad, and since those hotel-room conversations between Chicago and London, there were long silences between us.

One morning I rode my bicycle to the Post Office to mail my second quarterly report to the Averys. Under the hard blue sky, cloudless, reflecting the calm sea, I pedaled slowly home. I felt as though I had earned the right to leisure. Perhaps I would take a long swim with my mother, if she was in the mood. I wheeled into her driveway, propped my bike against the stone wall, and entered the house. Bloodcurdling screams greeted me. Grabbing a brass candlestick, I ran upstairs, at least three at a time.

"You're scalding me, you're scalding me," cried Pem from behind the closed bathroom door.

"Honora? Are you in there?" I asked.

"Yes, I'm giving her a bath," Honora said. "Mother, hold still."

"Can I come in?" I asked.

"If you dare," my mother answered.

I entered feeling nervous and shy. I had never seen Pem naked, much less in a bathtub. I worried that she would feel embarrassed by my presence, and I was afraid of seeing her body. She sat in the claw-footed tub; her head bent, she didn't notice me at first. Ah, Pem. Her skin was white and smooth, pulled tight over her humpback. The pillowy breasts I remembered from childhood had stretched, long counterweights to the humpback, flat as empty hot-water bottles. Her white hair, now wet, looked touchingly sparse, and crusty red sores covered her scalp. She had a few wisps of pubic hair, dark as her brows, but her legs were hairless; I remember her telling me that if I started shaving my legs I'd soon "have a regular beard down there," that she had never shaved hers, and after awhile all the hair had rubbed off or fallen out. She glanced up, saw me, and smiled. "Hi! What's this, a party?"

"Should I go?" I asked Honora, who shook her head. She stood beside the tub, wet patches covering her white blouse. She looked old, as if the battle to bathe Pem had defeated her.

"Having a bath, Pem?" I asked.

"I'll be damned if I have a bath!"

"But you're already having one—you're all wet."

She blushed, realizing I was right, then turned haughtily to stare at the towel bar.

"I'm trying to wash her hair," Honora said. "The doctor says that's psoriasis on her scalp. Doesn't it look terrible?"

We both bent down for a closer look and stood peering at the ugly sores. Pem splashed some water at us. "Heh, heh," she laughed.

"That's not funny, Mother," my mother said.

"Want me to shampoo her?" I asked, not really wanting to touch her head.

"I hate to say yes, Georgie, but I'm about to lose my mind."

I held the spray nozzle in one hand, then turned on the water to adjust the pressure. Spraying it gently against the inside of my arm, I tested the temperature. It felt perfect.

"Ooooh, freezing! You're freezing me!" Pem wailed. I made the water a little warmer.

"You're burning me! Ouch! Where's your mother? Honora, she's burning me."

Without adjusting the temperature again, I directed the stream at Pem's head, lathered up the medicated tar prescribed by the doctor, and began to massage her scalp.

"There, there, dear," I said, in my best hairdresser voice. "What'll it be today? Shampoo and a curl? Maybe a manicure?"

"You're freezing me! You're burning me!" Pem cried.

"How about we change that hair color of yours, you've had it for years. Want to go platinum? Or maybe auburn? Your hair's been white too long. Maybe we should darken it, match your brows . . ."

But Pem's distress was so great that even the chance to tell the brow story refused to cheer her up. She hunched even further, trying to hide her face, and wept. I heard Honora crying behind me. Pem's eyes were closed tight as a child's, and great, round tears rolled down her withered cheeks.

"There, I think all the soap's out," I said after I had finished rinsing. Pem tried to stand on her own, but the tub was too slippery. Honora and I each reached under one arm and hoisted her up. She stepped out of the tub like a cowboy climbing over the corral fence after falling off a bronco. Honora wrapped a pink towel around her.

"Thank you," Pem said. Then, with enormous dignity, she arranged the towel around her, the mantle of a queen, and strode towards her bedroom.

"My god," I said. "How often—"

"Once a week," Honora said. "She makes me feel like I'm her

torturer. I always wait till a sunny day, so the house will be warm, and I try to get her into the tub before she changes out of her nightgown. One curse of my meteorology background is that I usually know the night before whether it will be warm enough or not, and I dread it all night."

"You can't continue to bathe her alone," I said. "She's too heavy. Both of you could fall. From now on you have to call me or Clare."

"Thank you for offering, sweetie. I know you're right, but I didn't want you to have to see her that way. Isn't it sad?" Unconsciously, or perhaps not, Honora cupped her own breasts as she spoke. I felt like doing the same to myself, to make sure they were still full, that whatever had drained out of Pem's remained in mine.

We walked downstairs, onto the porch. Leaning back in wicker rockers we were silent, watching swans and cygnets fish the shallows. Just two months ago we had sat in the same places, watching fireworks, eating the Fourth of July cake. I wondered how long Pem would be in our midst. She was only eighty-six; she had a long way to go to reach the venerable ages of ninety-five and one hundred that her family regularly lived to, but that day on Honora's porch I felt something sliding away. Things couldn't go on forever, Pem and Honora taking care of each other, looking after the rest of us. I glanced at my mother; her face looked set and old, vaguely angry, as she stared at the swans feeding with their babies. Perhaps she was thinking that she had taken care of me and Clare, and now she was taking care of Pem. When would someone ever take care of her?

"Are you mad at Pem?" I asked.

She laughed. "Mad at her? You saw her—how can I be mad at her? I feel sorry for her. Do you remember when she was with-it?"

"Yes."

"She was a terrific mother. She loved taking me, and you girls, places. She'd take us to Providence or New York for the day at the drop of a hat. She and I saw the first night of many a Broadway show. I'm sad that she won't ever be that way again. I'd always hoped that we could be good company for each other."

Bennison Point was a maypole of good company, with colored streamers connecting the Swifts and the Symonds and the Mackens and the Bennisons. And here came Pem, shuffling through the house, appearing at the porch door in her pink towel, both hands stretched out, a mask of perplexity on her old face, saying, "I can't find my clothes." And Honora and I both started to laugh, we couldn't help it, and we walked to Pem and held her in our arms.

Nine

"This is marvelous," Helen said, tapping my quarterly report with one hand. We were sitting at the dining table in her apartment because she could not, as she had written in her note, "abide the stodginess of the Foundation offices." She lived in Chelsea, not far from the Gregory, with a view of the seminary gardens from her windows. Worn but vivid tapestries of life in the French court covered her walls. A gaudy parrot regarded us from a cage that resembled a Chinese teahouse.

"I'm so pleased you like it."

"Oh, I do—we all like your work. John appointed me to discuss it with you. As you probably know, he's all over the world these days. Your husband keeps you informed of John's travels, doesn't he?"

"Quite well, considering he's usually traveling with him."

"Oh, dear," Helen said, gazing politely out the window, leaving no doubt that she had definite views about those travels. She wore green eye shadow today, applied as patchily as her sister's had been, but somehow it seemed glamorous on her. Silver and

enameled bangles clanked when she moved her arm. Her move-
ments as she poured our tea were somehow theatrical; I wondered
whether she had been an actress. She wore the same yellow,
orange and green caftan she had on the first time I met her.

"Do you do much work for the Foundation?" I asked.

"Nowadays I do. I used to be a professional tennis player. I
did!" she said emphatically, as though she thought I wouldn't
believe her. "I played against Billie Jean King, Margaret Court,
Chris Evert when she was just a baby—all the best players. I
reached the semifinals at Wimbledon one year. I had to quit, on
account of a really bad case of tendonitis. I still have it," she said,
flexing her right arm.

"You look like a tennis player," I said, appraising her muscular
arms.

"I still love it. John and I play all the time, whenever he's free,
that is. When we both were married, we'd have great mixed
doubles."

"Oh, you're divorced?"

"Widowed. My husband dropped dead of a heart attack at the
age of forty-one. It was quite a blow. No one expects someone
young to die like that. I've been trying to analyze what it is that
draws me to your work so, and I think it's the stories about loss.
God, they kill me—that story about Caroline Orne, it could break
your heart. I sense that you know about loss."

"Well, my father died when I was young. But aside from that
I don't, not really," I said. I wondered: does constantly fearing
it count?

"Maybe that's enough."

"Helen," I said, not knowing quite how to ask the question.
"The last time I saw you, you told me your mother had been
murdered."

"Yes," Helen said. She twisted her bracelets. "None of us has
quite gotten over that. I'm the youngest, and I was twelve. Jasper

was twenty. You know, he was at Harvard then, and everyone said he had a brilliant future as a lawyer, but we'll never know. All the life went out of old Jazz afterwards. He was her favorite, I guess. At least he thought he was." She smiled in a wry manner, so that only half her mouth turned up. "Jasper is very big on things like that—'Mother's favorite,' 'eldest child'—you know. Poor Jazz, he's just a middle-level banker."

If Helen had been a subject instead of my patron, I would have asked her the details of her mother's murder. I wanted to know. Perhaps she was considering telling me; she was watching me carefully, but then her gaze shifted to her parrot.

"Back to your report," Helen said. "I liked the part about Dora Castile, though I must say it takes a far stretch of the imagination to understand what anyone, even a wife, could see in trash like Warren Castile."

"You should have heard her voice," I said. "It was defiant, as though she was daring me to question that she loved him, but at the same time it was shaky. He'd only been dead about two weeks."

"The two weeks after Leroy, my husband, died . . . they were terrible. Meetings with lawyers, insurance men, the funeral-home people. It was incredible. I felt desperately sad the whole time, but I never had a minute to sit still and think about it."

"I can't imagine that," I said, trying not to think about Nick, sensing it would be a bad omen if I did.

I was preparing to ask Helen about her mother when she cleared her throat. "Are you happy with your husband?" she asked, leaning forward to pour more tea.

"Yes," I said. "It's special between us. I don't think anyone has a marriage like ours. We do everything possible to be together. That's difficult, with his work, but we're vigilant. I try to spend nights in the city when he has to work late, and I travel with him on business trips."

"All the time?"

"Whenever possible," I said. The beauty of talking to someone new, someone far removed from my family, was that I could go back in time—restore the truth, by what I said, to what I wanted it to be.

Helen shook her head, stirring milk into her tea with an ivory-handled spoon. "Excuse me, but that sounds brutal. He forces you to do this?"

I stared at her. "No. I want to do it," I said.

She stirred silently for a few seconds before speaking. "Well," she said. "Everyone has their own ways of making their marriages work. But with the life I know you must lead, after years of observing it in my own family, I think that system would turn into torture."

I laughed. "But I love doing it! Nick tries to call me before the last train leaves for New York. Or he tells me we're going on a business trip, and our bags are packed within ten minutes."

"Oh, not you, dear. I was thinking it might be torture for Nick."

That was it, wasn't it? I felt my hands touch my cheeks, remembering that night at Vinnie's, when Nick had asked me not to come into the city on his late nights. Had he rehearsed the words? Here was Helen Avery casting a cool eye on the situation, naming it torture.

"I can see I've upset you," Helen said. "I mean, I know the pressures those guys put themselves under—sometimes unnecessarily, I think. And to have to worry about you, and your comfort, and making sure you are informed before the last train leaves, well—"

What an illusion, the idea that I could go back in time, reinvent my marriage for Helen. A great change had taken place in our house, and I couldn't pretend it hadn't. Even to someone new. Helen's words had hurt me; they were right on the money, and it bothered me that she could so glibly define Nick's and my great upheaval. I felt breathless, dangerous, as though I was balancing on something I was about to fall off of.

"I'm sorry I've upset you," she said. "Just understand that I've been affected by the Wall Street life, and the troubles and absences it seems to cause, and I was just thinking out loud."

"That's all right," I said, hiding the fact that it was not. *Something bad is going to happen,* I thought. I had a quick vision: Nick's face, mine, not smiling, not facing each other.

"Well," Helen said, studying my expression, gauging how upset I was. "I'll tell you why I invited you here. As I've said, we are wild about your work," she said, flashing a smile that was meant to enchant me, to make me forget being upset. "And we want you to publicize it."

"What do you mean?"

"We would like to arrange a few interviews with newspapers and magazines, to distribute your reports to a large readership. We think the Swift Observatory will be of interest to many people. Possibly we could arrange for syndication, for your pieces to appear in newspapers and magazines."

The idea would have intrigued me at the beginning of the conversation, but now I felt stiff, unable to act pleased. I tilted my head, and she took it as encouragement to continue.

"We would like you to give some interviews, to publicize the project on your own. John will then negotiate with several publications that have expressed interest."

"You mean you've already been discussing this with outsiders?"

Helen laughed, charmingly. "Of course, dear. From the day we saw your first report. That is how it works—call it putting out feelers, if you wish. We try to ignite interest in all our projects. It helps you, it helps the other grantees. Maybe you won't win the Nobel Prize, but Leo Guziewicz did."

"How does the Foundation benefit?"

"Not at all, except for the satisfaction it brings. It pleases us when the world recognizes the brilliance of our grantees. It proves to us that we know what we are about." Again the marvelous grin.

"I have no interest in publicizing the Swift Observatory," I said.

Helen continued to smile. "I know I upset you before. I didn't mean to. I think I feel close to you, because of what you write about and because you're living a life that seems very familiar to me. Wrongly, I tried to give you the wisdom of my age. I'm sure that the relationship between you and Nick is lovely—totally unlike the one between my mother and father, or John and his ex, or any of the others. From everything you tell me, it is. Will you forgive me?"

"Yes," I said, because in spite of how she had hurt me, I felt drawn to her as well. And I knew myself well enough to realize that the only people capable of truly hurting me were the ones I felt close to.

"Yawk!" the parrot croaked, making me jump. "Give us a kiss!"

Helen rose and made her way through the room's clutter, squeezing between the baby grand piano and an ancient lecturn supporting an open Bible to stand beside the cage. Then I saw how the parrot and her bright caftan were the same colors: emerald, gold, and orange.

"He thinks I'm a parrot," she said joyfully. "He's in love with me, aren't you, Didier?"

"Give us a kiss, give us a kiss," the parrot squawked.

"*Gros bisous!* Kiss, kiss," Helen said, laughing.

I laughed too. "I'd better go," I said after a minute.

"All right," Helen said. She held my arm as we walked to the door. "Promise me you'll think about our plan. I know it would be wonderful for you, for the Swift Observatory. And forgive me for hurting your feelings."

"I'll think about it," I said. "And I'm not upset anymore," I said, bending towards her to receive her kiss on the cheek, still feeling that uneasy dread that had come over me earlier. Wondering: how could I be upset over romantic advice offered by a woman in love with her parrot?

.   .   .

"I'm going back to London," Nick said, and his tone was an invitation to brawl. We stood in our yard beneath the hunter's moon. The plane had just dropped him off, and I heard it chattering across the bay to the Mendillos' dock.

"What do you mean, you're going back to London?" I said, feeling myself wind like a spring.

"Just what I said. Tomorrow I'll be leaving, probably for three weeks. My participation is crucial to this deal. I'm in charge of all the documents. I sit in on every meeting. I know more about the deal than anyone involved—even the client."

I walked three paces ahead of him, my arms folded across my chest. The wind felt chilly; I hadn't been able to find a sweater when I heard the plane coming in. At the door Nick dropped his briefcase and came to stand in front of me. "I am going to hold you for a minute, and then we'd better have a good talk," he said. His arms went around me, and we hugged tight, not moving, not even wanting to kiss. We might have stood there all night. I wasn't going to break it up. Moonlight slanted through the kitchen window, spilling across the floor and glossing Nick's wingtip shoe. We stood there so long the light slid away, leaving the shoe dull and black. Then we walked into the living room. Any thoughts I had had of cooking dinner were gone.

"Something bad is happening to us," Nick said.

"I don't think that's true," I said. "You're having a busy patch at work, and we don't see each other as much."

Nick shook his head. He sat at the edge of the sofa, his shirt-sleeves rolled up and tie loosened, his hands clasped and elbows resting on his knees. He looked at the floor. *Something bad is going to happen,* I thought again, remembering Helen's. Dread flooded me; I didn't want to hear what he was about to say.

"I don't see it that way," he said. "I've been busy ever since we've known each other. Law school, the bar exam, every year since then has been busy. You've been so supportive—more so than any wife I've heard of. But this is different. It's obsessive, the way you doubt my tone of voice, my motives for going to London without you, everything. I feel you doubting everything about us."

"Me? I'm doubting nothing about us," I said.

"About me then. You don't trust me. I hate that, Georgie. I call you up, and I sense you waiting for the worst. You're just waiting for a suspicious tone of voice or for me to tell you I have to stay overnight in New York, or that I have to go to London. Then, when I tell you, I know that I'm just confirming what you knew all along: that I don't want to be with you. Try to deny that."

"It's not true. I'm disappointed, of course, when we can't be together. But I know it's out of your control."

"But what if it's not out of my control? What if I think it's better that I go alone to London? I can concentrate better if I know you're not sitting in the hotel, watching the clock, wondering if I'll get back before the restaurants close."

"Oh, my God," I said, thinking it was exactly what Helen had said. I hated her at that moment, and I hated Nick. It didn't matter that I had expected something awful to happen; nothing could have prepared me for this.

"While I'm gone this time we need to do some serious thinking. I can't go on this way, hearing doubt in your voice all the time."

When my father had taken the job with Ordaco, he was always away from home; I had felt relieved, because it had diffused the tensions between him and Honora, serious tensions that might

have led to a real separation. But this relatively short business
trip of Nick's terrified me; it sounded like he was proposing
separation, the emotional kind where two people go to their
corners to consider the state of their love.

"Nick, don't do this," I said softly.

"Don't do what? Don't go to London? Or don't feel so unhappy? You so badly want things to go your way, there's no
room for my feelings. Do you see that, Georgie? Do you?"

"Unhappy? You feel unhappy?" I heard myself ask.

I was holding my head because I was about to faint. I felt
Nick's warm hand on the back of my neck, pressing downward.
"There, put your head between your knees," he was saying.

Blackness rushed towards me, but then I was all right. I sat
up straight. Nick kept his hand on my neck, the fingers gripping
lightly. One of them traced a gentle pattern across my skin. I
imagined he was spelling "I love you." His black eyes gleamed;
I saw the tears there.

"What's going to happen to us?" I asked, feeling numb.

"I don't know," Nick said.

We made love that night. I thought if I could remind his body
of how fine we were together, everything would be all right. We
undressed each other in the darkness, seriously, without speaking.
Moonlight illuminated his body: his silky skin, the dark hair
curling around his penis, which darkened as it grew. I made him
lie on his back while my hands rubbed circles on his chest, his
abdomen, his thighs. I was the witch, and my hands wrote spells
as I lowered my mouth to his erection, crazed with love and
danger.

· · ·

Nick and the Hubbard, Starr entourage flew to Britain on the
morning Concorde, so I was shocked to hear John Avery's voice
on the telephone.

"I'm not disturbing you, am I?" he asked.

"No, but I thought—aren't you supposed to be in London?"

"Not this week. I'm leaving this part of the deal to my able associate, man named Nicholas Symonds. Maybe you know him?"

"Maybe I do," I said, not at all sure I did.

"I'm calling to tighten the screws. I have arranged two interviews and a photo session for Miss Swift of Observatory renoun. Will you do it?"

"I don't think so, John. I've thought about it, and it doesn't seem right for me. What does someone want pictures of me for anyway? I can understand an interview, but why pictures?"

"I think it's a neat angle, a pretty woman who is the Swift Observatory. Excuse me for calling you pretty—I know professional women today think that ability is all, that men shouldn't notice anything else."

"That's okay. Thanks," I said, wondering whether he was making a mild pass.

"I'll tell you what—think about the publicity for another day or two, then call me. It would be a terrific thing, to get wide coverage for your endeavor."

"Yes, well," I said, anxious to end the conversation. I was sitting on my porch, thinking about Nick and Jean in London without John, which meant dinners for two, not three, when Clare came through the yard. She was wearing a turquoise bathing suit, dark glasses and rubber thongs.

"Mother has decided today is the perfect day for a picnic. Want to come?"

"Where are you going?"

"Candle Island." She meant the big rock half a mile offshore. For the first time I noticed the day was cloudless, one of those brilliant blue and gold August days with a breeze just strong enough to move the leaves and stir the stalks of aster and goldenrod.

"I guess so," I said.

"Are you depressed?" she asked, sitting on the porch step, her back against the railing. Removing her sunglasses, she shielded her eyes to look at me.

"Yes. Very. He'll be gone for three weeks."

"You can live with that."

"Did Nick—do you know if Nick said anything to Donald about the trip?"

"Well, Donald told me that Nick seems upset about something. He didn't say what, but I got the idea that he's pretty angry with you."

"Oh, thanks, Clare! Nick is thousands of miles away, and you tell me something like that. Thanks."

"Honey, tell me what's wrong."

"I think Nick wants to leave me," I said in a voice so small I could hardly hear it.

"I don't believe that."

"I think it's true. I'm making him miserable. You know why— the way I act when he's not here. I'm afraid of so many things, Clare."

"What are you most afraid of?"

"That things will change even more. That Nick and I won't be together." The idea was so hideous, I started to shiver. Clare sat on the arm of my wicker chair and put her arm around me. I felt her cheek press against the top of my head.

Honora walked into my yard carrying oars, the plaid beach blanket, and a basket from which protruded a loaf of French bread, a pineapple top, and a bottle of Evian water. She waved to us, then motioned to the pier alongside which our dinghy rocked. "Come on!" she called.

"I don't feel like a picnic," I said.

"Please come," Clare said. "I want you to be with us. I understand why you're upset, but everything will work out. I know you, and I know Nick. You'll both figure out how to manage this."

"I hope so."

"Come on," she said. I took her hand and allowed myself to be led towards the boat, noticing the red cross-hatching the wicker had indented in the backs of her bare legs.

At the pier we discussed who would swim and who would row the boat; Clare volunteered to row out if Honora would row back. Once everything was settled, we began our trip. I swam steadily, taking a breath every three strokes, keeping my eyes open and watching the bay's rock bottom give way to the deep Sound. Clare's oars splashed, lulling me into memories of other swims out to Candle Island. We always did it in groups of three or more, with someone in the rowboat in case of danger. Strong cramps? Shark attack? Nothing bad had ever happened, but we wanted to be prepared. I was lost in memory when Honora crashed into me. "Sorry, bad radar," she said, working herself back on course.

Twenty-five minutes later we had arrived at Candle Island. Honora and I clung to the rock, panting, while Clare hauled the scarred old dinghy across seaweed and barnacles to a flat surface. We spread out the blanket, and Honora passed out white tennis hats.

"What a splendid sunny day," she said.

"Hand me some salami, I'm starved," Clare said.

"So Nick is in London," Honora said. "Is it still that top secret deal where he's not allowed to take you along?"

"Mother—" Clare warned.

"Just because you and Donald have an arrangement that lets you each do your own thing doesn't mean your sister does. I know she'd rather be in London, and I think she should be. Why don't you surprise him, take one of those cheapo flights and hide in his hotel room?"

I was the volcano and rage was the lava, and it burst forth, covering everyone in its path. "Jesus Christ," I said. "For as long as I can remember you have been training me to sit at my husband's side, not let him out of my sight for fear that he might look at another woman. Just because your husband had an affair does not mean that all men have them."

Honora stared at me, shocked. "Georgie, of course they don't. It's not true that I ever told you that."

"It is true," I said. "It absolutely is and I believed you. I have the most wonderful husband in the world, and I can't let him out of my sight for mortal fear that he's going to fuck his secretary or some floozy on the street."

"Nick wouldn't do that—I know he wouldn't. I simply suggested you fly to London because I know you want to be with him."

"Say what you want, but that's not the reason."

"It is! Don't call me a liar, Georgiana. I think it would be sweet to surprise him that way. I can just see him, dragging home after a hard day in the City, to find you waiting with open arms."

"If I did that, he would leave me. That is what it has come to. I want to be with him in London more than anything in the world, but if I went there my marriage would be over," I said, and then I dived into the cool water. I started swimming home, and I didn't look back to see whether the rowboat was coming after me.

That night Honora knocked at my door. I let her in, and we stood in my kitchen, facing each other. She wore a black velour sweatsuit covered by an embroidered shawl. I had already put on my white nightgown.

"That was a very dangerous thing you did today," she said finally, "swimming away without the boat."

"I don't care."

"Clare and I followed you, of course, but you were swimming

so fast, I'm not sure we could have caught you in time, if something had happened."

Just like me, Mother—always waiting for something to happen, I thought. Instead I said: "I'm sorry I spoiled the picnic."

Honora raised her hand, to show me that hadn't mattered at all. "I want you to tell me what's going on."

"I'm not in the mood to talk to you. I'm very tired, and I want to go to bed."

Honora checked her watch, the big gold one that had been her father's. "It's only nine-thirty. You can't be tired yet."

"I am. Please go, all right? I'm fine."

"Listen. Out at Candle Island you accused me of instilling something in you that is going to ruin your marriage. I think you have a responsibility to explain that to me."

"I'm sorry. I was exaggerating," I said, thinking that if she didn't leave I would start crying and never stop.

"Every marriage has ups and downs. Yours has had mainly ups, from what I've been able to see, and I'm very grateful for that. Whatever is going on between you and Nick will turn out fine. I have confidence that it will."

"So do I," I said, smiling to assure her. She hesitated an instant, then returned my smile, kissed me goodnight, and left. Watching her cross the lawn, I thought of what she had said. What business did she have being "grateful" that my marriage had gone well? I could understand a mother's desire to see her daughter happy, but gratefulness seemed entirely disproportionate. Entirely wrong. In fact, it made no sense at all unless she knew some secret about why women were essentially unlovable, tricksters who duped men into staying with them.

·   ·   ·

My telephone conversations with Nick that first week had an unfamiliar air of reservation, as though the memory of our last night together and its implicit threat stood between us. He called me just as often, and we talked about all the important things: our work, our health, the Point, the weather. I cannot say that the reserved tone was exclusively his. Rather, I felt myself pulling back, wanting to give him less of myself. In this terrible courtship I was playing hard to get, to make myself seem more desirable.

I doubted that John Avery had intended for me to consider the two days he had given me to think about interviewing a deadline, but I did. Two days after his call, I phoned him at Hubbard, Starr.

"I've decided to do it," I said. "Heaven knows how it's going to help the Swift Observatory, but I'll do the interviews."

"Super. Let me pass you to Heidi, my secretary, and she'll set you up."

Heidi sounded so well-informed, so organized, that at first I thought John had taken for granted that I would capitulate and do the interviews; then I realized that probably she often arranged them for Avery Foundation grantees. She asked me whether I would prefer to see interviewers at my home in Black Hall or at a hotel in New York.

"At a hotel," I said, surprising myself.

"Do you have a favorite hotel?" she asked.

"Not really," I said, thinking, "Anything but the Gregory."

She named a hotel in midtown, I agreed, and she told me she would call me back with the dates and details. I thanked her, and we said goodbye. Leaning back in my chair I watched Eugene, Casey, and their babysitter swimming in the bay. Clare was reading in a folding chair. It would be good to leave this place for a few days, I thought. Even in the heat of August. Too much here was familiar, and everything I felt was brand-new. Maybe I would seem more alluring to Nick, giving interviews in my room at a fancy hotel. It would be better for him to envision me in New York than at home. In New York the possibilities were many: he could imagine me brave and lonely in my strange room, he could imagine me toasted and fêted and heralded in print for my beauty and brilliance. If I stayed at home he would imagine one thing only: me, Georgiana Swift, in the bosom of my family, burning the home fires until his safe return.

The hotel overlooked Central Park, and by some error in booking or the Avery Foundation's generosity, I was given a suite on a high floor. I walked through my rooms, noticing the antique writing desk; the gilded chairs; the little balcony that curved over the street, following the contours of the hotel's ornate facade, giving one the feeling that this was an aerie in the country. Only the tall buildings across the Park and the faint sound of traffic below testified that I was still in the city. Although I had several interviews scheduled that day, I wanted to make some Observatory calls. First I tried to follow up on Mona Tuchman, but no one was home. Then I called a two young dress designers I had read about in the Living Section who had succeeded in introducing their work to several big department stores. Later I took a walk down Fifth Avenue, looking in store windows, imagining how the clothes, shoes, and jewelry would look on me. I stared for fifteen minutes at a pair of amber and violet shoes before walking into the store to try them on. Usually in New York I was drawn into the Park, but not this trip. This trip I had things to prove that had nothing to do with the wonders of nature.

Steve Wunderlich, my first interviewer, worked for *The New York Times*. He arrived at the appointed hour, and we sat in the salon of my suite. I was wearing my new shoes. We chatted for a few minutes as he tested his tape recorder, set it in the best place to receive our voices. I observed how relaxed he seemed, as if this was his hotel room instead of mine. He appeared young, twenty-five or twenty-six, and he dressed like a professor in gray slacks, a light madras jacket, and a striped bow tie. He smiled to put me at ease. I wondered whether my manner was as easy as his, whether the people I interviewed felt as relaxed as I did.

"How did the Swift Observatory originate?" he asked.

"I am interested in human nature," I said, trying to explain my work without sounding pretentious.

"I've seen your reports, and I'm wondering about your interviews with people like Mona Tuchman and Caroline Orne. They told you very personal things, details they never told reporters. Can you explain that?"

"Maybe because our interviews were like conversations. Two people sitting together, talking about hard subjects. Both of them have been through hell, and they needed to talk."

"Why do you specialize in families?"

"The family fascinates me. Everything that takes place in families has incredible power. The strongest feelings occur between family members, and at the same time, the greatest sense of peace, of ease. For example, a woman can feel perfectly comfortable with her sister. They love each other, know each other so well that they have a private language, a sense of what each other is thinking before she says it. Suddenly one sister does the wrong thing—I don't know, makes eyes at the other's boyfriend, or tells her mother her sister's secret. Something fairly serious. If another person did it, someone outside the family, the consequences would be different. The friendship might end, or things might blow over. But in the family a bond exists that is so strong, it has to withstand everything. Maybe one sister wants to claw the other's eyes out, or maybe they give one another the cold shoulder for awhile. Rage is greater, so is love, in a family. Because you know you're going to be together at the end."

"What about divorce? Divorce has dissolved many a family."

"That's true, unless you fight tooth and nail to keep that from happening. Look at Mona Tuchman."

"That was just infidelity, not divorce," Steve said, a wry smile on his face.

"Just infidelity?" I asked, determined to control my scorn. The flip way he said "Just infidelity" seemed unworldly and immature; I had the feeling that Steve was single and spent undue amounts of time reading *Playboy*. For a few seconds we sat silently, and I was thinking about my family and Nick, how they had inspired the things I had just said, and how far away they felt at that moment.

"So you're committed to commitment."

"Yes. For myself, that is. But the Swift Observatory is just as interested in families where that goes wrong. Right now I'm working on a story about people who join cults or religious orders that prohibit any contact with their families. Some families are devastated, but I was surprised to find a few for whom it is actually a relief—for the families as well as for the cult members."

We talked for a few more minutes, and then it was time for my next interview. Steve and I shook hands. I admitted the next interviewer, Karine Bernadin for *Islander Magazine*. An hour later I saw Paul Tebib for *The Washington Post*, and an hour after that I saw Holly Roylance for the *Brussels Review*. All of them were bright, interested in what I had to say; only one of them, Karine Bernadin, wore a wedding ring.

That evening I had a drink in the hotel bar. The air conditioning smelled stale; I tried not to think of the cool breeze blowing through my house at Black Hall. I stared at the ice in my glass, imagining that all the men, sitting by themselves or in pairs, were watching me. The idea made me so uncomfortable, I paid cash instead of signing for my drink, so that no one could sneak a look at my room number on the check, and left.

"We took a chance and won our bet," came John Avery's voice as I walked through the lobby. He stood by the reception desk with Helen; they grinned at my obvious surprise.

"We're on our way home from a board meeting, and John suggested we stop by—to see if you're free for dinner."

"How wonderful! I was just starting to feel hungry," I said. The dinner hour had been looming, empty without Nick, and here was relief.

"Let's eat in the hotel dining room," John said. "That okay with you, Georgie?"

"Fine," I said. John left Helen's side, gave me his arm, and led me through the lobby.

We were seated at a curved banquette, with me between the Averys. "Nick's doing quite a job in London," John said. "He and Jean are holding down the fort."

"He told me Jean was there," I said. I found myself studying John's face, the sound of his voice: attentive to anything that might give me a clue about what happened between Nick and Jean when I wasn't there. "They work well together, I guess."

"Very well," John said, buttering a roll. "Some associates can't work as a team the way they can. Very efficient. Each handles different aspects of the deal, but they get together on the important things. They take a big load off my mind."

"That's nice," I said.

"Jean . . ." Helen said, her nose wrinkling. "Would that be the Jean I met in your office that time? Tall woman, very on-the-move?"

" 'On-the-move' describes Jean Snizort," John said, chuckling. "She's a very aggressive, able lawyer. She was handing complicated transactions early in her career—people trust her."

Some people, I thought. John turned to me. "And very attractive. A lot of wives would hate to think of their husbands in London with Jean Snizort." What is John trying to tell me, I wondered. He wouldn't be so blatant if sparks were flying between them. On the other hand, maybe this is his way of warning me.

"Now, John," Helen said, scolding. "Maybe Georgie and I don't like jokes like that. First you say the woman is a great lawyer, then you hint she's on the prowl. That kind of talk doesn't flatter you. It makes you sound like an old male chauvinist." Then, to me, "But I've seen her—I know what he means."

"She's pretty," I said, thinking perhaps dinner alone in my room would have been more pleasant.

"Now, how'd the interviews go?" John asked. "That's what we're burning to know."

"They went well. It was strange, being on the other side of an interview. The reporters seemed interested in my ideas, interviewing technique—things like that."

"I can imagine," Helen said. "You prompt people to tell you exceptionally personal things."

"It might be a form of therapy for some people," John said slowly. "There they are, in the midst of an extraordinary event— and you come along, asking gentle questions."

John saying "gentle questions" seemed intimate and flattering, and I felt myself blush as deeply as if he had taken my hand.

"There were no gentle questions after Mother died," Helen said. "Only terrible, nosy reporters out for blood."

I hesitated, then asked, "Would you tell me about that?"

"Oh. She was killed by her lover," Helen said. "He was a much younger man. That was partly why the reporters were so interested. Daddy hated the scandal so much, we almost never talked about her again from that day onward."

I thought of how horrible that must have been for all the Averys: to love your mother and not be allowed to talk about her when she was no longer there. At the same time, to be ashamed of her actions, furious at her betrayal, knowing you would never see her again.

"He was Jasper's soccer coach," John said, his mouth set. A waiter brought our dinners; we sat silently until he left, and no one touched the food.

"We all took it out on Jasper," Helen said. "As if he were to blame for being a good soccer player, and having a handsome young coach who of course came frequently to our house for dinner. Until he killed Mum, we all thought he was sweet. No one had any suspicions about an affair—we just assumed that Mum had taken a shine to him. She loved our friends." Helen sounded bewildered, as if she were telling it for the first time, as if in the telling the facts became more real.

"She was always dropping in on our parties, telling us how much she loved being with the young people," John said. "It was sad, really, when I think about it now. She was awfully lonely. Our father was always off on business, flying all over the world." He shook his head. "Like me. Like Nick, Georgie. Sometimes I see a young guy like Nick with a wonderful wife like you, and I wonder why he does it."

Helen placed her hand on mine. "Maybe that's what I was trying to tell you that day at my apartment."

"You were thinking about your father," I said.

"Among others," Helen said. "Men. The men of Wall Street." She leaned over, to see past me to John.

"Don't be sexist," John said. "Weren't we just talking about Jean?"

"Poor Mum," Helen said. "You know, I'm as old as she was when she died. She tilted her head. "I can't imagine loving a boy that age."

"Do you know why he killed her?" I asked.

"Heat, lust, I don't know," Helen said. "They got carried away for a while, and he thought she was going to leave Daddy for him."

"Naturally he was rather fond of her bankroll," John said. "But we know it was more than that."

"Jasper has never gotten over it," Helen said.

"You don't get over something like that," John said. "You get on with it, but you never forget."

We ate a little of our tepid dinners. Then John ordered three cognacs. I drank mine feeling sad. I thought of what John had said earlier, about my asking "gentle questions." I hadn't had to ask many that night; he and Helen hadn't needed much encouragement.

"It's quite a life, isn't it, Georgie?" John asked after a while. "What do you say we have the waiter bring a phone over here, give Nick a call?"

"Why, thank you—" I said, wondering whether I owed John's kindness to his reminiscence about the distance between his parents. But when he requested a telephone be brought to the table, the waiter told him they didn't have a cord long enough to reach.

Helen laughed. "Where do you think you are, John? Hollywood? They don't do things like that in these old hotels."

"That's all right," I said. "But thank you. It was a wonderful idea. And thank you for dinner."

"It was our pleasure," John said. For the first time in all the years I had known him, he kissed my cheek. Then I turned and kissed Helen's. We sat there for a moment, and then the maître d' came to pull out the big round table. We said goodnight and I went upstairs to bed.

.   .   .

That hotel bed was so big, a sprawling affair, and Nick was nowhere in it. During the night I explored it with my hands, my toes, pretending that Nick had fallen asleep and rolled just out of reach. All the particles of yellow light in New York, that brassy light peculiar to the city, were somehow concentrated in the air outside my window. Filmy window shades set the mood for romance, but did nothing to keep that light out. I lay on my back for a long time, then I tried my side. Finally I did what I had sworn I would not do: I called Nick in London. It was five A.M. there.

"Hi," I said. "I'm sorry to wake you."

"What? That's okay. Is anything wrong?" Nick asked, sounding perfectly awake, but I could envision him struggling up from sleep, his hair tousled, his pajamas half-unbuttoned.

"Nothing much. I can't sleep. I miss you. I had dinner with John and Helen, and we talked about their mother."

"Their mother."

"She was murdered when they were children. It was very sad."

"That's terrible." Long pause. "No wonder you can't sleep." Another long pause. I could see him lying in his hotel bed, holding the telephone, not really able to wake up. The image made me sleepy, and I smiled. "I'm going to hypnotize you to sleep, okay?" he asked.

"Okay."

"Lie back. Put your head on the pillow and close your eyes. Now think of the Point. It's a warm summer night, and we're taking a swim."

"You and me?" I asked, my eyes closed.

"Mmmm. We're treading water. It's nice and warm, but cool at the same time. Just listen to the waves. Whoosh, whoosh," he said, and I nearly laughed at Nick trying to sound like a wave. He must have been sleeping deeply.

He was silent for so long, I knew he had fallen asleep again. I loved the idea of drifting off myself, holding the receiver that connected me to Nick in London, but I couldn't bear the thought of the phone bill. "Nick?" I said, and when there was no answer, I said "Sweet dreams," and hung up the phone.

I did get some sleep that night, but the next morning I had a headache and felt confused. The phone call had reminded me of the old days with Nick: we were sweet and loving, always available for each other. Sipping coffee in my room, I felt anger building at the thought that one of us had played a trick on the other. Would he have been as kind if he hadn't been asleep? Had he acted loving simply out of habit? I realized that I was doing what he disliked, questioning all of his motives; I didn't want to do it, but that morning in New York, I had no choice. As if to drive away all the hope inspired by our sleepy phone call, every evil thought about Jean, about Nick's despair, about our sad destiny, came back to jeer at me.

My sole appointment that day was with a photographer. He was scheduled to take pictures of me to accompany an excerpt from my second quarterly report in *Vanguard Magazine*. I had felt comfortable during the interviews, but photographs made me nervous. I looked through my clothes, trying to decide what to wear. After a while I called Clare for advice, and she suggested I wear red, because it would look good with my dark hair. Honora was sitting at Clare's kitchen table, and although I didn't want to talk to her, she insisted.

"Wear lots of makeup, honey," she said. "I know you're not used to it, but believe me—you'll be glad you did. Years of experience has taught me that without lipstick, the camera makes you look like a washout."

"Thanks," I said, wanting to end the conversation before she started asking me about Nick. I could imagine the two of them speculating on what was happening between us. Of course they cared about me; I had no doubt of that, but their concern rattled me.

God, I felt angry at them, sitting on Bennison Point, lamenting my marriage's change of course. Honora didn't know romance. Neither did Clare. Did she care whether Donald came home or not? She considered his late hours inevitable, assumed that he would be home when he could. To Clare and Honora husbands were breadwinners. You had to make allowances for them; after all, they were only men. I thought of Nick's bare back, tan and muscled, and felt something so thrilling I had to cross my legs.

As my photo session grew nearer, I began to try on clothes. I had brought two outfits from home, and I tried each one three times. Each looked fine the first time, not quite perfect the second. By the third time, I wondered how I could ever have bought any of them. I ran to Bergdorf Goodman and took the elevator to the dress department. But did I want to wear a dress? Maybe I wanted to project a different image, something more intellectual and sophisticated. Slacks. In fact, Bergdorf's was the wrong store. I hurried down to street level, out the door, around the corner to Bendel's. But everything I saw seemed to come from animals: leopard spots, tiger stripes, belts of snakeskin and alligator shoes. Alligator shoes would look great with Chanel. If I hurried to Saks, maybe I could find a Chanel suit. Did they carry Chanel? Did I really want to spend all that money on a suit for one set of pictures? I imagined Nick picking up the magazine, seeing me on the page. I wanted to look beautiful, but a little mysterious, dressed perfectly. My photographic image would woo him. Makeup, I thought. Honora had said to wear makeup. I stopped at Bendel's ground floor makeup department and bought some lipstick called "Poppy Field."

Back at the hotel I dressed in the first outfit I had tried on that morning: tight black skirt with a full white silk blouse, Grampa's gold watch chain as a necklace, earrings made from my father's gold cuff links. They were monogrammed "TS," and had brought me luck before. I checked the time; I had forty minutes until the photographer arrived. I went through notes for my current report, checked myself in the mirror a few times, then decided to tempt fate. I called Nick again. Although it was only seven o'clock at night in London, he was in his hotel room.

"Hi, baby," I said.

"Thanks for my wakeup call," he said.

"I'm sorry about that. I hope you got enough sleep."

"Plenty. How are you? Did you finally fall asleep?"

"Sort of. Right now I'm waiting for the photographer. I'm a little nervous."

"Don't be—you'll look beautiful. Did you see your interview in the *Times*?"

"I think he said it would be out tomorrow," I said. "I'm surprised you're home already. Light day of work?"

"Not really, but things are stalled for the moment. We thought we'd go to the theater tonight."

I clenched my teeth to keep from saying "We?" Instead I said "Oh?"

"Yes. I thought I'd like the Lorca play with Glenda Jackson, but Jean's in the mood for a musical."

"Oh," I said.

"Anyway, she got us tickets to *Walking Shoes*." He laughed. "She claims she bought them from a scalper on the Underground. You know how hard it is to get tickets to that show? It's about to open in New York, and every American is rushing to see it here, so they can tell all their friends they saw it in London."

It would always be a fun little story, I thought, how Nick and Jean saw *Walking Shoes* in London the week it opened on Broadway. I felt very sad.

"I hope you enjoy it," I said.

"Well, I have my doubts, but you know I love the theater. I'd much rather be seeing the Lorca with you."

But you're not, I thought, and that seemed to be the important thing.

"Georgie, you're not saying anything," he said.

"I know. I'm mulling."

"Mull if you want, but don't worry. That call last night was really nice. I liked being your lullaby."

"Thanks," I said, feeling blocked, listening to him say the nice words.

We said goodbye. We each said "I love you," but I felt too depressed to remark on that. The words meant a lot to me. They were anything but hollow, but they didn't make up for the hateful fact that Nick was on his way to the West End with Jean Snizort.

Ten

The photographer arrived a little late. I'd been so nervous, anticipating his arrival, I kept hopping out of my seat every few seconds—combing my hair again, looking in the mirror, deciding the whole thing was a mistake, trying to get over my talk with Nick. Flushed and sweaty, I answered the doorbell; the photographer stood there holding two square camera cases. Everything about him was square: stocky, with the body of a wrestler, he had pale green eyes and hair the color of a palomino's mane. We shook hands. His name was Mark Constable.

"Do you need a minute?" he asked, obviously a reference to my disheveled state.

"Oh," I said, blushing. I touched my cheeks. "I look terrible, I know. Is there anything I can do? I mean, can you give me some advice? I'm not used to having my picture taken . . ."

He stood there watching me, expressionless. "No, you look pretty," he said, and for some reason that made me feel happy. "Let me fix up my cameras, and we can go out," he said.

I gestured at the salon, and he placed his cases on a low glass

table. He began removing an astonishing assortment of cameras
and lenses, screwing them together, holding his light meter in
the air and making it flash. I watched him. His smallest move-
ments seemed full of intensity. The way he removed a lens cap
and placed it in one of the many pockets of his big khaki coat
seemed deliberate, part of a great and elaborate plan. A glance
at my reflection in the glass cabinet showed me my lipstick had
worn off, but I didn't reapply it. I felt a peculiar mix of exhil-
aration and exhaustion; having my picture taken seemed like a
fun thing to do, but I wished I could lie down on the sofa and
defer it to another day.

"Where are you going to take my picture?" I asked, wondering
why he needed six cameras.

"I thought we'd walk around the city a little. My editor didn't
know what you looked like—you might have been seventy, for
all he knew. If you were, I'd have gone with a more sedate
shoot—in the Library, say. But you're young and pretty, so maybe
we'll try the Park."

"Well, thanks," I said, thinking it was the second time he had
said I was pretty. I was keeping track.

Traffic outside was crazy. We stood on the curb, waiting to
cross Central Park South, but taxis and trucks whizzed by with
barely a space in between. When two taxis nearly collided, we
grabbed our chance. "Come on," Mark said, holding my elbow.
I ran beside him, but he stopped me in the middle of the street.
He stared at me for an instant, frowning, as though he were
concentrating very hard. Suddenly traffic was streaming past us
on both sides; I stood perfectly still and prayed I wouldn't die.

"Fantastic," Mark said, focusing one of the cameras on me.

"Not here!" I gasped, feeling the hot wind of a speeding bus
in my face.

"It's great, you look so pretty with those skyscrapers in the
background and the yellow cabs going by." Three "pretties." I

began to relax a little. We'd been standing there thirty seconds and weren't dead yet. "It's dynamic, vibrant," he called over the traffic's roar. "Think of your work. Think of what these pictures will say about the Swift Observatory—you're in the fray."

I began to strike poses, like a fashion model. The velocity of passing traffic acted like a wind machine; my hair whipped around my face and I started to imitate Cheryl Tiegs, Christie Brinkley, then what the hell—Tina Turner and Madonna.

"Beautiful," Mark said, coming close enough to my face that I could hear his camera's clicks and whirs. His cameras dangled on straps around his neck. Dropping one camera, he took up another. Cars slowed down, their occupants craning to see whether I was someone famous. Mark stood inches away; beads of sweat trickled down his forehead, and I smelled the faint scent of aftershave. I was smiling at him and he was smiling back. We were having fun in the middle of the street.

From there we went into the subway; he took my picture on the platform, beneath the mosaic sign saying "Columbus Circle." We watched two new trains go by before one covered with grafitti came along. "Come on!" Mark called, and I jumped aboard. He snapped me hanging on the strap, studying the nearly obliterated map, sitting on the bench seat. We stepped off a few minutes later in the middle of Times Square. "Come on!" Mark said, running up the stairs.

"I thought you said we were going into the Park," I said.

"No, you're a city girl," he said. "You look so pretty in your black-and-white outfit, we need some color to set you off."

My memory of that photo session fills me with excitement and danger; the music of screeching brakes and blaring horns plays in the background. After two hours Mark looked at his watch and said he was hungry. "Do you have time for a bite?" he asked.

"Sure," I said. We started walking uptown, towards my hotel. The sun had already gone behind the tall buildings along Sixth Avenue, and I shivered slightly.

We stopped at a brasserie that reminded me of Paris. Tables lined the sidewalk. Mark glanced at me, saw I was chilly, said "Let's go inside." Mistaking us for a married couple or lovers, the maître d' seated us side by side on a banquette. We each ordered a glass of red wine; Mark ordered a hamburger.

"Tell me more about the Swift Observatory," he said, and I did while he ate. Then I asked him about his work.

"I'm mainly freelance, and I usually do news stories. An assignment like this is unusual for me." He sat erect, looking straight ahead, though his voice sounded relaxed and his eyes occasionally slid to look at me.

"What sort of news stories?"

"Well, I used to be based in Lebanon. I took a lot of pictures of fighting. Rubble and injuries, military installations. A lot of hurt people."

I imagined his pictures, the sort you see in news magazines. Bloody faces, bewildered children, bodies in open graves, holes in the sides of concrete buildings. For a second I flashed to our position in the midst of traffic, of the risks we had taken. Did he seek these risks, or was he simply used to them?

"What are you doing in New York?" I asked.

"I wanted to come back to the States for awhile. I was getting numb over there. My editor would call, tell me about fifteen people dying in a bus explosion. The next day it would be seven people killed by land mines. The events lost their distinction. My friend asked me if the child in one picture was a boy or a girl, and I didn't know. I hadn't bothered to notice."

We sat quietly; I studied his face for signs that he was remembering sad, ugly things, but it remained impassive.

"It's nice being back," he went on. "I see my family quite a bit—they live in New Jersey. And the work here is different, nice. I didn't get many assignments taking pictures of interesting women in the Middle East."

Interesting, not pretty, I thought.

"Are you married?" I ask.

He laughed. "No. I'm not sure it would be possible for me to get married. I had a girlfriend—we were serious. But I travel all the time, and there's no predicting the next assignment."

"Did your girlfriend travel with you?" I asked, leaning forward to see his face, really wanting to hear his answer.

"When she could. She's a reporter, and sometimes we had the same assignment."

What a bond that must have been, I thought, sharing the feeling of danger, the memories of death and destruction. I wondered why the relationship hadn't worked, if one had wanted more from it than the other, but I didn't feel like asking.

"Are you married?" he asked, though of course he had already seen my wedding ring.

"Yes."

"Is your husband here with you? He must be really proud."

"Oh, he is. Proud, not here, I mean. I mean, he's proud of me, but he's in London. He's working there."

"Really?" Mark asked, and I thought I detected disbelief in his voice. I imagined he was wondering how any husband could leave me, a woman he had called "pretty" four times, alone in New York. The thought made me smile.

"He's a lawyer," I said, and I betrayed Nick by thinking how much closer Mark's work was to my heart. I thought of Nick, of his deals, of the millions and billions that existed for him on paper and for me not at all except to indicate how busy Nick would be, and I suddenly felt sad for Nick, for all he was missing by living out his days amid papers and numbers.

"The pictures of you will be wonderful," Mark said. "Those shots of you in the middle of the street really fit the work you do. You're like a reporter. Everyone thinks reporters do desk work, but that's the least of it—they're always taking risks. They get very involved. I read those pieces you did on the women in

Chicago. You really entered their lives, and that came across."

"You read my pieces?"

"Yes. They're good. You didn't interpret, or try to make the story more dramatic than it naturally was. You just gave the facts. That's what I try to do in my news pictures." He grinned. "Shooting you was more fun. I wanted to make the surroundings complement the subject, which was easy. Still, I acted as editor more than I usually do."

"Oh," I said, wondering what that meant.

"We should go," Mark said, looking at his watch. "I have to take pictures of two prizewinning architects."

"Okay," I said, disappointed it was over already.

"I have to stop by your hotel, to pick up my camera cases."

We walked a few blocks along the Park, through the dark canyon of trees and tall buildings. On the street it felt like evening, but from my high room we could see the sun was an hour away from setting. Mark peered out the window. I saw that he wasn't simply enjoying the view: he was assessing the light, distances, composition.

"Let's take another picture," he said.

"Are you sure you have time?" I asked.

He nodded, placing his hands on my shoulders and guiding me onto the balcony. He was silent, setting up the shot. I leaned against the wrought iron rail, watching him choose which camera he would use. They hung from his neck, lenses of varying lengths pointing out. He found the one he wanted. Raising it to his eye, he began to twist the lens. He focused on me, lowered the camera to look at me with his bare eyes, raised the camera, then lowered it again. The declining light had turned the hotel's facade golden. I stood there, squinting slightly. He crossed the balcony to me, then gently pushed back my hair. It fell into my eyes again. He gazed at me, then pushed it back.

Can't you imagine how it feels when someone with six cameras around his neck, all pointed at you, walks across the balcony to brush the hair back from your forehead? Feeling faint, I closed my eyes. I wanted him to kiss me. But then I heard the shutter click; he was just taking another picture.

I opened my eyes and smiled. He took a few more shots, then put his cameras away.

"Maybe this is strange, asking you this," he said, standing at the door. "I know you're married, but would you like to have a late dinner tonight?"

"Tonight? Oh, I can't tonight," I said, thinking of how I had wanted him to kiss me.

"That's too bad. I would have liked that. Well, it was nice meeting you," Mark said, sounding disappointed. We shook hands, and he left.

Closing the door after him, I imagined the kiss that never happened: he would brush the hair out of my eyes, and his hand would slide to the back of my neck. Strong, but tender, he would stare into my eyes, then both of us would tilt our heads, our eyes would close, our lips would touch. I leaned against the door, thinking of his soft lips, and my eyes flew open.

"Oh my God, oh my God," I said, beginning to pace the room. I felt knifed by the agonies of loss, of betrayal; on one hand, I had betrayed Nick merely by wishing that Mark would kiss me. Like Jimmy Carter, I had lusted in my heart. On the other hand I agonized because Mark hadn't kissed me, and I had really wanted him to. I still did. If he knocked at the door, I would welcome him to my lips with open arms.

Madly I tore to the telephone and dialed Clare's number. "Hello?" she said. I heard Eugene singing in the background.

"Clare, I'm in deep trouble. I need to talk to you."

"Why? What's wrong?" she asked, sounding alarmed.

"I feel something for . . . another man."

"You mean another man than Nick?"

"Yes. That is exactly what I mean."

"Georgie, you only left the Point yesterday. What could have happened?"

"A lot. I feel attracted to someone else."

"You do? Hold on." I heard her telling Eugene to put water in the birdbath. She came back on the line. "Describe the feeling."

I had to close my eyes to get it right. "It's like, I'm wishing he would kiss me. I can just about feel his lips on mine. I think I'll die if he doesn't."

"Georgie, he's not right there, is he?" Clare asked in a low tone.

I opened my eyes to make sure. "No. But the feeling is very strong. His name is Mark Constable—he's the photographer who took my pictures." I described the photo session to her, and when I was finished, she laughed.

"What?" I asked, offended that she wasn't taking me seriously enough.

"It sounds like you had a fabulous time together, and you're just feeling a little carried away. Don't take this wrong, but you lead a very isolated life, and you're confusing ordinary, everyday fun with desire. Get your hormones under control." She laughed some more.

"Ha, ha. How do you know?"

"Trust me."

I remembered standing on the balcony with Mark, the sun setting across the Park. I recalled the look in his eyes. "I think he felt something too."

"Probably he did. Why not?"

"Listen, how do you know so much about it? You live on the Point too. You're just as isolated as I am. As a matter of fact, more so. The Observatory brings me into contact with a lot of people."

"Your isolation is a state of mind. You think you and Nick,

and the rest of the family to a lesser extent, are in the castle keep, surrounded by a moat. You don't want to let anyone in or out."

"Thank you, Hans Christian Andersen, or should I say Dr. Freud?" I said, angry at her analysis, even though it sounded reasonable.

"Anyway, Nick is now the Evil Wizard, tooting off to London, on the Concorde no less, and your photographer is the new Prince."

"That's not true. You're exaggerating. I love Nick. I just feel like kissing Mark."

Clare snorted. "Imagine what you'd say if Nick said he just felt like kissing that female lawyer you hate so much. You know, you're proving a theory I was developing about you. You're so obsessed with the fear that Nick might commit adultery, you're going to get drawn into it yourself."

"I am not. Shut up. What business do you have developing theories about me, all on your own, without letting me in on them?"

"That makes no sense. Maybe you really are lovestruck—you sound irrational. I'm sorry if you think I'm making fun of you. I'm really not," she said, sounding incredibly amused. "I just love you so much, and I've hated to see you hurt over Nick. I think this is healthy for you. Maybe it's your way of changing a little, being a little more flexible about your marriage. Remember, wishes don't always come true. Just because you wish Mark had kissed you doesn't mean he did. Right?"

"Right. You know? I just looked at the time, and it's seven-thirty. Do you realize that Nick took Jean to the theater in London, and I haven't thought of them once? It must be after midnight there."

"Good going, sweetpea!" Clare said affectionately.

"Thanks, Clare."

"You're welcome. Oh—here comes Donald's plane. They all

finished work early, and we're having a cookout tonight. I see it now, coming down. I'd better go."

"Safe landing," we said simultaneously, then hung up.

To celebrate my new flexibility and because I was feeling high from Clare's congratulations, I decided to call Nick. I asked the Savoy operator to try his room. The phone rang and rang, and there was no answer. I said maybe she had made a mistake and asked her to try again. No answer. I hung up, then stood by the window. The sun was down; a strip of rose gleamed in the west. They had gone to the theater and decided to have dinner afterwards. But surely dinner would be over by now? They had decided to go to a nightclub. They had decided to go to Jean's room because they knew I would find them in Nick's. At that moment they were holding each other, naked, in Jean's bed.

"Stop it, stop it," I said out loud.

Be sensible. Maybe the client called and they had to forego the theater and work after all. No, Nick had been ready to leave when we spoke earlier. The only way the client could have found him was to have him paged at the theater. Highly unlikely. An accident! I thought, losing my breath. Dear God, he's lying in a London hospital, unconscious, near death, and no one knows who he is because some street urchins stole his U.S. passport for an easy sale on the black market.

I was shivering and had been for heaven knows how long when the phone rang.

It was Mark, calling from the lobby. He asked if I had changed my mind about dinner. I said sure, come on up, we'll order from room service. By the time he knocked on my door I had stripped naked, and I greeted him with an open-mouthed kiss. We didn't even make it to the bed, but fell to the floor and made wild and passionate love on the carpet.

It was Nick calling from the airport. Guess what? he asked. I decided to surprise you and fly back early, quit my job, open a little landscape gardening concern in Black Hall. Meanwhile I'll take a cab to your hotel, undressing you in my mind the entire way. Order up some oysters from room service, baby—I'll be there soon.

All that happened, and the phone was still ringing. I answered it on the third ring.

"Hello?"

"Georgie?" came Nick's voice, fuzzy in its transatlantic state.

"Where in God's name have you been?" I shrieked. "Are you all right?"

"I've been at the office. Everything broke tonight—they called my room just as I was leaving for the theater. We never did see the play."

"I was calling in the middle of the night your time, and I didn't get an answer, and I've been so worried!"

"I know. I have your message."

"You should have called me, to let me know you were going to be out all night," I said. I didn't even have the strength to censor the torrent. "The things I imagined were horrible."

"I'm sorry. I really am. I wanted to call you, because I had the feeling you'd call again like last night, but I'd left the number for your hotel at my hotel."

"Whew," I said, considerably calmer, suddenly struck with disappointment that he wasn't calling from Kennedy to say he was on the way. "I feel better now. I'm glad you're all right."

"I'd better get some shut-eye. I'm really tired, and meetings start early in the morning."

"Sweet dreams, Nick."

"Sweet dreams, Georgie."

I snuggled into my nightgown, warm with the memory of Nick's voice. Room service had just delivered my lamb chops when the phone rang again. It was Mark.

"Sorry to call you so late," he said.

"That's okay."

"I just got the contact sheets of your pictures. They're really pretty."

"They are? Thanks," I said, flushing at the compliment.

"I thought maybe you'd like to see them. Would you like to have lunch tomorrow?"

"Yes," I said, without a moment's hesitation.

The next morning I read the *Times* story about the Swift Observatory. In print, my endeavor sounded serious and admirable, larger than life, or at least larger than my life. Had I really covered such diverse subjects as "love that leads to violence," "the devastation caused in families who lose a child to the greater security of religious cults," "the funny poignance of elderly twins reunited after a lifetime of not knowing of each other's existence"? The reporter had included my philosophy on families, and John Avery was quoted saying: "Miss Swift is a visionary." I glowed with pleasure; I could hardly wait to get home and hear Clare's and Honora's reactions. I planned to take a late train that afternoon. Calculating the time difference, I decided Nick would be impossible to reach until later. Meanwhile, I was glad I had arranged a celebratory lunch. It just happened to be with Mark.

We met at Boccador, an East Side restaurant with tall windows that admitted plenty of light and overlooked a private garden. I wore white jersey pants that ended above my ankle, a beige jersey tunic with gold buttons, and the Poppy Field lipstick. My white leather purse was trimmed with beige and shaped like a saddlebag; Nick had bought it for me on our last visit to Paris.

Mark waited for me in a banquette facing the garden. He rose as I approached, but the headwaiter standing by the table and the table's awkward position prevented us from kissing hello. We shook hands instead. I sat beside him. My heart seemed to be beating fast; I tried to forget my fantasies of the night before by concentrating on the table settings. White linen tablecloth, matching napkins, white plates rimmed with blue and gold, heavy cutlery.

"Congratulations," he said. "I saw that piece in the paper."

"I was really happy with it," I said, incapable of sounding blasé.

"I told you we needed dynamic pictures for a story about the Swift Observatory."

"This is a lovely restaurant," I said.

"Do you like it? I come here a lot." He looked around the room, perhaps trying to see it the way someone would for the first time.

"We hardly ever go out to dinner in Black Hall," I said, wanting to remind him that I was married. "Although there are lots of good restaurants."

The waiter came to our table and Mark ordered two glasses of champagne. "To celebrate your Observatory," he said, grinning; at that instant I felt a pang, because I was celebrating with Mark, not Nick.

"Would you like to see the pictures?" he asked, then removed two contact sheets from the briefcase beside him. Many tiny pictures of me covered each page, in the sequence he had taken them; they reminded me of a filmstrip. There I was in the middle of the street: looking left, looking right, sucking in my cheeks to make my cheekbones look like Jerry Hall's, my black hair tossed about, smiling, not smiling, stock-still in terror at the close call with that tour bus. I smiled, remembering the fun we had had. Clare had been right: we were just two normal people having a good time.

Then I saw the pictures on the balcony. One glance made the blood rise to my cheeks. I instantly recognized which photo Mark had taken after touching my hair. My yearning was so obvious, captured on film for all, especially Mark, to see. Lowering my head, I felt ashamed. I gazed down, so he wouldn't notice my red cheeks.

"These are fine," I said, erasing the emotion from my voice.

"You sound disappointed," he said, sounding disappointed.

"No, really. They're wonderful." I looked up then, smiled at him. He was leaning forward, frowning with concern. "I was just remembering how it felt, standing in the middle of Central Park South, risking life and limb. Do you do that sort of thing often?"

"No, hardly ever. But the feeling hit me when we were halfway across: take her picture. They're good, aren't they?" he asked, examining the contact sheet. I stiffened when I saw him pause at the balcony sequence. He looked at those for a long time, then tapped the paper with one finger. "These are pretty," he said. "If I were the photo editor, I'd have a hard time deciding whether to go with the drama in the street, or use one of these."

"The street ones are better," I said, relieved when the waiter gave me a menu to study.

We both had sole meunière. Mark told me stories about his life in Lebanon, the constant awareness of his own mortality, the way he began acting careless—crossing the street, getting too close to gunfire, straying into forbidden districts. Then we talked about our families. I told him about Nick, about Honora and Pem, about my wonderful sister and her family. He showed me another contact sheet in his briefcase, with pictures of a family party: his mother and father standing knee-deep in the surf; his older brother, surprisingly dark and bearded; his grandfather, home from the nursing home for the day.

"Oh, it must be sad, to have him living in a place like that," I said.

"He likes it. They have busy schedules every day—bingo, card tournaments, prayer services, discussion groups, movies."

"I don't know," I said, shaking my head. "That sounds like camp for grownups—basket weaving and bead stringing. Things to keep them occupied. I guess we're lucky my grandmother doesn't have to go into one."

"You are, but they're not all bad. My grandfather plays banjo, and there's a dixieland band at his place. He really enjoys it."

"That's nice," I said, not believing him.

Mark called for the check, and I looked at my watch.

"Well, I have a train to catch," I said. "I have to get my things from the hotel, check out. . . ." I smiled at him. The lunch had been fun, not half as guilt-provoking as I had feared it would be. What was so bad about having a meal with a member of the opposite sex? Suddenly I felt benevolent about the idea of Nick dining with Jean. I hoped their conversations were as pleasant, as stimulating, as Mark's and mine had been.

Waiters bustled to our table as we stood to rise. I hid a smile, watching Mark hand a folded bill to the maître d'.

"You have to do that when you're a regular," he said, seeing that I had noticed. It seemed endearing and intimate, the sort of thing a husband would say to a wife. Mark held the door for me. Pedestrian traffic had thinned, and I realized that we had spent a long time at the table, that the lunch hour was long over.

"Thank you," I said, turning to face him. "I really enjoyed that."

"So did I," Mark said. "You're . . . you're a wonderful woman, Georgie. I like being with you. I wish you weren't married."

Looking directly into his eyes, I realized we were practically the same height. He took one short step towards me, held me in his arms, and kissed me on the lips. His mouth was soft, and his tongue parted my lips just slightly. His fingers tangled in my hair. For the first time in eight years I was kissing a man without bending way back to accomodate his height. I remained purely analytical throughout the kiss, but the moment we stepped apart, my left hand clasped in his right one, I fainted.

. . .

Seconds and a lifetime later, I came to. I lay on the sidewalk, a crumpled heap, and Mark was trying to straighten me out. He was pulling on one leg, saying, "Georgie, please wake up!" He was so busy, he didn't notice that my eyes were open, watching him.

"I'm okay," I said, after a bit.

He crawled on his hands and knees to sit beside my head. He tried to slide his briefcase under my hair, as a sort of bulgy leather pillow, but I struggled to sit up.

"Lie back," he said. "You can't stand yet. What happened?"

What had happened? Staring at the pale summer sky, I reflected. The unthinkable had occurred and another man's lips had touched mine, but of course I couldn't tell him that. "I think the heat got me," I said.

"Really? I was just thinking it feels like autumn. Are you sure you're all right?"

"Yes. Yes, I think so," I said, though I did feel rather woozy still. "Help me up?" I asked.

By now the waiters and the maître d' had noticed me lying on their sidewalk, and had rushed out to help. "Madame, Señora, Missee Sahib, dear lady," voices were saying in all languages.

"If someone could just call me a cab," I said.

"That's ridiculous," Mark said. "I'm taking you back to your hotel."

The last thing I wanted was to go anywhere near a hotel with Mark, but I had no choice. I still felt weak, as though I might faint again. He directed the maître d', he of the recently greased palm, to fetch his car from a nearby garage, and he wouldn't let me stand until it arrived. Driving to the hotel, he kept casting sidelong glances at me, as if to make sure I was still conscious, or as if he had a question he could not quite bring himself to ask. In the hotel lobby he asked someone to vacate their chair, and he pushed me into it. Then he went to the reception desk, spoke to someone for a few minutes, came to me with my bill and a charge slip for me to sign.

"Thank you, Mark," I said, really touched by his taking care of me.

"You scared me back there. Are you sure you're all right?"

"I'm fine."

"Did it bother you that I kissed you?"

I smiled, because suddenly it seemed ridiculous that not only had it bothered me, it had momentarily stopped my heart. "No," I said.

"Well, I'm glad of that. Come on—I'll drive you to Penn Station."

The Colonial stood on Track 13. Mark walked aboard with me, found me a seat, heaved my bag onto the overhead luggage rack. He kissed me again, this time on the cheek.

"I think you should see a doctor," he said. "It's not that hot out, so I don't think you fainted from the heat. I'm going to call you this week, to make sure you're okay. Will you give me your number?"

I hesitated, but then I reached into my bag for a notepad. I wrote down my address and telephone number.

"Thanks," he said. "I think your train is about to leave, so I'd better get off."

He stood on the platform, waving at me. I waved back, watching his palomino hair shine like a beacon in the hellish murk of Penn Station, until the train pulled away. I think he blew me a kiss. As soon as we turned a corner, I changed seats, to one across the aisle from which I could see Long Island Sound when it came into sight. I wanted to get as far from New York, from the scene of the kiss, as soon as possible, while at the same time wanting to relive the moment he had pulled me to him. I trembled as the feelings dueled, and for a moment I thought I might faint again.

When people get married, they make private vows that have nothing to do with ceremony or tradition. Two of the great-aunts had told me they had not taken off their wedding rings since their wedding days. Pem and Granddamon had changed sides of the bed the 14th of each month, to symbolize their wish to never get into a rut. Adultery seemed impossible to me, so I had privately vowed to never kiss another man but Nick. The day of our wedding I stood beside him, in my white dress, in the little seaside chapel. I remember the priest speaking in solemn tones, the whir of the ceiling fan, Clare in her yellow dress in the corner of my vision. Nick held my hand so lightly, and I remember the secret thrill I had felt when he began making circles on my palm with his thumb. The priest had asked, "Do you, Georgiana Agassiz Mary Swift, take this man, Nicholas Gabriel Symonds, to be your husband?" My lips quivering, my heart racing, I had said "I do," and it was the most solemn moment in my life. As Nick kissed me at the altar, I was thinking, "From this moment on, I will never kiss another man." And that thought was comforting, full of pure joy, not unlike the feeling I had had walking out of algebra class one late May, thinking, "I will never take another math test."

My vow broken, I traveled eastward, towards home. The image of Nick, whom I had betrayed, filled my head and nearly broke my heart. Nick in London, working so hard, struggling in his career so that we could have a good life. I had cheapened that with one easy pucker. The image of Mark, with his worried green eyes and death-defying approach to life, wanted to enter my mind, but he was banished for the moment. This train ride belonged to Nick. I would confess the kiss to him at the first possible moment. I thought of him so intensely, repledging my love for him the whole way home, that by the time the train pulled into Old Saybrook, I had nearly forgiven myself.

Eleven

The local taxi drove me across the bridge to Black Hall. I welcomed familiar landmarks: the marshes, silvery in twilight; the lighthouses blinking across the river; the fish market. These things Nick loved so much, he was willing to fly into New York each day just so he had them to come home to. Forgiveness was total by the time I paid the cabdriver. I lifted my bag from the trunk, all feelings of faintness gone, and walked up the shadowy path to my house.

"Georgie!" came Clare's voice from Honora's porch.

"Hello!" I called. She ran across the yard, and I saw in her face that something was wrong. We stared at each other for a few seconds, and then she hugged me.

"Mother had a heart attack," she said.

We sat down together on the cool ground. "Don't tell me she's dead," I said. "Please don't say that."

"She's not. She's in the hospital, in New London. I just got home from seeing her. It was fairly serious, though. The doctors won't know how much damage there was for a while, and she's in intensive care."

Clare and I were crying, our arms around each other. "It was awful, Georgie," she said. "She was so happy about that story in *The New York Times*. I mean, she was at the drugstore by six this morning, waiting for the papers to be delivered. She bought about twenty copies, then had second thoughts because she wanted everyone in town to be able to read it. So she drove up to Middletown, where we don't really know anyone, and bought fifty copies."

"She had the heart attack in Middletown?" I asked, dreading to hear the details.

"No. She came back home and called me over. She was so excited! She was calling everyone, and I mean everyone—the Bennisons in Providence and Fort Worth, Dr. Nayab in Woods Hole, the Bouchers, Peg Malley. Her favorite part was where John Avery calls you a visionary."

"Then what?"

"Well, I noticed she was getting short of breath. I said, 'Mom, knock off the calls for a while.' Or something like that. I don't know," Clare said, frowning, trying to remember. "Then she touched her chest, then started flexing her arms a few times. She looked like she was in pain, and she said, 'Sweetie, I think I'm having a heart attack, call Dr. Cooke and tell him we're coming in.' God, she was so calm."

"That is just like Honora, in total control, even at a time like that. Clare, will she be all right?"

"We just don't know. She looks so frail, with the oxygen mask on and tubes in her arms. You can see her tonight, if you want. People in intensive care can have visitors all through the night. Donald's flying home now, to be with Eugene and Case. I tried to call you at the hotel, after I drove her to the hospital and the doctor said she was stable, but you had just checked out."

"What about Pem?"

Clare shook her head. "Doesn't have a clue. Keeps asking me, 'Where's your mother?', acts as though she doesn't understand the word 'hospital.' She can't bear the idea, so she's playing stupid."

"We'll have to take care of her until Honora comes home."

"I know."

I told Clare about the kiss. "I feel as though this is my punishment," I said. "My mother has a heart attack because I kissed another man."

"She would have one if she knew," Clare said, and we laughed for a second. Then she turned on me. "That really is self-centered, thinking Mom had a heart attack because of a little kiss. God, I'm so sick of the perils of your marriage and now the perils of your love life. Grow up, Georgie."

"I'm sorry," I said, stung. I thought of Honora in a hospital bed, a place I'd never seen her before. Was she conscious? Was she afraid? I had to be with her. "I'm leaving," I said. "I want to see Honora."

"Well, obviously you can't drive yourself if you fainted today. So you'll have to wait until Donald arrives, and then I'll go with you to the hospital." She sounded put out, but I knew she really wanted to go. I walked into Honora's house, to get away from her. She had spoken with such contempt. I thought it cruel of her to suggest I had a love life with anyone but Nick; she was making my kiss seem insignificant and momentous at the same time. I refused to look at her.

"Hello, Pem," I said, crossing the room to hug her. She stood by the window, a bow of pink yarn tied in her hair.

"Where's your mother?" she asked, both palms turned up.

"She's in the hospital."

"The hospital? What's she doing in the hospital?" she asked, twisting her hands in anguish. I held them.

"She had a heart attack."

"I'm hungry. Where's our supper?" Pem shuffled off to the kitchen.

"See what I mean?" Clare asked, standing beside me.

"Yes," I said, not ready to forgive her.

Donald burst through the door. In our daze, we hadn't even heard his plane land. He flung himself into Clare's arms, and they both sobbed. Missing Nick more than ever, missing Honora, bowled over by the force of Donald's emotion, I stood aside, sobbing also. They peeked over each other's shoulders at me, then shuffled over, to hug me into their circle.

"I love her like a mother," Donald said after a minute. His own mother had died when he was in college. "I've lived next door to her all these years, and I can't imagine her gone."

"God, you make her sound dead," Clare said sternly.

Donald, hurt, blinked at her sharp tone.

"She's the enforcer tonight," I said. "She's keeping everyone on their best behavior. She's not taking guff."

"Damn right," Clare said. Then, to Donald, "There's chowder on the stove and hot dogs in the fridge. Georgie and I have to go see her."

"I know. Give her my love," Donald said.

"How did this awful thing happen?" I asked suddenly, feeling fuzzy and bewildered. "Honora is so healthy."

"She swims all the time," Donald said.

"She's thin," Clare said. "How could she have had a heart attack?"

"Granddamon died of a heart attack," I said.

"But he was old. And Honora's not dying," Clare said, her voice trembling.

"I have to get ahold of Nick," I said. I called, but the phone rang and rang in his empty hotel room.

"I'll call him later, if you want," Donald said.

"Oh, would you?" I asked, kissing him. With a shock, I realized that I had kissed his lips, as I had many times before. How had I never counted that as breaking my vow? Certainly it was not sexual, the way kissing Mark had been, but lips were lips when it came to my vow.

Passing through the kitchen we caught Pem trying to hide a ragged sandwich in her pocket.

"See you later, Alligator," Clare said.

"Not if I see you first," Pem replied, laughing. Then, once more, confusion clouded her face. "Where's your mother?" she asked.

Neither Clare nor I had the heart to answer, so we ran down the steps, leaving her to Donald.

Honora lay in a hospital bed, the clear plastic oxygen mask over her mouth and nose. An emerald tube connected the mask with a silver plate on the wall from which air flowed. Several plastic tubes carried clear liquids into her arm from bottles suspended overhead. Her eyes closed, she looked unspeakably gray.

"Just a few minutes, girls," a nurse said.

Clare held Honora's hand, and I touched her forearm. Her eyelids fluttered, then opened. She grinned to see us. That look of happiness was so familiar, so unfettered, the same expression that crossed her face every time Clare or I dropped in unexpectedly, that it made me gasp.

"She just squeezed my hand," Clare said, smiling at her.

"I'm glad to see you, Mom," I said.

She nodded, then closed her eyes and apparently went to sleep.

"She'll tire easily," the nurse said, coming by to check the level in one of the intravenous bottles. "That's not unusual after a heart attack. Don't worry too much about it."

"Okay," Clare and I said at once, eager for any information.

"Can we see her doctor?" I asked.

"I'm afraid he's come and gone. But he'll be back tomorrow morning. I'll tell him to call you."

"Thank you," I said.

"You really should go now," the nurse said. "She'll sleep easier without you watching her."

"Not Honora," Clare said, but we left.

The parking lot was well-lighted, nearly empty since regular visiting hours were long over. A stiff breeze blew off the harbor. I felt moisture in the air; I could see no stars, and across the water I heard foghorns, the same ones Eugene O'Neill had heard from Monte Cristo Cottage.

"She looks terrible," I said, sitting beside Clare on the front seat.

"She looks much worse than she did this afternoon," Clare said, sounding frightened.

"Maybe that's common when someone's had a heart attack?"

"I'm thinking maybe we shouldn't leave yet. I mean, if something happened. . . ."

"You don't mean . . . if she died?"

"Yes, I do." We sat silently, considering the possibility of our mother's death.

"No," I said firmly. "We can't think about that. The nurse would have told us if there was any immediate danger."

"Georgie, there's nothing but immediate danger the first forty-eight hours after a heart attack. Anything could happen." In spite of what she was saying, Clare started the car and drove out of the parking lot. We kept our eyes straight ahead when we passed the funeral home where Granddamon's wake had been.

"She's so young," I said.

"It seems unnatural, her being so sick when all Pem's people go on forever."

"I can't stand to think of what's going to happen to Pem," I said.

"I need a cone," Clare said, pulling into Friendly's parking lot. We each ordered cones; I had watermelon sherbet, and she had vanilla ice cream with chocolate shots.

"Mine is delicious," she said. "Want a bite?"

We exchanged cones, tasted, gave them back. We climbed back into the car, cones in hand. Clare pulled onto Route 156. We stayed on back roads the entire way. Just before we turned onto the road to Bennison Point, I opened my window. My cone contained another few bites of sherbet, but I dropped it onto the road. A minor sacrifice for a very great cause. "Be well," I whispered to myself.

"I know what you just did," Clare said. "And I must say, I'm mildly disgusted that you would even think that something as tiny as throwing out your ice cream cone could save her life." But even as she spoke she was rolling down her own window, flinging her own cone at a street sign.

. . .

Inside my house, I answered my telephone.

"Donald told me," Nick said the instant I answered. "Will she be all right?"

"We don't know."

"What am I doing here?" Nick asked, not quite into the mouthpiece, as though he was talking to himself. "I want to be there right now."

"Can you come home?"

"What do you think?"

It was clever of him, having me answer my own question. That way the inevitable "No" would come from me. "Well, you're in the midst of a big deal for Hubbard, Starr. If you see it through, you get all the credit. If you fly home, you look bad. The partners would be very unhappy."

"That's how I see it. Maybe I can fly home for the weekend—that's two days away. I'd miss a few meetings, but I don't care. I want to be with you."

"Then just come back." Even though I understood, this time I didn't care. I wanted him home, and that was that.

"Georgie."

I stared out the window at barrels of fog rolling down the Sound. Chalky and lighter than the clear black night, they seemed evil, and I knew they would soon fill the house with dampness. I would have to peer through thick white air to see Clare's house, and I wouldn't be able to see Honora's at all. "Everything is changing," I said in a low voice. "I went to New York, and when I came back, I barely recognized this place. You're gone, Honora's gone. When you come back from London, you'll see what I mean. It's all different."

"What happened is terrible, but it's not permanent. I'll be home soon. This deal will be signed in one week. Honora will get well, and everything will be the same."

"No it won't," I said. I was thinking of Pem. She was spending tonight at Clare's; tomorrow she would come here or I would move into Honora's. A wish had begun, repeating itself in my mind: don't let this be her last summer on Bennison Point. Most often "her" meant Pem, but sometimes it meant Honora. Sometimes it meant me.

"Donald told me Honora was so proud of that piece in the *Times*. So was I—I had Denise send it to me by Rapifax. You're something, you are."

"Those interviews seem very far away. Maybe I was a fool to do them. This place is my life, Nick. Everything important to me is here, on the Point. You, the family—I started that bay profile so I could work at home, and even with the Swift Observatory I never intended to leave."

"Staying home is not an act of faith," Nick said. "If it were, I'd be guilty of something, coming to London. Even if you stay in that house for the rest of your life, things will change."

"Come home."

"One thing that won't change," he said, as if he had not heard me, "is that I love you. I will come home when I can."

We said goodbye. Wrapping my black shawl around my shoulders, I walked onto the porch. My house had never felt so empty, and I wanted to wait for the first wisps of fog, coming for us across the bay.

.   .   .

The doctor told us the damage to Honora's heart was extensive, but that she would recover. She was awake, he said, and wanted to see us. Clare and I debated whether to bring Pem to the hospital.

"It's just going to upset her," Clare said.

"Honora is her daughter. Doesn't she have the right to be upset?" I countered.

"Yes, if she understood what was going on. Taking Pem to the hospital is like taking a two-year-old into the frighthouse."

"Mom will want to see her."

In the end, I won. We dressed Pem in her best dress, a crimson paisley challis, and bundled her into the car.

"I don't want to go!" she said.

"See?" Clare asked.

Ignoring them, I started up the car. Driving through the fog with my sister and grandmother felt snug, oddly comforting, like a mug of hot chocolate after skating. Knowing Pem had once enjoyed Andy Williams, I pushed a tape of his into the cassette player.

"Aren't you afraid of seeing her?" Clare asked.

"Not really. You are?"

"Yes. I'm afraid she'll look as bad as she did yesterday. But even if she doesn't, I'll never forget the color of her skin. She'll never know how bad it was. Isn't it weird? She knows she's sick, but she'll never quite be able to see herself the way we did."

"She's seen sick people."

"But you never think you could be as sick as other people. Honora will think of herself as having had a heart attack, and

she'll have to live differently as a result. But she'll never see
herself wearing the death mask, the way we did. We know how
it's going to end."

"This is morbid," I said.

"Well, that's how I feel. Morbid."

"Her doctor sounds optimistic."

"I know. But don't you feel you've had a peek into the future?"

"Yes," I said, thinking of how bleak I had felt the night before.
Sitting on the porch, I had waited for the fog to surround me.
It had come slowly, first blurring the lights in Clare's house, then
shrouding them. When I finally went inside, my hair was wet.

We entered the hospital through a door reserved for doctors,
but our theory had always been if you do something with perfect
confidence, everyone will assume you have the right. Besides, the
doctor's entrance was much closer to Intensive Care, and Pem
wasn't capable of a long walk.

"What are we doing here?" Pem asked.

"Visiting Honora," I said. She shook her head.

We walked down a long corridor filled with patients on stretch-
ers and in wheelchairs, with inhalators, respirators, EKG machines and heart monitors: life-giving apparatus that filled me
with terror. Pem walked slowly, her feet shuffling the bright
floor, looking straight down. Occasionally she ventured to turn
her head a miniscule amount, just enough to glimpse the stainless-
steel wheel of a stretcher, the base of an IV pole, the white shoe
of a nurse.

"The Egyptian Wing," Clare said, and I nodded.

Once Clare, Honora and I had spent a day at the Metropolitan
Museum of Art. Walking through the Egyptian Wing, past the
tombs, mummies, sarcophagi, funerary figures of Pharoahs, we
had all recognized it as the sort of place that would horrify Pem.
She had childish sensibilities and was easily disturbed by ugliness
or reminders of death. That day, in the Egyptian Wing, Honora

had done an imitation of Pem walking exactly as she was doing now, in the hospital. After that visit to the Met it became impossible for me to believe Pem had not been with us. Whenever I visit the Egyptian Wing I see her perfectly, shuffling along, head down, trying to escape the macabre.

We entered Intensive Care, and all the nurses converged on us. "Only two at a time," they said.

Honora had already spied us and was waving. At once I saw her color was better, nearly pink, and she was smiling her square smile.

"Thank God," I said to Clare.

"She'd love to see all three of us together," Clare said to the nurses. "Please?"

"Well, for a minute," the chief nurse said.

Crossing the room, Pem kept her head down, but she looked up when we reached Honora's bed. "Take that thing out of your nose," she commanded, referring to a clear plastic feeding tube that extended from an IV bottle into Honora's left nostril.

"I like it," Honora said. "It distinguishes me."

"How are you?" I asked.

"Much better. Very tired, but aside from that, fine."

"Do you remember everything?" Clare asked.

"Up until the time they brought me to this floor. I remember you were with me, sweetie. Thank you."

"Oh," Clare said, surprised, as if there was nothing to say, as if she had never expected to be thanked.

"Come on, get up and let's go home," Pem said. She sounded agitated, and I watched her scan the room for exits without ever letting her eyes rest on people in the other beds. I was beginning to feel I had made a mistake by insisting she come. I didn't want her to upset Honora.

"Pem," I said, trying to calm her, "We'll go in a few minutes."

"I want to go now!" she said, her voice rising.

Clare and I looked around, trying silently to apologize to the nurses and other patients.

"That's okay," Honora said. She beckoned Pem closer. Pem leaned towards Honora's face. They touched each other's cheeks. Then Honora held Pem's old hand. They didn't say a word, but both were staring intensely. After a while Pem straightened up. Honora's mouth twisted down, fighting what it was about to say. "What's going to happen to her?" she asked.

"I'll go sit with her in the waiting room," Clare said.

We watched them disappear through the double doors. Lines on the heart monitor behind Honora's head zigzagged in a regular pattern. Faint beeps could be heard from around the room.

"We shouldn't have upset you, bringing Pem," I said. "It was my idea."

"Of course you should have brought her," my mother said. "I wanted very much to see her. The situation is upsetting, not Pem."

"She hated seeing you like this."

"I know she did. She's worrying about me, I'm her daughter, and I'm afraid of what will become of her."

"Clare and I are taking care of her."

"For now," Honora said, and the silence that followed felt as sinister as the fog had last night. "Heavens, I nearly forgot," Honora said after a minute. "What a writeup in the paper yesterday! Didn't I tell you you'd put the Swift name on the map? How did everything go?"

"Wonderfully," I said, feeling guilty for thinking of Mark at that instant.

"She needs her rest," a nurse said, standing beside me.

"This is my daughter," Honora said, "and yesterday she was called 'a visionary' by *The New York Times*."

"Mom—" I said, embarrassed.

"Well, it's true."

"That's really exciting," the nurse said. "But Mom does need her rest now, so you'll have to come back later."

Bending to kiss my mother's forehead, I heard her whisper: "Tyrant. No appreciation for the intellect. Bring me some copies of that article, so I can pass them around."

"Nick sends his love."

"Dear Nicky. Now don't let him hurry home from London on account of this."

"Don't worry about that," I said, betraying no irony.

. . .

I recorded a message, telling anyone who called that they could reach me at a different number, and I moved into Honora's house. I had thought Pem would be too disoriented, losing Honora even temporarily, to move to a different house. She sat on the sofa, occasionally casting a glance towards Honora's empty end, scratching the sores on her head. She had stopped asking, "Where's your mother?"; now she glared at me, accusing me of taking Honora's place.

Notes for the Swift Observatory's third report covered Honora's black lacquered writing table, but I had no desire to work. Staring into the fog was like sitting before a mirror. It threw my thoughts back at me. With fog enclosing Bennison Point, the only family under observation was my own.

I noticed and envied Donald's constant presence. Saying things were slow at work, he took four days off. Of all of us, Donald seemed the most profoundly sad. Clare and I felt sad, of course, but Donald seemed truly shaken. He couldn't visit Honora without tears spilling from his eyes. I would see him standing on the dock, staring out to sea. Eating dinner with me and Pem, at the Mackens' house or ours, Donald would sigh a lot. "It seems strange without her," he said more than once.

Nick sent flowers to the hospital, called Honora from London,

arranged for Liberty's to send her a red cotton robe. That same
day he sent me rain boots from our favorite store in Mayfair,
because my old ones had worn out. Our telephone conversations
were more frequent than ever. Although he didn't feel that he
could abandon the deal to come home, he did inform the clients
and other lawyers that he had to take phone calls from me any
time I called. Once I called him at the client's office. His voice
sounded casual as we spoke, and he let me trail on and on about
how I didn't feel the doctor was giving us adequate information,
how Honora seemed in no hurry to leave the hospital, how Pem
was withdrawing more every day, sitting for hours alone on the
sofa.

"I think it's too much for me," I had said, close to tears. "My
mother just had a severe heart attack, my grandmother is totally
senile, and you're so far away. I can't stand it."

"Neither can I. The timing of this tender offer is terrible."

"They're all going to be terrible," I had snapped. "No matter
what happens the rest of our lives, your work is going to come
first."

"That's not fair, Georgie," he had said. "And if you're going
to be mean, I have to get off because in order to take your call
I just walked away from a table of thirty people, and they're all
sitting there waiting for me to return."

Then I had felt guilty for interrupting his intense negotiating
session and making thirty people wait, many of whom billed their
time at hourly rates equivalent to monthly rents in some parts
of the country; at the same time I had felt touched that he had
considered me important enough to make them wait. In the old
days, I would have taken it for granted.

The same day rain squalls washed in, dissolving the fog, Mark
Constable called me at Honora's.

"I called your house, got your machine, and it sent me here,"
he said.

"This is my mother's house," I said. "She just had a heart attack, and I'm staying with Pem. You know, the grandmother I told you about."

"Georgie, I'm really sorry."

"I found out about it the night I came home from New York. A taxi drove me home from the train, and my sister was watching out for me."

"First you faint, then you hear your mother had a heart attack. What a day. And it started off so well. . . ."

"Oh, you mean—" I stopped myself, because I had been about to say "because of the kiss" when I realized that he meant the *Times* article.

"Did you see the piece in *The Washington Post*?" he asked.

"No—I can't believe it, it totally slipped my mind. Did you see it?"

"Yes, and I think it was even better than the *Times*. It described more of the issues you've covered and included an excerpt. Something about twins reunited after fifty years."

"Oh yes, Vivian and Doris."

"But the best part was the *Post*'s Saturday issue, where they run the best editorial cartoons of the previous week from papers all over the country. Have you ever seen that?" Mark asked.

"I know it well," I said, remembering Saturday mornings in Washington when Nick and I would cook pancakes and take them back to bed, spread them with raspberry jam made by Pem the previous summer. We had loved that page of editorials.

"You were in a cartoon! The *Cleveland Plain Dealer* must have run a wire-service story on the Swift Observatory, and their cartoonist did a drawing of the Swift Observer, this wise, kind-looking woman wearing spectacles, looking down on a map of the United States where all these things are going on—one family sitting on their rooftop during a flood, a plane crash in one state with their families waiting at an airport in another, a bunch of girls helping their sister adjust her wedding veil. Tons of things, little drawings all over the map, all telling stories. And the caption is 'All My Children.' "

"That sounds wonderful," I said, smiling.

"Too bad you didn't see it."

"I know, I really wish I had. Maybe the library has it."

"Because I was going to suggest I drop it by your house. I have to drive to Boston for the weekend, and I see that Black Hall is on the way."

He had already looked at a map. "That sounds like a lot of trouble for you," I said, not sure whether I wanted him to come.

"Not at all. I'll be heading by Friday night. Maybe I could take you out to dinner."

I was thinking it would be nice to talk to him at dinner. Conversations with Pem frustrated me, and when Clare was with her family she forgot our language and talked in theirs. "Mush, Casey," meant "Eat your dinner," "Egremont" said to Donald meant something sexy because he always blushed; in general the conversation covered topics of interest to a couple with young children. I thought of Nick, having dinner with Jean and other interesting people in his field. Why shouldn't I enjoy the company of someone with whom I had things in common, whose work fascinated me?

"Well, that would be nice," I said slowly. "Yes, I'll have dinner with you." I gave him directions to my house.

During the days before Friday, I called Mark three times. He was never home; I left all the messages on his machine. First I told him I couldn't have dinner after all. Then I called him to say I could. Then I called again to say I definitely couldn't. Since he didn't call back, I assumed he had gotten my final message and was taking no for an answer. I felt confused, because I really would have enjoyed his company and didn't see why I should deprive myself of it. On the other hand, every time I remembered the kiss, I felt overwhelmed. When I asked Clare about it, she thought for a moment before answering.

"Ordinarily, I'd say what's the big deal about dinner with someone. But you have such strong feelings about it, maybe you'd better resolve them before you get yourself in trouble."

"You mean before I have an affair with him?"

"No. But you felt so guilty about feeling attracted to him the other day, and then the kiss . . . I don't know, Georgie. With Mother so sick, and you in such a state over Nick being in London, not to mention Pem—maybe you should just lay low for a while."

"Anyway, he never even called back," I said, feeling a combination of things: hurt, relieved, insulted, disappointed.

"What about Pem?" Clare asked, happy to change the subject, though the subject of Pem was even more painful. The doctor had told Honora that she wouldn't be able to care for Pem after she went home. That Pem was incapable of taking care of herself, and that just looking after her daily needs required more physical work than Honora seemed to realize.

"Clare, the doctor says Mom should put her in a home," I said. "We can't have that." We were sitting at the harvest table in Honora's living room, listening to the waves, watching Pem scratch her head.

"Then what are we going to do? Look at her." Pem was working an especially large flake from her scalp. She deposited it in a pile of others on the arm of the sofa. "That's not even sanitary."

"Oh, God. Sanitary is the least of it."

"I know that. I also know that Honora is eaten up by this. I think it's why she's in no hurry to come home. She realizes that once she gets here, she's going to have to deal with it."

"Where's the boy?" Pem asked suddenly.

"London," I said. "New York," Clare said.

"He should be here, with the family, not in London, New York."

"Want to watch TV?" I asked, and it was my misfortune to tune the channel to Sesame Street. "Oh, shit," I said, watching Pem's lips tighten. Her face grew red; she leaned forward for a closer look at the Muppets. Two particularly hairy ones were frolicking beside a garbage can.

"Makes me so goddamn mad," she said, her voice rising, her fist pounding the arm of the sofa and crushing the pyramid of dandruff. "With all the people who would love to be on television, they're giving the job to that frog."

"What she says makes perfect sense, actually," Clare said. I left Pem to watch the show, reasoning that she had so little scandal in her life, a few minutes of scathing commentary would do her good.

"Think of it from Pem's point of view," Clare said. "Maybe the home will be good for her. Trained nurses to take care of her, people to play canasta with, aides to bathe her and change her when she wets herself."

"She would hate it. She should be allowed to grow old in her home, on Bennison Point. She's the only Bennison left, in case you haven't noticed."

"Oh, get off your high horse," Clare said.

The phone rang. My heart skipped for a minute, thinking it might be Mark, and in that instant I knew Clare was right: I had done the right thing, declining dinner with him.

"Hello," came Honora's voice, sounding stronger than I had heard it.

"When are you coming home?" I asked. "We miss you."

"The doctor says I can leave next Thursday, if all continues to go well. Of course, there are setbacks for someone in my condition."

"Oh, of course," I said in my best crooning tone. Covering the mouthpiece, I said to Clare, "Setbacks." Clare tilted her head back and forth.

"But God willing, I guess I'll be home then. How's Pem?"

"Watching the Muppets. Furious because a few of them are doing a dance number."

"Just be grateful it's not monkeys. The night before I had my heart attack she was having a fit over the *National Geographic* special, saying with all the poor starstruck young actors, how could they give the parts to baboons."

We laughed, and Clare laughed along, even though she had no idea of what Honora had said. Or perhaps she did. Such was the telepathy that went on among us. I suppose that is not uncommon among people who share the same ancestors, the same senses of humor, and a deep and abiding love. At that moment, hearing Honora's voice, I could pretend all four of us were together, and I felt happy.

Twelve

Honora's first request, upon release from Intensive Care, was for a roll of tape. Beside her bed in the semiprivate room, she attached the articles and editorial cartoon, which the Avery Foundation had sent to me. The Foundation also forwarded mail generated by all the press. One day I received a manila envelope full of letters from people praising the Swift Observatory, volunteering to work for me. Letters came from all parts of the country and Canada; people sent contributions, which the Avery Foundation promised to add to my grant. I took the letters with me to the hospital and let Honora read them while I tried to reply to a few. Her poor roommate had to listen to her telling the nurses, technicians, doctors, and orderlies what an important person I was.

"Listen to this," she said, reading aloud from one letter. " 'This is an idea whose time has come. The observation of humanity will make the world a better place.' Isn't that so true?"

"So true," I said, concentrating on my note to a woman from

Chesterton, Idaho, who had volunteered to send me regular updates on life in Chesterton. I was taking her up on it.

"Ooh, here's a nasty one," Honora said, frowning. " 'Who do you think you are, setting yourself up as an authority on the family? I am a trained marriage counselor, and I found that piece on Mona Tuchman to be horrifying, the way you condone her violence. Do we want a nation of avengers?' " Honora lowered the page, an expression of ecstasy in her eyes. "I love that. You are striking terror into the small minds of the world. This person is so threatened by you! I mean, in his own covetous way, he's acknowledging your influence—worrying that the world will turn violent if they read your reports."

I smiled at her pride, at her willingness to turn anything, even a poison pen letter, to my advantage. I continued writing.

"I mean, hasn't he ever heard of illumination? People discover what's good in life by looking at what's evil in life."

"I don't believe what Mona Tuchman did was evil," I said, putting down my pen, wondering whether Nick would want to run me through with a butter knife when I told him about the kiss. Oddly, I was looking forward to the moment when I would tell him about it. It was Friday; I had decided to tell Nick that night, the evening I had originally scheduled for dinner with Mark.

"Mona Tuchman," Honora said after a minute. "We used to hear so much about her, and now nothing at all. Are you in touch with her?"

"No," I said. I felt a pang of guilt. I had encouraged friendship with her, then cut her off when she phoned me. The details of her life and crime were not simply facts to me, but issues too close to my own soul.

"She was one of your first subjects," Honora said. "It was such a thrill when you would come over to tell us about your conversations with her. Such a thrill." Her gaze grew distant and troubled. When she spoke again her voice was thick. "I think that was our golden time. The early part of this summer, when you were establishing yourself as the Swift Observatory, and we were all happy and healthy."

"Mom, things will be good again. The doctor said it's natural and very common for people to feel depressed after heart attacks."

She shook her head. Her full chestnut hair swept her thin shoulders. "I know that, and I suppose I do feel a little depressed. But this isn't just a chemical reaction. Right now I am facing hard facts. I'm thinking about your grandmother."

"We can't let her go into a home," I said. "Clare and I can help take care of her. We can take turns having her stay at our houses. Every other week—"

Honora held up her hand to stop me. "It's too much responsibility for you. What happens when Nicky has to work late and you go to the city? Can you imagine Pem going along with you?"

"Maybe I won't be doing that so often," I said, searching my mind for a subject to switch to, anything to keep Honora from giving me a lecture on how a wife should be with her husband.

"Yes, I've sensed that that has become a problem," she said, staring at me long and hard.

"But I don't want to talk about it now."

"No. Okay," Honora said. Suddenly she seemed exhausted. Her head sunk into the pillow, and she began to cry. Tears rolled down her cheeks, into the corners of her mouth. Her shoulders shook. I tried to hug her, but the sides of the bed made it difficult.

"What? What is it?" I asked, but I already knew. The same things that broke my heart broke my mother's. Bennison Point was changing fast, and although I didn't want to admit it, I agreed with her that our golden time had come and gone. We would treat Honora with a certain fragility; I mourned my strong, invulnerable mother whom I now considered gone forever. She couldn't even control what would happen to Pem. My dear Pem, my grandmother, whom I had started calling "Pem" at the age of two when I couldn't pronounce her real name, "Penitance." I thought of her, and my shoulders began to shake. I pressed my cheek against my mother's, crying. I thought of Nick and knew that things would never be the same between us. Even if we loved each other forever, the obstinance to stay together, the refusal to be separated, was gone. That had been our act of faith; it had made our lives complicated, but until this summer we had fought to resist the ease of status quo, one partner taking a trip while the other stayed home. We had refused to do what others did, to oblige when our careers demanded that we be apart. We had been so special. I sobbed.

"This reminds me of when you were a baby," Honora said in a shaky voice, patting the back of my head. "You never slept. Never. I would be up late into the night, walking you around the house, patting your head."

"Would I finally fall asleep?"

"Well, after a while. But you never seemed to need as much sleep as other babies. So often I would check you in the middle of the night, and you would be wide awake. Not making a sound—you were quiet and vigilant. You had such wide blue eyes, and sometimes you scared me, you looked so alarmed. Sometimes I would walk into your nursery, just to stare at you—you were a wonderful baby. But sometimes the look in your eyes would make the hair on the back of my neck stand up. I'd check the room to make sure no one was there. You were just a baby, but you were keeping watch."

I had done it even then. Was keeping watch over the ones I loved a trait I had been born with? Or had the eddies of sadness and discord between my parents stirred me into watchfulness? The feeling that something bad was going to happen had been with me a long time. Prickles circled my lips and raced along the nerves in my forehead.

"Mom, I think I'm going to—"

Faint. I did faint, banging my chin on the bed railing as I fell to the gleaming white floor. I'm not sure whether I lost consciousness; I was aware of my mother ringing her buzzer, yelling "Help, Nurse!", of her roommate saying "Jesus, Mary, and Joseph," of the sound of running feet, of nurses huddling around my inert body.

"Hon, you okay?" one nurse asked, her brow furrowed.

"How many fingers am I holding up?" asked an orderly who had heard Honora's cries.

"I'm all right," I said, looking up at my mother, who was peering over the side of the bed.

"Sweetie, you just keeled over," she said. "Just like that. What happened?"

"No breakfast," I said.

"Nurse, get her some orange juice," Honora commanded.

"No food or drink until a doctor sees her," the nurse said, and I was touched by her concern until I heard the other nurse whisper, "Hospital liability."

Honora, looking frightened but determined to shore me up with a big smile, waved goodbye as the orderly pushed me away in a wheelchair. I closed my eyes, pressing my palm against my sore chin. People watched me pass. I considered the indignities of hospital patients, how everyone felt free to stare at them, perhaps thinking, "Thank heavens it's her, not me." The love I felt for my family was so strong, I wondered whether I was dying of it. I wept all the way down to the emergency room.

Dr. Fern examined me. She was my age, slender and athletic with a halo of curly red hair. The questions she asked seemed kind and insightful.

"Have you been under any unusual stress lately?" she asked.

"You could say that," I said, undamming another flood of tears. She passed me a tiny box of Kleenex.

"Have you ever been anemic?"

"Around my periods, sometimes."

"Have you had severe headaches?"

"No."

"Have you ever fainted before?"

"Once." I told her about the time in New York, omitting the part about the kiss. "It was hot, and I was experiencing extreme emotions," I said.

"Do you want to tell me what's been causing the stress?"

"Well, that was my mother I was visiting upstairs. She had a heart attack at the beginning of this week. She's always been so healthy," I said.

"I'm sorry."

"And my grandmother, who has always lived with her, can't take care of herself, and she's quite senile, and my mother's doctor says having Pem, that's my grandmother, in the house, is a terrible strain, too much for my mother and her heart to handle."

"That's really terrible. They've always been together?"

"Practically. And my husband is in London, it's the first time he's ever taken a long trip without me, we were never the types to go away from each other, really, we would move mountains to be together. He has this seaplane. . . ." But then I felt too choked to talk.

"That's all very difficult, especially coming at the same time. I'm sure you're just feeling the pressure, and that will explain why you fainted. But I'd like to run a few tests."

I nodded. She did an EKG, made me walk a straight line and hold my arms out like a sleepwalker, took blood tests, gave me an eye exam. When all the tests were done, I retired to my wheelchair. "Can I go upstairs?" I asked. "My mother will be so worried."

"Sure," Dr. Fern said. "As long as we know where to find you."

"Georgie!" Honora exclaimed the instant I was pushed through the door. "Why are you still in that wheelchair? My God, I've been going crazy. No one seemed to know where you were."

"I'm okay. I told the doctor about everything that's going on in the family, and she seemed to think fainting wasn't an abnormal reaction."

"Did she say that?"

"Not in so many words, but that was the jist."

"Georgie, if I teach you nothing else, never rely on the jist when it comes to medicine. It's not unlike meteorology. With a given fact pattern a meteorologist might be tempted to predict several beautiful days of high pressure. But add another factor, just one, and you have a hurricane. Oh, dear. Something else to worry about."

We returned to the letters, Honora continuing to read excerpts aloud and me continuing to try to write replies. I was lost in the work, planning a subsequent Swift Observatory study of the people who had responded in writing to the news accounts, when Dr. Fern walked into the room. Her expression seemed grave to me.

"What?" I asked, my heart fluttering, my breath so short I thought I might faint again.

"Perhaps we should step into the hall? I'd like to talk to you."

"This is my mother. You can tell me in front of her."

Dr. Fern began to smile. "You're pregnant," she said.

.   .   .

I tried to call Nick from the telephone beside Honora's bed. The secretary at the client's office told me he had left, and he wasn't at the Savoy. I left messages at both places.

"Oh, it would have been a great thrill to hear you tell Nicky about this," Honora said, beaming.

"I can't believe I'm pregnant," I said. "Nick and I have talked about it so often, and I wasn't being very careful with my diaphragm, but I never thought it would happen so soon." I felt dizzy with happiness, frantic to get in touch with Nick. I thought of the words I would say to him: we're going to have a baby, you're going to be a father, I love you so much.

"Why don't you go home and wait for his call?" Honora asked. "He'll call you as soon as he gets that message."

"Maybe I will," I said, kissing her. I couldn't wait to get to my telephone.

"Can we tell Clare?" Honora asked.

"Not until Nick knows."

"You're absolutely right, sweetie. Clare will kill me when she finds out I knew and didn't tell her, but I don't blame you one bit. I am so happy. I feel better than I have since my heart attack."

I kissed her again and left, proud of any credit I deserved for making her better, proud of myself for getting pregnant. None of the considerations Nick and I had endlessly discussed—his tough schedule, my determination to follow him into the city, the things we wanted to do before we had children—mattered now. We were having a baby; I was already thinking of names. Perhaps Bennison Symonds for a boy; we could call him "Ben." For a girl, it would be harder. Maybe Penitence Symonds, in honor of Pem. We could call her "Penny." Or Letitia Symonds, in honor of Pem's mother, who had celebrated her ninth birthday on the boat from England. We would call her "Tia." I could imagine holding Tia on my lap, telling her about her brave great-great-grandmother, for whom she was named, and about her great-grandmother Pem. About her grandmother Honora. Would she know Pem and Honora? Driving along, I was thinking of the baby in my womb as twins, Ben and Tia, and I was telling them family stories the whole way home.

That day I called London fourteen times. The client's office had long since closed for the day, and the sleepy night operator lost her patience with me: "I told you once, and I told you again, missus, there's no one here and there's no one likely to be here until Monday."

"Try that extension one more time," I insisted. But there was no answer.

"Where's your mother?" Pem asked for the first time in several days. Her blue eyes glittered. She refused to sit down; she walked through the house, breaking leaves off houseplants, chasing flies with a swatter, making little sandwiches and then hiding them. She had the wanderlust; she could not rest. Late in the afternoon I found her in the garden, picking roses. Her hands bled from the thorns.

"Pem!" I cried. "Let me see your hand."

She offered to me, and I examined, the shredded palm. I led her into the house, took hydrogen peroxide and cotton balls from the medicine chest, and settled her at the kitchen table.

"Doesn't it hurt?" I asked when she didn't flinch.

She shook her head. The spirit had left her again.

"Tell me about the three steamers to Newport," I said.

She regarded me for a few seconds, then shrugged. "There used to be three steamers that left the dock in Providence for Newport, and if you weren't there by nine o'clock, they'd be jammed." She told the story with no expression in her voice; I had never heard it told with less than great drama, excitement, verve. Now there was nothing.

"What were they called?" I asked.

"I don't remember," she said.

"Pem, you're going to have another great-grandchild," I said, hoping the news would give her something happy to think about. I knew Nick would forgive me for telling her before he knew. She looked at me as though she didn't understand. "I'm having a baby," I said.

"Where's your mother?" she asked.

Then I felt angry. I had lived with this woman ever since I was small. We had lived together through all the good and bad times of each other's life. I remembered sitting beside her at Granddamon's funeral, letting her squeeze my hand when the choir sang "Ave Maria," his favorite hymn. She had let me reminisce about my father, making him sound like a hero and martyr, without ever contradicting me, even though I was aware she had never really liked him. We had made apple pies, Christmas cookies, the Fourth of July cake, and many special family dishes. She had always asked me about the cute boys in my class, something Honora never did, and I had always told her.

I leaned close to her face, staring directly into her eyes. "I said I'm having a baby."

She said nothing. We were having a staring contest; she refused to look away.

"Do you know who I am?" I asked. "What's my name?"

"Clare. No, Georgie. You are Georgiana Swift."

"Who am I?"

"Why, you're my granddaughter," she said, giving a slight laugh to let me know she considered it a foolish question.

"Do you understand what pregnancy is?"

"Nine months of misery. Heh, heh," she said, pleased with her witticism.

"I think you're mean," I said. "I know you miss Honora, and so do I. But I've just told you that Nick and I are having a baby, and you won't act happy. Aren't you happy for me, Pem?"

"Yes, I'm happy for you, Georgie," she said. She lowered her head and started to cry.

"Then why does it make you cry?" I asked, taking her bandaged hand.

"I love the Point," Pem said. And although she said nothing more, for the first time I realized that she knew she was in jeopardy.

Someone rang the front doorbell. No one ever rang Honora's bell. Everyone just knocked and walked in. An Avon Lady, I thought. Or someone collecting for charity. I opened the door, and there stood Mark Constable.

"Oh," I said.

"I hope you don't mind, me coming early," he said, smiling shyly. He wore his many-pocketed photographer's jacket over a shirt and tie. His tan face gleamed. His pale hair had been neatly combed, and he held a bottle of wine, which he handed to me as he kissed my cheek. I nearly shuddered at the contact, and what it reminded me of, but I forced myself to smile.

"No, that's okay," I said. "Mark, didn't you get my message?"

"Uh, no. I've been out of town. In fact, I've been north of Boston, taking pictures of King Salah on his boat. I'm on my way back to New York now, instead of the other way around. Why? Was it something important?"

I considered: what was the harm in one dinner? That folly of a kiss was long behind me, and all I could think of was talking to Nick, telling him about the baby. Poor Mark was a bachelor on his way back to his empty apartment; the least I could do was give him a home-cooked meal. "No, nothing important," I said. "Let me show you around."

I introduced him to Pem, who regarded him with surprise. While he stood at the window, admiring the view, she asked in a stage whisper, "Who's that bird?"

I put my finger to my lips and gave her a stern look. "That's our house over there," I said, pointing. Mine, Nick's, Ben's and Tia's. "And that's my sister Clare's." I spied Eugene and Casey snorkeling in the shallows. Playmates for my little one.

"What a great place," Mark said. "The whole family living near each other. Like the Kennedy Compound."

I smiled. We walked outside, through the rose garden and past the herb garden, to stand on the rocks. Waves broke a few feet away, spraying us with mist. Mark stepped back, but I loved the way it felt on my face. Within fifteen seconds Clare was coming towards us.

"Hello," she said, shaking his hand when I introduced them. "I've heard so much about you."

"Good things, I hope."

"You know, the story about how you took my picture standing in the middle of the street," I said giddily, shooting Clare a dark look. She mouthed "Be careful" when Mark looked away from her.

"Well, I just wanted to say hello," she said. Then, to me, "Mother sounded fantastic on the phone—I just spoke with her. Did she seem good when you saw her?" She sounded puzzled.

"Yes, I think this is a good day for her." Smiling at Clare, I simultaneously yearned to tell her my news and enjoyed keeping the secret.

"I'd love to stay and talk," Clare said, subtly accenting the "stay," "but Donald and I are going to the Mendillos.' They caught all that bluefish yesterday, and they want us to help them eat it."

"They left some in Honora's refrigerator," I said. "It's bluefish season. Last week Henry McPhee gave us some, the week before I cooked the one Eugene caught. Will you thank them for me?" I asked.

"Nice to meet you, Mark," Clare said, but she was looking at me, her eyes communicating caution.

"Maybe we'll grill bluefish outside," I said to Mark, watching Clare walk away, amused at her protective role as housemother.

"That sounds good. I'm an excellent barbeque chef. I did a lot of outdoor cooking in Lebanon."

We returned to the kitchen. I served Mark a gin and tonic, myself a glass of cranberry juice. No liquor would pass my lips until the baby was bouncing on my knee. Every time I passed the phone, I stared at it, willing it to ring. Why did I no longer fear what might be happening between Nick and Jean? Every explanation for where he might be was a reasonable one: dining with the clients, a night of theater, maybe even with Jean? After all, it was Friday night, and Nick had the right to enjoy it. Sitting on the terrace, watching the sun set into a golden bank of clouds, I was anxious for Nick to call, but not suspicious of his where-abouts. I silently toasted myself for turning a dangerous corner.

Mark was telling me about close calls in the Persian Gulf. I nodded avidly, but I was thinking of how strange it was to be having dinner with him instead of Nick. I liked him; his stories were vivid and poignant, and I thought of him fondly. But that night I should have been sitting opposite Nick, telling him about the baby, listening to his expressions of wonder and admiration for the two of us and what we had accomplished.

Mark lit the grill while I made a salad. I mixed Dijon mustard, mayonnaise, lemon juice, and fresh black pepper, and rubbed it

on the bluefish filet. Then I carried it outside. The sun had set,
and a light wind blew off the Sound.

"Chilly?" Mark asked, watching me hug myself.

"Oh, no," I said, smiling. I shivered with pleasure every time
I remembered the baby. Mark stepped towards me, and for a
second I thought he was going to put his arm around my shoulders. But instead he pointed at the horizon.

"What's that land out there?" he asked.

"Plum Island. And that's Orient Point, and that lighthouse
way left stands on a rock called Gull Island."

"This is nice." He smiled at me. "Thank you for having me
here."

"Oh, you're welcome. Well, the fish must be done," I said,
moving away. His closeness was making me nervous. I suddenly
had the feeling that Mark had an agenda for the evening that I
wanted no part of. Any sparks I had felt for him in New York
could, as Clare had told me, be attributed to the thrill of a photo
session in heavy traffic. But I wondered whether he realized that.

We sat at the dining table. Pem refused to join us. She scowled
when I told her my feelings would be hurt if she didn't.

"Eat with your friend," she said, making "friend" sound unspeakably dirty.

For the first time in my life of fixing dinners and setting tables,
I did not light candles. I turned on lamps around the room that
cast a cozy glow but did not suggest romance. This was a meal
to be gotten through.

"Excellent fish," Mark said. "That's a delicious sauce."

"Thank you. Bet you don't have bluefish in Lebanon."

"No, we don't. A visionary, a great saucier—what can't you
do?"

I blushed. "Don't flatter me, Mark," I said. "You know, the
reason I started the Swift Observatory was that I wanted to work
at home. I'm really just a homebody."

He shook his head. "Maybe that's true, but I think you would have found a way to do it no matter what. You're too good at interviewing people, getting into their lives. Why do you try to make your work seem insignificant?"

"I don't know," I said, but I was thinking it was because I wanted to distance myself from Mark. Originally I had felt attracted to him for his work, how it complemented my own. One sleepless night I had had fantasies of his photographs illustrating my reports. Now I wanted to remove the traces of things we had in common, convince us both they had been illusions.

"Well, I consider it significant. I don't think I've met a person my age who's been the subject of an editorial cartoon. Which I have in my briefcase, by the way," he said, beginning to rise from his chair.

"That's okay. I've seen it," I said. "The Avery Foundation sent me a copy."

"Oh. So I didn't have to stop by after all." Mark grinned, waiting for my reaction. He was testing me, letting me set the stage for what would happen next. If I wanted romance between us, I would lower my head and say prettily, "But I'm so glad you did." Inflection was all. I leaned forward, grinned, said, "But I'm so glad you did," in a tone reminiscent of the one old folks use, somewhat patronizingly, to young people.

"So am I," Mark said. "To tell you the truth, I've been looking forward to it. I've thought of you all week, Georgie."

The tone hadn't worked. "Well, thank you," I said.

"You look pretty tonight. You know, I told the photo editor he should use the balcony photo. You look so soft in it, without any hard edges. That's what makes the picture so striking."

"Why?" I asked, curious in spite of myself.

"Well, I take pictures of a lot of accomplished people. They come from all fields—the arts, business, politics, the army. Usually they have a sharpness to them; nearly all of them have it, even pretty women, and I've figured it's part of what makes them successful. It's not aggressive, or ugly, but it's there. In the eyes, sometimes in the jawline. Maybe the average reader wouldn't even notice, but I take the pictures and I see it."

"Do you notice it in person? When you're in the photo session?"

"Not always. It usually shows up after the shots are developed. It hardens in the darkroom. Not you, though. All your photos have a serene expression. Peaceful."

Like a Madonna, I thought. Perhaps Mark had captured my pregnancy on film, a contentedness realized by my body but not yet by my mind. I was still swooning over motherhood when Mark let his fingers trail across the back of my hand.

"Oh, Mark. I think you have the wrong idea," I said.

"I don't know how to say this—oh, what the hell. I've fallen in love with you. I've thought of you all week—you can't imagine how often I wanted to call you but forced myself to wait until tonight. It's crazy, I know you're married."

"I love him. I love Nick," I said.

"I know that. I mean, I can tell you're not the kind of person to take marriage lightly, and the way you talked about your husband the other day . . . I don't know." He smiled at me, a cute, rather dazed look in his eyes, and I had to smile back. He still held my hand; I eased it away.

"I like you," I said. "I had a wonderful time that day in New York."

Mark shook his head. In lamplight his yellow hair turned deep gold. "I've been telling myself all week to not make a fool of myself. I have a bad habit of stating my case, no matter what the circumstances are. I can't stand beating around the bush."

"No, I can tell," I said, sounding amused, inviting him to make light of the situation, wishing desperately that he would.

"I don't fall in love all the time," he continued. "Don't think that. But you're pretty, so pretty, and I think highly of your work, and all week, everything that happened, I wanted to talk over with you."

"That's nice, Mark," I said, feeling really uneasy and wanting to finish the conversation, "but that's exactly how I feel about Nick. Everything that happens, I want to tell him about it."

"But he's in London."

"We talk on the telephone."

"You make me want to settle in the States, not go back to Lebanon. I don't understand how he could have left you."

"He didn't leave me. He has business in London, and this time I couldn't go along. Usually I do. We're very close."

My radar picked up a familiar sound, the rackety sound of the local cab. I heard a car door slam outside Honora's gate. "Excuse me a second," I said to Mark, hurrying into the kitchen.

The taxi's red tail lights disappeared around the corner, and I peered out into darkness. A shadow fell across the walk; I recognized it instantly. Slamming the screen door behind me, I ran into the night filled with scents of salt and honeysuckle, and I threw myself into his arms. "Nick," I said into his warm shoulder. We held each other for minutes and minutes without saying anything. My arms held him so hard they ached, and I didn't care.

"You feel so good," he said. "I've been missing you for so long."

I tilted my head back, and we kissed, a long wonderful kiss that went far towards erasing the weeks we had just spent apart. It was a kiss that tasted at once familiar and brand-new, that made me feel cuddled and aroused at the same time. "Nick," I whispered. "Georgie," he whispered back, reclaiming me.

"I have something wonderful to tell you," I said, and at that instant I remembered Mark. I pictured him waiting at the table, full of undeclared statements of love, waiting for me to return. I wished fleetingly that he had spied our reunion and fled the scene.

"I can only stay for the weekend," Nick said, "but I'll be back for good next Thursday. I would have called you, but everything was split-second. Negotiations broke up early, I grabbed a cab and got to Heathrow in time for the Concorde. I did call from aboard the plane, but I got no answer."

"I was visiting Honora. Uh, Nick," I said. We had begun walking towards the house, our arms around each other.

Mark came to the screen door. He stood there, his hand on the knob, his hair darkened by the fine mesh between us and him. Nick stopped dead, and so did Mark, who had opened the door an inch and was about to step out.

"Nick," I said, trying to steady my voice. "This is Mark Constable. Mark, this is my husband, Nick Symonds." After three seconds the statues became gentlemen and shook hands.

"Mark is the photographer who took my pictures for *Vanguard*," I said to Nick. "Nick decided to surprise me and fly home for the weekend," I said to Mark.

"You must be exhausted, flying all that way," Mark said.

"No, it wasn't too bad. Excited about getting home, I guess," Nick said.

"Oh, sure," Mark replied.

We stood there for a while, shuffling our feet on Honora's walk. I was sending telepathic messages to Mark, telling him to do the brave thing and beat it.

"Well, I'd better go," Mark said. I thanked my powers of suggestion.

"No, don't hurry away. I don't mean to interrupt something. . . ." Nick's voice rose with a little question, curious rather than accusatory. He looked at me for an explanation.

"Mark stopped by on his way from Boston to New York," I said, growing flustered as I remembered everything: the kiss, my expression in the balcony photos, Mark saying he was in love with me. Both men watched me intensely. Mark's mouth was open slightly; I wondered whether he was fantasizing that I would renounce Nick, say I was leaving with Mark. Nick appeared puzzled. "Uh, he had to deliver some clippings, and I invited him to stay for dinner."

"And it was delicious, but now I've got to go," Mark said, alert again, wakened from whatever reverie had held him spellbound as I spoke.

"Come on, stay a while," Nick said. "Have a cup of coffee— it's a long drive to New York."

Mark shook his head vigorously. "No, thanks. Let me just grab my briefcase—" He dashed inside, and we followed. In a few seconds he was back in the kitchen, shaking our hands. His face looked redder than I had seen it. The personification of guilt, I thought, wondering whether I was so transparent.

"I hate to chase you away," Nick said, looking from Mark to me and back to Mark. "I mean, it feels weird coming home and having a guest run off like this."

"No, I mean it—" Mark said, giving a final wave, and hurrying out the door.

Nick and I stood alone in Honora's kitchen. A gallery of finger-painted pictures covered the wall behind his head. Honora had saved and framed early works of art by me, Clare, Eugene, and Casey. Staring at the bright lines and splashes had a calming effect; I forced myself to look into Nick's black eyes. They were asking me a question.

"Strange, the way he ran off like that," Nick said.

"I think it was quite considerate, giving us time alone together. One minute before you arrived I was telling him how much I missed you." As I preceded him into the dining room, I examined the table for evidence. No candles—that was a good sign. Plates full of untouched food—an incriminating sign, as if we had been torn away from the table by raging passion.

"Tell me what's going on," Nick said. "I know you, and you're upset about something."

I turned to face him, searching his lean face, still ruddy and weathered in spite of weeks spent in fluorescent-lit boardrooms. His black hair curled endearingly, but his eyes were unrelenting. I felt frantic with frustration; this was not the way this night

should happen. There were so many wonderful things: his surprising me, my news about the baby, the simple fact of being
together. Mark's presence had spoiled everything.

"It seems ridiculous, wasting our first night together by talking
about Mark Constable," I said. The smell of bluefish sitting in
the sauce made me dizzy. I pulled a chair to the window and
sat in it. "Want to sit down?" I asked. Nick carried another chair
from the table to the window, sat beside me.

"If he seemed nervous, it's because he has a little crush on me
and it shook him when you came home."

"I can't blame him for having a crush on you," Nick said. His
grin made my heart melt. "I just don't understand why he ran
off. I mean, you're a married woman, and he knows that. Doesn't
he? What's so bad about your husband coming home?"

"Well, we both thought you were in London."

"Uh huh," he said, inviting me to go on.

"Maybe it's more than a little crush. He just told me he's in
love with me." I watched Nick straighten his spine just slightly.

"In love with you? How long has he known you?"

I waved my hand, wanting to dismiss the whole topic. "It's
not that I mind telling you about it, but it does seem like a waste
of time right now. I'm so glad to have you home, Nick. I just
met him Monday. I told you, he's the guy who took my pictures
in New York."

"Have you seen him since then?" Nick asked, his voice definitely full of jealousy.

I realized the only way to get away from the topic of Mark
Constable was to tell Nick about the kiss. I'd put it lightly, make
it sound funny. I had already begun to consider that day unreal,
my one moment in the spotlight. I had succumbed to narcissism;
I hadn't kissed Mark, I had kissed my reflection, a voice that
kept telling me, "You're pretty." Of course I had kissed Mark's
lips, but they were just standing in for his words.

"Until tonight I'd only seen him one time," I said. "But it was a fairly intense day for us. I told you about standing in the street, feeling like a model while he took my picture. It was fun. We were having a pretty wild time, racing around the city." I didn't mention the conversations we had had about our work and families, the more serious moments that could have spelled a real relationship. As I got closer to the climax of my story, I felt a line of sweat form along my brow. "So the next day he asked me out for lunch, and I figured, why not? After all, people have lunch together all the time. What's the harm in a little lunch?"

"None at all."

I swallowed. "I ordered the sole meunière," I said. "It was very fresh. Maybe a little too much butter."

"Too bad. You hate buttery sole." Nick sounded amused, as though he knew this story was a difficult one for me to tell, and he was enjoying my discomfort. Of course he didn't know the zinger, the kiss, and I knew I was about to dash that amusement right out of his voice.

"Nick. After lunch we went outside. We were standing on the sidewalk. And then, Nick, we kissed." I closed my eyes, to avoid seeing his hurt expression.

"Really? You kissed him?"

"No, he kissed me. But I wasn't totally unwilling." My voice started to quiver. "I swear I would never, never do it again. If only you knew how terrible I felt, still do. Will you forgive me?" I reached for him. His color was deeper than it had been.

"I can't believe you kissed that guy. I can't believe it."

"Oh, Nick. Say you'll forgive me."

Nick stood; he pulled me to my feet and hugged me close. "You don't care for him? Are you sure? Because I couldn't stand it if you did."

"I don't care for him, Nick. Will you forgive me?"

"God, I feel bad that you kissed someone else, but there's nothing to forgive." He laughed, but it may have been a sob.

"I'm glad he beat it to New York, because otherwise I'd kill him."

I couldn't help it; I made mental notes for the Swift Observatory. Nick was my first example of a male's desire for vengeance. And I had inspired it. I lay my head against his chest. "I love you," I said. "I love you," he said. "Will you look what the cat dragged in?" Pem asked, standing beside us, beaming up at Nick. Nick swung one arm around her and pulled her close. "How are you, Pem?" he asked.

"Okay," she said. Then, to me, "Do you think the boy will make us a drink?"

"I bet he will," I said, relieved.

"Three martinis?" he asked.

"Make mine a cranberry juice," I said. He gave me a funny look, and I smiled, but of course that was not the moment to tell him. I felt like taking a long walk alone with him, but Pem seemed so happy to see him.

Pem and I sat on the sofa, I in Honora's spot. It was the first time since I had moved in with her that I had dared sit there. Although it was easy to feel jealous of their love, I respected it.

Nick mixed drinks in the kitchen; I heard ice tinkling in the shaker, and I thought how amazing he was. The news I had given him could have ruined our short time together, but he wasn't letting it.

"Are you hungry?" I asked when he entered bearing a tray of drinks.

"No, I ate on the plane." He sat between me and Pem, his arm around my shoulders.

"Many happy returns of the day," Pem said, moving closer to clink glasses.

"How's Honora?" he asked.

"Much better. She's doing very well now. But you should have seen her that first night. Clare said she looked like death, and she did. Her skin was gray; she was attached to so many machines. Now they say she can come home next week."

"Poor Honora," Nick said to Pem, turning to face her. Pem shrugged and looked away.

"Very sore subject," I said quietly.

The rhythm of breaking waves and the joy of being together lulled us into silence. Nick's fingers drummed my shoulder. I pressed closer to him, wild about the secret I was about to tell him. The fact that Pem already knew made it no less intimate. I thought of the expression "in one ear and out the other," of how aptly it applied to Pem's reception of my news. His legs outstretched, Nick eased off one shoe, then the other. Occasionally he sipped his drink. Once I leaned forward to look at Pem. She was sitting upright, her eyes closed, a gentle smile on her lips.

"She's so happy to have the family together," I whispered. "Honora's being gone has been terrible for her."

"That's no surprise," Nick whispered back.

"Maybe we can go out for a little while," I said. "I have something to tell you."

We crept away from the sofa, to avoid waking Pem. Grabbing big sweaters, we walked onto the front porch. Nick sat in a wicker rocking chair; he pulled me down on his lap. Ever since we had married, I had fantasized telling him that I was pregnant. Even during the years when I doubted that I would ever want children, I recognized what a pleasure it would be for a woman to tell the man she loved that she was going to have his baby. We rocked back and forth, Nick's arms securely around my waist.

"Lots of revelations tonight," he said.

"This one may make you quite happy."

"Well?"

"We're having a baby."

"Georgie!" he said, lifting me in his arms. My arms circled his neck, and I pressed my cheek against his. He carried me out the door, down the slatted wood steps, across Honora's yard. We stood at the edge of the sea.

"We're having a baby," he said, surveying the waves. "This reminds me of the night I asked you to marry me. I feel so happy."

Actually I had asked him to marry me, but he always wanted the credit for it. It had happened in this very spot, after a long dinner with Honora, Pem, Clare, and Donald. Honora had had a date that night, but I couldn't remember the man's name. That entire dinner was a blur. I had sat between Nick and Clare, phrasing the question in my mind, much the way I had rehearsed the words I would use to tell him about the baby. In the end I had held his hand and asked if he would be mine forever. He had said yes, then bent to kiss me. Nick was so tall.

"How long have you known?" he asked, still holding me aloft.

"Since this morning. It seems such a miracle, you arriving here tonight. I was calling all over London, trying to find you. I would have hated telling you over the phone, but I wanted you to know right away."

"I swear it's destiny. I felt so driven to get here—it seemed absolutely necessary, as if I didn't hug you by midnight tonight I would die. Really die. I felt this terrible constriction in my throat, like I was choking. That's never happened to me before."

"Oh, Nick."

"It's fine now." He lowered me so that I was standing in front of him. "We have to commemorate this," he said. "What should we do?"

"Let's swim," I said.

We undressed each other standing in the middle of Honora's yard. I undid his silk rep tie, then hung it around my own neck while I unbuttoned his white shirt. He was struggling with the shell buttons on my blouse, and I let him finish before I reached down to unbuckle his belt and lower his zipper. Shivering in the

chilly night, we made a pile of clothes, topped it with our un-
derwear, and walked into the bay.

The water was warmer than the air and silky against our skin.
Side by side, we swam from Honora's dock to Clare's and back.
On the return trip we breaststroked, to make conversation
possible.

"Do you like the names Bennison for a boy and Letitia for a
girl?" I asked.

"Nice names," Nick said. "Would you like to know the sex
before it's born?"

"Oh, definitely."

"Me too. We'll want to know as much about the baby as soon
as possible. When will you have the baby?"

I smiled, siphoning seawater through my teeth. "Well, the
doctor thinks I'm about six weeks pregnant. So the baby should
be born in March."

"That's a nice month for a birthday. I've never wanted a baby
to be born too near Christmas." Nick's birthday was January 2.

"Maybe it will happen around March 21, the vernal equinox.
Spring is a perfect time to come alive."

Nick stopped swimming and let his feet touch bottom. He
held me close. "The baby's already alive," he said, touching my
stomach. We gave each other a long, salty kiss.

"I could kiss you for an hour," I said.

"But let's do it on dry land," Nick said.

We climbed onto shore. Nick grabbed our clothes; I ran ahead
of him towards Honora's house. We were shivering as we crept
around the porch, checking each window for Pem. She hated it
when anyone skinny-dipped; she didn't approve of night swimming at all. She was touring the living room, pulling leaves off
the jade plants. We entered through the back door. We stood in
the downstairs bathroom, rubbing each other with thick white
towels. "I'll run a bath for you," Nick offered.

"Not right now," I said, for I felt a desire so strong that it must have been the accumulation of all the nights I had spent without him. Wrapped in towels, we went through the house, dashing past the living room door, to the room that had been mine as a child.

We held each other tight, and for a while that was all I wanted. I remembered other times we had made love in this room, times when Nick would visit for the weekend and sneak down the corridor from his room to mine. The stealth had made everything more exciting, and I suppose that sneaking past Pem that night reminded us both of earlier times. We began to make love. We knew each other so well. My hands knew the contours of his body by heart: his narrow hips, the scar of his appendectomy, the gentle curve and ridges of his erect penis. This was the man I'd been longing to touch.

"Your hands," he said, kissing them, and the feeling of his lips against my fingertips drove me crazy. We were pressed against each other the length of our bodies. Nick's legs wrapped around mine; I felt his bony knees and ankles, his soft calves. I wasn't sure that making love with Nick could be as good as my memory of it, but, that night, it was.

"I remember this," I said.

"It's been a long, long time," Nick said; there was an expression of pure contentment on his face. He was touching me in ways that were new and familiar. My arms ached and tingled.

"Hold me all night," I whispered.

Nick held me tight, and he didn't let go.

·   ·   ·

First thing next morning we took a swim, then drove to the hospital. Honora dozed, her bed cranked to a sitting position, the morning paper spread across her legs. Nick stopped in the doorway to her room. I saw him register astonishment, and although

I had grown used to seeing Honora in the hospital, I realized that for Nick it would be a shock. He, like all of us, had thought her the picture of health and strength. Having seen her attached to tubes, the heart monitor, and an oxygen machine, I thought she looked fine today.

Nick stood beside her bed, lowered his head to kiss her. "Sleeping beauty. . . ." he said.

Her eyes opened, and she beamed. With a pang I remembered how she had smiled at me and Clare the night of her heart attack; that smile had been just as full of welcome and delight.

"Nicky! What are you doing here? Georgie, why didn't you tell me he was coming?"

"I've been away too long," Nick said. "It's only for the weekend, but I had to come home."

"Poor lambie, you've been homesick," Honora said. "Well, certain of us here have been going crazy without you." My mother and my husband exchanged knowing, significant glances, as if they knew something about me that I could never hope to understand.

"Are you okay now?" Nick asked.

"I think so. I have to say, I feel appallingly weak, sleeping all the time, no desire to move. I've gotten addicted to television. I watch the morning talk shows, the noontime news, a couple of soap operas, then a rerun of 'Weather Woman.' I made a pretty dashing heroine, I must say."

"Do the nurses know you were Weather Woman?" I asked.

"I've let it slip out to a couple of them. One of the young residents wanted me to autograph the newspaper's weather report."

"Still famous, and you filmed those shows how long ago?" Nick asked.

"Must be twenty years. Gad, thirty years, some of them. I've been remembering that time. What else is there to do in here except watch TV and relive your life? Anyway, I was thinking about Woods Hole, how those scientists made me out to be the Painted Lady of meteorology."

"They were envious of you," I said.

"Some of them were, but others enjoyed feeling superior to me. It was a very difficult place to live, Georgie. I don't know if you're aware of that. Everyone rallied around your father, treating him like a member of the club, no doubt feeling sorry for him having to put up with my frivolity. I think that's what came between us. I've been thinking about him a lot in here."

"It didn't seem that bad," I said, dazzled by the intimacy; this was not at all like Honora. Nick and I sat at the end of her bed, like children gathered around the feet of a great storyteller.

"I'm glad we sheltered you from it. I used to be afraid for you, being my daughter. Clare was fine; Clare was an excellent student, always tops in the class. Everyone said she took after her father. But you never wanted to go to school. Your grades were good, not great. You always wanted to stay home, or spend a school day pawing through tidal pools on Nobska Point."

"But you were always strict about making me go to school."

"Yes. Now, looking back, I so admire your imagination and the fact that you didn't fit the mold. *Then* it terrified me. I thought you had to do all the conventional things, and do them well. You read more books than the entire third grade, but I was so upset when you got that C in arithmetic."

"I remember that." Honora had set me up with a little desk and an abacus, and she had made me spend one hour after school every day adding and subtracting. I was always better at subtraction.

"Why do you think she wanted to stay home?" Nick asked.

"I'll tell you why," my mother said, looking straight at me. "She was afraid something would happen if she wasn't there to look after our house. She thought her father and I would have a fight that would end our marriage, or that one of us would simply disappear. I knew that, Georgie. Even back then."

"I always wanted us to be together. Poor Dad," I said.

"Yes, poor Timmy," Honora agreed. "I can't get him out of my mind. He died so early. To me, he will always be a young man, even though he died in his forties. He would be so proud of the Swift Observatory. And my God! Of his latest grandchild! Give the old grandmother a kiss and let me congratulate you, Nick."

Nick obliged, getting his arms all the way around her in a good hug. I watched him from behind, the way his suede pilot's jacket hiked up over his pants, revealing his blue pullover sweater. His waist looked so narrow. "In London I was thinking of you here in the hospital, and Georgie mad as hell at me for going without her. I never thought I'd come back to a homecoming like this."

I smiled, happy he considered the news about the baby his homecoming. He seemed to have forgotten Mark Constable.

"Well, I told Georgie I don't think she should be driving until the fainting stops. It's much too dangerous."

"I agree," Nick said. "You know, she drove herself home after she fainted here yesterday?"

"I had to get home fast, to wait for your call," I said, knowing the excuse was feeble, that all of us were imagining the crash and wreck.

"We won't even honor that comment," Honora said.

"Just don't do it again," Nick said.

I imagined the pleasure my pregnancy would bring to Honora, all the things it would give her to worry about: whether I was eating properly, whether I was gaining too much weight or not enough, the adverse effects of swimming on the mother and unborn child. "Thank heavens I established the Swift Observatory before I got pregnant," I said. "I don't see why I can't continue as before."

"What about your grant increase?" Nick asked. "I thought John told me those funds are earmarked for travel."

"That's true, but he said it was a no-strings-attached proposition. I get the money whether I travel or not. I think I'll go back to my telephone system, conducting my interviews over the phone." What about the fact that my best interviews, with Mona Tuchman and Caroline Orne, had happened in person? I dismissed that thought.

"Well, if you want to continue traveling, I think we can arrange it," Nick said. "We could hire a nanny to help with the baby."

"I was so lucky, having Pem to help with you and Clare," Honora said. "In Woods Hole we had a series of housekeepers, some of them perfectly fine but others dreadful. The problem was that none of them stayed long enough for you girls to get attached to them. Pem, of course, was terrific. Once we moved to Black Hall, our families seemed to merge."

"It feels that way now," Nick said, his voice a little thick.

"The doctor tells me I can't keep Pem with me any longer," Honora said. "Did Georgie tell you that?"

"I know. It's hard to believe." Nick said. He watched Honora intently, knowing the subject was hard for her; his eyes looked as sad as hers, and I loved him for it.

"Well, to hell with the doctor," Honora said. "I've given it a great deal of thought, lying in here. I have always intended for Pem to live on Bennison Point all her life. She has the right— she and my father bought the land, built the houses for us to enjoy. I want her at home."

Although Honora's decision thrilled me, I knew I had to speak carefully. Maybe she wanted to be talked out of it; I remembered her frustration with Pem before her heart attack. The bedwetting, the sandwich-hiding, the bathing scene, Pem's pugilism. "What about your health, Mom? The doctor said that having Pem around might be too stressful," I said, even though, deep down, I didn't believe that was so—we could hire someone to help feed and bathe Pem.

"She's my mother, and we've been together for all these years. I think it would be more stressful for me to put her in a nursing home. That I will not do."

Nick cleared his throat. In fine lawyerly fashion, he liked to hear all the facts before giving his opinion. "On the other hand, mightn't Pem get better care at a nursing home? We all love her, and we hate to see her sad or unhappy, but she's in pretty bad shape. This morning she made toast for herself, carried it into the living room, went to the window, forgot she had made the toast, went to the kitchen to make more. The toaster wouldn't work the way she wanted it to, so she held down the lever until it started to smoke, and she blew a fuse."

"She did? You didn't tell me," I said.

Honora held up her hands, to stop the discussion. "I know all that. That's why I make her breakfast every morning. She's just forgetful."

"She could have started a fire," Nick said. "What if we hadn't been there? If the fuse hadn't blown, the house might have burned down."

"If, if," Honora said. "The point is, I'm always there. When I leave the house, it's after Pem has been fed, and then I turn off the kitchen appliances at the fuse box."

"And you hide the gin, and you lock the gate to the street, and you make her go to the toilet before you leave," I said, thinking of some of the things I had vaguely noticed but not considered significant.

"That's a lot of work for someone who's just had a serious heart attack," Nick said. "And I'm not sure anyone you might hire to help out would be willing to take on what amounts to twenty-four hours a day of babysitting."

Honora's stony expression convinced me to change the subject.

"Well, it's a beautiful day out. Nick picked the best weekend in weeks. It's just like autumn."

"That's right," Honora said, glancing out the window at the blue sky. "You two get going. Thanks for visiting, but I want you to have a really super day together."

"I'm sorry if I upset you," Nick said, standing at the head of her bed. "But I love you, and I want you to live a long time. I think you should follow your doctor's advice."

Honora squeezed his hand, smiling up at him. "I'm just afraid it would be a half-life if I had to think of her in one of those places. I don't think I could manage it."

"I think you'd adjust," Nick said, and I wanted to pull him out the door, to make him stop trying to convince Honora that Pem belonged in a home. I wanted our family together, so badly that I might have sacrificed Honora's health to do it.

. . .

Nick's mood changed drastically. Entering the hospital we had been happy, in love. Leaving, he looked cross. He glared at me for spending too long in front of the gift shop's showcase. We drove slowly home along side roads. We had traveled this way often before. I stared out the window, feeling sad, wondering what Nick was thinking. He drove with a little frown on his face.

"Were you shocked by the way she looks?" I asked after a while.

"Yes, I was," Nick said. "Seeing Honora like that changes everything. It gives you the idea nothing is permanent."

"I don't like the sound of that," I said, thinking of my old fears of being left: fears that belonged two days in the past, before Nick came home from London.

"You should have thought of that before you kissed the photographer," Nick said.

"Nick!" I leaned across the gearshift to touch his wrist. The wrist was taut; he gripped the wheel with both hands. "Nick," I said again, in a softer voice.

Nick stopped the car in a dusty turnaround beside a salt marsh. He continued to grip the wheel, as though he were still driving. Although it wasn't hot, Nick's black hair curled sweatily at his temples.

"Are you telling me we're not permanent?" I asked.

"I don't know. I'm upset. Honora was fine when I left for London, and now she's in the hospital—it's got me thinking. Maybe I should ask what you're telling me," Nick said. "Last night I walked in on you having dinner with another man. That's weird enough, but it's no big deal—I know that. But I can't believe you kissed him, Georgie."

"I'm sorry."

"This is serious trouble. We've been playing a little—you always worrying about Jean and me letting you. It's unrealistic. Do you realize how guilty you've made me feel about her? The entire time in London. If she came to work wearing a pretty dress and I happened to notice, I felt guilty. She rubbed my shoulders at the office one night, and I felt guilty."

"She rubbed your shoulders?" I asked, wondering whether a backrub was more innocent than a kiss.

"She did. And it felt really good, because I'd been sitting at the desk for ten hours straight. You know how that can happen? We'd been together for hours—we're together late at night. She noticed my shoulders looked tense. It was a nice gesture."

"Nice gesture? How naive can you be?" I asked.

Nick exhaled, sounding impatient and disgusted. "Do you think you're the only one who can be attracted to someone else? Jean's pretty, and she likes to flirt with me. I liked her rubbing my neck, Georgie. I imagined something else happening—going back to the hotel with her maybe. But I didn't. And I never kissed her." He exhaled again. "I'd like to punch that guy, with his blond hair." Somehow Nick managed to make blond hair sound like the worst affliction on earth. "Platinum blond and tan. A regular surfer. Ten years too late on the wrong coast."

I reached for Nick's wrist, and this time he let me pry his hand off the wheel. "I'm sorry I kissed Mark. It will never happen again," I said. "Will you forgive me? So we can have a good time before you go back to London?"

"Yes," he said.

Still, I had to know. "Nick, did you really want to go home with Jean?"

"For a second—yes."

"I know," I said, realizing what I had known all along: that Jean was pretty and Nick would be likely to notice. Maybe even feel attracted to her. A little. Naturally.

"But you're the one for me," he said.

I nodded and he put his arms around me, and when we kissed we both were crying.

"Honora having a heart attack," he said. "It's so fucking unpredictable. She's too healthy for that."

"She's getting better," I said.

· · ·

Back at the Point we swam again, trying to get back to feeling comfortable with each other. We walked across Honora's yard to our house, planned which room would be the baby's nursery. I envisioned wallpaper covered with lambs or bunnies, a white crib, a shelf full of Beatrix Potter books. When the baby was old enough to look out the window, he or she would see Clare's house across the bay, the rocky headland pointing towards Long Island. My baby could send flashlight messages in Morse code to Eugene and Casey.

That night we invited the Mackens to dinner. They left us

alone all that day; although surprised and delighted Nick was home, and eager to see him, they wanted to give us time alone. We made the rounds of the fish market, the vegetable stands, the cheese and liquor stores, the bakery. Back in the car, I said, "Take two. Tell me about London."

"It's some tender offer, I'll tell you," Nick said. "Loaded with important issues, and John has left me and Jean pretty much on our own."

"You and Jean have equal responsibility?"

"I was in charge before I left London. That's one reason I have to get back right away—so I can reclaim my turf. Jean's incredibly competitive."

"John Avery spoke highly of her," I said. "He said you two work well together."

"We do a good job of playing 'good cop—bad cop' in negotiations. Jean pretends to hold out for a minor point, then finally gives in on it, in order to save the major ones."

"That's an interesting tactic," I said.

"It's a little like a poker game," Nick said. "You have to keep a straight face. Anyway, the clients are happy so far."

"I'm really glad," I said, breathing easier. Every conversation seemed a milestone towards a return to normal relations.

Dinner that night was raucous and festive. We all felt berserk with the solace of Nick's arrival and Honora's imminent release from the hospital. Eugene and Casey presented us with two buckets of mussels gathered from the rocks, and we steamed them with white wine and shallots. Frank Sinatra made us want to dance; we turned up the music and hoofed up a storm. When the stars came out, we lay on our backs in the yard, testing the boys on the constellations. Pem sat in a lawn chair, wrapped in a blanket, complaining about the chill, but we wanted her with us.

Later, in the kitchen doing dishes, Nick and I made our announcement.

"Georgie and I are having a baby," Nick said.

"When did you find out?" Clare yelled, tackling me with a hug.

"Just yesterday," I said.

"Oh, I'm so happy for you," Clare said.

"Having kids changes you," Donald said solemnly.

"Honey, don't scare them," Clare said.

"No, I just mean the experience makes you richer. It adds another dimension to your relationship," Donald said, sounding rather stilted. "I'm not saying it right, but I mean it's good."

"He's still shook about Mom," Clare explained, reaching up to stroke his cheek with the back of her hand.

"Aunt Georgie, are you having a baby?" Casey asked.

"Yes, I am. You and Eugene will have a cousin to play with."

"Can I feel the baby kick?" Eugene asked, staring intently at my abdomen. Bits of grass stuck in his red hair; I picked a few out.

"The baby's not big enough to kick yet," I said.

"Why, honey?" Clare asked. "Do you remember when we felt Casey kick?"

"Yeah. Now I get to kick him back," Eugene said, running after his brother.

"Mommmmmy!" Casey called.

Donald went after them. "Some of the joys you have to look forward to," she said wryly.

"Honora seems thrilled," Nick said. "We're going to call my parents tonight."

"Get ready for endless seminars on How To Do Everything Right. Whether or not to breast-feed, which books to buy them, whether or not to spank . . . everyone has an opinion. My relationship with Honora changed quite a bit after I had Eugene," she said.

"For better or worse?" I asked.

Clare frowned, trying to formulate her answer. "Hard to say. She drives me crazy, worrying about every blessed thing I do. I remember when we took Eugene sailing for the first time—I think she stayed on her knees that whole day, praying to the saints and apostles that he would survive. If you think she worries now, wait till you have kids. She has the most gruesome imagination of any grandmother alive. She doesn't just worry—she worries in detail."

"I know. I remember that day," Nick said. "You sailed to Fisher's Island, and we had Honora and Pem for dinner. She kept saying, 'What if he falls overboard, he's so little.'"

"That's right," I said, remembering. "She wanted to know how long it would take to bring the boat around, and then she started to worry about his life jacket, how no life jacket could possibly be small enough to stay on him—it would slip off, and he would sink, and you and Donald would be so devastated when you found his empty jacket. That led to worries that you might feel so guilty your marriage would break up, or you might commit joint suicide."

"Well, her worrying is nothing new. On the other hand, my motherhood brought us closer, because it's a major experience we share. That means a lot to me." Clare regarded me carefully, as if she had something else to say.

"What?" I asked.

"Well, I was just thinking, that aspect of it might mean more to me than you. Having children is my biggest connection to her."

"What do you mean?" I asked.

"It's funny. Honora started off thinking you and I would set the world on fire, but then you refused to go to college. So she concentrated on me, but all I cared about was nesting—staying home with Donald and the boys. I think that opened her eyes to you. She considers you an unconventional success, and I think she's prouder of that than if you were teaching at MIT."

"Oh, come on," I said.

"No, it's true. Even the bay profile—she thought that was wonderful. And the Swift Observatory! You've seen the way she feels about that."

"Maybe I'll go outside and throw the Frisbee around with Don and the boys," Nick said. They had a fluorescent Frisbee, bright enough to see on the darkest night. I knew he wanted to leave me and Clare alone, give us a sisterly interlude; although I appreciated that, I had begun to realize that he would have to leave for London tomorrow, and our time together could be measured in hours and minutes.

"Let him play," Clare told me, watching me watch him leave. "He's been sitting in offices a long time. He needs to move around."

"I was dying to tell you about the baby, but of course I had to wait for Nick. He came home the night I found out. Isn't that unbelievable?"

"You two send each other vibes—I've always said that."

"Too bad my vibes couldn't have kept him away until Mark left. That was unfortunate."

"Well, it's not your fault. You tried to cancel dinner with Mark. I nearly died when I looked out my window and stood you standing there with some guy. I hope you didn't mind me running over, but I had to take a look. He's cute. I can see how you might have swooned for a minute."

"Have you ever swooned for someone besides Donald?"

"Oh, sure. My obstetrician, for one. But nothing physical has ever happened between us. Except, of course, what you'd expect. But once I kissed Henry McPhee after a softball game. Of course I don't have your scruples, so it never seemed very serious to me."

"Did Donald find out?"

"I never told him. Lord, don't say you confessed to Nick—"

"I did."

Clare giggled. "You are too much. And he was destroyed, I suppose?"

"Yes," I said defensively.

Clare was laughing so hard she choked. I pounded her on the back, harder than necessary because she made me so mad. Always making light of my scruples. She whooped, trying to collect herself enough to say something.

"So now you're pregnant, and you're both hoping this baby will keep you together, save your marriage from foundering on that kiss. . . ." She went into another laughing fit.

"All right, enough is enough," I said, when she showed no signs of stopping. Then she kissed my forehead.

"Georgie, you're the only person I know who would have an affair to save your marriage," she said, trying to sound solemn but continuing to giggle. "For years you've been driving yourself crazy imagining that every woman is out to snare Nick into adultery. Finally your paranoia gets him so frustrated, he gives you an ultimatum and leaves for London. You're left alone. You develop an attraction to the first man you spend a little time alone with. You then tease yourself into a flirtation, which I humbly submit was one big test."

"What was I testing?"

"You were testing just how far you would let yourself go, because you thought it would show you how far Nick would let himself go."

"Do you think Nick has ever kissed anyone?" I asked sharply.

Clare shook her head. "That's not the point, and you know it. Didn't your little test teach you anything?"

"Yes," I said, thinking of the talk Nick and I had had in the car, feeling calm because I no longer feared Jean Snizort.

"Honey, this has liberated you," Clare said, pouring tonic water into two wine glasses, raising hers to toast. We clinked. I did feel liberated.

"If only Nick weren't leaving tomorrow, I'd feel perfect," I said.

"What time is his plane?"

"Seven at night."

"Donald told me Nick's a big cheese on the tender offer, that he's doing very well on it."

"That's the idea. This tender offer is a test for Nick, speaking of tests. But it'll be over Thursday, and he'll come home for good then. That's not such a long time to wait," I said.

"Nah, you can stand it. You guys planning to do natural childbirth?"

"I guess so. I thought everyone did it nowadays."

"Poor Mom, she told me she was knocked out for both our births. One of the most important events in a woman's life, and she isn't allowed to witness it."

"That's awful. I didn't know that."

"Those are the sort of confidences that made me feel closer to her after I had the boys. Maybe you dread her worrying, but you can look forward to long mother-daughter chats," Clare said.

"That sounds nice." Clare and I finished drying the dishes. We stacked the plates in Honora's neat cabinets. Pem shuffled into the kitchen, saw that we were there, and shuffled out. "In search of a sandwich," I said.

"Pem enjoyed herself tonight."

"She loved having us all together—I think she nearly forgot Honora."

"Thank heavens Honora has decided to keep Pem at home," Clare said. "It's the right decision, but it means a lot of work for you and me."

"We'll have to hire a full-time nurse, so someone is always available," I said. "Then you and I will do the rest. We have to make sure Honora isn't stressed."

"Exactly."

Hearing voices in the living room, we joined the men and Pem. Donald flipped the record; we did a little more dancing. Although it was nearly midnight, and the little boys were yawning constantly, no one wanted the evening to end. Even Pem joined in, dancing with each of us.

"I think Georgie and Nick want a little time alone," Clare said finally.

"Let's fly you to the airport tomorrow," Donald suggested. "I think the plane's free."

"That'd be great," Nick said. "Georgie's not supposed to drive, and I've been wondering how to break it to her that I don't want her taking me to the airport."

The Mackens stood at the door, taking stock of their possessions, making sure they had everything they had come with. A thermos, some Sinatra records, the fluorescent Frisbee. The telephone rang. Everyone froze. Who could be calling at midnight? The room sounded hollow as the phone rang and rang. Finally Nick answered. He said a few words and the color drained from his face. We all knew before he spoke.

"She just died," he said.

. . .

"We have to get to the hospital," I said, and no one argued with me. My sister and her husband, my husband and I went mad, hustling Pem and the children, who understood nothing, into the car. "Hurry up!" I said to Pem, who blocked the kitchen door.

"Where are we going?" she asked.

"To the hospital," I said, and that word terrorized her into silence and submission.

"It's a mistake—it must be a mistake," Clare said.

We filled Honora's station wagon, me and Nick in front, Pem and the small boys sleeping in back, Clare and Donald huddled together in the way back. Nick drove at breakneck speed. We wanted to confront Honora's doctor, the night nurse, anyone in charge. We all hoped that we would arrive to discover they had revived her, that she would be sitting up in her bed, a damp cloth across her forehead, grinning broadly, saying, "Whew, that was a close call."

No one spoke during that ride except to tell Nick to go faster. "Come on," Clare said, under her breath.

"He's going as fast as he can!" I cried, waking Casey, making him whimper.

Once I turned to look at Pem. Her head drooped. From the front seat it looked like a soft white ball, bobbing in time with the road. No one had thought to explain things to her, or perhaps no one dared. Suddenly she wakened, stared out the window at the Niantic Shell Station, a familiar point of reference, and dozed again.

I imagined Nick pulling into the hospital parking lot, stopping at the emergency room entrance. I knew the shortest route to Honora's room: we would tear past Admitting, up the doctors' elevator, down the West Wing to room 514. We could be standing at Honora's bedside in six minutes. We could scream at her doctor and maybe attack him, beat our breasts and wail, or, with the grace of God, we could hug Honora and scold her for scaring us. Nick slowed down for a red light, then sped through it. At the hospital zone's yellow flashers, he wheeled into the parking lot, tires screeching. He stopped the car beneath the emergency room's awning, amid ambulances awash in eerie sallow light. We stared at the open door where a police officer stood talking to a couple dressed in motorcycle leather.

Our upturned faces were green from the hospital light; beyond the awning, across the parking lot, we could see the West Wing curving out from the main building. Nick took his foot off the brake, and the car slid forward. We stopped in a dark spot away from the entrance. All of us leaned and craned for a look at the window we thought was Honora's. Yes, that was it, fourth from the end, up five flights. Even Pem gazed in its direction, noting the darkness, the peace, of the sleeping wing. Clare began to sob, and then Donald and Nick. I felt tears sliding down my own cheeks. I reached across the cold seat for Nick's hand. When I turned to look at Pem, I saw Clare's arms embracing her from behind. Pem's eyes were wide and puzzled. I hated us for what we had done to her that night.

"Where's your mother?" Pem asked.

My mother is dead, I thought, but said nothing.

"Do you think we can see her?" Nick asked.

"Yes, I want to," I said. "They have to let us see her."

Pem, Eugene and Casey sat very still, looking bewildered. "Come on, boys," Donald said, with a look at Clare. "I'll tell them," he mouthed. Holding their hands, he led his sons across the parking lot to a stone bench. Streetlight filtered through the trees; we could hear Donald's gentle voice telling about Honora.

"Pem," I said, turning in my seat to hold her hands. "It's awful—Honora died."

"How do you know that?" she asked sharply.

"Because the doctor called us. He said she died of a heart attack."

"Oh, no. Oh dear Lord. God bless Honora and Damon," Pem said. Tears slid down her wrinkled pink cheeks. Clare held her from behind. "You poor girls," Pem said, reaching forward to touch my cheek. "You poor girls without a mother or father."

"We're orphans." Clare wept, and the realization hit me like an icy wind.

"I'm going in," I said. Nick opened his door; he walked around the car to open mine.

"Pem and I will stay here," Clare said. She was heaving herself over the back seat to sit beside Pem. I left them there, Clare's arm around Pem's thin shoulders.

The walk between our car and Honora's hospital room seemed endless and terrifying, yet I felt calmer as it went on. Nick held my hand. "Are you okay?" he asked.

"No," I said.

"I know," Nick said. He left me at the elevator bank while he spoke to the security guard. The guard nodded, allowed us to pass. We took the elevator to the fifth floor and walked straight to Honora's room. The door was closed. We stood in the corridor for a second or two, and then I pushed it open.

Honora's bed was empty. The sheets had been taken away; the striped mattress was clean and bare. I walked to it. I put my hand on the spot where my mother had lain. That's where her head had rested; that's where she propped herself up on her elbows. I ran my hand over the mattress in search of indentations, but it was smooth.

A nurse I had often seen before stood at the door. "I'm so sorry," she said.

"Did she have pain?" Nick asked.

"It was a massive heart attack," the nurse said, and her expression left no doubt that there had been pain. "They've taken her body away. I'm sorry, but you can't see her right now."

Her body. "That's all right," I said. I felt numb.

The nurse left, and then I noticed the clippings. The newspaper clippings about the Swift Observatory were still taped to the wall. The ones Honora had been reading when she had her first heart attack. She had been so proud. Of me. I stared at them hanging over the bare bed, and the air moved. It was a gust so strong it might have been Honora's ghost flying by. It knocked me down. I sat hard on the floor, and I whispered her name.

I stared at the wheels of her bed, at the cuffs of Nick's pants. His arms came around me. "Put your head down," he was saying "Take deep breaths."

"I'm not going to faint," I said.

"It's the shock of seeing her bed empty," he said.

"We're never going to see her again," I said in the smallest voice possible. We stayed there for a long time, until we remembered the rest of the family waiting in the car. Then we walked out of Honora's hospital room, closed the door behind us, and took the elevator down.

Sixteen

Driving home to Black Hall I was thinking of Pem and Honora when Honora was a child. Every year they had traveled to Galway, to Granddamon's family home in Clifden. They had looked west across the Atlantic, to the spot they imagined to be Bennison Point. Honora, and Pem in her lucid days, had told me how they had held hands and promised each other they would be home soon. They had stood on the rugged coast of Connamara, thinking of their house on its rock in Connecticut. While Granddamon had smoked a pipe with his father and walked the hills with his brothers, Pem and Honora had dangled their feet in the North Atlantic consoling each other with tales of home.

None of us would sleep that night. In Honora's driveway Nick and Donald each lifted a drowsy child; Clare and I stood on either side of Pem, holding her elbows. She shuffled along the stone walk, head down. Clare and I exchanged tearful glances. Both of us choked, crossing the threshold, knowing Honora would never come home again. Donald took the boys to bed. We led Pem to the sofa.

"Maybe I'll get some brandy," Nick said, heading towards the kitchen.

"Where's your mother?" Pem asked.

"Pem," I said. "Don't you remember?" She put her hands over her ears, and Clare held them, easing them down. Her eyes were screwed tight. How often will we have to do this? I wondered. How often will we have to tell her Honora died?

"Don't you remember what happened?" I asked. My grandmother opened her eyes slowly, with caution, as though she feared seeing something perilous. They were bright and blue, and their sharpness shocked me.

"I remember," she said. I hugged her, and Clare wrapped her arms around us both.

Nick pried us apart, settled me in a chair. He handed me a glass of brandy. "I can't drink this. I'm pregnant," I said.

"Just a sip," he said.

I obliged because I thought I needed medicine. Pem downed her glass, then reached for mine. Before I could stop her she had swallowed it. "Let her," Clare said, watching me lurch. "We all need a good anesthetic."

Donald came into the room. "They want to see you," he said to Clare.

"Oh, I've dreaded telling them about death," Clare said.

"You don't really have to. They just want to see that you're all right," Donald said. He sprawled on the floor, his head on a big pillow. Nick passed him a glass.

"How did—" I began.

"They took it fine. I told them Honora had gone to heaven, that they would see her there someday. They can't understand that she won't be coming home from the hospital, but they accept it. Isn't that weird? Just because I'm their father, they believe me when I tell them something as bizarre as that."

"I know. Who can believe Honora won't be coming back here?" Nick asked. The room was full of her: her plaid blanket, the radio to which she listened daily for weather forecasts, the pictures she had hung, the rug she had hooked while pregnant with Clare. Pem held her head in one hand. Honora's spot on the sofa was vacant, and I stared at it, trying to conjure my mother. I saw her fingers curling elegantly around the brandy snifter; she was sitting on her feet to keep them warm. She was smiling her square smile, delighted we all were still in her living room at two in the morning. Only Pem troubled her. I saw that smile disappear when she looked across the sofa at Pem.

"They are such troopers," Clare said, rejoining us, shaking her head. "They just said, 'You must be sad, Mommy.'" The braveness of her boys made her strong. She sat beside Donald on the floor, her spine straight, her eyes dry.

"What about . . . a funeral?" Donald asked.

In one swift motion Pem unfolded herself, grabbed Donald's glass, and downed his brandy.

"Pem!" we all said, but she had already withdrawn, head in hand, eyes closed.

"Mother would want lovely music," Clare said. "She loves a lot of horns."

"She loves 'Ave Maria' when it's sung well," I said.

"She loves music in general," Nick said. "Did she ever play an instrument?"

"She took flute lessons when she was a little girl," I said. "Didn't she, Clare?"

Clare nodded, sniffling. "What do you do to plan a funeral? How do we let everyone know?"

"Well, we'll have to call a few people," Nick said. "And there will have to be a notice in the paper."

"Honora would want a wonderful obituary," I said, my throat so tight it hurt. "She loved being written about."

"I volunteer to write it," Donald said. "That is, unless you girls—"

"No, you write it," I said, touched that he would want to.

"Put in a lot about the family," Clare said. "About how much she loved us. Everyone thinks of her as a scientist and an actress, but you know—she spent all her time thinking about the family. Bossing us around and—loving us."

"Telling us what to do and how to feel," I said. "Honora: she always knew best. God, I can't believe this." I knew I was going to vomit. I rose, unsteadily, and walked towards the bathroom. Nick came to my side. Without speaking we left the room. The bathroom tile felt cold beneath my bare feet, and Nick held my hair while I was sick. Then he handed me a glass of water.

"I can't stand it," I said. "I can't believe Honora just died."

"Let's go to bed," he said.

"I'm not tired. I wish I was unconscious. I'd take a sleeping pill except—"

"The baby," Nick said, nodding. "I'm going to call your doctor and ask if it's okay."

"Nick, it's two in the morning."

"I don't care."

I looked at him, tall and dark and tired; I stared into his black eyes and beyond, at his back reflected in the bathroom mirror. Then I remembered London and his big tender offer. "London," I said, horrified. "You have to leave for London tonight."

Nick laughed. His eyes softened, and suddenly he looked as relaxed as a man on a picnic. "Of course I'm not going back to London tonight," he said.

But you'll miss your moment of glory, I thought. Jean will get all the credit. How will this affect your chances at the firm? But all I could do was rest my cheek against his chest and cry with relief.

"Did you really think I would leave you now?" he whispered. "I loved Honora too. Can you imagine I would just go back to work?"

A commotion jolted us apart. Breaking glass and a loud bang

sounded in the living room. We ran towards it, discovered Donald and Clare pulling Pem off the floor.

"She was reaching for Nick's glass," Clare explained. I leaned close to Pem, and she weaved, regarding me with liquid eyes.

"She's drunk," Donald said, sounding apologetic.

Donald and Nick hoisted Pem into their arms, carried her up to her bedroom.

"Up the golden stairs," Pem said.

They left me and Clare to get her undressed. She sprawled across the bed. Clare struggled to pull the dress over Pem's head while I untied her shoes. Her feet smelled damp. Clare made no progress. We reached under her dress to grab her arms, trying to pull them out of the sleeves.

"Let her sleep in her clothes," Clare suggested.

"We can't," I said. "I let her sleep in her dress once before, and she woke up confused, thinking it was daytime and she was just taking an afternoon nap. She refused to let me get back to sleep."

"Georgie, she's dead drunk. She'll sleep till noon."

"We have to get her into her nightgown."

"Oh, God," Clare said.

I'm not sure why it was so important that Pem was properly clad that night. Maybe I wanted her to have dignity on the night my mother died. Maybe dressing Pem, like driving to the hospital, gave form to chaos. It comforted me to wrestle with my grandmother, knowing that if I could free her arms, I could pull the dress over her head. We shook her like a rag doll.

Finally she was naked. "Jesus," Clare said softly, gazing at Pem's stringy body, the way I had when I had come upon Honora bathing her. I pulled a pink flannel nightgown from the top drawer. While I was sliding it over her head, Pem opened her eyes. She looked happy to see me.

"Hi, Pem," I said.

"Hail Mary, full of grace!" she exclaimed.

"Want to say your prayers?" I asked.

"Hail, Mary!" she said again.

"She thinks you're the Virgin Mary," Clare said softly, stupified.

"Holy Virgin, have mercy on my soul," Pem said.

"It's me—it's Georgie," I said.

Pem's eyes burned with fierce joy. She gripped my hand tightly. "Have mercy on me and all us sinners," she said.

Thinking it would be cruel to do otherwise, I sat beside her on her bed. The lamplight was dim and pink. "Sleep tight, my child," I said.

"Hail Mary, full of grace, the Lord is with thee," she said, staring at me.

"Thank you," I said.

"It has been four weeks since my last confession, these are my sins," she said. "I lied, I stole, I took the name of the Lord in vain."

"Georgie," Clare said nervously, uncomfortable with me hearing our grandmother's confession. But I was riveted in my role.

"I absolve you of your sins, my child," I said.

"Thank you, Mary," Pem said, closing her eyes. "Take care of Honora, who has gone to heaven."

"I will," I promised.

· · ·

The funeral was in the white chapel where Nick and I, Clare and Donald, and Honora and my father had been married. Standing in the middle of Black Hall, surrounded by waves of golden marsh grass, the chapel gleamed in the sun. We filed into the cool, dark chapel and we sat in the front row. Nick and Donald along with some of our neighbors carried in her coffin, plain oak. She's in there, I thought. I never did see my mother dead; she hadn't liked the idea of wakes. The priest, Father Clarke, walked onto the altar. He looked past our family, beyond the congregation, out the open doors in the back of the church. I imagined he was speaking directly to the Holy Spirit, bypassing the rest of us. Pem stared at the coffin. Once I looked over my shoulder and saw that the church was packed. There were Dr. Orion, Dr. Metcalf, Dr. Hawkins and others from Woods Hole, directors of the TV stations in New Bedford and New Haven, some Bennison cousins from Providence, the sons and daughters of the great-aunts and -uncles, clusters of young people I didn't know. Fans of Weather Woman? The obituary Donald had written had appeared in newspapers all around the country.

Father Clarke had a great mop of red hair. Honora had thought him a terrific young priest, handsome and intelligent. When it came time in the mass for the eulogy, he smiled directly at me and Clare and Pem.

"Honora Swift never came to me in the usual way," he said, and I knew he meant confession—Honora had a horror of going to confession. "But once in a while she'd pass by and ask if I'd like to take a walk. Who would turn down a walk with Honora? I've lived in Black Hall for five years, and she showed me things I never knew existed—like a beaver's dam on Gill River and the house of a lady who collects nuts and charges admission to see them. Everyone who knew Honora knows what I'm talking about. She was interested in everything.

"But nothing interested her so much as her family—her daughters. On these walks she would tell me about Georgie and Nick, Clare and Donald and Eugene and Casey. Every detail of their lives concerned her. From Georgie's bay profile to Clare's brownie recipe. 'Too sweet, Father,' she said to me one day. 'Clare should use bittersweet chocolate. And she needs more moisture. They're dry, Father—her brownies are dry.'"

I glanced at Clare, who had started to cry.

Father Clarke was going on about Honora, about her endless fascination with the family. Every anecdote was on the money—his stories were so vivid, he had conjured Honora then and there, at her own funeral. But I knew Clare's tears were caused not by the stories' content, but by the fact that stories were all we had left of our mother.

A gentle crossbreeze blew through the open doors and windows, but the sound of people fanning themselves with prayer books filled the church. Nick held my sweaty hand in his own. A brass section from the Hartt School played "Ave Maria," then "Galway Bay."

Back at the house we fed people we knew well and others we hardly knew at all. The neighbors came.

"Black Hall won't be the same without her," the librarian said.

Dr. Orion, now stooped and gray, held my hand and told me how Woods Hole had changed after we had moved away. "Your mother gave the place class," he said, and his apparent sincerity left me with my mouth open.

"She always said you considered her the Painted Lady of Meteorology," Clare accused.

Dr. Orion chuckled. "Some of us did, standing in our labs, watching her speed away in that black limousine. She was a pip, but she was a dedicated scientist."

At that, tears sprang to my eyes and Clare's.

"Thank you," we said.

John and Helen Avery had been talking to Nick. They made their way through the crowd to me. "We're so sorry," they said. "I remember my mother's funeral," Helen said, shaking her head. We stared into each other's eyes, remembering that dinner at my hotel. She wore a different caftan of black and orange.

"You were so young when your mother died," I said.

"It doesn't matter," Helen said. "It was hell for us, and it will be hell for you and your sister. A mother is a mother."

"I've told Nick to take some time off," John said. "Until you're ready to let him go. Jean has things under control in London."

"Oh," I said, wondering how Nick felt about that.

"You be brave," John said, giving me a big hug.

Aunt Kat's oldest son had put on weight. He stood with his arm around Pem, reminiscing with her about the old days, the many happy Fourths of July he had spent at Black Hall. She laughed, nodding her head, leaning into his soft body. He walked her across the room to me, tilted his head, said, "An era gone by," as if he had a lot of practice, knowing just what to say at funerals.

I nodded earnestly. "So true," I said.

"Who's the bird?" Pem asked, watching him head for the buffet table.

"That's John, Aunt Kat's son," Clare said. We hadn't seen him for years. Pem regarded him long and hard.

"He got hit with the ugly stick," she said.

"So true," Clare said.

"Will this be over soon?" I asked.

"Depends on how hungry they are," Clare replied. We watched people take bits of baked ham, potatoes *au gratin*, jellied salad. It seemed vaguely mysterious that they would accept our hospitality at a time like this, or that we would offer it. A hundred conversations filled the room. We heard the name "Honora" repeated thousands of times, even when they thought we weren't listening. Everyone admired the view from her windows, the architecture of our houses, the beauty of her daughters and grandsons, the pity of her mother's decline. Clare and I stood by the banister, taking it in. Pem leaned against the fireplace's cool stone. Donald was helping Eugene and Casey and some of the relatives' children fly a kite.

"I don't think that's too appropriate, do you?" Clare asked.

"Why not? They're little and bored. Remember how we felt at funerals?"

"I don't feel so different right now," Clare said.

"Neither do I," I said, checking my watch, wishing everyone would go. Clare went outside to help with the kite.

I nearly fainted when I looked up, and saw Mark Constable coming towards me. He clutched my hand. "I hope you don't mind," he said. "I saw it in the paper."

"No, I don't mind," I said, astonished because I had never expected to see him again.

"I'm sorry about your mother. I feel . . . I don't know, connected to her. She had her heart attack that day we were together in New York."

"She had another one," I said, not wanting Mark to feel too connected to anything as important as my mother's death.

"I'm going back to Lebanon after all," he said.

For an instant I felt the wild thrill of panic, the thought that I was driving him back to the war zone.

"They gave me a call, they need me there," he said, "and I'm ready to go."

I placed my hands on his shoulders, kissed his lips lightly. "Godspeed," I said, and he was gone.

Nick came to me from across the room. "He's leaving for Beirut," I said. Nick just slid his arm around my shoulders and nodded.

Funerals are a wonderful distraction. They are like giving a big party, only none of the guests expect much from the hosts except grief. You plan the service, choose the coffin, call the caterer, decide on the hymns. I looked around, wondering whether Honora would have approved of her funeral. She would have liked Father Clarke's eulogy, and the fact her old colleagues from Woods Hole had come. But mainly she'd be thinking of us—me and Clare. Worrying that it was too much strain for us. "Sweetie," she might have said to me, "just get it over with."

"Everyone wanted Pem to have a drink," Donald said after everyone had left.

"I think they thought I was mean, insisting she drink only juice and soda," Clare said, "but to hell with them. I couldn't stand another apparition of Georgie the Holy Mother."

"It's over," Nick said.

"Thank heavens it's over," I said.

But it was just beginning.

Seventeen

Honora was nowhere. Her body was planted in the cemetery bordered by the Gill and Laurel Rivers, the closest we could get her to the water. Her soul had gone to heaven, if you believed in heaven. But her spirit was gone from Bennison Point. She was absent from every conversation. Clare and I would be talking, and we would pause at places where Honora would have wanted to comment. One morning before dawn I wakened to thunder and lightning, and I worried because Honora wouldn't call to tell Nick not to fly.

"You can't fly today," I said, shaking him.

"Maybe the storm will pass," he mumbled, still asleep. An hour later, when his alarm rang, the sun shined brightly.

Every morning Nick and Donald chattered across the waves in the seaplane, waving at me and Clare standing in Honora's front yard. Together we walked to Honora's house, where Nick and I were staying, to fix breakfast for Pem and the boys. Then we would dress Pem, and Clare would go home to her house. One of us would phone, or we would run across the yards to visit, several times a day. I tried to pull together the pieces I had

been working on for the Swift Observatory, but I couldn't concentrate. I stopped thinking about my baby. All my energy went
into missing Honora. I tried to remember the things we had
talked about the last time I saw her. Clare and I compared
conversations we had had with her, excursions we had taken with
her. At night I lay awake feeling that once my life had been rich
and now it was poor.

I kissed Nick until he woke up. "Hold me," I said.

"What is it?" he asked kindly. He wasn't getting enough sleep
these nights, but I couldn't stop myself.

"I'm scared. I'm afraid of dying."

"We're not dying," he said.

"But we will someday."

There was nothing he could say to that, but I wouldn't let him
go back to sleep. I couldn't stop worrying. I began to worry with
a vengeance: about plane crashes, ptomaine, shark attacks, aneu-
rysms. Danger from without and danger from within the body;
Honora had been killed by her own heart. I thought of all the
terrible things she had feared. She had worried the family might
be torn apart by natural disaster or nuclear war. Didn't that mean
she feared death? I lay awake thinking of her last minutes alive,
much as I had thought of my father treading water in the North
Sea. Had she known what was happening to her? Had she been
afraid?

That week we had several dinners with the Mackens, as if we
were leery of letting one another out of sight. Pem poked listlessly
at her food. Once Eugene asked if we were sure Honora wasn't
coming back, and Clare snapped, "We're sure," making him cry.
Donald and Nick talked about their work. Nick was handling
his part of the London deal from New York. But how well could
he handle it? Everything familiar seemed to totter: Nick was
worrying about his work, Eugene and Casey were worried about
their mother's bad humor, everyone worried about Pem.

One night rain beat down on the roof and fogged the windows.

"She's not eating," I said after Pem left the table without saying a word. "Not even sandwiches."

"She's depressed," Nick said.

"Very depressed," Clare said. "I'm not sure she knows where she is or who we are. She doesn't respond at all."

At that, the four of us followed Pem into the living room, made her identify each of us. "You're Georgie, you're Clare, you're the boy, you're the boy," she said.

Satisfied, we returned to the table. "We'll have to do something about her soon," Nick said.

"Like what?" I asked. "Because if you're talking about a nursing home, forget it. Honora decided Pem would live here for the rest of her life. In fact, it was her last wish."

"Hey, don't talk to me like I'm your enemy," Nick said darkly.

"I'm sorry."

"We have everything under control," Clare said. "Georgie and I are sharing responsibilities, and we've arranged to hire a nurse."

"I'm looking forward to moving back into our own house," Nick said.

"I can't blame you for that, especially with the baby coming," Donald said.

"I'll always be so happy Honora was with me when I heard about the baby," I said, beginning to cry, my hand straying to my stomach.

"So will I," Nick said, smiling into my eyes.

"Mommy, Pem smells funny," Eugene called. Our noses twitching, we sniffed our way into the living room. Standing in front of Pem, Nick and Donald gagged. Everyone formed a wide circle around me, Clare and Pem. Horrified, they watched as we tilted her, examined her seat.

"Honora always dreaded this day," I said to Clare, feeling as though I might vomit.

"This is much worse than urination," Clare agreed. "I've changed many diapers, but it doesn't seem right to have to change my grandmother."

"Pem!" we shouted into her ear, rousing her from deep stupor.

"Huh?" she asked, startled.

"Come on." We led her to the bathroom. By now both Clare and I were choking on the smell. "Don't come into the kitchen," I warned the others; the idea of closing the bathroom door seemed impossible.

"Why couldn't this have happened before dinner?" Clare asked.

Pem had sat in her own excrement, and it covered her entire rump, her underpants, and parts of her dress.

"Burn these," Clare said, when we had gotten the clothes off.

"I didn't do that, I didn't do that," Pem protested. "Who put that there?"

"You did it—it's okay," Clare said.

"You're a goddamned liar," Pem said. "Oh, I'll smash you." She made a fist and wound up for the punch, but I grabbed her hand.

"Come on, get into the tub," I said.

"I am so fucking sick of seeing my grandmother's boobs," Clare said between her teeth.

"Shut up—you think I like it?" I said, straining to support Pem as we lowered her into the tub.

"You shut up! Can't I say what I think?"

"Oh, you're freezing me!" Pem cried.

Clare had one foot in the tub for purchase as she sprayed warm water on Pem's dirty back. "This is really vile," she said.

"Pem, we'll give you a martini when you get out," I said.

"That nurse better get here soon. Can she start tomorrow?"

"Monday," I said. "Can you imagine Mom doing this all alone? How could we have let her do it? No wonder she—"

"If you say 'No wonder she had a heart attack,' I'll kill you," Clare said, standing up straight, one foot still in the tub. She held the spray nozzle like a weapon. "I really will. We had no idea how bad Pem was because Mom didn't want us to know. If you hadn't walked in on that bath scene, we wouldn't have known until this minute. If she wanted help, she would have asked for it. But oh, no! Honora and Pem, the closed corporation."

"Clare, you bitch," I said. "If that's the way you feel, why don't you pack up and get out of the bathroom. I'll take care of Pem." I grabbed for the hose.

She sprayed it straight into my face. The hot water made me blink, and I reached out to slap my sister. Pem, enthralled by the fight, was splashing us with filthy water.

"Selfish pig!" Clare screeched. "You want to do everything yourself."

"You're just jealous because Honora told me about Mrs. Billings instead of you," I yelled, scratching her, trying to hurt her. She grabbed my hair and twisted until I screamed.

"Ouch!" Clare said, ducking to swat Pem. "She's pinching my ankle," she explained, and I joined forces with Clare to pry Pem's claw-fingers loose.

"What the hell—" Nick said, grabbing me. I saw Donald grab Clare and in one motion lift her away from the tub.

"Hee, hee," Pem laughed, as if she hadn't had so much fun in months.

Nick and Donald gagged from the stench, both spellbound by the naked Pem.

"What are we doing here?" Donald asked, but he helped fill the tub with clean water.

When Pem was clean, powdered, and dry, we put her to bed. Then Clare, Nick, Donald and I took a cleansing swim. Although it was September and the air chilly with falling rain, the water was as warm as it had been all summer.

"Clare, I'm sorry," I said, breathless with amazement at all that had happened.

"Me too." We kissed, bobbing underwater for a second. "I think I went crazy. It hit me, giving Pem that bath. I'm just so sad. About Honora, about Pem too. It's just so sad."

"It's so sad," I said, and then the four of us were silent, treading water in the bay of Bennison Point that drizzly September night.

. . .

"She's a tyrant," Clare said of the nurse. "A regular Tartar." We were sitting at Honora's kitchen table, drinking coffee while the nurse dressed Pem upstairs. This distracted me from Nick's work troubles. The tender offer had wound up, as predicted, on Thursday; Jean, not Nick, had handled the closing and attended the closing dinner. While Nick was in New York, tying up the tender offer's loose ends and going to meetings for a new deal, Clare and I had charge of training the nurse.

"I twig your lay," I said, nodding my head. "She certainly makes herself right at home, doesn't she?"

Glumly we surveyed the changes she had made to the kitchen: photos of her family, total strangers to us, were attached to the refrigerator. Cartons of her favorite granola, her favorite pretzels, her favorite spaghetti cluttered the counters. When I had summoned my courage and asked her to please put them out of sight, she had said leaving them out made her feel at home. Most hideous of all, she called Pem "Shortcake."

"She's not even a registered nurse," Clare said. "She's not qualified to give injections, administer medication, anything like that."

"Clare, Pem isn't sick. She doesn't need medication."

"But we're paying all that money."

"Imagine the alternative—" Pem in a home.

We heard them descending the stairs. Loretta Bryant, tall with a blond bun and a jutting lower jaw, dressed in a snug sea-green uniform, preceded Pem into the kitchen. Pem followed like a sullen child. When she caught sight of me and Clare, she stuck out her tongue at Loretta's back.

"Good morning, ladies," Loretta sang to the tune of "Good Night, Ladies."

"Good morning," we chirped back, trying not to laugh.

"Let's see. Hot cereal, buttered toast, some nice orange juice—how does that sound, Shortcake?"

Pem shrugged, settling herself at the breakfast table. White salve covered the sores on her scalp. Loretta's unfortunate manner notwithstanding, she was taking good care of our grandmother.

Loretta bustled around for a few minutes before I noticed her lips were pinched. She kept glancing at me, as if she had something to say. Finally she stopped, her hands on her broad hips. "I understand that the family wants to spend time with the old ones," she said, "but I have to do my job."

"You mean we're in your way?" Clare asked.

Loretta nodded. "Don't get me wrong, but I have a job to do. My job is to make sure your grandmother gets her nourishment, and she eats better with you out of the room."

"We're going," I said as soon as I caught Clare's huffy expression.

"This is a real intrusion," Clare said, when we were out of earshot.

"No kidding, but it's working. I'm glad to let Loretta take the heat for a while." Slowly I had begun to reorganize my Swift Observatory files; Loretta's presence enabled me to work.

Clare's eyes filled with tears. "It galls me, it really does, to see her treat Pem with such indignity."

"I know. Me, too," I said. But I was so relieved to have help, I was willing to overlook it.

"I'd better get home," Clare said. "Casey's having a tough time at nursery school, and I want to make him some peanut butter cookies."

"Remember how Honora always made us cookies?" I asked.

That stopped Clare in her tracks; she turned to catch my grin. Honora had never been famous for her cookie-making. Clare smiled back, then walked out the door.

My new report was called "Death in the Family." I wanted to explore all aspects of how death affected the loved ones left behind. Honora's writing table had become my desk; I traced my fingers across its smooth, lacquered surface, then turned to the articles I had clipped from newspapers. I had pieces on war widows, orphans, parents whose children die young, adults who lose siblings. My only criterion was that the family connection be close and loving. Reading the articles, I had to feel the loss.

I sat there for a long time, my hand gripping the receiver, but I could not dial. How quickly I had phoned Mona Tuchman, Caroline Orne; how cavalier I had been about loss and suffering! It had been something to be studied, dissected like a dead frog. Of course I had felt sympathy for the victims, but it had been sympathy of a mild, analytical sort. Now I read and reread the articles about people who loved people who had died, and I felt too sad to call them.

Impulsively I dialed Mona Tuchman's number.

"Hello?" she said.

"Hi, it's Georgie Swift," I said.

"I read about your mother. I'm sorry," she said.

"I've been thinking about you," I said. "I've been feeling guilty about not calling you back after your last call."

"Why should you feel guilty?" she asked sharply.

"I—I don't know," I said, taken aback by her tone.

"You certainly have no responsibility to me," she said, more softly. "I did see those excerpts from our interview in the *Times*. You know, the article about the Swift Observatory?"

"Yes, I know."

"I liked the way I came off. You made me sound real, like

myself. Not like some of the other interviews. I'd read them and wonder who the bimbo was."

"We liked each other," I said. "I don't have the same connection with other people I talk to."

"Still hooked on infidelity?" she asked, giving a harsh laugh.

"No," I said truthfully. "How are you? What's been happening?"

"Dick and Celeste are going to give it a try," she said. "That's the big news. Me, I'm free as long as I stay in counseling. Counseling helps."

"I'm glad."

"The kids live with Dick. I've lost my kids, but right now I don't feel that I deserve them." Her voice sounded bitter; I wondered whether the counseling would force her to feel bitter before allowing her freedom. No wonder the court had spared her from prison—prison would have been redundant.

"I hope you get them back."

"Yes, well—listen, I'd better go. Thank you for calling."

"You're welcome," I said. Neither of us mentioned calling or meeting again, and I hung up thinking of Honora, of how, during our last time alone, she had asked about Mona Tuchman.

For the next hour I paged through news stories, looking for possible topics. I found many possible subjects for "Death in the Family," but no one I could bring myself to call. Then I looked around the room: at Pem sitting on the sofa and Honora's empty spot, at Loretta crocheting an afghan, at the teak table where the Mackens and the Swifts and Pem Bennison convened without Honora to dine every night, and I knew that the Swift Observatory was about to turn its gaze homeward.

Eighteen

That night I heard the seaplane coming home, and I stepped outside. The rising moon rode low in the sky; it seemed to light the plane from beneath. Loretta stood at the kitchen window.

"I don't care what you say," she said. "It's not good for the old ones to eat late."

"She wants to eat with the family," I said, keeping my eyes on the plane.

"Feed her at five o'clock, then let her have dessert or a bowl of cereal with the family. Ten o'clock at night! This is no time for a ninety-year-old woman to be having her dinner."

I suspected Loretta's real problem was that she had been eyeing the leg of lamb, resented having to wait so long to be offered a slice. She had been grumbling for days about our eating habits. Nick stepped onto the stone jetty, and I went to meet him.

"What a moon!" he said, giving me a kiss. I recalled the last full moon, the night our problems had surfaced. Honora had still been alive then. The tides wash in and the tides wash out. Were we any happier? We took our time walking back to the house.

"The Mackens aren't joining us tonight?" Nick asked.

"Casey has a little cold, and Clare thought they should stay home."

"I'm just as glad. I'm getting a little tired of the togetherness scene."

"It does get trying," I said, not wholeheartedly.

"How's the den mother tonight?" Nick asked. He meant Loretta, and I smiled.

"Put out by our dinner hour."

"Will anyone suffer unduly if it's a little later?" Nick asked, leading me onto the porch. We sat on the glider. I started it rocking, then tucked my feet beneath me.

"Tell me," I said.

"I want to go home," he said.

"This isn't home? It's practically home."

"Why can't we move into our own house?"

"Because Pem is used to this place. She's been through so many changes—Honora dying, Loretta coming to live with us. Just imagine how frightened she must be by the changes in her own head. She's very confused, and I'm afraid to move her."

"Then let her stay here with Loretta. You and I will be right next door—we'll see her every day."

I shook my head. "I don't think—"

"It's not fair to subject her to our routine. I agree with Loretta about that. When Honora was alive, Pem ate at seven o'clock every night. Tonight she'll eat at ten, last night it was nine-fifteen, tomorrow it could be midnight."

"She needs the family around."

"Georgie, you're being stubborn. You know I'm right."

"I do not," I said, but the idea of going home alone with Nick held me like a magnet.

"We're having a baby," Nick said, grinning. He put his hand on my stomach. I felt his thumb circle my belly button, newly protruding. "When I least expect to—it will hit me—you're pregnant with my baby. Does it ever just knock you out when you've practically forgotten about it?"

"At this point it's not something I forget about," I said, resting my head on Nick's shoulder. I couldn't stop smiling.

We walked into the house. Pem brightened when she saw Nick.

"How about a martini?" he asked.

"Make it a good one!" she said.

"The old ones shouldn't drink," Loretta said.

"It's not a real martini," I assured her.

Nick, Pem, and I sat at the dining table; Loretta preferred to eat alone in the kitchen, a preference for which I was grateful. Pem had not mentioned Honora since the funeral. Gazing across the table at her that night, I wondered about the ease with which she had accepted the transition. Perhaps she was so grateful to be with the family, she feared that any show of strong emotions might jeopardize her position. Or perhaps she didn't notice.

"Did Jean get all the credit for the tender offer?" I asked Nick.

Nick grinned. "It's great you've taken my advice—instead of worrying she's after me, you're worried she's after my job."

"It's a fair question," I said.

"No, she didn't get credit. I put the deal together, the client knows about Honora. Everything's okay, Georgie."

"I'm sorry anyway."

"For what?"

"For—I don't know, the timing of everything. You had to miss the closing."

"The timing of Honora's death?" he asked, and I felt my throat close and choke. He held my hand. "There was no good time for that. I still can't believe it. It hits me once in a while during the day. I'll be concentrating on work, and then I think of Honora."

We all lay down our forks, and tears slid down Pem's big nose. "We miss her, don't we, Pem?" I asked.

"I miss her very, very much," Pem answered.

I thought of the natural course of events, of how, in Pem's family, people lived to be very old, then died, then their children lived to be very old, then died. Honora had broken that chain. Pem had outlived her own daughter. Perhaps Granddamon's genes had short-circuited. I sat there feeling sad I would not get to nurse my mother through her old age, feeling too young to nurse my grandmother through her old age. Then I thought of the Swift Observatory, of how I wanted to give everyone in my family the chance to speak.

I rushed from the dining table to Honora's writing table and back again with my tape recorder.

"I want you to talk about Honora," I explained to Nick and Pem. "I'm not going to ask any questions. Just talk into the machine and say what's on your mind."

"What's the machine?" Pem asked, suspicious.

"A tape recorder." Was it possible she had never used one? I told her to sing "Do Re Mi" into the microphone, and then I played it back for her. "That's your voice," I said.

"It is not," Pem said; she refused to believe me. So Nick said a few words, then I sang "Jingle Bells," and we played it back. She remained unconvinced.

"Will you do me a favor?" I asked. "Even if you don't believe me, will you talk for a little while?"

"Not into that," she said, her arms folded across her chest. Loretta came through the door just then. She examined Pem's plate.

"That's a naughty plate, Shortcake," she said, casting a meaningful glance at me. "What did I tell you about their eating habits? No old person will eat a decent meal this late at night."

"Maybe you're right," I said. "Tomorrow you can feed her at seven."

"Five."

"Five's fine," Nick said quickly, grabbing my wrist. "Come on—let's go onto the porch and I'll talk into the machine."

I let him go alone while I stayed inside to help Loretta put Pem to bed. When I play back Nick's tape today, I hear the waves splashing the rocks in front of Honora's house. The tide had swelled under the full moon, so the waves were unusually full and soft. The wind rustled the porch screens, and a whippoorwill sang in a far-off marsh.

· · ·

NICHOLAS GABRIEL SYMONDS

"When people get married, the woman usually takes the man's name. But for a long time after I married Georgie, I felt as though I had become a Swift. This was a family of women, strong women, and they were used to each other and to having their own way. Once I had a dream they were witches, brewing spells in a cauldron to make men do what they wanted them to. In my dream, Honora was the head witch, and she was in life, too. But the thing was, the spells worked; I loved Georgie, and I loved the other women in her family, and I wanted more than anything for them to love me.

"My mother was jealous of the Swifts. She was always used to us kids coming home for holidays, not even considering going anyplace else. No one ever went to Florida for spring break, or to a girlfriend's for Christmas. But after I met Georgie, I never wanted to go home. Georgie thinks she was sneaky, arranging ways for us to spend holidays at Black Hall, but that was exactly what I wanted. There's a rhythm here that seduces you. Everyone's afraid of whether it can continue without Honora, and I am too. That's why we're all so skittish, not giving each other much peace or distance. I wonder whether there will be a power struggle between Georgie and Clare, because everyone is so used to having one dominant Swift.

"Georgie is the watcher. She'll be a wonderful mother, but totally different from Honora. We all love Honora so much, no one wants to say she wasn't the perfect mother. She made those girls dependent. Don and I too, in a way, but that was our choice. Georgie tells me about when she was small, sitting at the head of the stairs, listening for her parents to start a quarrel. I asked her, 'You mean, you heard them fighting and you listened?' 'No,' she said, 'I was waiting for them to start.' That is what I mean by 'dependent.' In a way, Georgie's watchfulness nearly came between us. When I left for London, I didn't know what I'd come home to; for a while I thought I couldn't continue to live here. I only knew Georgie had to change. I couldn't take the suspicions and hints, and I have the feeling Honora was behind a lot of it. I could almost hear her whispering in Georgie's ear, 'Don't trust men.'

"Sometimes in the plane Don and I joke, saying someday this place will be called 'Macken Point' or 'Symonds Point,' but of course it won't. When I'm fifty-five I'll walk into Poole's Hardware, and the guy behind the counter will say, 'Here comes Honora's son-in-law.' On the other hand, they said of Honora, 'Here comes Damon Bennison's daughter.'

"Damon must have been a willful character. In his pictures, his profile is even stronger than Pem's. I'll never know how he got Pem and Honora off this peninsula for a visit to Ireland every summer. Though I will say this: when one of the Bennison or Swift women falls in love, she means it. That's why I wonder about Timothy. Everyone thinks Honora got tired of him, outgrew him, but I'll never believe that. He hurt her so badly, having that affair, that she never forgave him and she never forgave men.

"I wish Honora could know our baby. Georgie was so funny, suggesting names. Bennison and Letitia. Didn't it ever occur to her that I might want to use a Symonds family name? Of course it did. But she thought she'd present her names so surely that I'd accept them at once. I did. I love her family names. But I know Georgie, and she'll suffer for it. She'll feel guilty for conning me. I'm telling you now, Georgie, don't. The names are fine. I'd suggest Honora, myself, only there can't ever be another Honora. At least, not on this Point."

· · ·

Pem set the house on fire. One morning I left Loretta to fix breakfast and do a little laundry while I took a swim. When I returned, Pem stood alone in the kitchen, beside a flaming toaster, shaking the burning sleeve of her robe.

"I'm afire!" she called when she saw me. "Ooh, ooh, I'm afire!" Flames licked the length of her sleeve, and her wild thrashing spread some to the voile curtains.

I threw her to the floor, rolled her in the rug, then flung her over my shoulder and carried her outside like a sack of grain. "Help, fire!" I yelled. Honora's smoke detectors clanged from all quarters. When I unrolled Pem, her sleeve no longer burned, but I smelled scorched skin and fabric. "Stay here," I commanded, and she sat on the grass, still, facing the burning kitchen.

Clare came running with a garden hose. "I called the fire department," she called. "They're on their way."

"Loretta's inside," I said. Smoke billowed out the front door.

"No, she's at my house, doing laundry. She said Honora's machine isn't big enough for Pem's sheets."

We heard the sirens far off. Clare directed the drizzle at the kitchen window; with her thumb partly covering the nozzle, she forced a bit of pressure. I stared at Honora's house, the silvery shingles already stained black with smoke, and tried not to weep. Then I turned to Pem. She was examining her extended arm. It appeared red, mildly blistered, but miraculously not burned.

"We should put some ice on this," she said, ignoring the fire.

"That's a good idea," I said. The red hook and ladder truck stopped in the road, unable to fit through Honora's gate. The men in black rubber coats and fire hats tore up the driveway, dragging monstrous hoses that they pointed at the fire.

"How'd it start?" asked one of the firemen, but years of marriage to lawyers had taught me and Clare to never blurt out information to officials.

"Electrical fire," I said simply, in case that would affect their methods of controlling it.

"Can you save the house?" Clare pleaded.

"We'll do our best."

Neighbors, summoned by the smoke and sirens, ran into the yard with buckets and wet blankets. They spread the blankets across bushes. "Thank heavens there's no wind," Mrs. Tobin said. "But if it picks up, you girls will want to spray water on your own houses, to keep them from catching."

Loretta stood near the edge of the crowd. Clare and I saw her at the same time. We left Mrs. Tobin in charge of Pem, then stalked over to Loretta.

"Where the hell were you?" I asked.

"I only left for five minutes, just to throw the laundry in Mrs. Macken's machine." She cowered, and I felt almost sorry for her. "Your grandmother already had her breakfast, and I left her in a nice sunny spot in the living room, watching you swim around that rock."

"Loretta, I told you she forgets whether she had breakfast or not—that's why I hired you, to watch her when I leave the house. Thanks to you, Pem set herself on fire."

Loretta's lower jaw gathered strength and jutted with full force. "Excuse me, lady, but don't accuse me of that. This is the hardest job I've ever taken, and I've taken hard jobs. You want a maid, cook, babysitter, and nurse all rolled into one body. Last night your grandmother soiled her sheets for about the twentieth time since I came to this house, and I was just taking them across the way to wash them at your sister's. Don't go accusing me of anything."

"She's sorry. Aren't you sorry, Georgie?" Clare asked.

But I was watching Honora's kitchen turn into a charred skeleton. The sturdy frame was now splindly and black, like an evil charcoal forest. Although the fire was out, billows and tendrils of smoke continued to pour through holes that had once been walls. I thought of the mornings Clare, Honora and I had sat in that kitchen, wondering whether the plane had landed safely in New York. I thought of the family meals we had cooked, of the cakes we had baked. I thought of Honora's gallery of finger paintings, now ash.

"It's just the kitchen, Georgie," Clare said. "It's not the whole house." She squeezed my hand.

"Loretta," I said. "You're fired."

"And good riddance!" Loretta said. Somewhat hysterically, I thought. I was aware that we were paying her more than the going rate. "You won't find anyone to do what I did, not even if you pay dollars more an hour. And the person I feel sorriest for is your grandmother, the way you force her to eat at all hours, give her liquor when it's terrible on her system. I might consider reporting you."

"Let her go," Clare demanded when I started to follow Loretta. "Why did you fire her? What are we going to do about Pem?"

"First of all, I'm going to take her to the doctor. Then she can stay in my house. Nick's been wanting to move home anyway."

"I think he meant you and him, not the whole entourage," Clare said. "Come on—I'll drive with you to Dr. Cooke's."

The firemen reported extensive smoke damage, but told us the house would stand. They wanted to stay, to make sure the fire was out. Dr. Cooke's office stood high on a hill, overlooking Black Hall and the mouth of the Connecticut River. I refused to look towards Bennison Point. I didn't want to see plumes of smoke.

Dr. Cooke treated and bandaged Pem's arm. Then he gave her a complete physical and pronounced her in excellent health. "It's a shame about your mother," he told us.

"You never saw any sign of a heart problem?" Clare asked. Dr. Cooke had been Pem and Honora's doctor for many years.

"It's a mystery. She had a little high blood pressure once in a while. I never treated it because it always went away."

"Really?" we asked. She had never told us about it.

"Why don't I check yours, while you're here?" he suggested, and although he was neither Clare's doctor nor mine, we eagerly accepted his offer.

"Hmmm," he said, loosening the cuff on my arm. "Yours is a tad elevated."

"Oh, no. . . ."

"Are you pregnant by any chance? Because high blood pressure can sometimes occur during pregnancy. But I'd have it watched by your doctor."

"I will," I promised.

Clare and I were silent in the car on the way home.

"Can you believe Honora had high blood pressure and didn't tell anyone?" she asked after a few miles.

"No. It gets me so mad."

"I'm going to drive you to the doctor myself," she said.

"The doctor says it's not uncommon during pregnancy."

"Still."

"I promise to take care of it. Will you drop me and Pem at my house? I'm a little tired. I want to take a nap."

"That's definitely common during pregnancy. The desire to sleep constantly." She glanced at me. "It must have been awful, seeing Pem on fire like that."

"It was." I couldn't get the image out of my mind, the gentle curls of flame creeping along her sleeve.

"Listen, you go to sleep, and I'll take Pem. And I'll take your tape recorder and do my part for the Swift Observatory."

"Thanks, Clare," I said. I'd been asking her for days, and that was the first time she'd agreed to do it.

. . .

CLARE SWIFT MACKEN

"Georgie, this feels too anonymous, talking with no one here. We're not used to that, are we? There's always someone here. Remember how we always wanted to share a room, even though we could have had rooms of our own? Everyone thought we were crazy. Eugene and Casey would die if they had to share a room.

"So, Mom's dead. Honora's dead. That's what I'm supposed to talk about. You told me you wanted to hear all my reactions to her death. Why don't I feel anything? I'm too self-conscious doing this. Let's just say I'm really sad.

"Let's see. I'll tell you this—you made her very proud. She loved the Swift Observatory. That's why I'm doing this, recording this message. It's for the greater glory of something Honora cared about, in memory of her. Some mornings we'd all be sitting at her kitchen table, the three of us, and you'd excuse yourself, to hurry home and wait for Nick to call. Honora always applauded that—she thought you were an exemplary wife. But sooner or later we'd get around to talking about your work. First the bay profile, later the Observatory. She'd say, 'Sweetie, with all these degrees between us, why can't we come up with something that interesting to do?' She was afraid I was bored, which I never was. I think she was, though. After 'Weather Woman' went off the air, and she became a real homebody, I think she wanted something more.

"She kept trying to convince me to show my work, or to go into biochemical research. She was endlessly passing me clippings about classmates of mine who had made it big. The big giveaway was always 'Donald will find you more interesting if you pursue your career.' Look where it got her and Dad!

"She was great when I found out about Donald, though. God, I wish I could see your face right now. Yes, Georgie, Donald had an affair. A big one, too, not some cute little kiss after lunch one day. Six years ago he had a six-month affair with someone from his office. They were in love. They wanted to open their own firm. Mom told me, 'Give him the heave-ho, you don't need a bastard like that.' I was ready to do it, too. I always wondered why you never noticed. I think it's because you didn't want to see my marriage breaking up. You'd see me crying and ask me what was wrong, and I'd say I had my period. That year I had my period forty-one times, and you never noticed. Mom and I talked all the time. After I kicked Donald out, he wanted to come home. I wasn't going to let him. But Mom had a long talk with him and convinced me he meant business. He wanted me and the boys, and that was that. 'Forgive but never forget' is what Mom said. At first I thought that would be impossible, but I found out it wasn't.

"I know how you must have felt seeing Pem burning today, because I saw Honora having her first heart attack. At least you could do something—roll Pem up in that rug and put out the fire. I couldn't do anything. Just drive Honora to the hospital. I was so afraid she would die. I sat in the waiting room, saying my prayers, wishing someone was with me. I felt terrible in that waiting room. You were in New York, giving those interviews, and I was so furious with you. I thought Honora was dying of pride for you. Because her last act before the heart attack was to drive all over the state in search of fifty copies of your interview.

"Isn't it strange, the way we've always thought we'd live to be a hundred because of Pem's people? Name one who died younger than ninety. I hate myself, but I almost cried today when the doctor told us Pem was in good health. What's going to happen to her? Her mind is already gone. She's worse than a retarded child. At least nature makes a place for retarded children. But what about an old lady whose body has outlived her mind? No one wants her. I don't, and I don't think you do either. I love her, but I don't want her anymore.

"I don't know. I dream of Honora every night, and I keep wishing she'd give me a message about Pem. She refuses. Last night she came out of the sea, draped in seaweed. She looked beautiful. She glowed with bioluminescense. The kelp was brown and shining, luxurious. The other seaweed, I can't remember its name, was green like lettuce. 'We need to have a chat, my dear dearie,' she said. 'Things have changed, or haven't you noticed?' When I woke up I wondered whether she was trying to tell me something about Pem, but it wasn't clear.

"She was a good mother. *Is* a good mother—just because she died, she doesn't stop being our mother. But I'll tell you, Georgie: I'm not sure she'd approve of what we're trying to do with Pem. Taking care of Pem was Honora's job, and I'm not sure she'd want us to do it as well as she did."

. . .

Nick and I moved Pem into our house, and he told me not to let her alone for a minute. All her clothes and many of ours reeked of smoke. Every day I hung more on the line to flutter in the wind, but nothing made the smell go away.

"Let's go home," she kept saying, so often I thought I would strike her.

"We *are* home," I would answer, my teeth clenched. "Honora's house caught on fire, remember?" I never reminded her of how it had started.

The Avery Foundation continued to send me correspondence generated by my interviews. The piece in *Vanguard* had appeared, accompanied by Mark's photo of me. In the end, the editor had chosen one of the traffic scenes, with a bus barreling at me from one direction and a taxi from the other. There I stood, cool as a model in a wind tunnel, loving the moment.

One weekend John and Helen were passing Black Hall on their way to Watch Hill, and we invited them for lunch. It was a brilliant day. The Averys and I sat on the porch, watching the waves, while Nick was inside, taking a call from a client. I felt nervous; I hadn't yet told them about my new plans for the Swift Observatory.

"Great spot," John said. "No wonder Nick's willing to do that crazy commute." His gaze kept sliding to the living room door; we could hear Nick speaking to the client. Perfect timing, I thought—for once, with John here, I was glad for Nick to get a business call at home.

"Have you been able to work, Georgie?" Helen asked. "Or is it still too soon?"

"Well, as a matter of fact, I do have a new idea," I said, clearing my throat. "I know you want me to travel, to expand my focus. I'm afraid what I have in mind is the opposite—I'm turning inward in a way. I'm interviewing my family."

Helen gasped. "But that's courageous!" she said.

"Do you think so?" I asked.

"Of course. It's much more difficult to put your family under scrutiny. It's a challenge to be objective, and you need to be."

"That's true," I said, thinking of Clare's recording. I didn't know how to approach her; her revelation about Donald made me shy away from her. With a subject more distant, like Mona or Caroline, I would have probed. With Clare I felt frozen.

"You must know I've wanted you to go farther afield," John said. "I voted in favor of increasing your grant to promote travel. Still, this idea interests me."

"We trust your instincts, Georgie," Helen said. "Take your ideas where you find them."

John was so obviously leaning towards the door, trying to listen to Nick, I laughed. John tilted his head. "That's my client on the phone to Nick. My client, and he's calling Nick Symonds."

"You've got to pass the baton sometime," Helen said.

"Let's not hear a lecture about growing old gracefully," John snapped, so harshly I felt startled. I had never thought of it from John's angle, with young men like Nick moving in on their work, their clients. Helen sat very straight, her mouth set in a thin line.

Nick stepped onto the porch. "Claude wants to know if this is the Black Hall branch of Hubbard, Starr. He'd like to speak to you, John."

John nodded and went inside to take the call. Helen relaxed. "I've got to learn when to keep my mouth shut," she said. "I guarantee he'll give me the silent treatment until we get to Watch Hill." But I was thinking of Nick, of how he had saved the lunch by asking John to come to the phone.

. . .

The recording done by Clare gave me pause. As the Swift Observer, I had to treat it as an artifact, as evidence, as the thoughts of a person who had recently suffered loss. She had spoken freely; I considered that an invitation to ask more questions, but I was afraid to. Of what I might hear? I avoided Clare all that weekend, and then she came to find me. I stood in the kitchen, washing dishes, when she walked in.

"I spill my guts and you give me the cold shoulder? Is that right?" she asked. "No questions? Not even a sympathetic pat on the back?" She appeared frazzled, maybe three pounds heavier than she had been on Friday.

"I didn't know what to say," I said.

"God, I feel nervous," Clare said. She sat down at my kitchen table. "I put away a pint of rum raisin before I had the nerve to come over. What did you think of what I told you?"

"I've been thinking about Donald. How could he have done that to you?"

"We've never figured it out. Even he doesn't know. He says he's never stopped loving me—but he loved her too."

"Were things . . . bad between you before it happened?" I asked, wanting the answer to be "Yes."

"Not that I could tell. A little duller than at the beginning of our marriage. It was a big shock."

"I never knew. I never suspected. Donald!"

"I was so unhappy. Georgie, now you know why I get so pissed at you for those affair-attacks you have about Nick. Why borrow trouble that way? Some days I listen to you talk about that Jean Snizort, or some other imaginary lover, and I feel like hitting you."

"I don't blame you. Nick feels like it too. But I'm training myself to stop." I watched Clare move the salt and pepper shakers around the table, like skaters doing figure-eights. "Honora was a brick during that time?"

"Completely. She was great."

"That's strange," I said. "Because when Nick went to London without me, she drove me nuts with that motherly concern of hers. It made me really wish for privacy."

Clare laughed. "Privacy? In this family? I won't say it doesn't exist, but . . . we don't keep secrets from each other for long. Look at me—I'm practically letting the Swift Observer read my diary."

"The Swift Observer had a hard enough time deciding whether she wanted to read it or not," I said, smiling at Clare. Leaning towards her. Giving her a hug.

. . .

A new nurse arrived, and everyone liked her better than Loretta. Beth Wilton had shoulder-length red hair; she wore bright sweaters over her uniform. Pem seemed mezmerized by the colors, like a child looking into a kaleidoscope. Beth dressed Pem every morning, then supervised her breakfast. She told me she wouldn't bathe Pem or wash her clothes; I would have to do it myself or hire a different aide.

"This is getting really expensive," Nick said.

"It's Pem's money," I said. "It should be spent to keep her in her home."

"Except this is our home," Nick said, although he agreed with me in principle. He worried about the amount of time I spent caring for Pem. "Go shopping with Clare for baby things," he said one day. I did go, only to please him. But to my surprise, the shopping was fun, and Clare and I had a long lunch. We talked about being pregnant; she told me about the births of Eugene and Casey. For once, we both forgot about Pem.

But not for long. Often I would find Pem asleep or crying. She never read or watched television; she hardly ever looked out the window.

"Isn't it gorgeous out?" I said one day.

"We have a beautiful view at our house," she said, thumbing her nose at my window, even though the view was essentially the same as the one from Honora's. I had given up trying to get her to record her thoughts. She feared the tape recorder. She hated to think a plastic box could hold her voice inside, then let it out when someone pushed a button.

One night when we were at dinner, I cornered Donald in the pantry. "Clare told me," I said.

"She told me she told you," he said, standing taller, as if preparing for a fight.

"You love her?" I asked.

"More than anything," he said. I stood aside to let him pass. And Donald and I never mentioned the topic again.

After dinner Donald asked me to bring him the tape recorder.

"Don't let him do that," Pem begged, watching him lift the microphone.

"This is Donald Macken reporting from Black Hall. Pem, will you tell us which three steamers used to leave the dock in Providence for Newport?" She shook her head, one finger held against her lips. "You know, the ones that used to be jammed if you weren't there by nine o'clock?" Again she shook her head. "Then I'll tell you. They were the *Nina*, the *Pinta*, and the *Queen Elizabeth*."

"The *Santa Maria*," Pem said, scoffing.

"Aha!" Donald said. When he played the tape back, Pem was grinning.

.   .   .

DONALD DESMOND MACKEN

"Pem always loved to play tricks, so she appreciates it when someone plays one on her. I have two little boys, and I'd be in deep shit if they raised half the hell their great-grandmother did. That's what's sad to see; Pem was so sharp when I married Clare. Nick didn't know her when she was all there; she had started her big decline before Georgie met him. Pem directed our wedding. She had it all planned, exactly like Honora's: where to have the ceremony, where to hold the reception, where to buy the wedding cake, which silver pattern to order from Lux, Bond. Clare and I didn't care. We just wanted to get married.

"It's probably Alzheimer's Disease. I wonder why no one has tried hard to get it diagnosed? We've always called it senility. Honora especially—it hurt her terribly when Pem turned ornery and forgetful, but she must have been relieved to take over as head of the Point. When I joined the family, she was really under Pem's thumb.

"Honora. Aren't the dinners different without her? She was comical, the way she played the worrier, and she knew it. She played it up. She knew if she got everyone pegging her as The Worrier, she could harass us with impunity. Those predawn phone calls of hers used to drive me crazy. You know, she worried, but she never played The Worrier until after Pem started to go. I think Georgie is destined to step into that role.

"I remember when Georgie brought Nick home for the first time. They had met in Washington, I guess, when he was still in law school and she was working for that pawnbroker. She used to go to the ends of the earth to get a weird job, and Nick was the first decent guy she brought home. Of course I instantly saw a fellow lawyer, someone I wouldn't mind having around here. An ally in this House of Bennison. The first night we met him, Clare told me Georgie was going to marry him. I asked her if Georgie had said so, and she said no, she just knew. That's the way those sisters are—tight as tight.

"After they got married, I could tell Honora really liked him. She'd play up to him, trying to get him to laugh at her jokes or, I don't know—get him to ask her about her early days when she was making it big as a meteorologist. She must have thought I was jealous because one day she said to me, 'I love you both like sons, but you'll always be first.' That meant a lot to me, and I've never known why.

"I think of Honora as a stable influence on the Point. The rest of us might rock the boat, but not Honora. All of us want her on our side. Isn't that true? Who would want to displease her? I remember once she acted very disgusted with me, and I couldn't stand it. She gave me the feeling I was rocking the boat, making it tip, and she made me sit down and steady it. That's it. She likes things to move on an even keel. If I could pass anything of Honora on to Eugene and Casey, it would be that. Go ahead and rock the boat, but carefully, and know when to sit down."

Nineteen

They say when someone is dying they can relive their entire lives in a matter of minutes. I wondered whether Honora had had time for that. Had she lain in her bed watching the ghosts of people and events play before her eyes? Or had she died before they had had the chance? Had her pain lasted long? I found myself spending time, when I should have been answering correspondence, reliving my own life, as if I hoped to cheat sudden death by having already run through my memories. One afternoon, sprawled in a sunny patch on the floor, knitting yellow booties, I was struck by what a homebody I was. I had gone from being a shrinking violet afraid to leave home, to a rebel who searched the world for, as Donald had said, weird jobs, back to being a homebody again.

For a period Honora and I had fought all the time. She had been shocked when I hadn't wanted to go to college.

"My daughters have to go to college," she had said, as if it were that simple, case closed. Dutifully I acquired and completed application forms. I went on interviews, often accompanied by Honora who would coach me on what to say, then pump me afterwards for a sense of how I had impressed the interviewer. We had many pleasant lunches in the college towns of Massachusetts, New York, and Vermont.

After receiving my acceptances on April 15, I enrolled at Wellesley. For the first time in my life I had nametapes to iron into my clothes. I subscribed to a linen service that picked up my dirty sheets and towels every Monday and left clean ones. My mother gave me a season's ticket to the Visiting Orchestra series. She and Pem drove me up to Boston in September, and I was home the second weekend of October.

"I'm not going back," I said. "I've always hated school, and that was before you were paying thousands of dollars a semester for it."

"The money doesn't matter," Honora said. "We've saved for your education since you were a baby." Her fingers twitched, probably itching to strangle me. "Do you want to see a counselor? Would that help?"

"I want to work."

She emitted a gutteral howl, as if someone had murdered one of her children; in a perverse way, I guess someone had.

"Mom, it's not so indecent. Not everyone goes to college." But of course everyone did; the only people my age who didn't go to college were either severely disturbed or dishwashers.

"You'll never get a good job. And I'm not thinking of tomorrow—I'm thinking ten years down the road. Do you want to waste your life in an office, typing someone else's work? Are you out to get married, meet some guy who will support you and expect you to cook his dinners and have his babies? Georgie, you are in for the shock of your life."

"I don't need a college degree to succeed."

Her breath was coming quick and shallow. "You'll do it on

your own. You're not going to live at home, supported by me, while you waste your life."

That came as a mild shock, and I took it as fighting words. "Fine. You want to kick me out of the house?"

"Yes. See how you do on your own."

I turned towards my room, to throw a few things into my knapsack and hit the road before dark, and she threw a lamp at me. It struck the small of my back. Then she tackled me, and I realized I was running into my room with my mother riding piggyback. "Get off, get off," I shrieked, but I couldn't shake her.

"Are you taking drugs? It is some boy?" she cried.

I wiggled out of her grasp. I ran out the front door, past Pem, who passed me a handful of dollars, and I didn't come home for six months.

I visited Clare at Radcliffe, where she was doing a dual major in biochemistry and studio art. She let me spend the night in her room. "You realize of course that Mom is terrified by the idea of a daughter ill-equipped to be anything but the best," she said. "She maintains that is the way to avoid domination."

"Right. Only she is allowed to dominate us."

Clare laughed, then went back to working up her lab report. She lied when Honora called to ask if she had seen me. The next morning she lent me a hundred dollars. I kissed her, then hitchhiked to New Bedford where I got a job on a scallop boat.

I went to sea with men, shucking scallops. We would spend a week on Georges Bank, dredging for sea scallops. It was the most degrading job I could find. In retrospect, I wonder why I was trying to punish myself. I would lie in my bunk, enduring rude comments like, "If it smells like fish, eat it." They rustled my curtains; in a way that sickens me now, I mildly enjoyed it. The men called me their mascot. I fell for a bearded sailor on a different scallop boat, then quit going to sea, to stay in his house and cook for him. Just as Honora had predicted.

One day I met Professor Arthur, someone my parents had known at Woods Hole, buying live bait on the wharf. I was so happy to see a familiar face, I told him the circumstances of my life. He rescued me, leaving his minnows on the counter, as urgently as if he were saving a kidnap victim. He took me to Woods Hole where I lived with him and his wife and worked as Dr. Nage's research assistant. We were studying wave heights in the Bermuda Triangle. On one of our cruises into the Atlantic, the scent of danger and mystery spelled romance for me and Dr. Nage. Soon afterwards, I fled Woods Hole.

My quest for, as Donald says, "weird jobs," lasted years and took me to Mad River Glen, where I worked as a chairlift attendant; Salem, Massachusetts, where I directed a children's theater; Ozone Park, New York, where I worked the afternoon shift in a soup kitchen. The letters I wrote home managed to convince Honora that interesting, if not high-paying, work existed without university degrees. I was developing a love for observation. All of those jobs were preparing me for the Swift Observatory, but only one was preparing me for Nick.

I stood behind the counter at the Brer Rabbit Pawnshop on the north side of Dupont Circle. I was surrounded by dusty astrolabes, brass bookends, a Queen Anne highboy, leatherbound volumes of Shelley. Under the glass counter sat gold pocket watches, diamond earrings, WWII medals, and antique cameos. Mr. Big, as the shop owner referred to himself, had stepped out for coffee and a corn muffin. Although I had been hired to dust and answer the phone, he sometimes left me in charge of the shop, telling me to "Stall the sellers as long as possible." This shop was an observer's dream. I watched the sad faces of people who parted with family treasures, the greedy faces of thieves who fenced their goods to Mr. Big. Families whose houses had been robbed would arrive, asking whether anyone had recently sold a Seth Thomas steeple clock or a pair of silver candlesticks. This was the sleazy fringe of breaking and entering; I felt guilty by association, but I was too mesmerized to quit.

One day Nick walked in. He wore a tan trenchcoat; his black eyes flashed. He looked like a private eye. From the moment he entered, he was casing the merchandise. If he hadn't been so fantastically handsome, I might have been afraid he was about to rob me.

"May I help you?" I asked.

"Yes, please. Do you have any diamond earrings for sale? I'd like to buy my girlfriend a birthday present."

I whisked my feather duster along the glass tabletop. "If you don't mind waiting, I'm sure the owner will be back in a minute."

"Don't you work here?"

"Yes, but I'm just the cleaning lady." He peered at me through the raven curls falling across his eyes. If he was trying to assess me, this is what he saw: a pale face, dark hair in a pixie cut, white blouse with lace collar. Mr. Big had recently told me to quit dressing like a librarian, but that was my style and I was stuck with it.

"When's he coming back?" Nick asked, leaning forward.

"I don't know," I said, catching his excitement.

"Then we don't have much time." He explained to me that his girlfriend's apartment on Capitol Hill had been robbed, that he was spending that afternoon away from his incredibly demanding legal studies, looking for her diamond earrings. He described them to me. I told him I never saw the merchandise until it appeared in the glass cases. "Are they here?" I asked.

"I don't see them," he said. "Listen, I've got to get home to study Torts. If you happen to see some diamond earrings with little pearls dangling from them, will you call me?"

"Sure," I said, thinking how in love he must be to spend his valuable time chasing after his girlfriend's baubles, how clever he was to set me up as a watchdog for them.

The earrings appeared the following Friday. I called the number he had given me. I had half-expected a girl to answer, but Nick did. "They're here," I said.

"Be right there."

Hours passed. Finally Mr. Big told me he was going out for some tea and toast; the minute he left, Nick rushed in.

"I've been sitting in the park, waiting for him to leave," Nick explained. He held up his Criminal Procedure book and grinned, letting me know his brain hadn't been idle. I showed him the earrings; he said they were Allie's.

"The case is locked," I said. "Mr. Big keeps the key on him."

"Shit. I can't afford to buy them back. How much do you think they cost?" We tried to read the little white tag. Mr. Big always attached tags to the jewels, but tucked them underneath where no one could possibly read them.

"I'm going to do what a woman must do, but this means quitting my job," I said. I broke the glass with a brass bookend, grabbed the earrings, and ran out the back door with Nick close behind. We took the endless escalator into the Dupont Circle Metro station, and lost ourselves in the crowd.

Nick was beaming with admiration. "I can't believe you just did that. It was fantastic. You wound up, you broke the glass, just like that. What's your name?"

"Georgie Swift."

"What made you work for a creep like that in the first place?"

"It was interesting," I said, wondering what I was going to do next. I couldn't go back to the place I had been staying, because Mr. Big had the address. I had heard about the leg-breaking techniques of shysters like him.

"I'd like to take you out to dinner," Nick said. "Please—it's the least I could do."

I felt so disappointed. This great romantic hero who would risk his legal studies for his true love, was inviting me out for dinner. But not so disappointed I wouldn't accept. "What about Allie?" I asked.

"She's busy tonight. In fact, she's out of town."

"Oh. Okay," I said.

We dined at the Foundry, a canal-side place in Georgetown full of hanging plants and pale wood, every law student's idea of the perfect restaurant. I wore the same clothes I had been wearing all day, since I could never again return to the fleabag I shared with two waitresses. Nick had changed into a gray tweed jacket and yellow wool tie. He ordered the wine with grace. He seemed not to notice the way my eyes darted from side to side, watching out for Mr. Big or his henchmen.

"That was a lovely thing you did, searching for Allie's earrings," I said.

"She'll be happy to get them back."

"Have you been together long?"

"Since our sophomore year at college."

"Oh." I calculated—four years. They must be very serious.

"But we're not exactly 'together' anymore. We still care for each other, but we see other people. In fact. . . ." He explained that he had fallen out of love with her, then felt guilty about it since his enrollment in law school had motivated her to move to Washington. "She felt so terrible when her apartment was robbed. She told me it was my fault, luring her here. She accused me of convincing her we'd be together for the rest of our lives, then leaving her."

"Did you do that?"

"No. I did think we would get married—I thought I wanted that. But then I found out we're very different in the real world than we were at college. She likes parties every night, getting dressed up in pretty dresses and diamond earrings, meeting new people and dancing till midnight. She's very bored with me because I have to study all the time." Nick stared intently at a wild philodendron hanging just beside my head. "The sad thing is, I like to study. I can't see myself turning into a socialite the minute I finish law school. She keeps trying to convince me I'll change, that the circumstances of my life are constraining right now, that I'll see things differently later. But I don't think I will. Once I told her I'd rather talk than dance, and she laughed."

"But if you're breaking up with her, why did you go looking for her earrings?"

"She looks pretty in those earrings. She loves them. I'm not really sure why."

"Where is she now?"

"In New York, looking for an apartment."

Oh," I said. Then he asked me about my life, and I told him about Honora, Pem, Clare, and Donald, then about my string of weird jobs, which made him laugh. He paid the check, and we went for a slow walk along the canal. In a dark spot beneath a willow tree he pointed at the water.

"I just saw a fish jump," he said. We stared for a few seconds at the whirl of concentric rings, and then he leaned down to kiss me. I fell in love during that kiss. We slept together that night and, with few and necessary exceptions, we have slept together every night since.

"I'm mad about him," Honora said the first night I brought him home, which was also the night I asked him to marry me.

"What's his name again?" Pem asked, already starting to slip.

"Nicholas Symonds."

"He has a first-rate mind," Honora said, glowing. "I've never met a lawyer who can talk the way he does about Blake's metaphysics."

I smiled; I had told Nick that Honora was notorious for testing Clare's and my boyfriends by asking them about Blake's metaphysics. Donald had failed the test, but Honora had embraced him anyway.

"Did you see how he polished off his lunch?" Pem asked. "I like a boy who likes to eat."

For their own reasons, Honora and Pem had loved Nick from the start, and he had loved them. If he could discuss Blake with Honora, he could just as easily discuss the Providence Steamrollers with Pem. And he could discuss anything with me.

One night Pem was walking from her bedroom to the bathroom when she tripped on a braided rug and sprained her ankle. The next morning was Saturday; Nick and I drove her to Dr. Cooke's. The doctor's expression seemed stern as he wrapped the bandage around her foot and up her black-and-blue leg. He checked her burned arm, pronounced it healed. Then he asked her to sit in the waiting room, under the watchful eye of his nurse, while he talked to Nick and me.

"This can't go on. You must see that," he said. "It's time to put Pem in a nursing home."

"No," I said.

"Yes," Dr. Cooke said. "What will be next? Will she succeed in lighting herself on fire? Will she drive you two so crazy you'll start to hate her? Don't think it can't happen—I've seen old people whose families have loved them forever, then start to neglect them horribly because they just can't stand the responsibility anymore."

"We have a nurse."

"One nurse needs to sleep at night. At nursing homes they have shifts, where someone is always on duty. Have you ever looked at Sussex Gardens? Or Steamboat Landing?" He named two rest homes on the same road in Sussex, a stretch to which my family had always referred as "Convalescent Promenade." Old people were always hobbling or being pushed in wheelchairs down the road.

"No, I can't say I've ever visited those places," I said pleasantly, glaring at Nick, wanting his help. He sat there with his hands folded, looking straight ahead. I noticed three gray hairs behind his ear.

"Georgie," Dr. Cooke said. "I know your mother intended to keep Pem at home. That was admirable and understandable. They're mother and daughter. They've lived together for years. But you and Nick shouldn't bear the burden. You're starting your own family. Free yourself."

"I don't want to free myself," I said bitterly, starting to cry. Free myself? From what? Did I want to put my grandmother away, bury her as deep as Honora? I imagined her sitting in a rest home, surrounded by other old people, the hum of air conditioning, the stink of urine.

"I do," Nick said quietly.

My eyes flicked: traitor!

Dr. Cooke was writing on a pad. "These are the names and addresses of three good places. I sit on the board of the first, and I'm on the staff of all three. I'll phone ahead, to tell them you're coming for a look."

"Don't waste your time," I said.

"Thank you," Nick said.

We rode home in silence. Pem sat in back, gazing out the window. Had the landscape of Black Hall changed much since she and Granddamon had bought the property? She had told us about the men who had delivered fish, ice, and vegetables in their wagons. I tried to imagine our car as a horse and buggy, failed, turned on the radio.

Beth had Pem's lunch ready when we got home. Nick and I took sandwiches outside to a shady spot near the rock jetty. Ever since seeing Dr. Cooke I had felt mad at Nick, but now I rested my head on his shoulder. Across the bay the Mackens were climbing into their daysailer. We had called to tell them what Dr. Cooke thought; they agreed with him. Clare waved to us; Nick waved back. The boat tossed as everyone took their places. Then Donald hoisted the white sail; it luffed, then filled, and the boat took off on a starboard reach.

"You know it's the right thing to do," Nick said.

"You mean loving you?" I asked, humming a little of Carly Simon's song, stalling for time.

"I mean putting Pem in a rest home. It's not fair to her, keeping her with us. She could injure herself very seriously," he said, giving me the chance to be noble and at the same time deny the real reason.

"Nick," I said, "when we put her in the rest home it won't be for her sake—it will be for ours." I felt so sleepy, I could hardly keep my eyes open. Nick stretched out his legs so I could lay my head in his lap. He covered me with his sweater. I fell asleep, and I dreamed of sweet things, of a warm summer day full of the sounds of children playing, of blue sky and fair weather clouds, of me and Nick pushing our baby around the bay in a white inner tube.

.   .   .

"And here's the dining room, and here's the TV room," the administrator of Steamboat Landing was saying. "We have special events every afternoon: bingo, travelogues, reading groups. . . ."

"Isn't it cruel to have travelogues when they'll never travel again?" I asked, thinking of places Pem had gone with Grand-damon: Ireland, Rio de Janeiro, Paris, Cuba, Venice.

"Some of them enjoy reliving their memories," the adminis-trator said. "Others enjoy seeing places they've never visited."

"Oh," I said. The place gleamed, just like Honora's hospital room. I heard Nick asking whether she could spend weekends and holidays with the family, whether she would have a room-mate, whether she could have a choice at dinner. The answers seemed reasonable and positive. The place overlooked a perfect green lawn and a harbor beyond. It was neither better nor worse than I had imagined. It smelled of urine. The nurses were pleas-ant. I hated it.

"Come on, let's go," I said.

"We do have a space available; she could be admitted right away," the administrator said. "Space at Steamboat Landing is very tight, but Dr. Cooke said to consider your grandmother an emergency." The administrator was squat and round. His belt circled his body at its exact midpoint. He smiled happily. "It's a hard decision," he said, knowing we would make it wisely.

"Can we talk it over?" Nick asked.

"Certainly," the administrator said, taking a giant step in the opposite direction.

"It's fine," I said.

"We haven't seen the others," Nick said.

"I can't take seeing any more. Sign the papers and let's get out of here," I said, wondering, if I couldn't take seeing any more nursing homes, how Pem could take living in one.

"You can bring her anytime after noon tomorrow," the ad-ministrator said after Nick told him "Yes." "Give us a list of her preferences, and we'll see that she's taken care of."

Our ride home was bleak. There was nothing to say. The day was clear as only a sunny September day can be. Wedding bells tolled for a couple standing on the sidewalk leading to the chapel where Nick and I had been married, but I heard the death knell and thought of Honora's funeral. I felt as though I had just made an appointment to have a beloved dog put to sleep.

"What do you want to have for dinner?" Nick asked.

"I don't care," I said.

"This is going to be a special dinner," Nick said. "I want it to be."

"Nick, it's too sad—let's not commemorate it any more than we have to."

At home I called Clare, to tell her the news and to invite her, Donald, and the boys for dinner. Pem was napping; I felt glad, because I didn't want to see her again. I wished I could fall asleep, wake up, have someone tell me it was taken care of. Nick paid Beth. "You're doing the right thing," she said, but there were tears in her eyes. "We had to put my grandmother in a home," she said. "Everyone hated it. It was the worst thing we've ever had to do. It takes real courage."

Her words hardened my heart. They made bile rise in my gorge. Beth Wilton's statement symbolized the reason Honora had prided herself on keeping Pem at home. No one ever claims it is easy to send an old person to a home. The heart of the person most eager to be free of an incontinent mother or a senile father aches when the time comes to send them away. We had seen it happen to Aunt Kat's son, Aunt Gert's daughters. Did the fact that they had sent their parents to nursing homes mean they loved them less? Of course not. Did the fact that Honora had kept Pem at home mean she loved Pem more? Honora thought so, and so had we.

Nick said he would cook dinner that night. I took a walk far out the peninsula and sat with my feet in the water. The sun was setting earlier every day. I looked across the Sound, at the water tower on Plum Island. It glowed like fire for that instant; then the sun set a little more, and the water tower was just dull metal. I thought of what Clare had said to the Swift Observer, of how Honora wouldn't want us taking as good care of Pem as she had. It was true. I knew it. She would sacrifice Pem to the nursing home, just so Clare and I wouldn't take her place in Pem's affections. It turned into a big conspiracy in my mind. Sitting there, looking across the water, I was counting Honora's manipulations, her wily ways of keeping each of us for herself so that she got the best of us and others in the family got what was left over. God, I longed to confront her. If the cemetery were nearer, I would have kicked her gravestone.

"Hi," Clare said, startling me.

"Hi."

"Nick told me you were out here. He and the guys are having a big game of fluorescent Frisbee, and Pem is home base."

"Don't tell me that. I don't want tonight to turn into one long, poignant goodbye."

"Don't you think that's inevitable? This is very hard."

"Wait till you see the home. It reeks of sincerity. 'Oh, we'll take such good care of your loved one—by the way, what's her name?'"

"Does she know she's going?" Clare asked.

"Not yet. I don't want her to worry all night. I'll tell her tomorrow morning. Nick's taking the day off to help me."

"I'll help too. I have to admit, it came as a big shock when you called me today. I didn't even know Pem had sprained her ankle. You should have called me before you went to Dr. Cooke."

"Well, I didn't think it would turn into such a big thing. He practically railroaded us into visiting the home. Are we doing the right thing, Clare?"

"Yes," she said. Then she laughed a little, and I laughed too. "'Are we doing the right thing?'" she asked in a Providence accent, and I knew she was imitating one of the great-aunt's children.

"Won't it be a barrel full of monkeys without her here?" I asked. "Just think of the fun things we can do—go shopping in Hartford at a moment's notice, plan a dinner party without worrying if Pem's going to say something embarrassing. . . ."

"Just like when Honora was alive," Clare said.

Then it had been really perfect. The family had been together, and Honora had had responsibility for Pem. The rest of us had simply enjoyed her company. Her company, I now knew, was a great deal easier to take when one was in it for only an hour or two a day.

"Dinner!" Nick called, his strong voice carrying across the bay.

"Come on," Clare said, and we walked home holding hands.

Candles flickered in the breeze blowing through the open windows. A platter of summer's last corn sat on the table. Smoke from the grill wafted in. "Can we please have some light?" Pem asked, gazing pointedly at the lamp hanging above the table.

"We have candles, Pem," Nick said.

"I like to see what I'm eating," she said. She took her second ear of corn.

"We love corn, don't we, Euge?" Casey said, nudging his brother.

"Yeah."

"Aunt Georgie, can we talk on the tape recorder?" Casey asked. "Mommy said you'd let us."

"Sorry," Clare said, grinning.

"Of course," I said, even though I hadn't thought of it before. The idea gave me the chance to escape; I could be the Swift Observer instead of Georgiana. I could view the scene with detatchment. My eyes could view Pem coolly, instead of filled with tears. She ate her corn with such gusto, butter dripping down her chin. Would they serve her corn at Steamboat Landing? Would it be native, just-picked that same day? I looked around the table. Nick had moved his chair closer to Pem's, to fill the space where Honora's place had been. Soon Clare would have to move in from the other side, to fill the space where Pem now sat. In a year they could push apart again, to make room for the baby's high chair. I had to look away.

·   ·   ·

EUGENE SWIFT MACKEN &
CLARENCE BENNISON MACKEN

"We have so many grandparents we don't know! And we're almost sick of hearing stories about them. Because it's weird to hear stories about people you know were real but you're never going to meet. Like our grandfather who drowned in the sea, and our great-great-grandfather who was an Indian, our grandmother who lived in China when she was little. She was Daddy's mommy. We don't visit any of Daddy's relatives.

"At the beginning of summer we saw an octopus. Granny saw it too. It had eight tentacles that moved around a lot, and she said it wouldn't eat us. We miss Granny. She got mad on the Fourth of July. The fireworks were long and red."

·   ·   ·

"I was born in the land of Uncle Sam, the good old U.S.A.!" Pem sang at the mention of the Fourth of July.

"Pem loves the Fourth," Donald said.

"Maybe we should clear the table," I said. "Thank you very much for recording your message," I said to Eugene and Casey.

"Is it going to go on the radio?" Eugene asked.

"No," I said.

"How come Pem is the only one who won't talk?" Eugene asked.

"Give me that thing," Pem said, and she grabbed the microphone. She stared at it long and hard, as if it were an ice cream cone she wanted to eat. Finally Nick held it, and Pem began to talk.

· · ·

PENITANCE ISABEL BENNISON

"I shall tell you the story of my life. I was born in the land of
Uncle Sam, the good old U.S.A. We lived in Providence, Rhode
Island. I worked at the hosiery when I was a girl, and I loved
to go to Aunt Florence's, at Silver Lake. She had a big basement
kitchen with windows that went all the length of the house. And
a window seat! We used to put on our skates in the kitchen, then
walk right out on the ice. Could my aunts skate! My aunts could
do anything on skates. They did the Grapevine, the Covered
Bridge, even the Vienna Waltz. We would eat hot apple pie in
the snow. And then, you know, the Grand Trunk Railroad bought
up all those places out by the lake. They filled in the lake, and
they never even went through. That was such a shame. I never
forgot that. My aunts had a basement kitchen with windows that
ran all the length of the house . . .

"I hated school, but I won a reading medal. Gert was jealous
and she was hitting me, so I put a bean in her ear, and the doctor
had to take it out her nose. She was a pain in the neck. All the
contestants had to read in front of all the principals of every
school in Providence, and I was the one they chose. I had malaria
then, and every other day I threw up. The only way I could feel
better was to put my cheek on the cool grass. I was too sick to
go to school, but I had to go anyway.

"I had my ninth birthday on the boat from England. No, that
was Ma. I must have had my ninth birthday in Providence. When
I married Damon, he took me to Connecticut. Everyone said to
me, 'Oh, you'll never like Connecticut,' but I did! Everyone in
Connecticut was nice to me! We had such lovely neighbors. I
can't remember who they were, but they were lovely. I had a
daughter, Honora. I remember her, all right!

"One of our neighbors, Martha Tobin, was a pain in the neck.
She had all the money in the world, and do you think she'd have

anyone to her house? She was always coming over for a meal. She was a chiseler. Oh, Lord, we'd see her coming through the gate every night at seven o'clock. Honora would never pull the shades or pretend we weren't home. Martha Tobin was one pain in the neck, and Father Lavery was another. Martha Tobin always thought her view was so wonderful. She thought she had the nicest view in Black Hall.

"You know, so many people say to me, 'Where can you see Long Island Sound from your house?' And they're looking right at it! It's funny.

"So many people say to me, 'What do you do to your brows?' It's funny! My hair turned gray when I was only thirty years old, but my brows stayed dark. They don't believe you; they call you a liar. I had Honora when I was only twenty-seven years old. Honora was my only daughter. And you're her daughters. Clare and Georgie. Georgie, porgie, pudding and pie . . . heh, heh.

"Honora was a good daughter. I miss her very, very much. When you have a daughter, so many people say to you, 'Oh, don't you wish you had a son?' But I never did. I only wanted Honora. She had straight brown hair, and when she was very young, she learned to play the piano. Do, re, mi, fa, so, la, ti, do . . . she could play the Vienna Waltz, all our favorite songs. She loved school. Sometimes I'd ask her if she didn't have a little sore throat, something that would make her stay home from school, but she always wanted to go. She was a very neat girl. Her bookcovers were as neat as could be. ABCDEFGHIJKLMNOP . . . P for Penitance!

"Damon and I were very proud when she became the weather girl. We couldn't see her on our set here, so we would drive to Providence, where they could pick up the New Bedford station. 'Wendy Swift'—that was her stage name. Wendy Swift. She had two little girls, and you are those little girls. Your grandfather would smash anyone who asked him if we wished you were boys.

"I can't believe Damon is gone, and I can't believe Honora is gone. Every night I pray for them. I love them very, very much. I'm the old grandmother, alone with her granddaughters and grandsons and great-grandsons, and I love you all very, very much."

Twenty-one

Pem was old. That was her only problem. That night I lay awake making magical arrangements: if only Pem were ten years younger. If only Honora was alive. The rest of us could stay the same. Nick slept beside me. His gentle breathing was as rhythmic as the waves. My hand moved under the white sheet, came to rest on my belly. I felt crazed with sorcery, prepared to deal with the fates: my baby in return for the Point as it had been at the beginning of summer.

What if Rumpelstiltskin had confronted me in June, said, "Give me your firstborn, and I'll let you keep Pem and Honora"? I pictured him humpbacked and hook-nosed: Pem in disguise. With a Providence accent and a leather jerkin, a whalebone walking stick, and a bag of fool's gold, he was waiting for my answer. After I told him no, he let me roll over and go to sleep.

· · ·

Pem sat very still as Clare and I told her she had to go live at Steamboat Landing.

"You've been hurting yourself, Pem," I said. "They'll take better care of you there."

Her lips tight, she shook her head. Her white hair was proud and wild, and looking through it to her scaly scalp, I felt relieved that I wouldn't have to touch it again.

"It's true," Clare said. "And of course you can come home on weekends and for vacations. You'll have people around all the time—you'll make a lot of nice friends."

"Dr. Cooke will be there. You like Dr. Cooke, don't you?" I asked, but Pem refused to answer. She was giving us the silent treatment. All that morning she sat on the sofa, refusing to look me or Clare in the eyes. We were her betrayers. Sobs choked me every time I passed her, so I avoided the living room.

The afternoon was brilliant and windy; September 21, the first day of autumn. I packed Pem's bag while Clare marked her clothes with an indelible marker. I used a cheap vinyl suitcase, one no one would miss if it were stolen. Beth had told me thefts were common in nursing homes. I packed Pem's pajamas, her dresses, her toothbrush, some lipstick, and pictures of Honora, Timothy, Clare, Donald, Eugene, Casey, Nick, me, Granddamon and Pem at their wedding, Granddamon in his Navy uniform, the great-aunts and -uncles on our porch one Fourth of July, and a family photo Nick had taken with the timer last Christmas.

"I can't go," Clare said when the time came to leave. She stood in my kitchen, leaning against the refrigerator. Pem sat at the table, wearing her winter coat, lipstick, and amethyst earrings. Clare's eyes focused on her, and tears ran down her cheeks. I held my sister tight.

"That's all right," I said into her ear. "You don't have to." I could afford to be generous; I had Nick with me.

Nick entered the room. He wore a business suit; he had just shined his wingtips. Perhaps he thought his respectable appearance would work in Pem's favor, make the staff realize she had responsible people looking out for her. "Come on, Pem," he said, holding out his hand. She ignored it.

"Pem, don't leave like this," Clare sobbed. "You know we love you. This is terrible for us—"

"Clare," Nick warned. We had agreed we would stay calm in front of Pem; we hadn't wanted to upset her even more. But Pem seemed not to notice Clare's tears. She walked towards the door, head held high. She did not shuffle. She moved as though transported by air currents.

"Take my arm and call me Charlie," Nick said, slipping his arm through mine.

As we drove away I watched Pem, to see whether she would cast farewell glances at Honora's house or her own, at the bay, at the stone gateposts, but she did not. She stared straight ahead. The drive to Steamboat Landing passed quickly, with Nick trying to distract me with talk about John Avery and a tender offer for shares of some movie studio. It must have worked, because what I remember about that ride is not Pem alone in the back seat but the names of the actors who were filming pictures at that studio. Nick pulled into the home's circular drive.

"I want to take her in alone," I said.

"Georgie, no—" Nick said.

"I'm going to," I said, and I meant it.

Pem held my hand as we walked through the front door. A smiling nurse greeted us, shook our hands. She took Pem's suitcase, just like a good hostess, and led us to Pem's room. The windows overlooked a garden with chrysanthemums and a sundial. Pem's roommate, an old lady with jet-black hair, dozed on top of her bed covers.

"Oh, it's a shame Leslie is asleep. You're going to get along fine," the nurse said. Then she left me and Pem to get settled.

We looked at each other. Pem's arms hung at her sides, and she seemed more stooped than usual. She shook her head slightly.

Pem was eighty-six; this could be her home for the next fourteen years. I had to leave. I couldn't stand being there for another minute. I leaned to kiss Pem, and her arms clutched my neck. "Don't leave me alone in this place," she said, and her voice turned into a wail.

Nick stood at the nurses' station, giving instructions to the head nurse. "Get me out of here," I said, and he broke off his conversation in mid-sentence, and we ran through the double glass doors.

With Pem gone, the Mackens stopped coming for dinner so often. We all felt relief, returning to our old lives and separate families. Every morning Clare and I would convene in the yard, to watch the plane take off. We would talk for a few minutes, until the plane disappeared into the clouds, and then we would part. We were maintaining a little distance. This was new territory, and we both needed to learn the lay of the land. Every day I called Steamboat Landing to inquire about Pem; Dr. Cooke had suggested she would adjust better if we left her alone for about a week. It took Clare days to ask me about details of the place.

"It's what you'd expect," I told her bluntly.

"Is it . . . institutional?"

"Clare, it's an institution. Yes, it's institutional. There's always someone washing the floors, music plays in the elevator, school groups visit the place for their good-deed projects."

"How can Pem stand it?" Clare asked sadly.

One afternoon Nick called to tell me he had a late meeting and would spend the night in the city. I tested myself: did I feel compelled to chase after him, spend the night by his side whatever the cost? No, but I wanted to look for maternity clothes, so I took the train to New York. I shopped a little, looked at some Rembrandt etchings at the Pierpont Morgan Library, then went to the Gregory. That night Nick and I met for a late dinner at Vinnie's in the Village.

"I'm glad to be in New York tonight," Nick said. "The Point's a sad place these days. Everyone is remembering Honora and Pem."

"I know. Nick, today I was walking through the thirties on the East Side, and I started thinking about living in New York again. You wouldn't have to commute. After the baby is born, it's going to be so hard on you, flying off every day." As I spoke I thought about Black Hall. No one had mentioned it, but we would have to sell Pem's and Honora's houses. Things fall apart.

"I think I can manage the commute. I want the baby to grow up on Bennison Point," Nick said.

"Clare and I can hardly stand to be together," I said. "We remind each other too much of Mom and Pem."

"It will be a long time before we get over missing them."

"Everything happening is unnatural," I said. "Honora wasn't supposed to die young, and Pem was supposed to live her entire life on the Point."

"I know," Nick said. "It's killing us all that she's in the home."

"The home," I said, and I snorted. It was a place to live, but it wasn't a home. Listlessly we twirled our spaghetti; we both left full plates, and we returned to the Gregory where we lay down but did not sleep.

The next day I called Helen Avery. "Do you have some free time?" I asked. "Could you take a walk with me?"

"I'd love that," she said.

We met at the corner of West Tenth and Fifth Avenue, and we embraced like old friends. We headed south, towards Washington Square.

"How's the Foundation?" I asked.

"Let's see. The Foundation itself is dandy, but some of its members are not so hot. Myself, for example."

"Why? What's wrong?" I asked, feeling myself draw back a little; I didn't want to hear any sad news about someone I cared about.

"I'm in the doldrums, I guess. For years, since my husband died, I've been putting all my energy into the Foundation. The Foundation and tennis. The only people I ever see are relatives. John and I are driving each other crazy—we keep each other company at social functions, and we've gotten dependent on that. Instead of finding dates. After all these years alone, I'm starting to think about wanting someone." She shook her finger at me. "And I have you to blame for that."

"Me?"

"Oh, that day John and I had lunch at your house. I can't tell you how often I've thought of it. I watched Nick slice those tomatoes—he was concentrating, making each slice the same thickness as the others. I thought—men don't care about things like that! Then I watched you walk into your mother's yard, to pick some basil. I want to be like them, I thought. Happy with someone."

"Oh, Helen," I said. And I thought: what if Helen could marry someone wonderful, move to Bennison Point, take over Honora's house so we wouldn't have to sell it. I was thinking of dinners, my baby in a high chair and Helen in Honora's seat, then stopped myself. Helen was not Honora, and I couldn't make her be.

"I haven't cared about men for a long time," she said. "I thought, oh, I've have my great love. I had one good marriage— that's more than most people can say. You love someone, and he dies, and it hurts terribly. I didn't think I wanted to go through it again."

"Now you do?"

"It seems worth it. I look at you and Nick. I remember that afternoon at my apartment months ago, when I told you you were torturing him. I'll never forget the look on your face. I wanted to shrivel up for doing that to you. You couldn't stand the idea of torturing Nick."

I smiled, remembering that what I couldn't stand was the idea of that incredible closeness ending.

We were standing beside the Stanford White arch. Helen took my arm, led me to a vacant bench. "It's perilous, isn't it?" she asked.

"What is?"

"Love," she said.

And I sat there, thinking of the perils: of Nick flying through the sky and landing on the deep sea, of the night he imagined making love with Jean, of my mother dead and buried in the earth, of my baby who would never know her, of my grandmother alone in a place with bare floors and the stink of old age, of my sister and her husband and their repaired marriage, and I loved them all so much I wanted to whisper their names.

Helen frowned, staring at a pair of fire-eaters. "How do you think they do that?" she asked. "Why would someone ram a burning stick down his own throat?"

"It's a mystery," I said, thinking of other mysteries.

"Do you want a boy or a girl?" Helen asked, turning to me again.

"It doesn't matter," I said, though secretly I wished for a girl.

"This must be wonderful for your grandmother, looking forward to a new baby."

"You don't know?" I said, and then I told her about Pem.

"Oh, that's awful. You wanted to keep her at home." We were quiet for a moment, and then she cast me a sidelong glance. "I know you have your sister Clare, and there must be aunts and uncles on Nick's side, but I can't help this idea I have of playing a part in your baby's life. Sort of an honorary aunt?"

I hugged her. "Thank you," I said. "Nick and I would like that."

"I'm so sorry about your grandmother, Georgie. Just keep looking forward. Soon you'll have your baby."

"Won't that be a brave day?" I said.

.   .   .

Paul Mendillo was on vacation, so the next night I was offered his seat in the seaplane. After dark I met Donald, Nick, and Grey Tobin at the pier in Battery Park. All three men carried briefcases. Grey was flying: I got to ride in the copilot's seat. New York seemed hemmed in by small aircraft. I listened Grey talk on the radio to traffic control; I watched seaplanes and helicopters whiz past. Then we were cleared for takeoff, and we winged east, over the New York necklaces of bridges and highways, twinkling and gaudy. My heart beat hard with excitement until we tracked our way down Long Island Sound, the vast, deep, dark path to Bennison Point, and sadness closed in. Even over the engine's hum and Grey's voice telling about a major client in the midst of bankruptcy proceedings, I could hear Donald and Nick sighing. The two pitiful lights of Bennison Point came into sight. Grey banked the plane. We circled once, then set down with a gentle splash.

"See you tomorrow, guys. Hope the flight didn't bounce the baby too much, Georgie," Grey called after us as we stepped onto the stone jetty. The night was black and moonless, and at first we didn't notice Clare.

"What is it?" Donald asked, stopping dead still.

"We have to spring Pem," she said. "I can't take it one minute longer. We're bringing her home."

"But we decided—" I began.

"I don't care," she said, and I felt hope growing. "What the hell are we doing? We're four able-bodied adults, and we can handle one infirm little grandmother."

"I signed papers to get her into that place," Nick said. "It might take some time to undo them."

"But you want to?" I asked, looking into his eyes.

He nodded; his eyes smiled.

"We all want this?" I asked.

The answer was yes.

We climbed into our station wagon, drove to Steamboat Landing, and walked through the double doors. All four of us stood at the nurses' station. From somewhere down the hall a television played. Two old people dozed in wheelchairs; one was tied in. Although Nick and Donald wore their darkest, most lawyerly suits, the head nurse regarded us with suspicion, as if we were marauders.

"Visiting hours are long over," she said.

"We have come not to visit, but to retrieve," Clare said grandly. Leaving Nick and Donald to argue with the brass, I led my sister down the shining corridor to Pem's room. Pem sat upright in a straight chair, her head in one hand. She wore her pink pajamas and no robe. I thought she must be cold.

"Pem," I said, shaking her shoulder.

She looked up at once, and her expression was as delighted as Honora's had been the night I had visited her after her first heart attack. The memory filled me with a sadness so deep I thought my heart would crack, but I had things to do. Clare threw all Pem's belongings into the ratty suitcase, which hadn't been stolen. I helped Pem put on her shoes, then eased her out of the chair. I draped her winter coat over her shoulders.

"Where're we going?" she asked, trusting us as if the intervening week had never taken place.

"Home, of course," I said. And the three of us walked out of that room, down the hall, and out the door with Nick and Donald. We left the nurse shouting after us, and we never went back.

. . .

GEORGIANA AGASSIZ SWIFT

"Now it is April. I couldn't file my share of the report until I knew what was going to happen. I tried, but last fall the story of my family would have been incomplete. My report will be brief. I am the Swift Observer. I've let the others tell the story.

"We had to wait two seasons for the cycle to come around. My water broke before midnight on the first day of spring, but Tia wasn't born until the next day. She is so beautiful. I stare into her deep blue eyes looking for traces of me and Nick, Honora, Pem, but what I see is Tia.

"I remember that day last summer when Clare said one of us should have a daughter and make it four generations of Bennison women living on the Point. Even though Honora died before Tia was born, I think of us that way: four generations. I have never accepted loss easily. I know I'll never talk to my mother again, but I think of her every day. I know how proud she would be of Tia, how she would tell her the old stories, how happy she would feel to have a granddaughter. Pem, Honora and I are all the mothers of daughters.

"Pem has never mentioned her week's sojourn at Steamboat Landing, and neither do any of us. It was right to bring her home. She is difficult; four nurses have quit in six months. We shuffle her between Clare's house and mine, sharing the burden and confusing Pem in the process. She never seems quite sure of where she is, but she acts happy to be among us. She holds Tia in her arms. Sometimes she calls her Honora, sometimes Georgie or Clare. When I told Pem the baby was named 'Letitia,' after Pem's mother, Pem smiled for a long time before she forgot.

"Nick hates to leave every morning, and I hate for him to

leave. Tia and I wave goodbye through the window; the weather is not yet warm enough for me to take her outside every day. 'Maybe we should move back to New York,' Nick said one night last week when he had to stay overnight in the city, but right away he corrected himself. Bennison Point is where we belong. This is our home."

S.O., April, 1988

Bennison Point, Black Hall, Connecticut